DAMSELS IN

DISTRESS

VOLUME 2

Damsels in Distress
Volume 2
By S.S. Skye, Caitlin Ricci, Cari Z., Camilla Quinn, Anastasia Vitsky, Valerie Mores, Alex Powell, Kai Schalk, Annabelle Kitch, and Althea Claire Duffy

Published by Less Than Three Press LLC

High and Mighty Edited by
Hunting a Lady Edited by
Lies and Reverie Edited by
Living in Sin Edited by
Open Waters Edited by
Sky Knights Edited by
The Adventures of Monkey Girl and Tiger Kite Edited by
The Mercenary Edited by
Treason Edited by

Cover designed by Aisha Akeju

First Edition Month 2015

Printed in the United States of America

Print ISBN 9781620045619

High and Mighty | S.S. Skye
Lynley has been stuck in a tower for over a month, and each day is worse than the one before. She doesn't know why she's there, or who's responsible for it, but the very moment her feet touch the ground there is going to be hell to pay.

Hunting a Lady | Caitlin Ricci and Cari Z.
Shortly before completing her journeyman training in leather working, Jessa's master dies, leaving her at the cruel hands of his son Brent. When the local lord's daughter, Marguerite, is kidnapped and a reward is offered for her rescue, finding her first is a chance at escape Jessa can't ignore.

But when Jessa locates Marguerite, the story isn't quite as simple as a kidnapping. Unfortunately, Jessa's not the only one out for the reward, and if she hopes to claim it she's first got to keep them both alive...

Lies and Reverie | Camilla Quinn
Liddy spends the majority of her life minding her father's shop and trying to keep her sister, Caroline, out of trouble. What little time she has to herself is spent largely in daydreams about kissing beautiful princesses.

Then her sister catches the eye of a nobleman, and the sisters are thrust into the tangled world of high society. Liddy crosses paths with the beautiful, compelling Lady Sophia, the most powerful woman in Dunnshire. But what chance would a poor shop girl ever have with a real life princess?

Living in Sin | Anastasia Vitsky
Sick of playing "roommate" for the sake of her girlfriend's religious, tight-knit family, Audra issues an ultimatum: Tell your family, or I move out. After all, Audra's family supports her and loves Ciara as a second daughter. Why would Ciara's family be any different? Audra's tired of hiding the reality of their lives. She puts Ciara first, why can't Ciara do the same?

Caught between her family and her girlfriend, Ciara resents being forced to choose. She tries to keep the peace by accepting her aunt's endless blind dates and comforting her mother, who cares for Ciara's dying grandmother. How can Ciara shatter her family by forcing the truth on them? How can she face life without Audra if she does not?

Open Waters | Valerie Mores
Captain Jane of the Tantibus has been pirating for more than ten years. With a crew at her command and a ship under her feet, she is a terror to anyone that crosses her path. Her latest conquest is just one more on the list. When they find a common whore aboard, Jane orders the woman be brought along, never realizing the impact one decision can have, and that even an unstoppable pirate has a weakness...

Sky Knights | Alex Powell
Dounia and Ira are part of the Nightwitches, an elite squad of night bombers determined to help bring down Axis forces. They are proud and fearless—until tragedy strikes and their plane is shot down behind enemy lines, and their determination may not be enough to get them home safe.

The Adventures of Monkey Girl and Tiger Kite | Kai Schalk

High school would be a lot easier to deal with if Sunny Wong did not have to balance schoolwork with superhero shenanigans. But superhero she is, gifted the powers of Chinese folk hero Monkey, and when zombies start appearing it's up to her and her sidekick, Delia, to figure out who's responsible for raising the dead and why...

The Mercenary | Annabelle Kitch

Pidge is a mercenary: uncouth, poor, far from the type of beautiful woman the royal court would deem appropriate for Princess Trina, her childhood friend and lover. Life is easier, even kinder in many ways, on the road and in run-down towns where nobody cares about anything but how well she wields her sword and if she can pay for her drinks.

But when she learns that Trina has been trapped in an unwanted engagement, Pidge is determined to save her. According to the rules of the Church of Tamren, whoever returns the holy relics long ago stolen by the Kimbrar has the right to marry any member of the royal house. Provided she can first slay the beast that most say doesn't even exist.

Treason | Althea Claire Duffy

In the port city of Auragos, seven merchant Houses vie for control of the trade that has made the city wealthy. Raised as a spy for House Corellis, Elunet has played so many roles that she's sometimes unsure of who she really is.

Sent to uncover proof of treason by their greatest rival, House Mellas, Elunet will be more than happy to see such a despicable family brought down. Then she meets Tavia—heir to House Mellas, student mage, and nothing that Elunet expected. And the treason she hoped to unmask instead proves to be an entirely different, but equally dangerous secret...

Damsels in

Distress

S.S. Skye

Caitlin Ricci

Cari Z.

Camilla Quinn

Anastasia Vitsky

Valerie Mores

Alex Powell

Kai Schalk

Annabelle Kitch

Althea Clair Duffy

TABLE OF CONTENTS

HIGH AND MIGHTY

S.S. SKYE

The only window was at least fifty feet off the ground. Lynley had dropped a fork from it, vainly hoping that the distance would reveal itself to be smaller than it seemed. She wasn't exactly anxious to follow it, but there were few other options she could see to get out of this *fairytale tower*. She glared down at the ground; even in her head the words dripped with disdain.

She turned on the too-delicate window stool, her back to the unchanging view as she fixed a sullen glower on the bed sheets instead. She'd tested them and already knew they wouldn't work, but that didn't stop her from imagining a world where someone hadn't anticipated she would try exactly this to get out of this thrice-damned tower. The sheets were thin and weak though, completely unusable for rope if she actually wanted to be alive when her feet hit the ground.

Lynley had briefly considered attempting to scale the wall, safety line or no, but she had taken one look at the silk slippers that had been left in the tower for her and she had written it off as a last-ditch resort. Even if she somehow managed not to slip and go plunging to her death, she would still be stranded in the middle of a forest that continued past what she could see from the tower's window. She still didn't even know how she'd gotten here. Last she knew, she'd been with her company in the hills, rousting out bandits. She remembered being in their camp, and sleeping in her tent, but after that there were only hazy memories of some dream, and then waking up in this godsforsaken room.

Most of the initial furor of her anger had burned up in the first couple of weeks that she had been trapped here. Now, Lynley had given over to a slow burning rage that she was keeping banked at the back of her mind, waiting to be unleashed on whoever had locked her in. If she ever got out, anyway.

It seemed increasingly more unlikely with each passing day. The first thing she had done upon waking up here had been to explore every square inch she could access. The tower offered the very basic necessities for living, but the food was only that which wouldn't spoil, the water kept in large barrels at the bottom of a spiral stair, and the rest of what she had found was merely the odds and ends which might occur to someone if they were furnishing a house—an ivory backed brush, a mismatched collection of dishes and cutlery, and a single book that Lynley could almost quote now that she'd perused it so many times.

The tower made for comfortable enough living, but it wasn't stocked with anything that would come close to helping her in surviving long enough to figure out who had kidnapped her and locked her here. Whoever it was knew her well enough, apparently, to know that she wouldn't be content to wait around in this tower for something to happen. Unfortunately, Lynley had already exhausted every other possibility that had occurred to her, still unable to figure out a way to get to the ground without outside assistance.

Speculatively, she looked at the table knives that she had found stashed with some other miscellaneous cutlery. She really hated feeling like a helpless damsel waiting to be rescued.

~~*

The first audible jingle of tackle had Lynley up and across the room, one of the pitiful table knives clenched in her hand. She pressed against the wall, trying to see through the window without giving away her own presence. She wasn't about to throw caution to the wind and holler at the first person to come within earshot of this damnable room. It was like as not to leave her dead and—she told herself for the third time that day—she was not yet that desperate.

When the source of the noise finally emerged into the clearing, Lynley nearly rolled her eyes at her vigilance. The man that rode into the clearing would be laughable if he wasn't also suddenly looking like Lynley's most promising shot at freedom. His seat on his horse was decent, she supposed, but even from here she could see that his sword was belted on backwards.

There was a second horse, though. That was really what convinced Lynley to stay at the window, eyes on the man below. If it had just been that one sad rider on a single horse, she could have comfortably gone back to rereading the book for the umpteenth time and letting the man go about whatever business brought him to the middle of a forest. At the very least though, that horse implied that he was here for her, and might actually be of some help, despite the air of incompetence. If nothing else, he might be in possession of the tools Lynley would need to save herself. Certainly that sword would be better off in her hands.

She almost scoffed aloud as the man dismounted, the sword knocking him off balance. The horse seemed used to it, which spoke better of the horse than its rider, and Lynley had to forcefully remind herself of the weeks that had already passed without any sign of another human being. This tower wasn't located anywhere near a busy hub or thriving metropolis. Nearly a month had passed and the man below was the first creature she'd seen in the forest beyond birds and the occasional deer. If this man couldn't assist in her escape from the tower, there was no telling when next someone would come across this clearing.

With only slight reluctance, Lynley laid her blunt knife on the windowsill, leaving the cover of the wall to lean out the window slightly. It struck her as a bad sign that the man continued to mill about the clearing below, rifling through his saddlebags, without ever looking up at her window. It was a wonder someone like that would be traveling alone, and she would wager that he had come from relatively close. She couldn't imagine any other way he would have been able to arrive with his possessions still intact, and a second horse with him.

Lynley's patience began to wear thin about the same time that he returned to his second saddlebag for its third inspection. "Were you planning on announcing yourself at some point, or were you trying to kill me with the suspense?" she called down, not kindly. She felt only a momentary twinge of guilt as he startled, almost unsurprised when he managed to send something from the saddlebags clattering to the ground. She couldn't help the unimpressed eyebrow lift he earned by looking wildly around, turning in a full circle before finally thinking to look up the length of the tower to where she was leaning against the window. He was too far away, she thought, to fully appreciate the expression being leveled at him, but she figured it might be prudent not to vocally rebuke him until after she was free and on firm ground once more anyway.

Lynley propped her chin in one hand, continuing to watch the man closely, taking notes on his general incompetence so she could critique him later. He shouldn't be saving princesses with that sort of performance.

Several long moments passed in silence as the man continued to stare up at her, apparently frozen in place. With an aggrieved sigh, Lynley caved, brusquely prompting, "Well? You still have yet to announce yourself."

Even at this distance she could see him start again, and he bent over suddenly in what she realized only belatedly was meant as a bow. It also seemed like he was saying something, but she couldn't make it out from so far away. She waited a beat, honestly trying to give him the benefit of the doubt that he would eventually remember that she was half a dozen stories above him. She sighed again, fighting the urge to both roll her eyes and let her head thunk down on the windowsill. This was going to be a very trying endeavor.

"It has possibly escaped your attention," she called out, interrupting whatever the man had been saying and causing him to jerk back to look at her. "I am, however, quite high up here. I am sure you are speaking at a perfectly respectable volume for court, but the space between us is slightly greater than the proper speaking distance. Perhaps we could hang propriety for the moment." In the back of her head, Lynley could hear her tutors tutting about her sharp tongue and caustic tone, but she figured they could hang for the moment too.

There was an awkward moment of silence before the man actually started speaking loud enough for the sound to carry. "Forgive me, Your Highness. My name is Willerd, of the Western Thorny Mountains and I am honored to—"

Lynley cut him off before he could launch into what would no doubt be a very pretty and entirely trivial speech. "Lynley will do just fine, Lady Lynley if you absolutely insist on formalities. Am I correct in assuming that you have come with the express purpose of helping me secure my freedom?"

The man—Willerd, what an unfortunate name—gestured to the horses behind him, the movement likely meant to encompass the contents of the horses' cargo as well. "Yes, Your Highness. I am here to rescue you," he declared, rather grandiosely, she thought, for someone who couldn't even wear his sword belt properly.

She barely resisted the urge to snort, but she couldn't begin to bite her tongue. "That remains to be seen," she called down. "And Lynley will still do just fine." She could almost see him ramping up to argue that point, so she plowed forward. "Did you come prepared for the tower?" There would need to be a conversation later about how he had come prepared for anything at all, but she preferred to have that one face to face. "If so, please show me your provisions, post-haste. I am most anxious to be on the ground once more; I am sure you can appreciate just how much."

"Of course, Your Highness." Lynley rolled her eyes without compunction. "I am indeed prepared for a tower, and it shall be but the work of a moment for me to assemble my supplies."

He stood looking up at her in expectant silence, and she rolled her eyes again, fairly certain that he wouldn't be able to see it. "By all means," she called drolly, waving at his horses carelessly.

Willerd scrambled toward the horses then, and Lynley was gratified to see that the first thing out of the saddlebags was a very generous amount of rope that looked like it should actually be able to reach from her window to the hard packed earth below. He held it up triumphantly, as if she might not have been watching and therefore might have missed its appearance. "I have a grappling hook, as well," he yelled up to her and Lynley actually took a moment to reconsider whether Willerd really would be as unhelpful as she had assumed.

She managed some semblance of patience as he crouched to fiddle with the rope, presumably securing the hook to it, though Lynley already knew she would be double checking the knot before she trusted it to hold her weight while she scaled a wall several stories off the ground. It wasn't that she didn't trust Willerd's skills, per se. She just didn't have a lot of faith in his competence. She was hardly being unreasonable considering her life was very nearly in his hands. It wasn't a feeling she relished and Lynley was more than a little anxious to have her future firmly back in her own control.

Lynley's misgivings were thoroughly vindicated when Willerd finally straightened, grappling hook and rope held awkwardly in hand while he stared up the length of the tower. She tried to keep herself in check, but there was only so long that she was capable of waiting when he seemed to be frozen in place once more. "Did you not think that you would have need to actually get the hook to a higher point so that I could climb down the tower?" The urge to smack her head into the wall was steadily growing stronger.

"I... forgive me, Your Highness, I had not..." Willerd cut off on what she thought might be a sigh, though she was unable to hear it. "I had not thought the tower would be quite so high. I am afraid I have not the athleticism necessary to propel the hook up to your level."

Lynley sighed, allowing herself only a moment to wonder why she couldn't possibly be rescued by a proper knight. She knew she couldn't possibly be the only one who lived in the kingdom, but times like these truly made her wonder. It also meant that the plans that immediately came to mind would be all but unworkable with... whatever Willerd was. Inept as he was, though, Lynley was unwilling to give up on the first chance off getting out of this tower that had presented itself in the month she'd spent cooling her heels. She was not wired for isolation, even less for this confined seclusion.

With a fresh wash of determination, she turned to survey the room, hoping something would occur to her that she had somehow missed in the last weeks. Perhaps something she had previously discounted would now be possible with the addition of another person.

Her eyes landed on the bed and nearly glanced off, before her brain caught up and she drew closer, hands speculatively grabbing up one of the bed sheets. Lynley had already established that no amount of braiding or knotting would be able to turn the sheets into a rope that could hold her weight. A grappling hook attached to a rope, however, might be an entirely different story.

She leaned back out the window, hands planted firmly on the sill now. "Willerd, yes?" she called, more to get his attention than for affirmation. She waited until he was looking up at her instead of off into the distance. "If I were to lower some sort of rope, could you tie it to the hook?"

He was nodding before she'd even finished speaking, following it up with a rather high-pitched "Yes, Your Highness."

They were going to have a serious conversation about that once she was on the ground, but Lynley let it go for the moment, already moving toward the bed. With no small amount of prejudice, she began shredding the sheets into long strips, using her teeth to start it off before savagely ripping it the rest of the way. She had the feeling that any amount of travel with Willerd was going to prove to be very trying and the more frustration she could take out on these god-awful sheets, the less would be left for the man who was assisting in her escape. It would be shamefully ignoble to kill him when he seemed to be sincerely trying to help.

But she was taking that damn sword as soon as she was on the ground.

The rope formed quickly beneath her fingers, soothing the twist of anxiety that had been growing in her chest over the last month. Lynley wasn't an optimist by nature and the past weeks had proven that painfully clear. Every day had brought her a step closer to risking the drop and attempting to scale the smooth stone walls. The length of the rope was Lynley guessing more than anything, and she made sure to overshoot what she thought would be a sufficient length.

When she came back to the window, Willerd was sitting on the ground, grappling hook in his lap and gaze fixed forward on the wall. She didn't bother calling out, just dropped her makeshift rope down, the end wrapped securely around her hand. Willerd jumped back a bit where he was sitting, jerking to look up at her before silently reaching for the rope. She waited while he fiddled with the hook, tamping down the impatience to yank the hook up to her and get *out* already.

She took a deep breath as he finally stood, holding the hook above his head like it would help reach her sooner. "It might behoove you to back up, in case this rope should fail." Lynley bit off yet another sigh when Willerd stumbled backwards into one of the horses.

It seemed like an eternity before the hook was scraping against the stones just beneath her, and she let out a small crow of victory as her fingers closed around cool metal. It was reassuringly firm, solidly built and without obvious lack of craftsmanship. There was no urge to rush now, not when she was so close to being free and a careless move could cost her both this chance and her life.

She went over the knot first, tugging and testing for several long moments before she was more certain that it would hold. She supposed Willerd must not be wholly useless at everything, if he knew how to tie a secure knot. Lynley wedged the hook against one of the bottom corners of the window, casting what would hopefully be her last glance back at the room. It held only the barest essentials, and there really wasn't anything that she had any desire to take with her. Certainly she would rather never be reminded of this tower ever again.

Her thoughts strayed for a moment to the still questionably competent man waiting at the bottom though, and Lynley couldn't help the second look that swept the room, double checking that there was nothing that might prove useful on a journey when she had no real idea about the preparedness of her traveling companion. It suddenly occurred to her that though Willerd might be helping her from the tower, that didn't ensure the purity of his intentions. The two table knives were quickly tucked into her sash as she gazed despondently at the room's remaining offerings.

The only useful item left in the whole of the tower was the food, so Lynley quickly bundled some together in one of the three skirts she'd been cycling through for the last month. They were made of gossamer and silk, and she was already cringing at the thought of having to travel in what she was already wearing. She might have tolerated its like for a court function, but for any amount of time on the road, it would grow tiresome quickly. After a moment's hesitation, she yanked on the bloomers she'd eschewed for the last several weeks. They weren't the riding breeches she rather wished she had with her, but they would do better than nothing. With a final look around her short-lived prison, she turned back to the rope.

"What in the nine hells are you doing?" was out of her mouth before she could think to hold it in. Willerd was at the bottom of the tower, apparently attempting to climb the rope, though he couldn't be more than a foot or two off the ground.

"I am coming—" He broke off, and she could hear him grunt as he tried to drag himself higher. "—up to rescue you." The last word sounded punched out of him, and several beats passed while Lynley stared down at Willerd in fascinated horror. He *actually* believed he would be able to make it to the top. More insultingly, he seemed to believe that not only would she need some sort of assistance, but that *he* would be capable of supplying it.

"Get down and stand back," she barked, no longer in the mood to humor him. "I am perfectly capable of making my own damn way down from this tower."

The cursing was what brought Willerd's gaze up to stare along the tower at her, and she was preparing to growl out another curse when he quickly scrambled down, backing up several paces. He managed to avoid the horses this time, at least.

Lynley took a final look around the room, futilely wishing she could burn the thing to the ground. Instead she settled for promising herself—as she had every morning she had woken up in this place—that she would seek retribution once she discovered who had trapped her here and for what purpose. Kidnapping a princess was crime enough, but so soon before her coronation, Lynley was more than willing to see it as treason.

She hopped up onto the window ledge, grumbling to herself as her skirts billowed around her. Impatiently, she yanked up the edges, tucking them into the tight legs of her bloomers until they no longer fluttered around her. She'd used another sash to secure the bundle of food to her back, the knives still comfortably tucked in at her waist. She gave the rope a last tug, still perched precariously above the hook on the sill, with her back to the open air. She wrapped the rope around herself, over her right hip, across her chest, dropping it over her left shoulder. Her fingers clenched involuntarily and she took a steadying breath, focusing only on relaxing her grip. She'd give anything for her hide gloves right about now, would give her kingdom for a proper harness.

With a last deep breath and a short prayer to her gods, Lynley tipped back, feet against the wall, and hoped that the rope would hold.

~~*

Being a lady's maid had never been her parents' idea of success. They had had higher hopes for Corrissa, had always talked about marrying her off to a baronet and lifting themselves in society by proximity. By her age, she likely *would* have been married off already, if it hadn't been for Lady Isolda. The Duchess's family owned the duchy that Corrissa had been raised in, and she had turned to the wealthiest merchant families when it came time for her to choose the ladies who would be attending her.

Corrissa would never say it aloud, but she owed Lady Isolda a debt. Her parents' ambitions had never been her own, and she could have been content living out her days as a lady's maid. When the news was passed along that Lady Isolda would be marrying royalty, and had every intention of taking her ladies with her, Corrissa had breathed easy for the first time in years. Her parents had made their disapproval plain when she had accepted her position and had been explicit that they would allow it only until a match could be made for her. Lady Isolda's imminent marriage however—particularly to royalty—meant that it would be socially unacceptable for Corrissa to leave her service. Moving up to a lady-in-waiting meant that Corrissa finally had some protection from her parents' machinations.

It didn't, in the end, mean that she was free from a world of political scheming though. Life with Lady Isolda had started out peacefully, the days of a country duchess requiring relatively few social engagements and only carefully controlled personal obligations beyond those. The duchess wasn't gregarious by nature, and she seemed to hold few people as dear friends. There were certainly few enough people who could match Lady Isolda for either wit or austerity. It had all come together, though, to make Corrissa's first couple of years as a lady's maid relatively easy, more so than she had expected, and made the change to a life at court rather more shocking that it might otherwise have been.

She'd heard about the complexities of living at court—her parents had spoken of it often as if they were a part of it all—but nothing could have prepared her for being there. Lady Isolda had brought all of her lady's maids with her, adamantly refusing to add any new girls to their midst once they had arrived at the palace. It had confused most of them at first, because country duchesses didn't bring country daughters to wait on them in the palace. Lady Isolda should have had proper ladies waiting on her, daughters of knights and barons, girls who knew the proper customs and etiquette and who were apprised of the latest fashions. They had all felt woefully outclassed those first couple of months at court. Their duchess had flatly refused to replace them however, no matter what rumors flew or how many times her counselors tried to demand it. She remained obstinate that she would be surrounded only by ladies she had chosen and trusted, even if they were sorely undertrained.

Eventually—thankfully—they had adapted. Court fashion changed all the time and it was easier to catch up then, easier to find the ebb and flow of gossip as new scandals rose up and others faded away. They had all briefly floundered under a social calendar suddenly laden down with engagements, struggling to balance the flocks of people that began clawing for the duchess's attention against the time she actually had to spare for any of them. They had become proficient by necessity. Corrissa had gone from a country lady's maid to lady-in-waiting for a queen to be. Somehow, she had thought it'd be more glamorous.

~~*

Corrissa pounded on the door for the third time. "Lady Isolda! It is far past time for you to be about your day, milady!" She groaned, leaning her head against the door. Being named head lady-in-waiting to a duchess had seemed like an honor at the time, but Corrissa had since started to wonder if she hadn't somehow insulted someone to have ended up here. Lady Isolda was reserved, and conversationally razor-tongued, and an absolute nightmare to wake up in the mornings.

She hammered on the door again, trying to remember that giving up and damning the daily schedule to hell wouldn't actually accomplish anything, other than possibly her termination. Her hand was poised to bang again when a voice barked, "What?" more sharply that Corrissa thought should be possible for someone who had only just woken.

"Forgive me, milady, but you have a full schedule for today and if you fall behind this early, you shall never catch up." Corrissa tried to keep her tone pleasant, like she hadn't spent the last half an hour trying to wake the duchess.

The door was abruptly yanked open, Lady Isolda glowering at her blearily for a moment before turning and trudging back in, leaving the door open behind her. Corrissa shut it softly behind herself. She no longer needed to let her eyes adjust to the gloom in these chambers, used to the dimness that greeted her every morning. The bell pull was next to the door, the first thing she always did so that the kitchens would know to send breakfast up. Lady Isolda took the same chair next to the hearth every morning, even though no fire was lit because she would allow no one in her chambers without her presence. To her knowledge, Corrissa held the only key besides Lady Isolda, and it was explicitly for emergencies only. Late mornings unfortunately didn't fall into that category.

The room was silent as Corrissa attended her other morning chores; lighting candles so the servant who brought breakfast could see to set the table while Lady Isolda blinked and glared at the flames, laying out the day's first ensemble, and finally turning to dress Lady Isolda's hair where she was curled, mostly asleep, in her chair. Once she'd gotten the duchess up and out of bed, this was the calmest and quietest portion of Corrissa's day.

Sure enough, breakfast arrived in a cloud of silks and gossip, her fellow ladies-in-waiting chattering as they filled the room with noise. They were responsible for many of the other chores required for the upkeep of their lady's chambers and wardrobe, and Corrissa was glad for it. She just also sometimes wished that the peace of her mornings wasn't automatically forfeit.

She took some small pleasure from the flat looks Lady Isolda leveled at anyone who fluttered too closely to her as she tucked into her breakfast, daintily working her way through lacy looking pastries and several cups of strong coffee. Lady Isolda was always fair in her treatment—and indeed she treated her ladies-in-waiting better than most mistresses might have—but she was not a woman who invited bosom companionship or warm confidences, and certainly never gossip. Corrissa was hard pressed to imagine a woman more thoroughly devoted to propriety and the appearance thereof. She couldn't even say that she knew the duchess's preference for how she liked her hair to be dressed.

Corrissa pushed the last hairpin into place with a satisfied air, terming it a personal victory that Lady Isolda had finished her breakfast only minutes prior. The duchess kept a tightly packed schedule now that they had arrived at the court proper, and it was difficult enough to maintain it without falling behind first thing in the morning. She would never gossip like the other girls who tended the duchess, but even she could admit that Lady Isolda was more easily managed in the mornings if she arrived to her first appointment on time.

It was always something of a reprieve once they ushered Lady Isolda out of the room in the mornings. Part of the relief was borne of the desire to have the duchess out of their hair when she was still sluggish and grumpy, but the real reason had more to do with the fact that on mornings when things were running particularly late, she began council meetings in her chambers.

The first time Corrissa had seen Lady Isolda make the switch from grouchy and still half-asleep country duchess to cold and razor-tongued queen-to-be, she had nearly dropped the tea service in surprise. The transition had happened seamlessly and without warning. Any lingering drowsiness had fallen away in the blink of an eye, replaced by a cold harshness that made Corrissa exceedingly grateful that this wasn't the Lady Isolda she had to rouse from bed every morning. This was a woman she fully expected could rule the kingdom by herself.

Corrissa always felt a little guilty any time that particular line of thinking crossed her mind. It wasn't treason strictly speaking, but it certainly felt awfully close. Lady Isolda wasn't yet married to her betrothed, who was away on a quest and had been for some months without any word. It was such that whispers had started spreading through the castle hallways, speculations that the crown royal wouldn't be returning or had been killed while away on quest.

She couldn't say if Lady Isolda was aware of the content of all the rumors, because she never gave the indication that she might find herself jilted by an untimely death. There was never so much as a hint that she might be worried about her royal affianced, or that the long absence weighed on her in any way. From the moment of their arrival to the castle several months ago, Lady Isolda had assumed the mantle of queen, as though it was her due.

Sometimes, Corrissa forgot that Lady Isolda was to be queen only by marriage, her betrothal arranged by her parents at her birth. Most of the Royal Council seemed to have accepted the duchess's presence in their midst, even if she had spent only a few of the social seasons at court before the late king's death. The sole person who stood opposed to her inclusion was the Chancellor, cousin of the heir apparent.

It wasn't difficult for Corrissa to speculate as to why, of course. Chancellor Brayden was the nephew of the erstwhile king, most trusted of his advisors on the council up until the day of his death. She could easily understand why the Chancellor might be wary of allowing a country duchess into the kingdom's center of power, particularly when her betrothed remained just that—*betrothed*. Having had the king put such trust in him, she couldn't begrudge him for being cautious about his cousin's kingdom. Somebody had to look after the throne while it sat empty.

~~*

Somewhere in the world, she thought, there must be someone that she had greatly wronged for the gods to punish her like this. Lady Isolda had returned to her chambers in high dudgeon, her cool mask slipping away as the door clicked shut behind her. She was too well-bred to slam it, but it seemed a near thing, eyebrows pulled down in a thunderous scowl.

The duchess returned to her rooms most afternoons in order to change for the second part of her day, usually allowing her sole opportunity to sit and have a moment's peace without councilors and courtiers alike vying for her attention. It was a quiet affair, exchanging her morning dress for an afternoon gown, repinning any hair that had come loose. Lady Isolda usually took a light tea too, as she was reluctant to eat too heavily under the gaze of the court, and the council often ate late.

Today, she seemed to have no patience for any of it. She batted away the first girl to try to help her with her clothes, and hissed as another tried the same. "Do not touch me." The words were soft but venomous, and the handful of ladies-in-waiting who stood around her froze as she bared her teeth. "Do I look as though I require assistance?"

Corrissa could see at least two of the girls look to her, eyes wide and frightened. This was not a side of the duchess any of them had seen, and some of them had been with her for half a dozen years. With a sigh, Corrissa stepped forward. Lady Isolda's head whipped around, glower landing on Corrissa with a ferocity she had never been subject to before.

She put it aside for the moment, keeping her attention focused on the other girls. They were looking particularly skittish, some actually clutching their skirts as though the thin layers of cotton might be able to function as some sort of shield against Lady Isolda's ire.

"If you ladies would please excuse us." It may have been phrased as a request, but Corrissa left no room in her tone for argument. Rarely did she take advantage of her status as Mistress of the Robes, but in this instance she lacked the ability to balance both Lady Isolda's anger and the terror of a handful of flighty country daughters turned royal maids. "I will attend Lady Isolda. If I do not summon any of you, return at the ninth bell to assist our lady in preparing for the evening. Otherwise, you are to go about your day as usual."

Corrissa waited a beat, until all eyes were focused on her. "I am certain this is unnecessary for me to say, but I will do so anyway; if any of you are incapable of being discreet or if I find that any of you have been speaking out of turn, you will be released from our lady's service without reference. Have I made myself perfectly clear?"

She looked to each of the girls, getting some sort of affirmation from every one before she nodded decisively. "Very well. Go then."

There was nearly a jam as the ladies-in-waiting inelegantly scurried for the door. She offered a wan smile as Marian gave her arm a squeeze in passing. They two had been longest in Lady Isolda's service, both hailing from the same small village adjacent to the duchess's manor. Marian collared two of the girls trying to rush through the door at once, herding the last of them through and closing the door quietly behind her.

The soft click was all it took for the fight to go flooding from Lady Isolda. She collapsed gracelessly to one of the armchairs in the sitting area, like a marionette with its strings abruptly cut. Her face was lined by exhaustion, clenched fists releasing to hang limply over the edge of the chair.

Corrissa's plan hadn't extended beyond removing the less staid girls from the situation. She was unsure of whether Lady Isolda's anger had truly blown over so quickly or if she had simply banked her rage until something new set her off again.

While she was debating the best approach, images of cornered wounded animals in her head, Lady Isolda took the lead and broke the silence. "I must apologize, Corrissa. That was poorly done of me." She sighed, sinking further into the cushion, proper posture entirely abandoned, delicate fingers coming up to rub at her temples. "I have no explanation for what overcame me. Thank you for dismissing the other ladies. Certainly none of you deserved such treatment."

Corrissa crossed closer slowly, steps careful as she approached the sitting area. She froze as Lady Isolda's gaze snapped from the rug to take her in. There were dark circles under her eyes, cheeks looking almost gaunt despite the early afternoon light that filtered through the windows. "You may have the afternoon as well. I am able to dress myself for my meetings." Her voice was unusually devoid of both the steel and ice that it normally carried.

A sigh caught in Corrissa's throat. "With all due respect, milady, I have already dismissed your other ladies-in-waiting. It would be the highest impropriety to allow you to attend yourself. I appreciate the sentiment, but I must decline, milady."

Lady Isolda opened her mouth, brows pulled together like she meant to argue. Just as quickly though, she drooped again, sighing out a long breath and sinking further into the chair. "I am without the energy to argue with you now, Corrissa. If you will not leave, so be it. Only let me have a few moments to myself, please. I would like some privacy to regain my composure."

"Shall I go down to the kitchens and fetch some tea, milady? I am sure it would help you feel more yourself." Lady Isolda studied her for several minutes, expression caught somewhere between confusion and gratitude. Finally, she nodded slowly, waving off Corrissa's curtsy.

Outside in the hallway, Corrissa took a breath to lean back against the door and let the tension drain from her shoulders. She was in need of something a little stronger than tea herself before she headed back into those rooms. Honey and lemon weren't up to this particular challenge.

~~*

The palace kitchens never experienced any kind of respite, the fires always burning, and kitchen servants constantly flitting between pots, pans, and the pumps outside. Corrissa had become accustomed to the bustle over the last couple of months, unsurprised by the activity that ebbed and swelled every couple of hours.

She had found herself in the kitchens enough times in the first few weeks after their arrival to the palace that she'd become acquainted with more than a few of the kitchen's workers. There were a number of stools scattered around the kitchen, tucked out of the way.

Corrissa thought they were meant for any of the kitchen servants that might need a minute's break from the constant flurry of the kitchens, but in all of her visits down here, she'd never seen anyone but visitors using the stools.

She took her usual seat on the stool tucked next the baking counter, bracketed by the rack where dough was left to rise. Jacques was already well into the swing of his day, meaty hands buried in a bowl of dough, shoulders rippling as he rhythmically worked the dough. He continued kneading as he turned to smile at her, bobbing his head a little in greeting. Corrissa managed a small smile in return before sagging back against the wall. "The duchess is trying your soul, yes?"

Corrissa lolled her head over to look at Jacques, his hands never ceasing even as he turned his full focus on her. "*No.*" She sighed, tempering her tone. "No. I have simply not been sleeping well. The duchess has nothing to do with it."

Jacques barked out a short laugh, giving her a look that quite clearly said he didn't believe a word she had said. "The rumors would say otherwise, lass. Word in the kitchens is that your lady stormed from the council meeting after throwing a fit." He arched a brow at her. "Mayhap it is proving more difficult to take the throne than she thought it would."

Corrissa jerked up from the wall, shocked. "And what do you mean by that?"

The look on Jacques's face could only be described as confused pity. "Corri, you have been in the capitol for months. You cannot still be so naïve, lass. The whole castle knows your lady seeks to hold the throne by herself. The most popular bit of gossip right now says that she is the reason her betrothed remains missing.

The girls down in the laundry have some very good stories for they think she accomplished it, though some of the plans seem more complicated than I believe your lady would bother with."

Her stomach sank, an uneasy knot forming, as she tried not to line up Lady Isolda's behavior over the last couple of months with how such a plot might unfold. It was dishearteningly difficult. With a dismayed sigh, Corrissa sank back against the wall. "Does everyone believe this? Not the stories, Jacques!" she interrupted impatiently as he raised a brow at her, tone sharper than she remembered it being since she'd left home. "That Lady Isolda might have committed treason so she could rule by herself." Her skin felt too tight, and the kitchens were suddenly stifling.

Jacques shrugged with studied nonchalance, hands never stilling. "Who can say? She is a hard woman, is your lady, and she has few friends here in the castle, I hear tell. She does not endear herself to people, but who am I to say? I bake bread. I leave the intrigue to the toffs with that sort of time on their hands."

He let silence lapse between them then, and Corrissa couldn't figure out how to break it again. She had befriended Jacques at the urging of his niece, a sweet girl apprenticed to the baker back in Corrissa's home village. She also happened to be the girl Corrissa's brother was not-so-secretly in love with, but she would hardly hold that against Anna.

More important was the fact that Anna had pointed Corrissa in the direction of this very first friend she had made in the palace and the one who had initially shown her the ropes. If he was passing a rumor on to her, more than likely it wasn't just passing talk. With a fortifying breath, Corrissa slid from her stool, squeezing one of his thick forearms. "Thank you, Jacques."

He let out a light scoff. "Keep your chin up, lass. It might not be so dire as all that."

Corrissa nodded dully but said nothing. She had tea to bring to a treasonist.

~~*

Lynley—it had taken several weeks, and one black eye, but he had finally given up on the honorific—was one of the least pleasant people Willard had ever met. From the moment her feet had touched down on solid ground, she had taken over what was supposed to be *his* rescue mission.

Willard wasn't incompetent, no matter how frequently she chose to mutter it under her breath, knowing full well that he could hear her. He had come prepared for this quest, the slight hiccup with the hook notwithstanding. He had scoped out suitable inns on his way to the tower, had brought more than enough gold to see that the princess would be able to travel in comfort and that they would arrive back at the castle with all due haste.

Lynley had brusquely shot down each and every plan he had tried to put forward. He hadn't thought they would fall madly in love immediately or anything like that. He had thought they could surely be friends heading into this though, could foster a sort of mutual respect between them. That delusion had died a spectacularly quick death. Lynley had barely been on the ground for a full breath before she demanded that he hand over his sword, as she didn't trust him not to accidentally stab her with it. It felt rather unfair of her to have judged him so quickly, especially considering the fact that he had reached the tower before any of the others. He would have thought that would earn him the benefit of the doubt, at the very least.

She had made it rather brutally clear that she held no favorable expectations whatsoever for either his conduct or his capabilities. Every instance in which he did something right was greeted with surprised condescension, like he hadn't gotten her out of the bloody tower when she hadn't been capable of doing so alone. If he were being perfectly honest, it had taken only a couple of weeks for Willerd to realize that Lynley was the last person he would ever want to marry. Unfortunately for him, he had also come to the realization that there wasn't any way to convince his parents of the unsuitability of the match.

He had been trying to avoid thinking about that too often during the weeks that they traveled together. In the beginning, he'd been able to tell himself that it was only natural for Lynley to be cross. She'd been locked in a tower for some time before he had rescued her, so it would be strange if that hadn't put a damper on her spirits. The first night had given him pause, of course, when she had insisted they forego what he'd thought to be a rather charming forest inn in favor of sleeping under the stars. Willerd had seen the sense in it though. If he'd been trapped in a tower for a month, he would probably shy from being indoors so soon too.

It hadn't been just the one night though. It hadn't been the first week, or the second, or the third. Lynley categorically refused to sleep in any of the quaint establishments he had vetted on his trip to the tower. She had scoffed—*scoffed*—when he tried to determine what she had found wrong with them. She hadn't bothered to answer either. Rarely did she bother to answer any question he posed to her.

Lying on the cold and hard ground every night had, unfortunately, given him far too much space in his head to think about things. This hadn't been the life that Willerd wanted for himself to begin with, and with every day that passed, it seemed a little bit further than what he might deem livable. He had already abandoned his dream of owning a modest shop in the village where he had been raised, and had already made peace with the fact that he would never marry the girl he truly loved. This course of action would hardly have been his choice in the matter, but he had bent to his parents' wishes for too long to think that he could defy them now. When they had heard that a quest had been set for *Princess* Lynley's hand in marriage, they had ordered him into motion, and he had protested very little.

The reality of the situation with Lynley was verging on untenable, though. Mutual respect was laughably far from plausible—he winced at the memory that he'd ever thought more than that a possibility. The closer they came to reaching Lynley's home, and the conclusion of Willerd's quest, the more seriously he considered abandoning the mission altogether. His parents would be livid of course—he was their chance at a better life, after all—but he thought a future as Lynley's husband might just be worse.

"Willerd!" He startled guiltily at what had become the all too familiar sound of Lynley barking out his name. She had a voice that carried, even though it was merely the two of them, no more than a couple horse lengths separating them. He hadn't known it before rescuing her, but he could well believe her when she had told him that she was a blooded knight. It had nothing to do with his sword still strapped comfortably at her waist. He hadn't been able to find the words to ask for it back, and after their sole run-in with some rough types, he was only a little ashamed to admit that the weapon did more good in her hands than his. Even if it had meant he had watched the scuffle from the sidelines like a dimwitted clod.

He sighed and turned before she could yell at him again. "Yes?" He avoided using any sort of name outside of his head now, as one black eye had been more than enough.

"We should reach the capital in a few hours time, but I have no wish to go directly to the palace. We will stay the night outside the wall and then make our way in the morning." Willerd didn't bother trying to give his input; it had all been summarily ignored up until this point anyway. "If you desire to go into town, I will not hinder you."

Weeks in and Willerd still had no idea how anyone held full conversations with Lynley. As now, he mostly just nodded and let silence fall again. It was easier than any of the other options that had occurred to him. It made for peaceful traveling most of the time as well, though that really just gave Willerd more time in his head to wonder how well everything was really going to turn out. He could now say with confidence that a marriage to Lynley was probably the worst way he could imagine spending his future. He could also say without a trace of doubt that he couldn't see any possible way out of it.

That was it, he thought, as the capitol came into view in the distance. He was going to marry Lynley, and then she'd run him through on their wedding night. With his own sword too, probably, just to add insult to injury. It'd wrap this whole misadventure up nicely, he decided, even if he did end up dead at the end of it. He tried not to think about the fact that he probably wouldn't be in this situation right now if he had just dallied longer in getting to the tower.

~~*

He wished he could have been surprised when Lynley insisted on setting up camp outside the capitol walls when they finally arrived, instead of seeking accommodations at an inn. He wished he could say he had expected her to ask his opinion or consult his requests in any way. Mostly, he wished it was three months ago and he could tell himself that taking the long way to his destination would be better in the long run.

"I am going into the city," he started as they tethered their horses for the night. "My sister—" He sighed as Lynley stalked off toward the forest without a word. "Works at the palace," he finished to himself, not a little sarcastically. He didn't bother going after her, or ensuring that she would know where to find him. It wasn't like she needed him to take care of her. She'd made that point abundantly clear.

The walk through the capitol city was oddly chaotic after traveling with Lynley for a month. They had spent the duration of their travels on side roads and forest trails, eschewing the more well-worn roads that Willerd had scoped out on his way to the tower. Only twice had they run into any other travelers, and both times had found their fellows abandoning the trail and taking to the woods, as if Lynley and Willerd were bandits to be avoided.

By comparison, the city was teeming with life, even as the sun crawled lower in the late afternoon. It was difficult to decide whether he actually preferred it to the silence that had marked his travels so far, but it certainly made for a refreshing change of pace. Once through the palace gates, some of that died down, the people hustling past with a more reserved purpose.

It took him long enough to find the kitchens that servants had passed him in the hallways, lighting candles to keep the growing evening at bay. There were only two people he knew in the castle, and there was only one he actually had some idea how to find. He'd met the man when Jacques had visited his brother one year, the sole baker at the time that resided in Willerd's sleepy little village. Willerd couldn't even be sure the man would recognize him, but without him he had no chance of tracking down his sister.

As it turned out, he needn't have worried about that. Jacques called out to him before he could even find his bearings in the bustle of the kitchen, reeling him in and clapping one of his big meaty palms to Willerd's back. "Well met, lad, well met. Your sister gave me no warning you were coming to visit the capitol."

Willerd was unceremoniously pushed onto a stool next to Jacques' station as the man looked at him expectantly. It took him a long moment to realize his participation was actually required for a conversation once more. The weeks on the road had thrown him for a loop. "She had no warning herself," he blurted, rushing a little to get his words out now that someone was actually bothering to listen. "I have been on the road for nearly four months, so this will be a surprise to her too."

Jacques threw his head back to laugh, hands stilling where he had been aggressively beating what looked like a dozen eggs. "Then I am glad I will see the reunion. She will be down soon; she usually passes through for tea at the seventh bell." He fixed a shrewd eye on Willerd as he reassumed his bowl. "Tell me, how did you find my brother and his daughter when last you saw them?"

Willerd's mouth opened but no sound came out, and he could feel his ears flush pink. He was saved from having to answer by a laugh from one of the kitchen's entrances, familiar even if he couldn't see her face yet. *Corrissa.* Jacques's smirk slid into a smile as he turned to call around the racks blocking their view. "Corri, what perfect timing. I have something just in this minute, from your home village no less."

There was a murmur as she said farewell to whomever she had been speaking to, and then she called back, "What could it be to have you so excited to show me?"

Jacques's bulk blocked Willerd from view, but he could hear the mirth in the man's voice as he said, "Come see for yourself," and stepped aside. Willerd caught a glimpse of wide honey eyes just before there was a high pitched squeal of "Will!" and he found himself tackled by Corrissa.

It was only the wall behind him that kept them from crashing to the floor, but he only clutched her tighter as he laughed into her hair. "Good to see you too, Corri."

It took some moments before Corrissa finally let up, loosening her hold so she could hold him at arm's length. "Will, it is so good to see you. I thought you must be very busy not to have sent me any letters in months. What have you been doing?"

Willerd slumped back against the wall with a groan. "Do not make me relive these past months, I beg of you. Suffice to say I have been traveling for far too long and I will be very glad to see the end of it." He could see Corri beginning to pout and soldiered on quickly. "But come, tell me how you have been. Working in the castle—it is beyond imagining. I can scarcely believe you are lady-in-waiting now."

Corri's smile was crooked. "I suppose. It has certainly taken some getting used to. You would be amazed by how few secrets anyone in the palace has. Word travels far too quickly for that sort of thing, though I could not begin to guess how anyone finds these things out. Certainly our lady is far too discreet to let the secrets of another person slip." There was something like a grimace that crossed her face, but it was gone as quickly as it had appeared. "Lady Isolda has always been fair to her ladies-in-waiting, too. There are certainly girls whose mistresses are far crueler, and the duchess is never that. She is only a little cold, and certainly no one would expect differently of a lady with her servants. She has been most forgiving of the time it took us to adjust, and it has been a relief she does not ask what is said of her."

Willerd scoffed gently. "Surely it is not so different from the village. Everyone and their mother knew what everyone else was about, and no one was immune from being the subject of gossip. Even duchesses must do something worthy of gossip at some time." Corri grinned, but it seemed more forced than he remembered.

"I suppose you are right," she allowed, but there was no teasing in her voice like there should have been. She shook her head, almost as if to cast off the odd heaviness that seemed to have enveloped her. "Are you staying in the city?" she asked hopefully, and he tried not to notice how she wilted immediately when he shook his head.

"Not tonight," he rushed to console. "But after tomorrow, I should be much closer. It is only this night that I shall be out of the capitol walls." She dredged up a smile for him, but he thought they could probably both tell it was strained.

The shadows lingered in Corri's eyes as she bid him goodnight some time later, but he didn't know how to ask her what was wrong. She'd never had any problems bringing her troubles to him when they were young. What was it that stopped her doing so now? As he walked back through the darkened streets of the capitol, he couldn't help but think that something at the castle must be terribly wrong.

~~*

The morning came almost too quickly for Willerd's taste. Traveling on the road with Lynley hadn't been pleasant, but there had been a sort of routine to it, and he'd known what to expect at the beginning of each day. This morning was a giant unknown. As the city streets passed beneath their horses' hooves, Willerd's stomach clenched into tighter and tighter knots.

The palace was significantly more intimidating from this angle. Yesterday he'd been able to use a side entrance, slipping in through a servant's door and able to bypass all of this front gate grandeur. Lynley seemed not to notice it at all as they rode through the gates, more than a few people merely standing agape as they passed.

The horses were whisked away the moment they dismounted, Lynley striding forward without looking back to see if Willerd was following or not. Maybe after so many weeks she merely assumed he was. More likely, he thought, she probably couldn't be bothered to care either way. She certainly had no problems with ignoring the tumult that they left in their wake as they delved ever deeper into the castle.

Lynley seemed completely at ease with brushing past the guards, heading straight for the throne room without hesitation. They hadn't seen a proper bath in more than a month—or a bed, or brush, or change of clothes—but Lynley didn't seem bothered by her state of disarray. He supposed it might be hard to be a queen if one was overly concerned with that sort of thing, but he couldn't help but cringe with every clean, well-dressed person that laid eyes on them. Silently, Willerd tried to steel himself, internally berating himself that this was exactly the kind of behavior he would have to stamp out soon. He would never survive in court otherwise.

The guards standing at the doors to the audience chamber came to startled and sloppy attention, eyes wide as they swept over the pair. Lynley didn't so much as break stride, kept marching forward with the sure knowledge that the doors would be removed from her path before she hit them. Sure enough, the majordomo sprang to life, looking a little wild around the eyes as he gestured frantically for the heralds to open the doors and announce Lynley. Apparently, Lynley had traveled through the palace halls quicker than the news that she had returned.

The majordomo's announcement was proven entirely superfluous the moment the doors were opened. Every head swiveled to take in whoever had the gall to use the main entrance to the hall after audiences were already in session, instead of entering discreetly through a side entrance. Willerd couldn't be sure, but it seemed like Lynley puffed up further under that scrutiny, chest expanding as she stood up straighter, chin taking on the same upward tilt she'd gotten when she had convinced him that a bear shouldn't drive them from their campsite.

There was more than one gasp from the courtiers gathered, a low mumble rising from the crowd. It parted like water before a bow as Lynley strode forward, gaze fixed unerringly on the throne at the front of the room and its occupant. The woman seated there was coldly beautiful, hair meticulously coiffed, eyes hard and flat as she considered their approach. She'd be quite pretty, Willerd thought as they finally drew close, if she smiled, softened her hair, relaxed the rigidity of her posture, and *wasn't sitting on Lynley's throne*. The bottom dropped out of his stomach as she continued to sit there impassively, hands folded precisely in her lap, attention focused solely on Lynley. It gave a further swoop as Lynley stopped just short of the dais and *bowed*.

Willerd lurched over into an awkward bow, feeling like the floor had suddenly been revealed to be the ceiling. None of this had been part of his plan—or rather, his parents' plan—and he was feeling increasingly out of his depth. So far, very little had gone the way he had been told it would, and it seemed that his hopes that reaching the castle would fix that had now been thoroughly dashed to pieces.

After a long beat of silence, the woman on the throne finally rose to her feet, gracefully sinking into a curtsy, her skirts swept to the side with a soft rustle of silk. "Lady Lynley." Her voice was smooth and low, cultured in a way that Willerd's parents and tutors both had failed to teach him. "I am gladdened to see you returned to us. I have feared it would not be so for some months, and it is a relief that you appear to be as hale and hearty as ever I have seen."

Lynley inclined her head, seeming unbothered by this woman who appeared to have all but usurped the throne in her absence. "Lady Isolda, well met again. I am pleased to see that my court has endured under your guidance, though I expected nothing less." There was the hint of a smirk at the corner of Lynley's mouth that hadn't once made an appearance during the long weeks that Willerd had traveled with her.

The woman—Lady Isolda, *his sister's Duchess*—arched a delicate eyebrow. "You flatter me, truly. But come, you must be weary from your travels." For the first time, her eyes strayed from Lynley, flicking almost imperceptibly to take in Willerd and their travel-worn clothing, her lips pressing into a thin line. "I am sure you would welcome the opportunity to refresh yourselves. There will be time aplenty to... celebrate your return, later." There was the barest pause at the end as she glanced at Willerd again.

Apparently, he thought, he hadn't factored into her plans either.

~~*

Isolda flushed hotly as she led the way away from the audience chamber, heart hammering in her ears loudly enough that she was sure everyone around them could hear it. She couldn't say what she had said or done after Lynley showed up, couldn't say what excuse she had given. She hoped it had been adequate, tried to trust that her training would have taken over, and seen her through the moment. It was impossible to be sure though, and there was no one she could trust to ask.

Her eyes strayed for just a moment over her shoulder, a quick glance sliding over Lynley before she jerked her gaze around to the front. Staring was unladylike regardless of reason, even if that reason was the mud-stained and torn layers of silk and satin that clothed Lynley. To think that she had actually traversed the capitol and the castle in that was absolutely appalling, no matter that a small part of Isolda—a very small part—could only marvel at her sheer audacity. An even smaller part of her envied Lynley her gall, but the loudest part of her was already deliberating how best to quash and mitigate the rumors that were sure to crop up as a result of that, and that part had no time for pointless jealousy.

She checked the sigh that was building in her chest, letting it out as a slow controlled breath instead. It should have been only relief coursing through her right now, with visible proof before her that all of her plans weren't quickly and effortlessly slipping from her control. Somehow, none of it felt truly reassuring, and all she could do was wonder what would go wrong next. She had spent months now balancing a throne that—by all laws—she didn't yet have a solid claim to. With Lynley back in the capitol, that was one problem that would be remedied. She thought that should probably make her feel better than it did.

"I know you must be tired," she started, voice cool and controlled and pitched to carry back to the travelers. "But there is much of which you must be apprised as soon as possible." She paused minutely, before deciding to continue. "And there are questions that remain as to your long absence."

"You are correct on all counts, Lady Isolda." Lynley's voice was higher and rougher than hers, but it carried just as well. "If a bath and some real food could be called to my chambers, there is no reason to delay." Isolda fought the urge to check over her shoulder as Lynley paused, and then wished she had checked her facial expression as she continued. "There are deceivers in our midst. I would like to know soon who they are."

Isolda didn't bother replying when she knew it would be redundant, merely adjusted her course for the royal wing. The hallway off of which her own rooms were located wasn't far off, so her steps trod familiar hallways for most of the way. She didn't think about the fact that soon the royal wing would be her own.

She only paused at the intersection of two corridors to flag a servant, relaying Lynley's request for food and a bath. With the ease of long practice, Isolda continued to ignore the second weary traveler dogging her steps, silently wondering who he was but unwilling to seem too eager to find out. The answer would likely come out soon enough, and even if it didn't she could be patient. Isolda prided herself on that patience. It's what had gotten her this far in life, and it would see her through now. She just had to remember that.

Her feet were thankfully not strangers to these floors, because she spent most of the walk lost in her own thoughts. Most of that familiarity had come from exploring this hallway, usually at the darkest part of the night, when no one else would be wandering the halls with her, but she had been here a handful of times outside of that. She couldn't be seen avoiding the wing anymore than she could be seen actively prowling it, and there had been private correspondence that had needed attending to during Lynley's absence. As far as anyone needed to know, that was the only reason she had acquainted herself with these halls.

The guards were nodding to her politely, doors to the suite of rooms already half open, before they caught sight of Lynley. One of them jerked awkwardly to a stop, door only half open, while the other tried to straighten into a proper salute while still opening the door for Isolda. It was second nature for her to hold in an unimpressed snort, continuing smoothly into the room. Out of the corner of her eye, she could see Lynley waving the guards off.

Isolda had been in here enough times to be passingly comfortable making her way to the sitting area, back facing the wall as she sank gracefully onto a chaise. A twitch of fingers settled her skirts back into place as the door clicked shut. Her gaze came up immediately, focused in on Lynley as she paced the perimeter of the room. Isolda couldn't tell if it was borne of discomfort or if it was soothing, but Lynley's hand glanced over nearly everything she passed: the back of a sofa, the edge of the desk, the chest set next to the hearth.

The man who had accompanied her hung back, wringing his hands as he stood just inside the doorway. Isolda gave him her attention as Lynley paused to more thoroughly peruse the papers on her desk. He wasn't especially tall, probably just a bit taller than Isolda herself, though they both would be able to look straight over Lynley's head when standing behind her. She wondered idly if he'd tried to use his height against Lynley during their travels, since it was obvious the two had journeyed together from wherever they had been.

Knowing what she did of Lynley, Isolda didn't think it would have turned out terribly well for him if he had. Lynley was as fierce a knight as any and—if the stories Isolda had picked up over the months were to be believed—was not especially forgiving of perceived slights to herself or her character. The man might not have been gangly, but he certainly didn't look like he would prove too much of a challenge against a battle-blooded knight.

A knock at the door broke the silence that had grown just short of uncomfortable. Lynley barely looked up from the papers still occupying her attention, waving a hand at the man in a way meant to convey action. With a put-upon sigh he opened the door, stepping back uncertainly as two large servants shuffled in, a vast copper tub between them. Isolda pointed in front of the hearth as one directed a questioning look at her, settling back to watch the procession. They were followed by a string of servants, bucket after bucket of steaming water being dumped into the tub. In their midst came another servant with a tray laden down with food, another with a tea service just behind her. It was all over in a flurry of skirts and buckets, Isolda waving the last of them out as they hovered by the door. "If we have further need of anything, we shall ring the bell." One darted a look at the fireplace, and only long practice stilled her eye roll. "We are more than capable of lighting a fire should we require one. You may leave now."

She stood as the last scampered out, Lynley's traveling companion looking rather lost as he closed the door. Isolda ignored him, crossing to the chest beside the cold fireplace. It held what she supposed Lynley deemed bath essentials, and she plucked one of the vials of oil from the bottom, giving it a curious sniff before adding it liberally to the tub.

Lynley looked up sharply, eyes narrowing at the vial. "There is no call for that sort of frippery. I can bathe without that sort of floweriness."

Isolda glanced at her through hooded eyes, a single brow arched. "I suppose you *would* have become accustomed to that smell by now."

Lynley's brows shot up, and for the first time since arriving at the castle, Isolda found herself struggling to hide a smirk. There was something intimately satisfying about dealing with someone who didn't play the games and wore their emotions so openly. Lynley's surprise was plain to see, though it quickly shifted into something else. There was a glint in her eye and a stubborn clench in her jaw that nearly made Isolda want to back up as Lynley stalked closer.

She wouldn't allow herself to show that manner of weakness though, so Isolda stood her ground. After months of infuriating meetings with the council, her expression defaulted to cool attention, eyes soft and bland. She almost wanted to laugh at the way it caused Lynley's eyebrows to pinch together in the middle. Instead, she tipped her head slightly, blinking slowly in a way that had goaded more than one council member to snap.

"I am sorry to have offended your sensibilities, Duchess. I was trapped in a tower for some time, and have traveled extensively since. I shall endeavor to remedy the problem for you posthaste." Lynley gave a mocking bow, straightening with something between a sneer and a smirk. What might have once been silk slippers were kicked off without ceremony, revealing feet grubby and *bare*, Isolda realized. Lynley wasn't wearing any stockings. Her outer layers were just as quickly and abruptly removed, unrecognizable as anything befitting her station under the tears and mud. Isolda fought a grimace as she dropped them carelessly to the floor, before suddenly realizing that Lynley stood in nothing but the saddest excuse for chemise and bloomers that had ever graced the palace.

Isolda froze her face, unwilling to give anything away. Lynley didn't seem the type for games, so this was a power play, pure and simple. With the slightest uptick of her chin, Isolda allowed a small, pleasant smile to cross her face. "Well? I would hate for the water to cool before you had a chance to appreciate it."

Lynley's eyebrows jerked up, but whether she was shocked or impressed, Isolda couldn't tell. Either way, the chemise was off and billowing down to the floor in the next moment, bloomers following to pool on the floor with a soft thud. Isolda kept her eyes locked on Lynley's face, standing firm. She wouldn't allow herself to be scared off by a naked royal. She was a queen-to-be and she was not going to back down because an improper amount of skin was showing.

They remained at a standoff for several long minutes, eyes locked while the tub steamed fragrantly beside them. Isolda refused to be the first to look away, keeping her eyes soft as she stared Lynley down. In the end, Lynley tipped her head to the side, mouth relaxing into a smirk as she turned away with a small huff of a laugh. Isolda let her gaze flick curiously over the planes of her back as she climbed into the tub, attention averted safely away by the time Lynley had settled herself. Lynley raised a brow in challenge, but Isolda sniffed delicately and turned away, unwilling to become embroiled in another staring contest, particularly one which might prove unwinnable. Instead she strolled back to the sitting area, tugging an overly delicate chair around so that she could face the tub.

The first thing out of her mouth was not exactly what she had meant to ask. "Who is he?"

Lynley brows ticked up like she'd forgotten they weren't alone, and tossed a cursory glance over her shoulder to the man by the door, who was now very red faced and staring resolutely in the direction opposite the bathing area. She shrugged carelessly. "I have no idea, beyond his name."

The man's eyes widened and he whipped around before seeming to remember why he had been facing away in the first place. He whirled back to stare at the wall, managing to stammer out, "My name is Willerd, of the—" before a knock echoed through the room, effectively cutting him short.

The door was opening before Isolda could even gesture the man toward it, and she noted absently that Lynley made no move to cover herself. "Forgive me, milady," preceded Corrissa into the room, and she dipped into a curtsy as soon as she was fully through the door. "But you requested I notify you when—Will!" Corrissa had finally taken in the room's occupants, mouth dropping open slightly.

"You know this man?" Isolda tried to temper her tone, but she did not care for surprises.

Corrissa's eyes were still on the man—was it Will or Willerd?—and her eyebrows were up near her hairline as she answered. "He is my brother." She took a step toward him without seeming to mean to. "Will, what are you doing here?"

He shuffled uncertainly. "I helped Lady Lynley to escape from the tower," he started, looking over his shoulder at the tub again before turning away sharply, face burning anew. "I escorted her home, and now we are to be married."

Corrissa's jaw dropped, eyes blowing wide as saucers. Blood was suddenly roaring in her ears, but Isolda still managed a venomous, "I beg your pardon."

Both reactions were eclipsed as Lynley surged up in the tub, water sloshing over the side as she spun to face the man. "We are to be *what*?" she demanded, face thunderous. Something settled in Isolda's chest that she was not the only one to be so blindsided.

Willerd gaped around the room for several long moments, hands wringing furiously. He seemed to forget his agitation about Lynley's nakedness in the face of her outrage. His mouth worked soundlessly for some time, before the words started tripping off his tongue in a hurried jumble. "I—I was on a quest, at the behest of my parents. There was—there was a man, who came to our village. He said—there was a princess. A crown princess. She was locked away—she was locked in the tower. And the first man to reach her—noble or knight or not—would be granted her hand. I was—I was the first. I do not—my parents demanded I take up the quest."

Isolda rose from her chair and only just managed to refrain from stalking closer. "I will say this once and that shall be the end of this matter. I am Isolda, Duchess of the Western Thorny Mountains and the Crimson Valley. I have been betrothed to Lynley, then Princess of Fellinsoph and now Crown Princess and only remaining child of King Nikolai and Queen Talisa, since our infancy. The only person who is to be married to Lynley is I. Am I understood?"

Willerd had gone white as a sheet, wide eyes fixed on Isolda. He nodded jerkily, looking hopelessly lost as he continued to stand by the door. His pallor worsened as Lynley cleared her throat, bringing the room's attention to where she still stood in the bathtub.

"Claiming the right to my hand could well be construed as a treasonous plot against my intended. Is that clear?" Willerd's head wobbled in a shaky nod. "It is also true, however, that you assisted me in escaping from that tower and saw me safely back to the castle, and I am not unappreciative. So I will make you this deal: if you will tell us what you know of the person who called this quest, then I will see you are not brought up on charges of treason, and will furthermore see that you are properly compensated for the services you have rendered to the crown. Is that fair?"

"I had no wish to marry you." Willerd looked almost more surprised than anyone at the words that had come spilling from his mouth. They all stared for a beat, letting that sit in the open, like a dead fish that no one wished to touch.

"Well," Lynley broke the silence, looking almost amused. "I suppose that is for the best, in the end. Does that mean we have a deal?" This time Willerd simply nodded, still looking a bit horrified, and seeming to remember his discomfiture at Lynley's still naked frame.

Isolda's legs folded under her in relief, and she sank back into her chair as elegantly as possible. "Lynley, do resume your bath, for my sensibilities if not for the fact that we shall get nothing from him while he is preoccupied with your state of dishabille." She tried to keep her tone nonchalant, but even she could hear the quaver at the end.

With more grace than Isolda would have attributed to her, Lynley lowered herself back into the water. She settled back with a sigh, eyes narrowed to slits as she stared at nothing, lips pursed thoughtfully. "Who called for the quest?" Isolda wasn't sure if the question was merely Lynley musing aloud, but Willerd actually seemed to be giving it thought.

"I am not sure he called for the quest himself," he started, back to staring resolutely at the far wall. "The man who brought the pronouncement of the quest to our village did not appear to be of even the lowest of noble birth; it is hard to imagine he would have the power to call for a quest for Lady Lynley's hand. He called himself Christophe, though I doubt that will be helpful. I *can* tell you that he has a long scar that crosses his neck?" He sighed, slumping a little, and were he not still wearing his traveling clothes, Isolda might have offered him a seat.

"Is there nothing else about him you can tell us?" she prodded. The name wasn't unique by any means, and tracking a man with only a scar to go off would be difficult at best.

Willerd only shrugged. "I wish there was. He had a crooked nose and he looked rather rough, but that still leaves too many men. He was only in our village a couple of days before he moved on, and my parents insisted I leave immediately after that. They were afraid the quest had been brought to other villages before ours and thought I would already be behind."

Lynley sighed, letting her head fall back against the rim of the tub. "I suppose we will have to use that for now. I have not been back but a day, so I am woefully uninformed about what has been happening here, or anywhere in the kingdom for that matter, over the last several months. It will take me more than a night to catch up, I am sure."

Isolda reached up to rub her temple, only catching herself after her hand had started moving, and attempting to pass it off as merely fixing a stray hair. She had no time for headaches now, and certainly had no time to appear anything less than utterly in control. There were too many variables right now, pieces that didn't fit together into a cohesive picture. That made Isolda nervous in a way that she hadn't been since arriving at the castle. She had been alone then, that was true, but she had also known where she stood, and where those around her stood.

Part of the problem—most of the problem, actually—was that there were simply too many people who might have stood to benefit from this move. The fact that they had only the name 'Christophe' to go off of didn't help her temper any. There were whole lists of people who might be furthering whatever the goal was, as well, without being directly able to gain something from it. That uncertainty made Isolda feel far too exposed for her liking. This day had been one surprise after another, and only the first one had been anything approaching a pleasant one. Life had almost been easier before Lynley had returned. It had certainly been simpler.

"*Oh.*"

Isolda turned to Corrissa as she broke the silence, half startled since she'd completely forgotten the girl was still in the room. As three gazes turned to fix on her, Corrissa blushed. "Forgive me, Your Highness, Your Grace," she started, with a bob of a curtsy. "Only, there are rumors around the castle that make more sense in this light."

She stopped, gnawing her lip, but Isolda already felt her patience wearing thin for the day. "What sort of rumors?"

Corrissa winced minutely, unable to meet her gaze for the first time since she had come into Isolda's service. "That you are a traitor and wish the throne for yourself alone. There had been... theories... that Lady Lynley's long absence was by your hand."

Isolda had stood to pour herself a cup of tea, but her limbs seemed suddenly to be made of rubber. There was a tight knot forming in her chest, squeezing the air from her lungs, and she sagged back into her seat.

"Oh."

~~*

Over the years of their betrothal, Lynley had only been in the same place as Isolda a dozen times or so, more often than not in a court other than her own. She was aloof and entirely too proper, and the only thing she and Lynley had ever had in common was a mutual appreciation for horses. It couldn't be said that they were friends—or even that they were particularly friendly toward one another—but they had forged a sort of respect and understanding between them, on horseback, riding through the fields outside of the city walls.

The point was, Lynley knew that there were many worse people that her parents could have saddled her with. Isolda may have been aloof and proper, but she was also sharp, and had snuck *into* council meetings while Lynley was busy sneaking out. She thrived at diplomatic balls where Lynley was nearly to the point of gnawing her own arm off to escape, and had such a delicate way with words that Lynley honestly believed that most of the people who had ever talked to her had no idea that Isolda had just unashamedly insulted them.

Lynley thought, by this point, she had seen a fair range of the facial expressions that Isolda might show. She wasn't given to grand displays of emotion, nowhere near as obvious with her thoughts as Willerd had been over their weeks of travel. Balls, council meetings, and a banquet or two had given her enough of a stock though. She'd seen Isolda mildly irritated and grossly—blandly—smug and silently furious and calmly observant and whole dozens of others.

She didn't have a name for the expression that Isolda wore now.

Since the most interesting bath of Lynley's life and the revelation of what the rumor mill had been churning out in her absence, Isolda had been quiet. Not the same kind of focused, calculating quiet that Lynley had come to associate with sitting next to Isolda during council meetings, fighting to seem interested. This was the kind of quiet she honestly would have believed Isolda incapable of. It was almost... meek.

It was also highly unsettling. Lynley had been gone from the castle for nearly three months before she had woken up in the tower, dealing with some hill bandits in the south with her company before she and Isolda were to be wed. They had already been late by the time they had finally set their sights for home, and she'd known that Isolda would have already moved to the palace by the time they reached it. During her confinement, it had been an oddly comforting thought, that there someone she trusted in the castle looking after the throne, and she'd been so relieved to find that the

Isolda sitting in the audience hall was the same duchess she had come to know.

This Isolda seemed like a poor imitation of that. She remained unfailingly polite, and put on a good show at the banquet thrown to welcome Lynley home, charming the ambassadors who had come to extend the warm wishes of their rulers. She had floated around the ballroom with just as many diplomats as would be considered proper, and then had settled back in at Lynley's side with a soft smile. It bothered Lynley that she could see through the mask, when she never could before.

Lynley sighed as Isolda knocked. She knew it was Isolda because no one else knocked quite like that. It was oddly frivolous coming from her. "Come in," she called, shuffling the papers around on her desk, looking for an armory inventory she knew was in the stack somewhere.

Isolda glided in, avoiding even looking at the desk as she crossed to the chaise against the wall, sinking into the corner seat like she had every time she had visited these rooms. Lynley glanced up but Isolda's gaze was firmly focused on the short table in the middle of the sitting area. "Isolda?" She didn't look up, and Lynley fought another sigh, leveraging herself up and stationing herself behind a high back chair. "Duchess?"

Her gaze finally came up, and this was an expression Lynley knew well, determination drawing Isolda's lips tight, chin tipped upward resolutely. "There is a matter about which we must speak," she started, and Lynley nodded for her to go on, unease twisting her stomach. "I believe it would be best to call our betrothal off."

For a moment, Lynley found herself frozen in time, watching the scene from above: Isolda on the chaise, posture ramrod straight, eyes cool and weary, and Lynley standing across from her, using the chair more for support than as a shield now. It wasn't her shuffling her feet around the chair, knees buckling as she folded down into it, but she slammed back into her body, breath suddenly gone. "I must have misheard," she tried, voice sounding off in her own ears. "You think what?"

Isolda pursed her lips, glance dancing away for a moment before she turned back to stare Lynley down. "I think it would be the best course of action for all. You obviously cannot trust me anymore—"

"Where—" Lynley had to stop, clear her throat. "Why would you believe such a thing as that?"

Her gaze was cool and Lynley could almost see Isolda bracing herself. "You have delayed the wedding, even though finalizing our marriage would allow for the coronation to finally take place, ensuring that no amount of scheming could then take the throne from you. The only reason I can imagine for why you would postpone that is if you distrusted me, or believed that I might be part of whatever plot landed you in the tower. As such, it is only sensible that we call off—"

"Have you gone completely fucking insane?" At any other time, the look of unrestrained shock on Isolda's face might have made her smirk. "You believe the only possible reason I might delay our wedding is if I thought you capable of *treason*."

Isolda's mouth dropped open, just enough to be noticeable, brows pulled together in confusion. She opened her mouth, to say something else utterly ridiculous no doubt, so Lynley cut her off. "No. You are going to be silent for a moment while I process how entirely misguided you are capable of being." Lynley passed a hand over her face, trying to figure out where she'd gone wrong. She finally slumped back with a long sigh and studied Isolda, who sat staring away at the wall, hands clenched in her lap so tightly the knuckles had gone white.

"I apologize for whatever I have done to give you the impression that I no longer trust you." Isolda's gaze dragged over to meet hers, and Lynley tried to look as earnest as she was capable. "The reason I have delayed the wedding is for *your* safety."

Isolda opened her mouth to interrupt, forcing Lynley to raise a hand to stall her. "Hear me, please. Whoever orchestrated my capture does not want me dead, but just as clearly does not want me to marry you. I cannot fathom the reason behind this, but it seems clear that were I to proceed with our marriage that would put you in danger. And that was something I greatly wished to avoid."

Isolda nodded slowly, still looking uncertain. "Would it not still ease matters then, if we were to call the betrothal off?" she asked quietly, some of the life coming back to her as she continued. "I would not think any less of you were you to do so."

Lynley was shaking her head before Isolda had even finished talking. "I would not go back on the agreement made between our two families, certainly not at the threat of a traitor. My cousin could not convince me against our marriage, and I will not let a faceless stranger do so either. There is no one I have met better suited to ruling at my side than you."

Isolda narrowed her eyes at Lynley, but there a slight uptick at the corners of her mouth and two spots of color high on her cheeks, as she rose to her feet. "That was almost romantic, Your Highness."

The smirk crossed Lynley's face unbidden as she followed Isolda to the door, matter apparently dealt with to her satisfaction. "I would not become accustomed, your grace. We have reputations to uphold." Isolda hummed in acknowledgement. And Lynley couldn't be sure, since she was out the door in the next minute, but she thought Isolda might have winked.

~~*

Lynley was relieved to see Isolda return to something approaching familiar. She was back to biting at council members who tried to talk over her, and Lynley almost tripped over herself in her haste to accept when Isolda suggested they take an afternoon ride beyond the city walls. Things were finally comfortable, for the first time since she had returned. There was still the looming problem of someone having spirited her away to a tower to try to enact an as-yet unknown plan, but it helped that she had at least sorted out some of her personal affairs.

Naturally, just as she had fallen into some sort of routine—more than a month after she had returned and a couple weeks after she and Isolda had gotten back onto the same page—a horn sounded at the castle gate, signaling the return of the one of the royal companies. Lynley was on the front wall of the castle, leaning out between the parapets, before a messenger could even find her to tell her the news. She'd seen the standards at a distance. Her company had finally made it home.

There were at least two servants she knocked down in her race downstairs, and if she'd been a little less anxious, she would have slowed to apologize. But she had been trying for months not to think about the likely state of her company and the very real chance that most or all were dead. To see what appeared to be her full company marching through the city had been beyond anything she had been hoping for. She would simply have to hope that the servants understood her haste.

Knights and soldiers were pouring into the front hall when she reached the bottom of the staircase, and she had to stop a couple steps up and simply stare. It was almost unbelievable to see them here, so many months since she had been separated from them. She stood frozen on the steps then, unable to break whatever illusion this was.

"Lyn!" The shout brought her head up and about, and she didn't notice the stairs passing under her as she laid eyes on Sandros. The captain of her company was grinning broadly, and looked far better after his months of traveling than Lynley had after hers.

"San," she greeted warmly, accepting a hearty slap on the back, only a little surprised when he tugged her in to make it a real hug. She laughed, pushing him away. "Decorum, captain."

Sandros snorted, waving away her words like the joke they were. "We trekked after your ass once we found out it was in a tower, only to reach the tower to find it empty. If you were gonna get yourself outta that mess, you could at least have told us."

Lynley rolled her eyes, but the move was fond, and she honestly hadn't thought to ever be rolling her eyes at San's dramatics again. It was a good feeling, so she didn't fight the grin that felt like it was threatening to split her face in two. She was being jostled on all sides, but it was soothing, and the knights around her all smelled like they'd gone too long without bathing, but that was comforting in its own way too.

"That your dame there?" She jerked at the whisper in her ear, whipping to look at Sandros just behind her. He nodded toward the stairs that she had come down only a little while ago. She was unsurprised to find Isolda there, gaze already focused on her even in the midst of the crowd. She felt herself grin and turned back to Sandros, only to find him already smirking at her, eyebrows tilted knowingly. She pushed his face away with another laugh and swung around to wave Isolda over.

Instead of coming closer, Isolda shook her head. Lynley couldn't see her face clearly from here, certainly not enough to read the nuances of expression when Isolda had her face smooth and under control. Lynley could read the line of her shoulders though, the stiffness in her spine as she hiked up her skirts to disappear back up the stairs.

There was already a twist of guilt in her stomach every time Lynley remembered Isolda explaining that she should call off the betrothal, and Lynley couldn't allow another problem to get so far. She whirled to make her apologies to Sandros, but he was already waving her off with a smile, throwing in a wink that said he thought she was following Isolda up with entirely different goals in mind. She didn't bother correcting him, just slugged his shoulder like he was no doubt expecting and headed for the stairs.

Isolda was already back in her rooms by the time Lynley caught up with her, and she sighed at the closed door. Lynley took a deep breath before knocking, oddly relieved when Isolda called for her to enter. She poked her head in first anyway. Isolda was slumped in one of the armchairs in her sitting area, head in her hand. She glanced over at the door and started, surprise clear on her face. Lynley inched into the room, smiling uncertainly as Isolda's startled gaze followed her in and across the room.

She took one of the chairs opposite Isolda, feeling truly uncertain for perhaps the first time in her life. This country duchess had a way of making her feel like the first time she'd ever stepped onto a battlefield. It was more than a little disconcerting.

Across from her, Isolda was trying to straighten into and regain her usual amount of poise. "Was there something you required of me, Lynley?"

Lynley gave her a hard look, because Isolda wasn't dense. Sure enough, after a few moments she deflated, letting herself slump back into the chair. "It is nothing. Really," she insisted when Lynley raised a brow. "I ask only that you be discreet in your affairs. Other than that, you need not worry that I will get in the way."

There was a charged beat of silence before Lynley slunk from her chair, stalking across the sitting area. Isolda's eyes were wide as they tracked Lynley, the moment stretching taut as Lynley loomed over her chair. Isolda pressed back as Lynley leaned forward, one hand coming up to rest on the back of the chair, the other bracing on the arm of it next to Isolda's hand.

At this distance, Lynley could see that Isolda's pupils were blown wide. "Why do you insist on believing the worst of me?"

Isolda opened her mouth, but closed it slowly without saying anything. Lynley tried to hold onto the sting of anger, but the faint lines at the corners of Isolda's eyes were visible like this, the small confused pinch between her brows. In the end, there was only one thing she could manage. "I will say this as plainly as I know how, and maybe then you will trust that you are in this no more deeply than I. Once we are married, you will never again be alone. I am yours, and you are mine, and no one else will have me as you do. I will protect and defend you as I would myself, and I have faith that you will do no less. Whatever else you may think, will you try to believe all this is so?"

Isolda gave her a wan smile, delicate fingers moving to circle Lynley's wrist, squeezing gently. "I thought I was not to become accustomed to romance," she tried. Neither of them mentioned if it fell a little flat; Lynley just returned the smile. That was enough for now. She had never known Isolda to renege on an agreement.

~~*

"I saw the man!"

During the weeks since Lynley's company had returned, she and Isolda had established a new sort of routine. They met in Isolda's chambers for a breakfast that was still far earlier than she preferred, then Isolda would part from Lynley to attend meetings with the heads of the city's guilds, whichever ambassadors were visiting, and the Royal Council. Lynley would rejoin her for lunch, often at one of their desks over ever shifting stacks of papers and letters, and then they would resume their separate schedules. Some afternoons would be broken up when Lynley appeared to ask if Isolda would accompany her on horseback outside of the city, but those days were still too few to become the norm.

Corrissa bursting into Isolda's chambers while she read reports over afternoon tea was distinctly not part of any sort of routine. She was panting lightly, hair slipping from its plait like she had run here from another part of the castle. Isolda beckoned her in and pushed her onto one of the stools by her desk, offering a cup of tea that was waved away. "Which man?"

Still breathing heavily, Corrissa drew a finger across her neck. "The man with the quest—the one Willerd described for us. I am sure of it."

Isolda surged with excitement. Lynley had men from her company deployed across the kingdom searching for word of the man, and her spymaster had been tasked with discreetly sussing out anything about the origins of the damnable quest. So far, there had been neither hide nor hair of the man according to any of their sources. To think that he might be present at the castle was nearly too much to believe.

Before Isolda could press for more details, there was a knock at the door. She called for them to enter impatiently, unwilling to deal with any distraction now that the end of the matter might suddenly be at hand. Lynley strode in, smiling at something. Normally, Isolda might tease her about being an open book, but there were more important items to attend to.

"Corrissa has seen Christophe."

The smile fell off Lynley's face, to be replaced by sharp curiosity. "Where?"

Isolda nodded at Corrissa, prompting her to answer. "The kitchens, only just now." She hurried on before either could ask the obvious question. "I have already asked Jacques if he is familiar with the man. He is not, but if anyone else in the kitchen is, Jacques will know by tomorrow."

"And Jacques is...?" Lynley glanced over to see if Isolda was just as lost.

She was not. "The head pastry chef in the kitchens." Isolda waved Lynley off as she arched a brow, smirk tugging up the corners of her lips. "You have no call for smugness. You are just as likely as I to steal a second pastry." She allowed herself the barest smirk. "The difference is that I know who to thank."

Lynley narrowed her eyes but seemed to decide that answering Isolda's challenge could wait. She turned back to Corrissa slowly, obviously mulling over her options. "You are sure if there is anything to know in the kitchens, Jacques will know? And by tomorrow?"

Corrissa nodded surely, dipping a quick curtsy. "I am certain, Your Highness. There is not a single rumor that passes through the kitchen that Jacques does not hear. If anyone in the kitchen has information, he will have it soon enough. I told him you wished to know, so he will be discreet. The last thing he would wish to do is upset you."

Slowly, Lynley nodded, looking more than half lost in thought. Isolda nodded that Corrissa was free to leave, returning to her tea before it grew too cold to drink. It took Lynley several long moments before she looked around, brow creasing at Corrissa's absence but smoothing quickly enough when Isolda gestured to the tea service.

"I have actually come to see if you wished to join me for a ride," Lynley said, running a hand through hair that had long since lost its coiffure. "I suppose I shall just return—"

"Nowhere," Isolda cut in briskly, rising and brushing her skirts out. "A ride sounds perfect." When Lynley turned to her in incredulity, Isolda treated her to the blandest smile she could manage. "It will take you from the castle, and might manage to prevent you from going down to the kitchens to demand answers yourself."

From the way Lynley's mouth opened and then snapped shut abruptly, Isolda knew she had entertained plans of doing just that. She nodded in satisfaction. "Nothing will be gained that way, and indeed everything could be lost. Let me change and we shall be off." She paused, waiting until Lynley looked up to meet her gaze. "Tomorrow will be soon enough."

~~*

Tomorrow, by Lynley's standards, appeared to mean 'with the next sunrise', and Isolda didn't try to hide the glare she was leveling at her betrothed as Lynley strode into Isolda's chambers and threw the curtains open. She seemed entirely too cheerful for the time of day and grinned every time she met Isolda's glower.

Corrissa had blessedly greater survival instincts and arrived bearing a tray of coffee strong enough that Isolda could smell it the moment she stepped into the room. She pointedly took a few more minutes to glare over the rim of her mug at Lynley before finally turning her attention to Corrissa.

Her lady-in-waiting stood uncertainly at the edge of the sitting room, wringing her hands in a manner very like her brother and not at all like the rather stalwart girl Isolda had come to know her as. She didn't seem to want to look either of them in the eye, gaze focused on the rug at her feet. "Corrissa?"

The look on her face when her head came up could only be described as a grimace. "Jacques found the information." She shook her head, almost talking to herself as she continued. "I do not think you will be happy with this information."

Lynley was looking far more solemn now. "I am afraid that does not change the fact that we must know who has plotted treason against the crown."

Corrissa sketched a faint curtsy. "Yes, Your Highness. I simply wished to prepare you. From everything we have found, it would seem to be one of your council."

"My council?"

Corrissa nodded. "He knew you would not like rumor, so Jacques even went down into the city last night to make sure it was Christophe, and to be sure he had the employer correct." Isolda could see her swallow nervously as she glanced between the two of them. "He is in the service of your cousin, the Chancellor."

~~*

"Chancellor Brayden, you are found guilty of the crime of treason against the crown. You are hereby stripped of all titles and land, as well as citizenship to the kingdom of Fellinsoph. You are sentenced to exile from the kingdom and all lands held therein. If you are to be found within these boundaries after being escorted hence by the royal company, you will be executed without trial. May the gods have mercy on your soul."

The audience hall was crammed with more people than it usually saw in a week, unnaturally quiet as they had watched the proceedings. The trial had been nearly decided before Brayden had even been called to speak, witnesses coming out of the woodwork to support the crown as word had spread that the Chancellor's dealings had been tainted by treason. Christophe had disappeared from the city without a trace, only to turn up dead in a field two days later. Isolda knew Lynley hadn't pressed her men for information on that.

With Lynley and Isolda both in attendance, a second throne had been added to the dais so that they could oversee the trial. Lynley claimed it was a formality, but Isolda rather thought that maybe she wished to appear in front of the people as a united force with her betrothed. She kept to herself the pleased feeling that settled behind her ribcage at that, but the private smile that Lynley had shot her as they had taken their seats made her think it might not have been as secret as she thought.

Beyond that, the entire affair had been startlingly uneventful. Brayden had remained sullen and silent throughout, barely saying a word in his own defense. The only time he had even looked at the thrones had been to sneer at Lynley while Willerd gave an accounting of having rescued her from the tower.

Beyond that, he had directed his attention and all of his answers to the Arbiter of the Law, only just managing to remain respectful throughout the course of his questioning. Not once had he addressed Lynley or Isolda directly, though Isolda couldn't miss the way he had smirked when one of the witnesses spoke of the whispers that had traveled through the palace halls for months, pointing toward the treason against the crown being carried out by Lynley's own betrothed. Apparently, Lynley hadn't missed it either, since her hand had stretched casually across the distance between their thrones to brush Isolda's fingers where they dangled off the arm. Isolda had brushed the rough palm of Lynley's hand with gentle fingertips, feeling inexplicably better by the show of support.

As the Arbiter finished his pronouncement, the audience took that as a cue that talk was acceptable once more. After the relative silence of the trial, Isolda felt almost overwhelmed by the sudden onslaught of noise. No one seemed particularly outraged by the verdict, which she took for a good sign all things considered. Silently, she sent a prayer to the gods that their information had been correct and Brayden really had been acting alone. At least exile was unlikely to inspire a mob among the people, even if he hadn't been acting alone.

She stood when Lynley did, absently brushing her skirts, though she knew they wouldn't have wrinkled, even in the span of time the trial had taken. Corrissa had taken extra care that morning to wrap Isolda's braids around her head and pin them tightly, covering them with a jeweled veil so her hair would be one less worry. It also left her hands to dangle rather uselessly at her side now, with nothing to fuss over.

Lynley took the few steps that would bring them side by side, arms just brushing as she swayed closer. "I am unsure of whether I am relieved that the trial went along so smoothly, or if I should feel anxious that this was too easy for unraveling a treasonous plot." She sighed, leaning into Isolda's space the littlest bit. "I suppose I shall just be glad that he chose exile over execution. I am not sure I would have had the stomach to see such a thing through, though I know it is sometimes necessary of a ruler."

Shuffling just closer, Isolda shook her head. "I am sorry you are forced even to exile him, especially as he is the last of what remains of your family," she murmured, shoulder bumping Lynley's.

Lynley shook her head in response. "I am only sorry the last of my family would do such a thing. And I am sorry he was the start of the rumors about you. "

Isolda tried to shrug that off, though it still stung. "I wish this would not force you to be the last of your line," she sighed, knowing Lynley would immediately shut down any conversation about breaking the betrothal. With every passing day, Isolda found herself increasingly unable to so much as entertain the suggestion, even when she knew that it was the proper thing to do. She didn't examine that feeling too closely, though she had a suspicion that Lynley might feel the same toward her. There was, apparently, a limit to which propriety held sway.

Lynley scoffed, startling Isolda a little. "Our line has not always been carried on through blood, and it would do well for people to remember that. My grandmother was not her fathers', but our line has continued anyway. It will continue again," she maintained, confidently enough that Isolda found herself relaxing. "It is for the better that he is gone this definitively as well. I have always known that he would not suit for my council, certainly not after he tried so diligently to talk me from our betrothal. It is only particularly so now that he has tried to force my hand to secure his influence; Willerd might have been easy enough for his lower level machinations, but I think my cousin would have found it more difficult for him to pressure Willerd into truly standing against me. His competence may be questionable, but Willerd's character certainly is not. This is a more permanent removal from influence than I might have planned for Brayden, but it may prove better in the end. I doubt he would be pleased with me continuing the line as my great-grandfathers did, for starters." She wound her arm through Isolda's then, watching as Sandros put forth what was no doubt as threat that if he did not walk on his own, the once-Chancellor would be forcibly carried from the hall.

"There is some good news to come of this, at least," Lynley broke the silence as they watched the guards escort Brayden from the audience hall. Isolda turned to stare at her in disbelief, only further confused when she laughed softly before continuing, "At long last, we are to be *betrothed* no more." Isolda was smiling slightly before she could think not to.

~~*

The preparations for the wedding and the simultaneous coronation began nearly the moment the trial had concluded. The country had been waiting for quite some time to have a monarch again on the throne, and there were staggering amounts of work to do before the big day arrived. Horses laden down with invitations and notices were sent from the palace, and Isolda went down to the kitchens personally to ensure that the small army of pastry chefs that Jacques had acquired would be sufficient to ensure the success of the only part of the wedding feast that she cared about. Isolda nearly laughed when he informed her that Lynley had already been down to do the same, but managed to bite it back at the last minute. It was becoming surprisingly less automatic the more time she spent around her betrothed. She'd always known Lynley would be a bad influence.

The wedding clothes had been ordered shortly after the death of the late king, and the last few days leading up to the wedding left her distressingly idle. Much of the kingdom had shut down for a week of celebrations, and after the expulsion of Brayden, the council was—at least for the moment—docile as kittens. It was almost unimaginable after the stress and uncertainty that had plagued them both for months, but it seemed—somehow—things had finally fallen into place.

When the big day finally arrived, the wedding and subsequent coronation had passed by in a surreal blur, and Isolda found herself absently gazing out at the dancing that followed the feast, Lynley a warm presence at her side before it began to sink in. "I was certain that Willerd would be in attendance," she remarked, a bit inanely all things considered. "I made sure that Corrissa extended to him an invitation, and he seemed the type not to decline a royal invitation."

From the corner of her eye, she could see Lynley's face freeze halfway between expressions, and she turned to look curiously, brows climbing. Noticing her look, Lynley coughed self-consciously. "I sent him home."

Isolda's eyebrows shot the rest of the way up, and she drew out the moment to see if Lynley would answer on her own. "Why?"

Her curiosity only grew as Lynley avoided her gaze, staring resolutely out at the dancers twirling by. "So he could finally marry the girl—Anna."

"But his parents—"

"And to buy that shop for her, the bakery." Lynley cringed slightly.

The inkling of an idea grew in the back of her mind, and Isolda knew Lynley could hear the smirk as she prompted, "And how would he afford that?" she mused, pretending not to notice Lynley fighting a pout.

"It was the only just choice. I might still be in the tower but for him," Lynley protested.

The corners of Isolda's mouth tipped up, a single brow arched knowingly as she drawled. "Of course. You have to maintain your honor. Very noble; I understand completely."

"You are infuriating," Lynley bit back, the effect somewhat ruined by the grin that tugged her mouth up before she could force it back down. "I only did it because you and Corrissa kept on about his devotion and the damnable shop and how charming the whole affair was."

"I think it delightful," Isolda simpered.

Lynley rolled her eyes, pinning Isolda with her gaze. "You are simply hoping they will send confections in thanks, now."

Isolda shrugged lightly, looking up at Lynley through her lashes. "I do have a certain fondness for sweet things."

There was satisfaction in the knowledge that she was the only one who could draw a blush from Lynley. There was suppressed laughter in her voice when Lynley finally managed, "Come then, lady-wife. Let us see if you kiss as sweet at you talk. The happy couple is always superfluous at these banquets, anyway."

She let the answering laugh bubble out of her, just for tonight, edging with Lynley toward the edge of the dais. "You will ruin your reputation if you continue with these romantic declarations."

Lynley grabbed her hand, bringing it up to brush a soft kiss across her knuckles. "Who will ever know this but you?"

For once, Isolda didn't try to temper the smile that stole across her face then, content to revel in it for the moment. "Well? I believe I was promised both solitude and kisses. I find myself quite lacking in both," she taunted, smile brightening as it was returned.

Lynley tugged her out into the deserted hallway with a wink and a teasing kiss. "Yes, *Your Majesty*.

HUNTING A LADY

CAITLIN RICCI & CARI Z.

Jessa wiped the sweat from her brow before hunching her shoulders over the low wooden table and the deer hide laid out in front of her. The blade of her short, sharp knife glinted in the bright sunlight coming in through the door she'd propped open to release some of the stuffy fall air as she worked. She didn't use her knife while stretching hides, so there was really no reason for her to have it out. But seeing it there, just within arm's reach, made her feel better.

"You still working on that? Any other apprentice would have that hide stretched and ready to cut by now."

Ignoring the gruff voice behind her was a lot easier said than done, especially when Brent put a heavy hand on the bare skin of her tanned shoulder. His fingers curled over her smooth muscles, and she shook her head, getting back to work.

"Can't imagine why my uncle kept you around. No sane person would have a girl as an apprentice working under him. But maybe under a man is exactly where you belong."

Brent moved his hand to the back of her neck, where the fine tendrils of dark hair that had escaped from her bun curled over her nape. Jessa shivered and bit the inside of her cheek to keep from snapping at him.

After taking a deep breath, she turned around to face him. Brent had to move to avoid getting hit by her knees as she got comfortable again on the rickety stool. "Sir." The word hurt to say, but as her trade master, Brent was supposed to get at least that much respect from her. Too bad he hadn't earned it. He was nothing like his uncle in that regard. "The hide needs to be stretched by this afternoon to make bracers for the order due next week. If I delay, the leather won't have enough time to cure." Jessa let the implication linger in her voice. Brent was taking up her time and they, meaning she, had an order to fill or else they'd lose the sale and risk word getting around that they couldn't do it. They weren't the only leatherworkers in Pierce, and even before her master died they'd been struggling to compete.

Brent took a step back and blinked as the sunlight hit his eyes. "All right. Get it done before supper or you don't eat."

Jessa nodded, expecting such a condition. Her previous master had said it often enough as well, although she'd never gone hungry in her three years of apprenticing under him. "Anything else?" she asked him when Brent hadn't turned to leave her to her work.

He took a moment to reply, as if he was considering something. "My uncle's price to train you. It wasn't enough."

She raised her dark eyebrows, waiting for him to go on.

"Your work is shoddy. I'll have to work with you for much longer before you're anywhere near being a journeyman. That'll be time consuming."

Jessa leaned forward over her knees as she met his gaze. "What are you saying?"

"I'm extending the duration of your apprenticeship by two years. And meals, board, and the other expenses that my uncle ignored because he was too soft on you will now come out of your share of the earnings," he said sternly.

She jumped to her feet angrily. "That's impossible!"

Brent gave her an arrogant smile and nodded toward the door. "Then leave. My uncle is dead and you're a complication I don't need. Leave, if you think someone else will take you in. I hear they're hiring women in the capital, but it's not the kind of work you'll like—a lot less making armor and more taking it off of men... if you get my meaning."

Yeah, Jessa got it all right. It made her blood boil that he'd even suggest that. "There's got to be another way. You know I can't afford what you're asking me for."

He sucked on his bottom lip, and Jessa had the sick feeling she'd regret what she just said. "I suppose you could buy your journeyman's commission right now despite your deficiencies, if you could afford it, which we both know you can't." Nor would she be able to save for it, with him deducting all of her upkeep from her share of the earnings. "And, well, I wouldn't normally offer this, but since you're in a bind, and I can't simply toss my uncle's apprentice onto the street..."

"What is it?" she ground out, crossing her arms over her chest.

"Marry me."

Jessa laughed before she caught sight of his expression and realized he was actually serious. "No," she snapped at him. She barely knew Brent Harper, and what she did know of him, she didn't like. Spending an hour in his presence was difficult enough, a lifetime with him in her life... in her bed... No. Just the thought of such a fate made her shudder.

Brent shrugged as if her response hardly mattered to him one way or the other. "Then come up with the money for your journeyman fees. Six gold, in my hand, or no deal."

"And if I can't get it?"

He gave her a slow once over that made her want to scrub herself raw in the river. "Then you either leave with nothing, or agree to marry me. Do wash up before coming in to eat," he added. "You stink."

Jessa glared at him until he'd left the workshop and she was once again alone. Only then did she let herself wilt a little, hunching over the filthy table and clenching her throat against the shiver of impending tears. This was it, then? Years of hard work, rising above the loss of her parents and the skepticism of society to win an apprenticeship and master a trade, and now at the end, she was to fail? Due to her new 'master's' venality?

Well, she wasn't going to give in to him. Jessa would find a way to pay her journeyman's fee, and then she would bid and the town of Pierce farewell for good. There *had* to be a place she could ply her trade that was better than this.

A few hours later, Jessa finished stretching the hide and sighed wearily. It was late and cold, and she still had to bathe. There would be no hot water to ease the discomfort of it, but she could admit to herself that she did indeed stink. Damn Brent and his obsessive desire to hoard coin wherever he could. His uncle had never bothered to prepare his own raw hides, preferring to buy them from the tannery at the edge of town, but he'd made sure Jessa knew how to do it, and Brent had jumped on her knowledge and proclaimed it one more task for her to keep up with. It took so much time, though, and left her skin so raw and red...

No self-pity, Jessa reminded herself as she grabbed a clean shift from beneath the pallet where she slept and headed outside to the well. *You can do this. You'll get through it.*

If only she knew how.

~~*

The thunder of hooves on the cobblestone road and the raucous yelling of men woke Jessa out of a dead sleep that night. She groaned, pressing her face into her thin pillow, and restrained the impulse to scream out her window at them. After a moment they passed the shop by, and Jessa tried to fall back to sleep. She had but a few more precious hours before she would have to begin her day, and every moment of rest was valuable to her.

Her attempt was unsuccessful. After a brief silence, the streets began to fill with sound again. This time, it was the noises of her neighbors, shouting questions at one another and filling the night air with their chatter. Jessa wasn't worried that they would wake Brent up; he'd drunk enough to keep him asleep well into the morning, despite the noise. Perhaps she could block up her ears and get some sleep after all...

When ignoring their voices didn't work, Jessa got to her feet, wrapped her wool blanket around her shoulders, and slid her feet into a battered pair of leather sandals, then slipped out the back door of the shop and around to the street.

"What's going on?" she asked Grace Pruett, the wife of the baker, Crystal, across the way. Grace tended to know more than any regular person should when it came to the comings and goings of her neighbors and could always be counted on for the latest news. Two women bonded together as Grace and Crystal were was a rare occurrence, but not unheard of, especially for older women who had already had husbands and children and wanted a companion for their later years.

"A troop of horsemen riding down from the castle," Missus Pruett said excitedly, her gray curls falling haphazardly out of her night cap. "Oh, they caused such a ruckus! I sent my Jamie up to the castle to see what all the fuss is about. He should be back soon." Grace fixed her eagle-like gaze on Jessa's drawn face and swollen hands and asked, "How do you fare working with Master Harper's nephew, my dear?"

"I'm well," Jessa replied, unwilling to air her grievances to the entire town, which was what she'd be doing if she told Missus Pruett the truth. "Quite well."

"Hmm." Grace tilted her head a little. "You know, you could do worse than to make a match with that man. With you to work the shop and him to carry on Master Harper's good name, I'm sure your business would flourish."

Jessa bit back the curse on the tip of her tongue. "I fear we're not that compatible," she said at last, and let Missus Pruett take that as she may. In truth, Jessa had never met a man she felt compatible with, but hopefully Grace would attribute her reluctance to Brent's very public drinking habit.

Missus Pruett opened her mouth to speak, but whatever she would have said was lost to the burgeoning noise of another company of horsemen riding down the street, these ones dressed in the dark blue livery of Lord Barrington. Their expressions were stern and they moved quickly, although one held back at the end to shout at the assembled townspeople, "Return to your homes! There's nothing more to see tonight!"

"Which means that there might be tomorrow," Missus Pruett said speculatively. "Interesting... but, oh, my dear," she turned suddenly back to Jessa, "you must get back inside. You look fit to perish in this cold wearing just a shift! My Amber left behind some of her older things when she got married, and she was a slip of a girl just like you before her first babe. I'll bring you a bag of her clothes tomorrow."

"Really, it isn't necessary," Jessa protested, her fierce pride making her speak out against accepting anyone's charity even though she had but one shift, one old dress, and a few pairs of threadbare trousers to her name.

"Oh, it's no problem. You'd be doing me a favor," Missus Pruett said, her tone light but her eyes far too knowing. "I need the space for other things, and I'd rather not have to carry them all the way over to the convent in Lightly, not with my knees." The fact that she could have sent any of her numerous brood was politely ignored by both of them. "I'll just leave them behind the shop for you in the morning, shall I? No need to bother your master with such a trifle."

"Thank you," Jessa said after a moment, more grateful than she would let herself express.

"It's my pleasure, my dear." Missus Pruett shuddered theatrically and wrapped her shawl tighter around herself. "Goodness, I'm going to get back inside where it's warm. You should do the same."

"I will. Good night," Jessa said, then headed back to the shop before she could break down and thank Missus Pruett more honestly, and more embarrassingly. A weight she hadn't even allowed herself to think about had suddenly lifted, and Jessa got back into bed with a lighter heart. Her situation was bad, but it wasn't desperate. She would find a way out of this. She *would*.

She fell asleep and dreamed of horses carrying her to a place far, far away.

~~*

The first chore of Jessa's morning was fetching the household's water for the day. When the rain fell consistently, she could use the run-off to fill the barrels beneath the eaves, but most of the time she had to pull water at the well. The only public well was in the center of the town, thankfully not far from where their shop was located, but it still took upwards of an hour to haul her double buckets there, wait her turn in line to fill them, then lug them back home and repeat it three more times. Jessa was in the middle of her third trip that morning when a herald, dressed in their local nobleman's colors of blue and gray and with an eagle emblazoned on his tabard, came into the town square with four guards trailing behind him.

"Hear ye, hear ye," the herald cried out once he came to a stop, followed by a blast of the horn in his hand that brought most of the conversation in the square to a curious halt. "Last night, Lord Barrington's eldest daughter, the Lady Marguerite, was abducted from the castle by scoundrels and thieves. Our lord's efforts to find her continue, but any citizen of Pierce who brings her home will be richly rewarded with ten gold crowns, and our lord's eternal gratitude. Who among you is man enough to bring the young lady home?"

With the promise of riches lingering in the air, it didn't take long for men to begin stating their intent.

"Me!"

"Aye!"

"I'll do it!"

Jessa looked around at the men who had stepped forward and raised their fists toward the herald, signaling their promise. Were she a man, she might have done the same, for while there was glory in saving Lady Marguerite, Jessa's mind focused on the idea of what she could do with that kind of wealth.

"My son saw men riding west last night. Those must have been the ones that took her," she overheard one woman tell another.

"West! The riders went west!" another person yelled.

"Then that is where we'll go," Jamie—Missus Pruett's Jamie—shouted to his friends. "We'll rescue the young lady and be back by supper!"

There was a chorus of cheers and Jessa tried not to slosh the water as men began grabbing their horses—old, hard-ridden steeds the lot of them—and mounting up for what she was sure would be a memorable chase.

She glanced at a pair of men who stood off to the side of the crowd and wondered at the secretive smiles they shared. The first group of riders were good people; Jessa knew them well enough. These two she didn't recognize and didn't trust, especially upon seeing the swords buckled at their waists. No one wore a sword in Pierce, other than the castle guardsmen. Men bearing arms occasionally passed through the town on their way to the capital, but they were never invited to linger.

"What're you lookin' at, girl?" one of the pair sneered at her.

She gave them her back without a word and kept walking.

Jessa emptied the buckets into the barrels and tried not to think too hard about what was going on outside, but she couldn't help herself. Ideas kept popping into her head, distracting her as she stoked the fire and put a kettle on to boil. Her most persistent thought was this: just how foolish were these kidnappers, to abduct a noblewoman from her home in the middle of the night, then tear off through town with her like they were in a parade, yelling and shouting to wake the dead? It made no sense.

"If I were a kidnapper," Jessa murmured to herself as she poured hot water over the fragrant herbs in her cup, "I would keep my deed between myself and the family of my victim." If the family knew anything different about the situation, though, they were holding it close, and making everyone think that... that...

No, it didn't make sense. That the Lady Marguerite was missing, Jessa didn't doubt. Lord Barrington had a reputation as an honest man who wouldn't turn his town inside out simply to relish the frenzy it produced. But was riding away with the young woman really the best way of taking her? Perhaps it was simply a diversion. Perhaps that was the blind, meant to hide the hunter from the herd. Perhaps there was something to learn at the castle itself, not that they would grant a nobody like Jessa entrance. But if her hunch was right, she wouldn't need to go inside. She would only have to look over the forest that surrounded it on two sides.

But she couldn't. No, she couldn't, she had so much work to do, so much of the day to prepare for, and time was wasting. Brent would be up soon and when he saw the little she'd gotten accomplished, he'd...

Jessa's hackles rose. He'd what? She put down her cup and made her way quietly back to glance into Brent's room; he was still asleep, snoring like a thunderclap. What had he done lately to deserve her loyalty, much less her *fear*?

Jessa wasn't a fool. She couldn't just run off, not for any old reason, certainly not on a wild chase to look for a lord's kidnapped daughter. But they needed a new hide, not to mention fresh meat, which they could trade with and salt and store. She would take the day and go hunting. If she happened to find more than her normal four-legged prey, well... that was merely happenstance. She'd have to leave a note for Brent, to let him know where she'd gone.

Jessa left him sleeping with an arrow balanced on the bridge of his nose. That should be a sufficient message.

Being as quiet as possible, she took a pack and put the simplest of necessities in it: a leather drinking bag filled with water, a bit of salted fish, a hunk of bread, and her bow and quiver. She was out the door before Brent began to stir.

Though the morning had dawned unseasonably warm and bright, the clouds were starting to roll in and people moved to get inside before an afternoon storm caught them by surprise. Jessa would need to seek shelter if the ominous clouds above her lingered too long over the forest, but for now she walked on, keeping her pace brisk until she came to the mouth of the road leading west out of the town. This was the one all of the men had taken, including the riders from the night before. There was another exit, but it was barely more than a trail, and not nearly wide enough to safely gallop horses through as the forest lay on one side of it and a steep riverbank ran along the other.

Jessa sucked her bottom lip between her teeth as her concerns mounted. If the men who'd gone through town were simply a distraction, as she was starting to believe they were, that only left a few options: the forest, which covered the castle on two sides, or the fast-moving and hard-to-follow river. The forest, however, was neither dense nor imposing this close to the castle as most of the underbrush had been cleared to provide firewood over the years. A group of men travelling with a lady on foot would raise suspicion anywhere, but deep in the forest people could disappear quite easily.

Well, if they'd gotten away in a boat, there was nothing Jessa could do about it now. Either way, her next step was to get to the castle and see what she could find. It was a relatively short walk to get there, and although the castle guards eyed her suspiciously as she approached them, Jessa didn't let their scrutiny dissuade her. She turned toward the forest that lined the castle road and walked along the edge of it, scanning the forest floor for any signs of recent disturbance. Deer droppings and missing bark from a tree told her a stag had come through here recently, and she kept him in mind for her hunt should her hunch prove false.

Jessa might have given up if she hadn't caught sight of a bit of blue fabric dangling from a low-hanging branch at the edge of the woods nearly an hour later. She crouched down and used the side of her hand to brush the fallen leaves aside, revealing a faint trail and a few scattered footprints. They weren't the tracks of a man, much less a group of them, so she might have ignored them except that this wasn't a trail someone would have taken for a stroll in the woods. There were far easier paths than this. More obvious as well.

With her mind made up, Jessa stepped into the forest.

After a few minutes of following, it became evident to Jessa that whoever was walking this way, they had done a poor job of covering their tracks. As she got deeper into the woods, the underbrush grew thicker, the ground still wet and soft from the last rainfall. The woman's footprints—and they were either a woman's or a child's, Jessa knew that much after comparing the size to her own foot—were deep and regular, with no attempt made to obscure them. There were slips and hesitations here and there, signs of uncertainty and sloppiness but not of coercion. And how could a lone person be coerced, anyhow?

It was noon, and the sun was high in the sky, but even now the light filtered pale and gauzy through the prickly canopy above. Jessa looked back the way she'd come, then evaluated the path before her. The person walking here might not be good at concealment, but she—as good a guess as anything before Jessa knew differently—seemed to know where she was going. The trail meandered a bit, but its direction was consistently northeast, where the town of Lightly lay fifteen miles away by road, but only five miles through the forest. Jessa could make it there before dusk fell if she moved quickly enough, but... should she? What were the chances that these footprints belonged to Lady Marguerite, alone and free, when everyone said she had been kidnapped?

A faint rustle to Jessa's left had her freezing in place, completely immobile except for her eyes as she glanced over. Four long, delicate legs stepped through the underbrush, almost soundless. The stag blended in so well with the backdrop of light and shadow and dappled wood that he was nearly invisible. He hadn't seen her; it was a perfect opportunity for a shot. Jessa reached back slowly for her bow, fingers brushing the smooth fletching on the edge of her arrows as she went to grab a shaft.

The silky feel of the feathers reminded Jessa of the scrap of cloth she'd found earlier. She hadn't paid much attention to it at the time beyond noting it, but when she'd touched it, the fabric had been so smooth under her fingertips, softer than anything she'd ever felt before. Not a townswoman's coarse, serviceable linen, that was for certain. Not common at all, and therefore...

Jessa sighed and relaxed her stance, lowering her arm. The stag saw her movement and startled, leaping off into the forest, and Jessa watched him go with a conflicted heart. Bringing him back to Pierce would only have continued the life she was living now, not changed anything. Finding Lady Marguerite could mean real change. Perhaps Lady Marguerite had a reason for fleeing the castle under cover of darkness. Perhaps she had been fleeing from the men. Why continue on, though, once she'd lost them? Had she become addled, so scared from the attempt that she'd lost her senses?

Jessa wouldn't figure anything out by standing here watching her livelihood run away from her. She hiked up her trousers a bit and continued to follow the tracks. She nearly lost the trail more than once and spent a good chunk of an hour having to backtrack when she missed a thin broken branch where someone had stepped on it and snapped the wood.

Luckily, by sunset the trail was more obvious as the trees began to thin, and the forest underbrush slowly changed over to rural pastures. She'd reached the town of Lightly, which was little more than a few dozen homes and the convent which anchored the town. Travelling at night was risky since she couldn't see if there was a tangled root in front of her to trip on, so she decided to go into the inn for a little while. Jessa wouldn't stay there overnight, that was much too expensive, but she could likely afford a little supper before heading out to make camp in the woods.

She heard the boisterous laughter of drunken men from a few yards away from the inn and ducked her head to avoid their attention as she pushed the door aside and entered, taking a small table in the back. The inn's main area was dimly lit; only a few scattered candles in heavy brass candlesticks hung on the walls to chase away the growing shadows and darkness.

A blade-thin woman in a dirty apron approached, and Jessa put her bow and quiver down on the table next to her. "I'm Ana, the innkeeper's wife. What will you have tonight?"

"What's the least expensive thing you have?" Jessa asked her softly. She wasn't ashamed of her situation, but she didn't feel the need to advertise it either.

The woman gave Jessa a thin smile and clasped her hands together in front of her. "How about a bowl of potato soup and some ale?"

"I might not have enough for the ale..." Jessa slipped her hand into the pocket of the vest she wore and fingered one of the few copper coins she'd managed to save recently.

It hadn't seemed possible, but Ana's smile became even thinner. "'Tis but two coppers in total, and the first cup comes included with the soup."

Jessa flushed and nodded quickly to Ana, who moved away as one of the men clamored for a refill of their ale. She'd underestimated the chill after such a warm day and looked forward to a bowl of soup to warm her up before she made her cold camp. She couldn't follow the faint trail in the dark and knew better than to waste energy searching for it all night.

A few minutes later, Jessa received her soup and a small tankard of ale, more than she'd expected to get, honestly, and she smiled her thanks as she tucked into the meal. Eating was also a good way to conceal her observation of the room around her, and she let her gaze wander as she tilted her head back to drink, scanning from one side of the room to the other. There was the large, loud group of men by the bar, farmers from the look of them—Lightly was a farming town, its only real source of commerce the nunnery, which also functioned as a dairy. They seemed more interested in drinking than in anything going on around them. A few more scattered tables held quieter folk, less drunk or simply more polite, who cast the occasional glance her way. Most of the room's attention, though, went to the woman sitting at the far wall to Jessa's left.

She wore a long cloak, its hood pulled over her face for effective concealment, but at the same time it drew attention to her by its oddness. The cloak itself was quite fine, tightly woven green wool with a pattern of oak leaves around the edges. At the bottom of the cloak peeked her feet, clad in muddy leather boots, and the edge of a fine blue dress...

Ah. Jessa felt the pieces fall together in her mind. This, then, was the Lady Marguerite. Not stumbling with fear through the forest, or carried off to God knew where by horse or by boat. No, she was sitting at an inn, eating a meal of pheasant, fresh bread, and fine ale, and doing possibly the worst job of being covert that Jessa had ever seen. It was a wonder no one else had recognized her, but then Jessa supposed that with everyone in Pierce assuming the lady had been taken in the opposite direction, it was entirely possible that no one here knew of her supposed kidnapping. Seeing a noblewoman in a commoners' inn was a peculiarity, but no one wanted to draw attention to it for fear of censure.

Jessa felt excitement thrum through her body, casting off the last of her lingering chill. She had found Lady Marguerite. *She* was the first. The reward was hers as soon as she could get the girl back to Pierce. She forced herself to finish her meal slowly so she would have an excuse to stay inside and keep watch instead of heading out. Fortunately, Lady Marguerite finished eating not long after her, and headed out of the taproom and up the nearby stairs in a way that was probably meant to be furtive, tugging her hood closer around her face and moving fast. Speculative murmurs erupted as soon as she was out of sight, and Jessa knew she had to be quick. Someone was bound to figure things out sooner or later, and she wasn't about to lose this bounty. She pushed her empty bowl and tankard away, left her coppers on the table, and headed for the stairs herself.

There weren't many beds available in this inn, and only one of the rooms was private. Jessa headed for the door at the end of the narrow hall, the only one that was closed, steeled herself, and knocked.

There was a clatter inside, as though someone had been startled, then footsteps. The door unlocked and opened a crack. "Yes?"

"Lady Marguerite?" Jessa asked quietly. The door began to shut, but Jessa drove her shoulder against it to hold it open. "Please. We need to talk, my lady."

"Why should I talk with you?" Lady Marguerite demanded, trying for haughty, but unable to disguise the tremor of nerves in her voice. "Some ruffian who comes banging on the door of a complete stranger, an innocent young woman... Why, I could have you arrested for such behavior!"

"Not without giving yourself away you couldn't," Jessa replied. "Do you really want to have this conversation in the open? Because I can speak much, *much* louder than this, and people's ears are already open down there."

There was a long moment of silence, and then the door opened up. "Come in," Lady Marguerite said grudgingly.

"Thank you," Jessa said as she entered.

"Oh, shut up."

Jessa shut the door behind herself, never taking her eyes off Lady Marguerite who strode back and forth in front of her, clearly annoyed.

"I don't understand!" she exclaimed. "I was sure that I thought of everything. How did you find me?"

"My lady, I—"

"Oh, for goodness' sake, call me Marguerite. There's no sense in using courtesies when you've already barged your way into my room. Who are you, anyway?"

"Jessa, my lady, Jessa Lind."

Marguerite untied her cloak and laid it over the bed behind her, then turned back and faced Jessa, hands on her hips. "Well? Where did I go wrong, then?"

Jessa stared for a long moment, feeling surprisingly tongue-tied. She had known of Marguerite, of course, everyone in Pierce knew who the members of the Barrington family were, but she had never been this close to her before. Catching a glimpse of her through the crowd at a festival didn't carry the same impact as seeing her up close and personal did, and she was...

lovely. Quite lovely, actually. Her blue dress, probably the plainest thing Lady Marguerite owned judging from the simple cut and lack of decoration, was still quite fine. Her boots, now unlaced and sitting in the corner, came up to knee height, and were made of thick, sturdy leather. Jessa admired the craftsmanship even as she struggled to speak. It was easier through the door, when she didn't have to look at Marguerite's sparkling brown eyes, or see how the lamp light turned her braids to twisted gold.

"Jessa!" Suddenly Marguerite was much closer, and much more annoyed. "Can you give me an answer, or should I assume you a simpleton?"

The insult helped to clear the fog from Jessa's mind, and she frowned. "No need to be rude, *my lady*. As for my finding you, you're not quite as clever as you think."

"Nonsense," Marguerite scoffed, crossing her arms. "I'm exactly as clever as I think, which is rather a lot. I organized the distraction, I successfully followed my secret route, I made it all the way to this inn without anyone the wiser..." She frowned pensively. "I should have just continued on to the convent, I suppose, but I was so hungry, and the sisters never have very elaborate meals. One must get dreadfully tired of milk and cheese after a while, but with all those cows, what else can you do?"

"You left signs behind," Jessa said, ignoring most of the drivel about the convent. Cheese every day sounded nice to her, frankly. "Boot tracks in the mud, a scrap of your dress on a jagged branch. And honestly, if *I* wasn't taken in by your 'kidnappers riding around whooping and hollering' plot, there are bound to be others who weren't as well. Couldn't you have instructed them to go about faking things more quietly? Some of us were trying to sleep!"

"I didn't want you sleeping. I wanted you witnessing my capture!" Marguerite insisted.

"All anyone witnessed was a bunch of idiots riding about in the night, followed the next morning by your father's genuine distress and very generous reward offer."

Marguerite sighed loudly. "Oh, he's only distressed because my absence means he's not going to be able to foist me off onto my second cousin. Trying to marry me to that ignorant lout without even having the decency to speak with me about it first! Would you stand for it?"

"No," Jessa said after a moment, thinking about her own unfortunate circumstances. "No, I wouldn't."

"Exactly! What self-respecting, modern woman would? Besides, James is ridiculously in love with my sister Eleanor, and she with him. They both have more beauty than brains, so, hah, a perfect match." Marguerite tapped a long index finger against her chin as she looked at Jessa. "Well, despite my planning, the end result is that you found me before I got to the convent. So." She smiled brightly, and entirely falsely. "Let's discuss what it will take for you to forget you ever saw me. I have fifteen silver crowns in my satchel, and a number of copper coins as well. Would that do it?"

It was tempting, but it wasn't enough to buy her freedom with. And besides... "Your father offered ten gold crowns," Jessa said, enjoying the look of shock that appeared on Marguerite's face probably more than she should. "I think you might have underestimated his concern for you."

"Ten gold... That's a ridiculous sum of money! That's... that's a tenth of my entire dowry. That's absurd! How am I supposed to compete with that?"

"You're not."

"Oh, come now." Marguerite turned wheedling, twining the fingers of one hand into the end of her braid, batting her big eyes at Jessa. "There must be something I can do to convince you to let me go to the convent. I don't want to be trapped in a loveless marriage. I would much sooner be a nun."

"Obviously, given your choice of destination," Jessa replied. "Although I'm of the opinion that the sisters would have just given you back to your father."

"The laws of sanctuary declare that they could not!"

"The laws of patriarchy declare that they would," Jessa said, tired of arguing. "Come now, think less like a lady and more like a merchant. The sisters aren't stupid. They know where the biggest market for their wares is. Taking in the stubborn, spoiled eldest daughter of their lord and granting her sanctuary as though she were a refugee in fear for her life? That would *not* lead to prosperity."

"I beg to disagree."

"You may beg for many things, my lady, but I won't listen." Jessa squared her shoulders. "You're coming home with me."

Marguerite put her hands on her hips. "Absolutely not."

"Oh yes, you are."

"You shall have to drag me, for I am *not* going with you."

"I'll carry you over my shoulders like a carcass if I must," Jessa warned. "I've hauled heavier burdens than you over longer distances."

"Oh… oh, you're a hunter!" Marguerite's anger seemed momentarily forgotten as she looked at Jessa's unstrung bow. "Really, a woman hunter, how extraordinary! How did you ever convince someone to teach you that?"

"I learned out of necessity." The last thing Jessa wanted to do right now was get into the tragedies of her youth. "And you—"

"Wait." Marguerite held up a hand. "Do you hear that?"

"Hear what?"

"Hoof beats outside." Sure enough, through the window Jessa could hear the clip-clop of iron-shod hooves. "Arriving so late…"

"It could be anyone," Jessa said, but just in case she brushed past Marguerite and glanced carefully out the window down at the well-lit entrance to the inn. There were two horses, each carrying a man wearing a sword buckled around his waist. Jessa's blood ran cold.

"I recognize them," she murmured, backing away from the window. "They were in Pierce this morning when the reward was announced, but they're not native to our town. They're carrying blades."

"Oh." Marguerite's voice sounded rather small. "Oh dear."

Jessa had to agree with her. "We have to go." She moved away from the window and quickly walked to the door.

"Maybe they can help us," Marguerite said.

Jessa hesitated at the door and glanced over her shoulder. "Help us? How?"

Marguerite tried for a smile, but what ended up on her face was far less than comforting. She looked downright scared. "They might be good company... for the trip back."

"Other men, perhaps, but I don't trust these two. We'll need to be quiet as we leave. And we'll need to hurry as well. Grab your cloak, put your boots back on, and come." Marguerite didn't look so sure but she did follow closely behind Jessa as she opened the door and snuck into the hallway. Jessa could hear the new arrivals talking to Ana, and hugged the wall as she peeked down the staircase to see where they were.

"There's only one way downstairs. How are we going to get out of here without them seeing us?" Marguerite whispered. Jessa felt Marguerite grab her hand, and Jessa gave her a little squeeze to let her know she appreciated the gesture.

"They're not looking anywhere near us right now, but they could turn around at any moment. We'll have to go quickly." Jessa started down the stairs, but a tug on her hand from Marguerite stopped her.

"You'll protect me, won't you?"

"Of course," Jessa replied, pulling Marguerite down the stairs with her by her hand.

"And you'll do it because of more than just the gold you were promised for bringing me back?"

Jessa wasn't entirely sure what Marguerite expected her to say, but she still nodded. "Yes. Now let's get out of here."

She spotted the two newcomers talking to some of the men sitting around the bar and took the stairs as quickly as she could with Marguerite right behind her. Marguerite had put the hood of her cloak up before they'd left the room, and Jessa was glad to see it was still up now as they neared the bottom of the stairs.

"Back down for more ale?" Ana asked Jessa, surprising her. She hadn't seen Ana standing in the shadow of the stairway.

Jessa shook her head and walked toward the door. "No, thank you. We'll be going now."

"Already? Was the room not to her lady's liking?" Ana asked, following along and matching Jessa's long strides.

"Jessa..." Marguerite hissed at her, the nervousness clear in her voice.

"It was fine," Jessa replied as she hurried toward the door. Her hand was on the brass handle when she heard a voice from behind her call out to them to wait.

She slowly turned, Marguerite moving with her until she was between Jessa and the door. Jessa glanced back to make sure the hood was over her face, obscuring her identity.

"You two," one of the men called to them as he approached. His companion flanked them on the right.

"Yes?" Jessa said, meeting his gaze with her own. *Don't seem nervous.*

He cocked his hip and placed his hand on the hilt of his sword. "You two haven't seen a lone girl running around, have you?"

Jessa shook her head. "Not at all. Goodnight."

"What about your friend? She doesn't say much."

"No, she doesn't. Farewell." Jessa reached behind her and opened the door. Once she could feel the chilly night air on her bare neck she stepped back, forcing Marguerite out of the inn.

"Well, keep your eyes open. And if you see her, send her to me. I'll make sure she's taken care of."

Jessa didn't like the look in the man's eyes or the way his friend smiled, but she nodded anyway, hoping they weren't too suspicious of her and Marguerite.

"We need to run," Marguerite whispered once they were clear of the inn and the door closed behind them.

Jessa wrapped her hand around Marguerite's upper arm as she made to run. She glanced over her shoulder and saw one of the men watching them through a window in the inn. "We walk."

"But—"

Jessa turned back to her. "No running. But we can walk fast."

Marguerite didn't look convinced, but at least she didn't run.

Perhaps running would have been better, because they had barely reached the road that flanked the forest's edge before Jessa heard the door to the inn opening in the distance and the man calling out, "Just a moment, lass, you two can't head into the woods. It wouldn't be *safe*."

Jessa's hand itched to stop and ready her bow, but they needed to keep moving. She pulled Marguerite along into the tall grasses that preceded the forest underbrush. "You could get lost!" the man yelled, still sounding abominably happy about the possibility. "And then we'd just have to come and find you! Much better not to drag us out at all, ladies. Spare us the trouble of hunting you down… "

"Jessa," Marguerite murmured as they kept going, stumbling over roots and piles of rotting leaves in the dark.

"Be quiet," Jessa hissed, straining her eyes for the clearest path in the faint light. Thank heavens there was a full moon tonight, otherwise she would have been completely blind. There, where the ground rose up a bit... "Follow me closely. Step where I step."

"Well, may I at least have a moment to tie my boots?" Marguerite huffed.

"No," Jessa said, "you may not. The more time we waste, the sooner they'll be after us, likely with lanterns. So we need to find a place to hide, quickly."

"Why would they go to the trouble?"

"Do you not remember the amount of your reward?" Jessa asked. "There was nothing in your father's announcement about you being returned safe and sound, however, so for the love of God keep quiet until I'm sure we're free of them."

Jessa could feel Marguerite bridle, her body tensing with indignation, but she let herself be led in silence. Jessa moved carefully, more slowly than she wanted to, but she had to be cautious now, to find the places where they were least likely to leave sign of themselves. She had no way of knowing what kind of trackers these men were, but they'd been smart enough to get this far.

A distant shaft of light penetrated the misty gloom and Jess froze, pulling Marguerite flush to her back. One lantern... and there was the second, the light concentrated into beams with the help of lantern shutters. "Perfectly still now," Jessa whispered. "Wait for the light to move away." They clung fast to each other, breathless as the beam passed close to them. Once they moved off again, Jessa started moving again, this time with the intent of hiding them as soon as possible.

Fifty more painstaking paces led them to a partially fallen tree, its upper half long collapsed under the crushing weight of its own branches. Jessa pulled Marguerite around the base of it and pressed her low to the ground, hidden in a tangle of tree limbs. "Stay here," she breathed, restringing her bow and taking an arrow from her slender quiver.

"You can't mean to shoot them!" Marguerite protested.

"No, of course not," Jessa lied soothingly. "Now *stay*." She eased her head around the edge of the trunk and watched the lantern lights come closer. The brightness ruined her night vision, but it didn't matter. She didn't need to see her prey in the dark when they carried their own beacons.

She didn't want to shoot them, but she had experience with such men, more so than her coddled charge. Jessa wouldn't let either of them pass into these men's grasps. The lanterns worked their way closer, the owners pausing every now and then to inspect the ground, swearing and sounding angrier and angrier.

"Best to show yourselves, lasses, before you make my night any worse," one of them called out. "I've no wish to harm you, but I can't speak for my friend here."

"Tracks are gone," the other man grunted, swinging his lantern back and forth irritably. "They must've worked their way back toward the road. It's foolish to try and clear the forest at night."

"Just a little further," the first one said, pressing closer to their hiding place. Jessa very carefully nocked the arrow, then began to raise her bow.

"No, no further!" the second man protested a moment later. "My damn feet are so cold I can't feel 'em, and that wench of an innkeeper is probably rifling through our saddlebags right now. They've gone back to the road. We'll find them there."

Finally, the first man stopped his forward progress, less than twenty feet from the tree. "If they are foundering in the trees, I wish them many broken bones," he muttered. "Fine." They turned around and left much faster than they'd arrived, and Jessa released the tension in her bow with a silent sigh of relief.

Marguerite tugged the leg of Jessa's trousers. Jessa could just make out enough of her face in the moonlight to see the white of her teeth, bared in a surprising grin. "How terribly exciting!" she whispered.

Jessa rolled her eyes and sat down.

"Shouldn't you make a fire?" Marguerite said after a few quiet moments during which Jessa had been focused on the noises of the forest around them, making sure the men really had left them alone.

Shaking her head, Jessa pulled her knees up to her chest. "Not tonight."

"But it's cold... and wet," Marguerite protested, her voice growing louder in the night.

"It's too dangerous. They could see the light of it or smell the wood burning," Jessa said, hoping Marguerite wouldn't press the issue anymore.

Marguerite frowned and tucked the edges of her cloak around her feet. "So you mean for us to stay here? All night?"

"It's not as bad as all that," Jessa replied, a bit defensively despite the way she tried not to let it show. The fallen tree had been a lucky find, and she'd slept worse places during a hunting trip. Her stomach started to tighten, and she realized she was hungry. Pity. She'd expected the soup she'd had in the inn to last her longer than that.

"Hungry?" she asked Marguerite as she reached into her pack and pulled out her bread. Marguerite shook her head, but Jessa only took a small piece for herself. "If you change your mind later, it's there. We should try to sleep, though. I plan to have you home as soon as possible tomorrow."

Marguerite sighed loudly but did as Jessa suggested anyway, despite the sour look she gave. She lay down as well and put her arm up so that she was resting on it instead of the cold ground. The rain started up not long after that, and Jessa was thankful that the little place they'd found didn't seem to get too wet, with all the overlapping branches above it protecting them from the damp. It would be a miserable night even without that added discomfort.

Jessa closed her eyes and tried not to shiver as she wrapped her arms around herself.

"Are you asleep?" Marguerite asked after a moment.

"Not yet," Jessa replied, glad that her voice didn't shake as her teeth chattered.

Marguerite restlessly shifted this way and that, and finally Jessa opened her eyes to see Marguerite staring back at her. "I miss my bed," she confessed. "Perhaps running away wasn't my best idea ever, but I couldn't imagine being married to someone I don't care for."

"And now?" Jessa asked her.

Marguerite shrugged daintily and moved closer to her. "I still don't wish to be married. I want to go learn at one of the great universities in the capital."

She'd said it like it was a precious secret, and Jessa supposed that it was. Few women ever pursued such things. "Learn about what?" Jessa found herself asking.

Marguerite gave her a little smile. "The stars, mostly, and the celestial spheres that contain them. There is more than one sphere, you know, according to popular hypothesis. It's an endlessly fascinating field of study. What do you think is out there among the stars?"

Jessa had never spent much time thinking on it. "I don't know. I've only ever looked up to tell direction. You think there could be more?"

Marguerite looked excited as she said, "Oh yes. I dream of whole worlds beyond this one, beyond the planets that we see. Can you imagine? I would love to know of a world made of chocolate."

"Chocolate? What is that?" Jessa asked, scrunching her nose at the sound of the unfamiliar word. It sounded like something that would be burned over fire, perhaps a tough game bird that was only desirable as food in the dead of winter when nothing else was available.

Marguerite dropped her mouth open. "You've never had chocolate?" Jessa shook her head. "Well, you must. After you get me back, I'll come to you and bring you some. It is simply the most decadent treat in existence."

"Thank you. It's a nice thought. However, I doubt you'll have time to stop by and visit."

"Why ever not?"

Jessa frowned at her. "Won't you be getting married?"

Marguerite's face instantly fell. "Oh. Yes. Perhaps... perhaps my father will reconsider."

"Maybe." Of course Jessa didn't know Marguerite's father, but she didn't want to dash whatever little hope Marguerite had of living a life free of an arranged marriage either.

"I know that tone."

Jessa frowned. "What?"

"That one that says you don't believe me. That says I'm a silly girl with silly ideas who doesn't know the first thing about the real world. I hear it quite a bit at home, believe me."

"I didn't mean to insult you," Jessa began, but Marguerite's impatient sigh interrupted her.

"But you don't particularly care that you did, do you? There's a distance between us that no amount of chatter can breach, especially not now that you've essentially saved me from my own poor decisions." Marguerite wrapped her arms more tightly around her frame. "You are in a position of knowing far more than me about our current circumstances, and nothing I say can be of any value to you." She sounded close to tears.

Jessa didn't know what to say to comfort the girl, but she did recognize a person courting illness from the cold. She was cold herself, tired after a long day's tracking and the release of tension once their hunters turned back. Silently, she scooted over to sit next to Marguerite and put her arm around her shoulders. Marguerite stiffened for a moment before her dignity relaxed enough for her to accept the touch.

"I would never say your words are without value," Jessa told her. "They're simply... Perhaps I consider them fanciful, but that's not a bad thing. There is very little room for such thoughts in my life."

"What is it you do?" Marguerite asked, turning a little more to face her. Jessa was the taller of the two by a good bit, and it wasn't surprising when Marguerite settled her head against Jessa's shoulder. It was a familiar gesture, and one she had no right to accept from a lady of Marguerite's stature, but she was glad for it all the same. It had been so long since she had been graced with the company of another woman. "Apart from hunting down wayward ladies."

"I'm an apprentice leather worker," Jessa said. "I would have been a journeyman this year, but my master died, and the man who took over from him is...

unreasonable. Before I learned of the reward for your return, before I found you, I was looking at a future of interminable service, and possibly an unwanted marriage of my own." She sighed, imagining how furious Brent had to be right now. "So in a way, you should look upon yourself as *my* savior. I was beginning to feel quite hopeless before you came along."

"Hmm. Do you like leather working?"

"I like it well enough," Jessa replied. "It's better than many of the options for young women of my common background, and if I can become a journeyman, it could afford me true freedom. The ability to move on, found my own shop..." She stopped speaking, afraid she was giving too much away, but Marguerite just hummed thoughtfully.

"That is how I feel about pursuing my education. Not that I anticipate it being a means to support myself, necessarily, but that it would broaden my world and offer up new opportunities. There is so much to discover, if one can only move beyond a certain level of expectation. For me, it has always been marriage, but I've never met a man that interested me in that way."

"Neither have I," Jessa confessed. "I'm not sure I will. And yet a man alone is a bachelor, while a woman alone is merely pathetic," she continued, and Marguerite turned her face into Jessa's shoulder and chuckled. Jessa smiled and pulled her a little tighter. If questioned, she might have said that the gesture was simply to share more warmth, but in truth she simply wanted to have Marguerite nearer to her and any distance felt like too much. It was surprisingly comfortable, holding Marguerite close like this. Despite her fatigue, Jessa didn't want to go to sleep.

"We shall have to be alone and pathetic together," Marguerite said.

"But together we aren't alone," Jessa pointed out.

"Not in any way that counts," Marguerite agreed. Tentatively, she wrapped her arm around Jessa's waist, and sighed when Jessa only pulled her closer.

"Tell me about the stars," Jessa requested, closing her eyes. She wouldn't sleep, but she might drowse comfortably for a bit.

"The stars... there is so much to know about them. There are stories about them, histories from all around the world, each one a different explanation for the heavens. There are lenses that gather light on clear nights, and let you see them closer and more brightly than you can imagine. All of these are enormous, of course, and kept in institutions of higher learning, but I've seen pictures of them before. The stars help sailors plot their courses, and they tell the turning of the seasons just as accurately as any weather. My favorite story about them..." Marguerite kept speaking, her voice smooth and soft against Jessa's neck, and Jessa, despite her best intentions, fell asleep with the sweetness of her voice still echoing in her mind.

The next morning, Jessa awoke to the call of mourning doves above her head and the sound of something moving through the woods. It was heavy and cracked the twigs under it when it walked, but it didn't speak so she doubted it was a person. Knowing that there were bears about this time of year, she kept still and waited for whatever it was to pass by before slowly sitting up.

"Marguerite," Jessa said, laying a hand on her shoulder and shaking her awake. "Marguerite, it's time to wake."

"Not now, Papa... Such a wonderful dream..." Marguerite sleepily replied.

Jessa smiled and shook her harder. When Marguerite opened her eyes, she let her go and got to her feet, barely spending a moment to brush the dirt and fallen leaves from her trousers. "I would have liked to let you sleep, as I'm sure you need it, but it's morning and we best get you home."

Marguerite stuck her lower lip out in a pout but got to her feet as well. "Do you have any of that bread left?"

"It's stale by now," Jessa warned her even as she got it out and handed what was left of it to Marguerite, along with the little bit of fish. Marguerite tried to take only half of it and hand it back, but Jessa waved her offering away. It wasn't that she didn't feel the first of her morning hunger pangs developing, but she was used to being hungry at times and doubted Marguerite had much experience with such discomfort.

Once Marguerite finished off the meal, such as it was, Jessa began leading them back through the forest toward her castle.

"Are you sure you know the way?" Marguerite asked her only a few minutes into their walk.

Jessa nodded and kept going. "I am. There's a stream to the west of us, much smaller than the river that goes through town, but still flowing. Sometimes there are decent-sized fish in it that are easy to catch since most everyone else thinks only the river can provide them with food. We'll follow that for a ways and get back on the path you took here."

She heard Marguerite sigh from behind her, and Jessa looked back to see her smiling. "Oh, that's impressive. I used a compass to find my way."

"A compass?" Jessa had heard of the devices but had never seen one for herself.

"Yes, my father bought it for me last year. They're the most marvelous little things, look..." She reached into a pocket of her cloak and pulled out a small bronze case, its face covered by glass, with a needle at the center. "They've been around forever, of course, but it's only recently that someone worked out a way to mass produce them. The needle always points north, so I simply had to head northeast of the castle and knew I could come to Lightly eventually."

"Clever," Jessa admitted, touching the edge of the bronze casing.

"Perhaps, but your way required much more skill. You're very resourceful, it's quite admirable. Someday we will have to come out to these woods again, and you can show me everything you know. I think it will be a wonderful adventure, and quite a bit more fun than the one we are on right now."

Jessa smirked and turned back to the woods ahead of her instead of getting lost in Marguerite's fantasy. "You think of this as an adventure?"

"Well... yes. Up until a few nights ago, I'd never dreamt of running away. And now I have."

"And would you do it again?" Jessa asked her without turning around.

"Certainly not. At least, not so late in the year. Are the summer months any better for sleeping outside?"

Jessa shook her head and kept walking. She had to pick her way over a tangle of roots that jutted up from the ground, but once she was clear, she heard Marguerite screech and turned around just in time to have her fall on top of her.

"I'm very lucky you were there to catch me," Marguerite said as she began to right herself.

Jessa smiled at her and waited for Marguerite to get up before she rolled over and rose to her feet as well. "And I am lucky you do not weigh more than you do." She was joking and expected Marguerite to laugh with her, but what she got instead was a stick thrown at the back of her head.

Marguerite was staring at her when she turned back around. "That is a rotten thing to say." With that, Marguerite began storming ahead of her, her footsteps loud as she tromped through the woods. When she would have tripped over a rock that was hidden by fallen leaves, Jessa reached out and grabbed Marguerite's arm to keep her from falling.

"I fear I am not as comfortable in the forest as you are," Marguerite admitted when she had found the rock for herself by stubbing the toe of her boot on it.

"Perhaps we should walk together, then," Jessa suggested.

Marguerite gave her a soft smile and offered Jessa her hand, which she was glad to take.

They held hands whenever they could, and eventually it was all Jessa could do to tug Marguerite along by their grip, cajoling her with the promise of food and fresh water at the forest's end. Marguerite moved like she was bone-tired, so much so that eventually even her warring optimism and occasional complaints failed her, and she saved her breath for the trail. The walk took time, and despite their early start they didn't make it back to the outskirts of Pierce until well after noon.

In some ways, that was perfect. The tradespeople of Pierce tended to relax after the midday meal, which meant more people were inside napping than walking the streets, especially on a chill day like this. Marguerite unsurprisingly wanted to postpone her coming confrontation with her father until she looked less worn, so Jessa led her through shadowed alleys back to her master's shop, bringing her through the rear door as quietly as possible.

Marguerite looked around, stunned. "But this is a workshop. Where is your bedroom?"

"This is where I sleep," Jessa explained, searching for the water bucket. There was a spot where Marguerite could shower outside without being seen, but she'd need something to use to scoop the water with. Cup, cup... Ah!

"You sleep in the same room you work in?" Marguerite wrinkled her nose. "And why does it *smell* so?"

"Experiments in tanning," Jessa said abruptly. "Just be grateful the weather is chilly today, it's much worse in the heat."

"I shall take your word for it." Marguerite dropped her sodden cloak on the work table next to Jessa's abandoned hide, then bent to untie her boots. "Will you help me with the laces?" she asked, straightening up and lifting her hair out of the way.

"Certainly." Jessa reached out and untied the back of Marguerite's dress, loosening it around her shoulders and neck until the garment hung down off her pale frame. Her skin was clammy and cool, but soft as well. Jessa forced her hands away from the tender flesh and back by her sides. "I'll get you water." She took the bucket and went out to the nearest rain barrel, which was nearly overflowing today—at least that was one chore she wouldn't have to do. She pulled some water, made sure to clear it of leaves and the occasional bug, then set it next to the shower area. "Out here," she called quietly.

Marguerite joined her outside, clutching her bodice closed with one hand. "Have you anything I can use to dry myself with?" she asked.

"Yes, let me get it." Actually, Jessa never usually bothered, but her wool blanket would likely be dry again in a few hours. She went in to fetch it off her cot, only to run out again a moment later when she heard Marguerite's muffled shriek.

"What?" Jessa demanded when she reached the shower area, trying for quiet but probably failing in her anxiousness.

Marguerite was bent over, clutching her barely dampened shoulders. "It's so cold!" she hissed. "How can you bear to use such cold water to bathe? Is there no way to warm it? To take the edge off?"

Jessa forcibly held in both her temper and her strange, sudden desire to rest her eyes on Marguerite's bared form. Tired, it was simply that she was so tired, and now this... "No, my lady."

"Please," Marguerite begged. "I'm so cold after the woods, and I just know that this water will make me ill if I use it like this. You have no kettle, nothing?"

There was a kettle... and although Jessa hadn't been there to light a fire beneath it that morning, if Brent wanted his hot tea, then he'd have had to take care of it himself. Perhaps it was still warm. She would have to sneak into the kitchen, but he was probably out drinking at this time of day, seeing as the workshop was abandoned. "I will check for you," Jessa said with a sigh. Marguerite beamed at her. "But for the love of God, stay quiet!" she added before heading back inside.

A quick glance through the workshop door showed that the hall was empty, and Jessa tiptoed across the way and into the kitchen, where the kettle was indeed on the hob, and the fire from this morning still smoldered gently in the grate below. Jessa grabbed a rag from the table and wrapped it around the kettle's handle, lifting it off the metal run carefully.

An enormous hand dug into Jessa's hair and jerked her head back roughly, bending her over in a painful arc. She cried out and dropped the kettle, spilling warm water all over the floor. Jessa clutched at her hair and tried to turn to face Brent, but he held her at arm's length, his grip fierce and unrelenting.

"Here she is at last, the wandering apprentice," he said with a sneer. "No game to accompany you, wench? Over a day spent wandering the woods with nothing to show for it? Or did you find a warm place to sleep on your back, with a man between your thighs?"

"Brent, let me g—"

"No," he said, shaking her head furiously. Jessa's eyes filled with unwilling tears as she felt strands rip. "You can't talk your way out of this. You wanted to see if you could survive without me? You're *nothing* without me! I'll have you here forever, one way or another, and you—" His tirade stopped suddenly, his grip on Jessa suddenly loosening.

"Very good," Marguerite said calmly. "You know enough not to struggle. I take it you recognize this knife, then?" From her low vantage point, Jessa could barely see Marguerite standing behind Brent, but the blade she held at his throat was unmistakable. Jessa used it to scrape the hides clean, and it was wickedly sharp. "It's quite nice, isn't it? I've never held anything so sharp in my hands before. I'm quite afraid I might slip at any moment, which I would hate to do. It would make such a terrible mess of the floor. Do let go of my rescuer, now."

Brent complied silently, and Jessa instantly surged away from him once she was free, standing up and refusing to rub her head to check for dislodged hanks of hair. "My lady, are you all right?" she asked shakily.

"I'm very well, thank you," Marguerite said cheerfully. "I heard the commotion and decided my shower could wait. How fortunate that I did! I feel I prevented a terrible misunderstanding from taking place." She smiled at Brent, but it was all teeth. "After all, this man doesn't yet understand that you don't belong to him anymore. Your time here is over as soon as you pay your fees, which will be amply covered out of the cost of your reward for my safe return. So, your master gets paid and you get your freedom. What a wonderful turn of events." Marguerite finally removed the knife from Brent's throat, and he stumbled away from her, one hand pressed to his neck.

"You... you're actually..." he choked.

"The daughter of your lord? The friend of the woman you just threatened? Ready and willing to utterly ruin you if you try to interfere with either of us in any way?" Marguerite asked sweetly. "Why, yes, I actually am. I think we've spent enough time in your unforgettable company, sir." She turned back to Jessa. "I think bathing can wait. I'm ready to go home. I would appreciate your escort."

"Of course," Jessa said faintly. "Let me get my shoes."

"And grab your bow!" Marguerite called after her. "I want Father to see you in all your glory. She is amazing with that bow," Marguerite confided in Brent, who

Hunting a Lady

looked dumbfounded. "Why, she shot a man who dared to try and steal me away right through the eye. Astonishing."

Jessa didn't know why Marguerite was lying, but she did like the way that Brent's hands trembled as he looked at her when she came back, bow in hand. "At your service, my lady," she said.

"Wonderful. Let's be off, then."

"How did you know to threaten him like that?" Jessa asked Marguerite once they were a good distance from the workshop.

Marguerite flashed her a little smile and pulled the hood of her cloak up, covering her face from anyone that might have been curious enough to look their way. "I must know how to protect my virtue, mustn't I?" Marguerite replied. Jessa supposed that made a good bit of sense given Marguerite's station in life. "My father says that pretty young women like myself have to. Do you think I'm pretty?" Marguerite continued, startling Jessa, who had no idea what to say to such a strange question.

"Y-yes." Jessa licked her lips. "I suppose so, anyway." She tried to ignore her own admission, but the deep blush covering her cheeks gave her away.

While Jessa might have been called pretty, if she really cleaned up and did something with her hair, Marguerite seemed to be beautiful despite what the forest had attempted to make of her overnight. Her hair was tangled and her dress was soiled from sleeping in the dirt, but somehow she still looked ready for one of those fancy balls Jessa knew Marguerite's father held at times.

They made their way quickly through town and up to the castle. Its heavy iron gate remained guarded by two solemn-looking guards. "The lord isn't taking visitors at this time," the one to Jessa's left said.

"Come back another day," the one to her right continued.

Jessa stopped walking just in front of Marguerite. "He'll want to see me," she told them both confidently.

"He'll want to see us," Marguerite corrected her. She stepped up and dropped her hood so that the men could look upon her fully and see her for who she really was.

They dropped their gazes and then fell to one knee. "Open the gate! Lady Marguerite has returned to us!" one of the guards called behind him. Jessa wondered what it would be like to have that sort of respect from the men around her instead of the more disturbing sort of behavior she was used to. It must have been nice to be seen as a young woman instead of a thing to be used. In that moment, she both respected Marguerite and was jealous of the life she thought Marguerite must have led, despite her arguments with her father.

The gates opened from inside the castle grounds, and a page ran forward to escort them onto the castle grounds. Guards joined them as they walked, becoming an escort of sorts to take them along the path to the castle Jessa had only ever had glimpses of through a closed gate. Marguerite's home was even grander than Jessa had imagined it to be, with what must have been at least a dozen rooms and plenty of well-kept gardens surrounding them.

"You live here?" Jessa whispered to Marguerite, knowing that of course she did but also not knowing what to say.

Marguerite nodded. "Yes. It's a nice enough place, I suppose, but it does get awfully dull at times. I do hope you'll come to visit. I would greatly miss your company if I never got the chance to see you again. After such an adventure together, you must know you're my greatest friend." She put her fingers against Jessa's palm and Jessa welcomed the chance to hold her hand as they walked.

The page opened a set of wooden doors and they were led into the castle. The room Jessa and Marguerite stepped into was awash with bright sunlight coming in through the tall windows all around them.

Jessa thought Marguerite would want to drop her hand as she led Jessa further into the castle, through narrow passageways and torch-lit rooms, but Marguerite kept hold of her.

"Does Father know I've returned?" Marguerite called back to one of the guards.

"Not yet, my lady. He's in the garden taking his afternoon peace."

"What's that?" Jessa asked Marguerite before she could stop herself from uttering a question some people would consider rude at the very least and, at most, completely beyond her place.

But Marguerite only swung their hands together and answered her as if Jessa had only asked about the weather. "Father likes to have his quiet time. It's when he reflects on how his decisions best help those of his people. He's a good lord."

"Yes, he is," Jessa replied, instantly agreeing with her. She hadn't lived under another lord in her admittedly short life, but she knew Lord Barrington had a reputation as both kind and fair.

Marguerite led her past the page and through a side door that opened to a small courtyard. Another two guards blocked their path to Lord Barrington, who Jessa could see seated just beyond them, but they quickly stepped aside once they caught sight of Marguerite.

"Father!" she called, letting go of Jessa's hand and running toward him. He stood up to greet her and they embraced as Jessa stood off to the side, watching a scene of fatherly affection she'd never gotten to experience for herself. Her master had been a decent man who had treated her with respect, but he hadn't been her father, though he had tried to fill that place in her life the best he could with what little he'd had.

Lord Barrington let her go and Jessa caught sight of a bright smile on Marguerite's dirt-smudged face. "My dear girl, I'm so glad that you found your way back home! However did you escape from those men?"

The smile quickly fled from Marguerite's face. "Father, I'm sorry, but there were no men. I paid four of our stable hands to ride out and make it seem like I had been taken by them while I secreted myself away into the woods. It was all a ruse. I am dreadfully sorry for making you worry." She gestured to where Jessa stood, watching their private moment with great discomfort. "This is Jessa. She found me at the inn and brought me back home to you."

Jessa ducked her head and gave Lord Barrington a little bow. "My lord."

Lord Barrington shook his head, staring between Jessa and his daughter. "A ruse? You lied to me? Child, why would you do such a thing? I was so worried about you."

"I know, and I feel awful for trying to deceive you. But I don't wish to be married against my will to someone I do not love," Marguerite said, her voice taking on a higher edge with her impassioned plea. "I would rather live as a nun than a reluctant wife."

"You ran away... to be free of a marriage?" Lord Barrington asked Marguerite, sounding incredulous. Jessa looked to Marguerite and frowned at the sight of tears in her eyes. She wished that she could go and comfort her, but knew it simply wasn't done. The tender embraces they'd shared earlier aside, it was not her place to be so familiar with Lady Barrington here in her castle.

Marguerite nodded. "I did, Father. And I would again. I cannot stomach the idea of being trapped in such a thing. I abhor it."

Lord Barrington looked like he was about to say something more on the subject, but closed his mouth as he remembered Jessa was still there. "I thank you for bringing back my daughter," he said to her, formal but sincere. "You're a brave young woman. Please, follow my page, Martin. He will ensure that you have your reward for my daughter's safe return."

Jessa looked to Marguerite and wished she could say goodbye to her properly, and that they could have a moment of privacy. Instead she simply nodded to Lord Barrington. "Thank you, my lord. Goodbye, my lady."

Marguerite was looking at her, Jessa could feel it. But she did not dare look back at Marguerite as she turned to follow the page boy back out. "Goodbye, Jessa. I hope you have a good life, now that you have the means to do so. Do come back and visit, and thank you for bringing me home."

Jessa waited at the doorway as Marguerite's soft words worked their way into her heart. She hoped Marguerite would find happiness in her life as well.

~~*

One month later, Jessa sat alone at her small table, eating stew made from a rabbit she'd caught only an hour before. The meat was tough but the broth had a good taste, and a rabbit was more than enough to make a meal for one person. She'd paid off Brent in order to become an official journeyman leatherworker, and he'd taken her money and signed her certificate and rid himself of her as quickly as possible. Jessa was glad to have no more contact with him. But as the days trailed by and her thoughts continued to center around Marguerite, whom she hadn't seen since their farewell at the castle, Jessa wondered if it wasn't time for her to leave town. After all, it did no one any good to pine after a person she could never have.

She lost interest in eating, got to her feet, and went toward the shed's open doorway. She looked beyond the town square to the top of the castle, which was just barely visible above the line of trees that lay bare in the autumn chill. Jessa propped her shoulder up against the wall of the shed and chewed on her lower lip. There was hardly space for a table, a chair, and a bed, but Missus Pruitt had insisted she stay there after Jessa had left Brent's company. Brent still had the workshop, though word had quickly gotten around about his sub-par craftsmanship and so customers were going elsewhere for their needs. Jessa had enough left over from the reward to let her live comfortably for a time while she figured out what to do next.

She'd meant to go see Marguerite shortly after that day in Lord Barrington's garden, but she'd become too busy with moving herself out. The next time she'd thought about it, something else had come up, and that pattern had repeated until Jessa was forced to face the realization that she'd been making excuses to avoid going up there. It wasn't that she didn't want to see Marguerite—quite the opposite, in fact—but she didn't want to hear word of an impending marriage or something else that would be equally upsetting.

In the quiet moments when Jessa laid down on her cot to sleep at night, she had faced the truth of her feelings for Marguerite. Though they were friendly, they were far from innocent fantasies, and nothing a girl should have for someone who, however briefly, had been her charge. Having thoughts of someone so far above her station was inappropriate as well, and so she had kept her distance from Marguerite in body, if not in thought.

"Hello."

Marguerite's voice was such a constant in Jessa's head that she paid no attention to the sudden onset of lunacy that made her believe she was hearing Marguerite speaking to her.

"Jessa? Jessa? Oh, *Jessa*?"

Frowning, Jessa had to admit that sounded not at all like someone in her head. She turned to look at the open doorway and her mouth fell open a bit. "Marguerite?" She moved to go to her but stopped before she could embarrass herself.

Marguerite nodded. "I'm here. You never came to see me, so I insisted on coming to you. Did you forget about me entirely this past month?"

"Never," Jessa told her instantly. "I just... How did you find me?"

"My father knows where everyone lives in the town." Smiling, Marguerite pulled Jessa into a hug. Today Marguerite smelled like roses, not rainwater, and Jessa was glad to hold her again, however briefly. "I didn't forget about you either. In truth, I've hardly had a moment in my mind where you were not also in there with me."

"I'm honored that you remembered me."

Marguerite pulled back, not far enough to let go, but far enough to look into Jessa's face. "Oh, honor has nothing to do with it. It isn't honor that kept you in my mind, and I hope it's not just honor that's kept me in yours." Marguerite bit her lip for a moment before saying, "I dream about you. When I think about you, it's not simply that I've missed you. I... Do you understand what I'm trying to say? It's something *more* than that. Please, tell me that you feel the same, or help me salvage my dignity and stop me from saying any more."

Jessa could hardly speak, and so she didn't try. Instead she cupped her hands to Marguerite's rounded, rosy cheeks, and kissed her softly just beside her fingertips. Before she could pull away, though, Marguerite surprised her with a brief kiss on her lips. It was a moment she might have been flogged for, had anyone seen her kissing Lady Barrington, but in that instant Jessa couldn't begin to care. It lifted her spirits and brought up ideas she'd only dreamed of. It wasn't love, not yet, but it might be someday. "Something more like this?" she murmured when their lips parted.

"Yes, exactly like that." Marguerite stepped back and Jessa was glad to see her smiling. "Come away with me."

"Where?" Jessa asked, though there were a dozen other things she should have probably said instead, but Marguerite's smile only grew brighter.

"The capital, of course. I've been given leave to become a scholar, and I wish to learn of the world and the stars above us. Will you join me on an adventure?"

"But your father—" Jessa hedged.

Marguerite shook her head. "My father has realized that my happiness is important to him. I won't be caged in a loveless marriage. Eleanor has graciously agreed to follow her own heart and find love with a man I neither want nor care for. Does that news quiet your concerns for the moment?"

Jessa nodded.

"Good. Then it's settled. I have a carriage waiting to take us when you're ready," Marguerite said as she stepped back and looked at her expectantly.

"What, now?" Jessa demanded. "Today?"

"This very instant, if you can," Marguerite affirmed. "The university is expecting me directly, but I will postpone the journey if you need more time." She started to blush. "I realize this is rather… sudden, but everything came together all at once and the only thing I could think of that would make it better is having a friend with me. I don't want to take you away from Pierce if you don't wish to come, though."

What did Jessa have holding her here? She was officially a journeyman, no longer bound to any master. She had no home, she had no family, and she had some tools but no shop of her own yet. Never in her life had she had more freedom, and never had she had more opportunity to do something with it. And being with Marguerite again, after a month apart… Jessa thought she'd been imagining things, that time had conflated what she felt into a falsehood, but here was Marguerite asking for her, dreaming about her, kissing her. There was no falsehood in that, despite its suddenness. "I do want to come with you."

"Now?" Marguerite asked hopefully.

"Now is good."

On unsteady legs, Jessa managed to stand and get her things together. She was packed within the hour, settled her bill and bid a silent farewell to the small shed she'd been renting from the baker and her wife.

"I was so afraid you'd turn me down, and my father would have never let me go alone. I would have had to leave with men-at-arms, and those filthy creatures never stop to bathe," Marguerite confided as she walked out into the street where a carriage was waiting for them.

Jessa snickered and followed her out into the bright sunlight. She had the means to practice her craft and would find work in the capital, she was sure of it. She could have a new life there, and Jessa looked forward to discovering all its potential, with Marguerite by her side.

LIES &

REVERIE

CAMILLA QUINN

Liddy Farrows dreamed of slaying dragons and kissing princesses. In her mind, she charged headlong into battle, her dark curls unbound. Around her, steel clashed against steel and lines of blue fire shot through the sky. The enormous dragon roared, its wings fanning the flames. Meeting its emerald gaze, she brandished her broadsword, blessed the blade with a palmer's kiss, and thrust hard into the monster's breast. With a sharp cry, the beast looked from its gaping wound to Liddy, its eyes narrowed as it retreated into the clouds. Around her, fires crackled. Enchanted green blood stained her battle-worn armor. Still, the fight was over. The dragon would not soon return.

Riding back to the fantastical kingdom of Dunland, Liddy was met with cheers. At the castle, she received a knighthood from the gray-eyed king and his doubtful queen; her first quest was to track the dragon and return with its head. She bowed in acceptance. During the following banquet, Liddy ruefully sipped at mulled wine until a nameless, faceless princess drew her into a dance. Her hands were delicate against Liddy's callouses, her laugh high as a crystal bell. With wide-eyed awe, Liddy was gifted a single patient kiss which spawned warmth in her belly, sweet and rich as spring honey.

Unfortunately, Liddy's daydreams never lasted as long as she'd like. She started from a dark alcove off the banquet hall at the soft tap on her shoulder. She blinked down at the shop accounts she'd been balancing and over her shoulder to see her father. Mr. Farrows hunched forward, his narrow frame drawn thin with age, and he gently thumbed the battered volume under his arm. "Away again, my darling?"

Liddy blushed and tucked a stray brown curl behind her ear, her scalp prickling from the tightness of her bun beneath her white spinster's cap. She looked over the stocked shelves. A pair of ladies in gray frocks holding fans browsed the produce outside, and Robert Pike, her father's apprentice, tended to them, holding their selections patiently. The June heat burned away Liddy's image of Dunland and returned her to her father's tiny shop. At her father's knowing look, Liddy shook away her disappointment. "I'm sorry, father. I get lost sometimes."

Feeling her father's gaze, Liddy took up her quill, heedless of the ink splattered on her fingers. She breathed deeply as she studied the figures, carefully balancing their meager profits. She barely heard the dull thump of her father placing his book on the counter. Then an arm slunk around her shoulder, and she pulled her quill pen away from the page. "Liddy," Mr. Farrows began, "I remember a time when we could scarcely get a moment's silence between your stories. And these days, I wish there were a mite less silence in this house."

A cry of shock sounded, followed by a flurry of footsteps and the shop door banging open. "Mr. Farrows!" called a small, rosy-cheeked woman dressed in an almost lurid shade of pink, her voice shrill and sharp. "Miss Liddy, you simply must make Miss Caroline see reason."

"Papa, please," said Caroline Farrows, the elder sister, her blond curls pulled into a beautiful knot, her green eyes wild and desperate. "It's an impertinent and unnecessary suggestion."

Mr. Farrows stiffened and whispered to Liddy, "Though it appears today, silence will not prevail." Then Mr. Farrows drew himself into his full height and smoothed down his gray hair. "Mrs. Pike, Caroline, whatever has you in an uproar?"

"Oh, Mr. Farrows," began Mrs. Pike. "Miss Farrows and I were taking tea in the garden when Collin Monroe, you know, the bookseller's nephew, peeked in at the sound of our voices—"

"It was uncalled for," interrupted Caroline. "We were enjoying the fine morning, not inviting every ruffian with a full head of hair and an easy smile to supper—"

"—and being a good hostess, I offered to have another setting brought out, which he declined, but he asked to take a turn about the garden with Miss Farrows. And Miss Farrows—"

"We had already been engaged in a lively debate. It was rude of him to interrupt—"

"—said no!" said Mrs. Pike, her mouth tight at the impertinence. "It is not to be borne. A young lady in want of a husband does not turn down prospects."

Liddy stifled her chuckles as Caroline gaped at Mrs. Pike. Though Mrs. Pike had taken on the role of mentor and matchmaker for Caroline some years ago, Liddy couldn't recall a time where the two hadn't squabbled when the subject of marriage was broached. Caroline folded her arms across her chest. "Collin Monroe would no sooner make me an offer of marriage than he would enlist in the Royal Navy. He's most vocal on the subject. He plans to take no wife."

"Collin Monroe is but twenty, and impressionable as mud," Mr. Farrows replied sternly. "All these young men swear by bachelorhood, but do not doubt it, the world will be peopled."

Liddy looked down at the counter. She felt Caroline's gaze sweep from her to their father. "Papa, you cannot be serious."

From the corner of her eye, Liddy watched as her father's posture drew firmer. He clasped his hands together on the counter. Unconsciously, she mirrored the gesture, nervously rubbing the dried ink from her fingertips.

The front door swung open again to admit the ladies in gray and Robert. At once, Mrs. Pike flitted over to the pair, like a butterfly moving from flower to flower, pollinating blooms. Liddy looked between her sister's stern brow and her father's weary frown. She swallowed, hoping it might somehow alleviate the silence; it did not.

Mr. Farrows ground his teeth and eyed his elder daughter. "Caroline, you know I cannot support the two of you on a shopkeeper's living. While Liddy is clever and well-mannered, you will attract a husband, but you must first calm your heart. It would be prudent, my dear."

The skin on the back of her neck prickled, and her instinct pushed her to stand between the feuding factions of her family. Instead, Liddy only rocked forward onto her toes as Caroline's gaze snapped to her, at once fiery and pained. Her throat ran dry, but she knew not what to say. Then Caroline huffed and spun on her heel, grumbling as she went. When the door slammed behind her, Liddy looked just in to time to see her father deflate, shoulders slumping forward and elbows resting on the worn counter. He hung his head and sighed. "Every day your sister reminds me more of Eliza. Headstrong. Willful. Utterly unstoppable."

"Is that a good or bad thing, Father?" Liddy asked, her head angled to make out her father's expression. He rarely spoke of his sister. In fact, Liddy could not recall ever meeting her.

Mr. Farrows looked down at the worn counter, his eyes misted by the memory. "Eliza was very dear to me, but her wild spirit led her astray of society. Had she been married, it might have been forgivable, but she was alone in the world. And alone she passed into obscurity and ruin." Then he pushed himself off the counter, joints popping like a firecracker. "Pray, go and see to your sister, my darling. You've an uncommon knack with her."

Liddy regarded her father's slouched posture and drained expression. The puffy bags under his eyes spoke of sleeplessness, and the downturned slope of his mouth told of worry. But when Mr. Farrows looked at her, Liddy noticed an unconscious smile pulling at his eyes. It did little to ease the rolling in her gut. Her stomach was always uneasy these days; she suspected it was merely a fact of getting older. Briskly, she folded the ledger and wiped her inky hands on her apron. "Of course, Father."

With a downward tilt to her head, Liddy moved to the front of the store. Creeping along the walls, Liddy stilled at the corner where Mrs. Pike engaged the ladies in gray, Miss Elinor Hamish and her London-born cousin, Miss Cynthia.

"Oh to be sure, Barron is the finest dressmaker in London, but I find his designs too opulent for country wear," Mrs. Pike said matter-of-factly, looking up at the taller ladies without a tick of self-consciousness. "But I have heard Lady Sinclair from our own Piedmont Downs has an account with him. True, her attire is a little garish for day wear, but fine all the same. Even Lady Stanley of Stratfield Gardens, my Benjamin's employer, has all her gowns ordered from him. Oh, that reminds me! Robert," Mrs. Pike said, turning to her elder son who stood at attention behind the ladies, the tips of his auburn hair catching on the rafters. "I almost forgot to tell you! Benjamin has been given holiday. The Stanleys have decided to summer on the continent, and Benji's been given the whole season off. Isn't that wonderful news?"

Robert cleared his throat and shifted the produce from one arm to another. "Quite wonderful, mother," Robert said, his deep voice strained to remain civil, "but perhaps we might move this conversation toward the counter so Miss Lydia may pass."

Suddenly, four pairs of eyes fell on Liddy and she stiffened under their gaze. Mrs. Pike, her back being turned to Liddy, gave a small squeal and spun about. "Oh Miss Lydia, dear, you've given me a fright. What a light step you were gifted! If only I could teach your sister a fraction of your reserve. Men do like that in a woman."

Liddy felt her cheeks flush under such attention. Behind her back, her fingers knotted together, and she picked at her callouses. "Even if reserve suited Caroline," she began meekly, "I dare say you'd be hard pressed to force her into any activity she did not wish. Please, excuse me."

Curtseying meekly, Liddy snuck between Miss Hamish and the wall only to stop when Robert called her name. "Mr. Monroe is looking into something for me," Robert said, fumbling the ladies' goods as he retrieved a folded note from his apron pocket. "If you would drop this by the bookshop. It's on the way."

Liddy smiled and took the rough paper. "Of course, Rob—Mr. Pike," she corrected quickly, and silently cursed her slip. The Misses Hamish giggled politely into their fans while Robert flushed as red as his hair. She gave another small curtsey and raced out into the dusty streets.

Summers in Dunnshire beat hot, and this June was no exception. Around Liddy, the humid air hugged close to her, unnaturally still and heavy, like the space before a convict's last breath. Ladies and gentlemen kept under the shade of awnings, parasols and hats. Liddy felt a line of sweat forming beneath her bosom and wished desperately to tear off the damn corset that kept her posture straight and her pace slow. She kicked up dust and before long, her dark green frock bore a line of dirt around the hem and her underarms were sticky. It was unpleasant to be sure, yet passing the open windows and infrequent bystanders, Liddy's mind wandered back to the fantastical landscape.

In man's breeches astride her horse, she rode down the lone village road away from the castle. A crowd had gathered to send her off. As she studied the passing faces for any potential enemy, she noticed her princess dressed in pauper's robes which did little to mask her grace. She nodded in reverence, but passed on. At the outskirts of the village, a crone clad in dark rags with a hobble and a sly grin stumbled into her path. Liddy palmed the hilt of her sword.

"Good day, Miss Lydia," said Widow Jennings, her voice ground to gravel by the years, but her eyes sharp as ever. "Another errand, I see. How your father keeps you busy."

Liddy curtseyed and held the gate open for the widow to pass. "Good afternoon, Mrs. Jennings. I'll send your groceries round tomorrow morning."

"Such a good girl," Mrs. Jennings continued as she hobbled up the overgrown walk. "You'll make a fine, considerate companion one day."

Liddy let the gate swing closed and smiled as she turned up the lane. The way to Mr. Monroe's bookshop was well worn in her memory, like a rut through sodden ground. She'd made the trip many times, usually to exchange one book for another. Absently, Liddy scolded herself for not retrieving her most recent novel from behind the counter. She'd finished *Twelfth Night* days ago and had not had the opportunity to return the book. Liddy sighed; *it will wait until tomorrow*, she thought as she straightened her skirt, quickly tucked another curl behind her ear, and stepped into the doorway of Mr. Monroe's store.

The smell of leather, ink and dust greeted her like an old friend's embrace. In the cool shadows of history and literature, Liddy's shoulders eased and her steps fell lighter. She ran a gentle hand along the books' spines, feeling the embossed lettering beneath her fingertips. Beneath her feet, the old floorboards squeaked and groaned, a melody which never failed to calm her spirit.

"Mr. Monroe?" Liddy called as loudly as she dared. She instantly regretted it; anything above a hush seemed like disturbing the dead.

"The store room," a soft voice replied, distracted and gruff with frustration. "One moment—oh, you useless thing!"

Liddy grinned and carefully wound her way through the cases and stacks of books, past the counter covered in candlewax, and into the rear of the store. Here the books were stacked perilously high, and the smell of musty paper and dank earth hung strangely sweet. Light poured in from a narrow window at the rear of the shop, and Liddy saw particles of dust dancing in the air. Liddy turned at the end of the narrow hallway and found Mr. Monroe on his hands and knees fiddling with a cast-iron stove. He scowled and bashed his tool against the metal. "Infernal contraption."

"Might I be of assistance?"

Mr. Monroe gave a huff of frustrated laughter. "Forgive my foul mouth, Miss Liddy, but damn the inventor of this insufferable thing to the darkest reaches of hell and damnation. How I relish the day such a device becomes obsolete. Bah, the stove can wait. Not like we need another degree of warmth."

Mr. Monroe quickly shuffled out of the alcove and pushed onto his feet, knees popping as he went. He ran a swift hand through his graying locks and turned toward Liddy. Mr. Monroe was a man of no great height, though he held himself so well, few realized. While he'd never married, he had a handsome face with a smooth brow, a strong nose and dark, mirthful eyes. With a quick tip of his head, Mr. Monroe brushed his sooty hands on his work apron. "How may I be of service, Miss Liddy? Finished with the Bard already?"

"I'm only a messenger today," Liddy said, holding Robert's note out in her small, ink-stained hands. "Mr. Pike asked me to bring this for you."

With a quirked brow, Mr. Monroe stepped forward and took the offered paper. As he ripped the seal, he righted a stack of books with his knee. Liddy flinched for fear they would topple, but Mr. Monroe's gentle pressure kept the volumes upright. He hummed quietly as he read the letter. "What trouble has young Robert devised?" Mr. Monroe murmured.

Liddy perked at the word 'trouble'. In all the years she'd known the man, Robert Pike was nothing if not sedate. The thought of him putting so much as a toe out of line seemed as ridiculous to Liddy as a dragon descending on Dunnshire and snatching her up into the sky, though it would make for no less a spectacle.

Mr. Monroe chuckled to himself and carefully tucked the note into his pocket. With a mischievous grin, he opened his mouth to speak. Leaning forward on her tiptoes, Liddy waited for the words, but instead she was met with the ding of the doorbell and the staccato creak of the floorboards under unpracticed feet. Mr. Monroe's mouth snapped shut, and he turned in the narrow hall and pulled back the curtain leading into the shop. Liddy waited a moment and followed at a respectful distance, her head tucked down as she crossed to the other side of the counter only to see the hem of dark gown. Who would wear black in this heat?

Instinctively, Liddy's eyes swept up the full silken skirt, the embroidered bodice, the indelicate neckline. She did not stop at the pale neck, the modest chin or the plush lips; but at the blue eyes fair as winter sky, Liddy froze. The woman—no longer a youth but far from an elder—gave Liddy a look of cool disinterest, like a sorceress regarding a fly buzzing around her experiments. Liddy's heart leapt into her throat, and when the woman subtly raised an eyebrow, Liddy dropped her gaze and curtseyed deeply. The motion sent her backward into a bookcase which wobbled precariously. Flushing with embarrassment, she turned and stilled the case with both hands. *Fool*, she chastised herself as she made for the door.

"Good day, Miss Liddy. Don't forget *Twelfth Night.* Another volume waits for you," Mr. Monroe called after her, his voice warm with amusement. "Good day, Lady Sinclair," he continued sedately.

"My order from London," the woman began. Her voice rang low and resonant, surprisingly deep for a woman. Every syllable was pronounced clearly, bringing music into the simple phrase.

"It arrived just this morning."

"Excellent."

Liddy kept her steps fast and light, and she pulled the door shut behind her. When the latch clicked, Liddy deflated against the doorway. Her hand settled against her chest, her breath suddenly easier despite the corset. *Oh, what a fool I must look, young and stupid compared to such an elegant lady,* Liddy thought. *But she'll soon have forgotten me. They always do.*

Righting herself, she stepped out of the shadows of the doorway and was met with a carriage drawn by four gray horses. Of course, a lady would go nowhere without her carriage. Liddy politely acknowledged the footmen and hurried past the whispering townsfolk.

"—still in mourning garb," one woman with a newborn on her hip observed snidely. "Almost oppressively so. Lord Sinclair has been dead almost two years."

"The whole mess is suspicious," said her companion. "Lord Sinclair was the best rider in the country. It would take more than a spooked horse to throw him."

"—and she kept his name? The nerve of that woman," griped a middle-aged man to his wife.

"—never belonged here. She should've taken herself back to London the moment he was buried—"

"And I heard," whispered another woman some yards away, "the marriage was never consummated."

Liddy's cheeks heated, and not from exertion or the weather. She nodded quickly to the bystanders, but the cruel gossip turned her stomach. What good was chattering about people one hardly knew? And what had her ladyship done to deserve such ridicule? She couldn't say. Other people's business was none of hers, and she knew she was infinitely happier in her own daydreams that she ever would be delving into those lives. With every step, she let the townsfolk's mumbled words ebb away. Besides, Liddy had other matters to attend to, and Caroline would take every ounce of her focus.

Just outside of town, Liddy carefully stepped through a field of wildflowers, picking long stems of cornflowers and daisies. She swallowed her apprehensions and made toward an elm tree near the center of the field. Seated in the shade, tying knots in the long grass, Caroline quietly seethed. She eyed the tree line, mouth pursed, shoulders tense. Liddy shuffled her feet, and Caroline's gaze snapped toward her. Then the elder sighed, tugged off her bonnet, and mussed with her hair.

"Papa sent you," Caroline said. "How brave of him, sending his daughter into the lion's den."

"You're hardly a lion, Caro," Liddy said, standing a few feet off in the sun. "A lioness, perhaps, fiercely protecting your independence."

Caroline chuckled and looked up at her younger sister. Liddy pointedly ignored the rosy tint to her nose and the puffiness of her eyes. Liddy quietly stepped into the shade and knelt beside her sister. Her grip on the wildflowers tightened reflexively. She gently laid the bundle of flowers on the ground and set about weaving the stems into a chain. Liddy kept her eyes on her work, though she could feel Caroline's gaze shifting from her eyes to her moving hands to the tree line and back again. Liddy sat in quiet reverence of the countryside. In the limbs above them, wrens and doves chirped and called. Leaves rustled in the breeze. Warm earth scented the air. Bit by bit, Liddy noticed how Caroline's shoulders eased and the line of her back smoothed. Her frown flattened, and the elder sighed. Liddy hummed a gentling tune as she threaded stems together into a circlet. Rising on her knees, she placed the wreath on Caroline's head. At Caroline's furrowed brow, Liddy kissed the crown of her head and whispered, "Even a lioness deserves a crown."

A smile pulled at Caroline's mouth, and she ran her fingers over the feather-soft petals. "You are too sweet, little sister."

Liddy grinned and settled back on the hot earth. "Is it still sweet if I hoped it would make you sensible to father's argument?"

Caroline looked down and fisted her hands in her skirt. "Always, Liddy. You know how my temper has its way with me. Some days, I wish it were possible to do away with it entirely."

Shaking her head, Liddy laid a hand on Caroline's shoulder. "Never wish such things," she said. "Your temper is a part of you. Wishing it away would leave you somehow less than you deserve. Between your temper, passion, and independence, you're the fiercest creature any man would dare to behold."

Caroline smiled, but it spoke more of melancholy. "But?"

Liddy swallowed around the urge to be silent. How she wished things could remain as they were, where Caroline marched against a disbelieving world and her at her sister's side. But she'd told father she'd counsel Caroline, and that spurred her to speak. "But father is right. Impudent and overbearing, but right. And as much as we may wish it otherwise, our futures are paved towards husbands and families and settlement. Well, yours at least. It appears I'm already branded a spinster."

"No, Liddy. There will be someone for you."

At Caroline's kind insistence, she shook her head. "If there is someone, it will only be their pity. Pray, Caro, no more protests. I am well enough acquainted with the ways of this world, and they suit me ill. Just as I will not long endure in the company of strangers, you will not survive out of it. For all your wild spirits, I fear they would die without some force to rebel against."

Caroline sat silently for a moment. Liddy held her gaze intently, and kept close to her sister should she need further counsel. But the elder blinked twice, tears clinging to her eyelashes, and she looked away from Liddy to her own fisted hands. Caroline bit her lower lip and forced herself to smile. "You always had sense enough for both of us, Liddy."

The tension ebbed out of Liddy's shoulders, and she smiled in return. "Only when others are watching."

"And are there others watching, little sister?" Caroline said, a laugh pulling her voice higher.

"Always, Caro. Or have you forgotten what monsters hide in the shadows?"

"Oh," Caroline said dramatically, throwing herself against the tree and crying out, "help me, someone. There are monsters in frilly bonnets and shopkeeper's attire who will marry me off at a moment's notice. Help me, somebody! Save me!"

Liddy laughed so hard her sides ached, and she toppled down against the tree. She'd forgotten how Caroline would always play along when they were younger; even if her imagination couldn't fathom a magical world, Caroline never begrudged Liddy her fantasies. Caroline's laugher quieted, and Liddy saw the same darkness in her eyes, the same fret. "As if I need saving," Caroline muttered.

"Everyone needs saving from something," Liddy said as a horse whinnied just down the road. They looked to see a horse and rider approaching from the direction of town. The rider pulled the horse to a stop a few feet from their tree and gracefully slid from the horse's back. He tipped his hat before removing it to reveal brown curls and vivid hazel eyes. "I heard a shout from farther up the road," he said, approaching quickly. "Are either of you injured?"

Liddy regarded the rider with a small smile. His countenance was pleasant though his mouth was drawn into a thin line of concern. Between his strong jaw, broad shoulders, and respectable height, he struck Liddy as something out of a fairy tale, a lone knight diverted from his quest to render aid. At that moment, his boot snagged on a root, and he stumbled. Liddy's smile only broadened. She composed herself to speak, but Caroline spoke up. "No, why ever would we be?"

Liddy shrank back, subtly sensing the severity of Caroline's retort. She saw the gentleman turn between them before his gaze settled on Caroline, his bright eyes full of wonder. For a moment, she wondered if others looked at her and Caroline with such intent, like they were two peculiar puzzles whose solutions eluded answer. Liddy couldn't guess; she would swear that understanding herself and Caroline was the simplest task devised.

The gentleman averted his eyes and bowed his head, hiding a blush. "Forgive me. I assumed someone must be in peril."

Caroline stood quickly, slipping the circlet from her head and grabbing the wildflowers and her bonnet to occupy her hands. Liddy followed her sister's motions with a short delay. The gentleman briefly looked again at Caroline, and when their gazes met, Caroline's posture stiffened and she drew a sharp breath. "Pray, sir, perhaps you should not assume in the future. It will save you from embarrassment."

"My apologies," the gentleman said. "Might I enquire to whom I must beg forgiveness?"

"You may," Caroline said coolly with a brief curtsey, "but I choose to give no answer. Good day, sir."

Without another word, Caroline brushed past the gentleman, her head held high and her mouth tight. He turned to watch her go, his hands clasped on the brim of his hat, his mouth half-open. Liddy stepped forward after a few moments and stood beside the gentleman. "I beg your pardon, sir," Liddy began. "My sister has been out of sorts of late. I fear you've come upon her during her ill-humor."

"She is a unique creature, perhaps the most surprising I've ever come upon," he said, all the while staring after Caroline's retreating figure. "Such passion."

Liddy nodded. "Caro does embrace her passions wholeheartedly. To her, anything less would be a lie."

The gentleman started at Liddy's words, as though he did not expect her to be there. He inclined his head respectfully, but his eyes shone with hope. "Caro? Short for Caroline?"

"Yes, sir. Miss Caroline Farrows. And you are?"

"Henry Bennett," he said. "I am a guest at Piedmont for the season."

All at once, Liddy's mind drifted back to the beautiful woman clad in black silk and her icy eyes. Her voice briefly caught in her throat before she asked. "You're one of Lady Sinclair's guests?"

"Yes, she's my sister. And here she is now," the gentleman said, his eyes turned back toward the road. Liddy's head snapped in the direction of town. Through the rising cloud of dirt, she made out the same gray ponies from outside the bookshop. Mr. Bennett quickly pulled his horse to his side as the black carriage bumped past, its curtains drawn. As Liddy bowed her head after the carriage, her mind fluttered, and in place of the carriage roamed a great black beast, its wings cutting a wide swath in its wake. Her hand balled into a fist for lack of a weapon in her weary world. But Lady Sinclair's carriage did not stop, not even for her brother, and as the dust settled, Mr. Bennett bowed to her and mounted his steed. "Fare you well, Miss Farrows," he said with a smile, looking once more down the road after Caroline. "I trust this will not be the last time we meet."

Liddy curtseyed and raced up the lane after her sister. Somehow, a strange feeling settled in her gut from the look she'd seen as Mr. Bennett watched Caroline, a queasy sort of happiness. She hadn't seen such a look in years, perhaps not since her mother had died, and she knew it had never been trained on her. Low disappointment threatened to rear its head, but Liddy shook it away. If it meant Caro's future happiness, she would ignore her own sense of loss. Besides, a man like Mr. Bennett seemed exactly the sort to win Caroline. She could not stop the smile on her lips as she caught up with Caroline and wound their arms together.

"Why ever did he keep you?" Caroline asked quickly, her cheeks flushed and her eyes bright.

"He asked for your name."

"And you gave it?"

"It would have been impolite to deny him."

"He was a stranger!"

"Perhaps," Liddy said, looking over her shoulder to find Mr. Bennett had yet to turn his horse up the road. "But not for long."

~~*

Liddy was returning from Mr. Monroe's shop the next morning, already escaping into the forest of *A Midsummer Night's Dream*, when she noticed Caroline coming out of Widow Jennings's garden accompanied by the widow and none other than Mr. Bennett. Mrs. Jennings was beaming, holding Mr. Bennett's arm at the garden gate, Caroline standing just ahead of them, her expression schooled into something civil though her brow was furrowed deeply. Liddy marked her page with her finger and held the book closed. Caroline brightened on seeing her sister, and she pulled Liddy to her side. "Dear sister, you would not guess who I ran into on my delivery this morning," said Caroline, her eyes wide with strained civility.

Mr. Bennett and Mrs. Jennings broke from their conversation to greet Liddy. "Your Mr. Bennett is quite a merry gentleman, Miss Lydia. Why, he offered to help put them away, too! Your mother taught you well."

"You flatter me, Mrs. Jennings," said Mr. Bennett with a smile, "but I cannot accept thanks for only doing what is right."

Mrs. Jennings chuckled and patted his hand. "Oh, Mr. Bennett, you are too good. You must come see me again. You make most entertaining company. Now," she said as she dropped his arm and turned back up the walk, "I leave you with the Misses Farrows. They'll see to you."

Mr. Bennett tipped his hat and stepped beyond the garden, his step lively and his smile merry. From the corner of her eye, Liddy noted a subconscious smile pull at Caroline's mouth, but all too quickly, she buried it in a twisted grouse. "We should return to the shop," Caroline offered quickly, steering Liddy down the lane with no further ado. Still, at the quick crunch of footsteps behind them, Liddy knew Mr. Bennett would not be cast aside so easily.

"I shall join you," he said, falling into step beside Caroline. "I am expected there as well."

They strolled in relative silence, something Liddy found no fault with as they crossed toward the shop. She tried to focus on Caroline's subdued reactions to Mr. Bennett, but her eyes were drawn by the mounting crowd as they came closer to the shop. Before Liddy could ask what had drawn such eyes, she glimpsed the black carriage from yesterday and the same footmen in dark livery. So that was what Mr. Bennett meant by "expected." And no wonder the townsfolk were crowded so close. It was rare enough to see Lady Sinclair in the village, but twice in as many days was unheard of. Keeping her book tucked tight to her chest, Liddy followed as Caroline pushed through the onlookers, Mr. Bennett hopping ahead to open the door.

Inside, Robert met them with a look of cool confusion, but she let it go unspoken. Instead, he nodded politely and went to the store room. From the back counter, Mr. Farrows looked up at the newcomers, stricken with relief to see his daughters; he raised a gentle hand to wave them back. Opposite the counter, again in a fine gown, stood Lady Sinclair. She half-turned toward the newly arrived party, her eyes sweeping from Mr. Bennett to Caroline and finally to Liddy. Liddy's fingers clenched on the spine of her book as though it were a wooden shield poised against a leaden mace.

Mr. Bennett stepped forward quickly, attending to his sister and shaking Mr. Farrows' offered hand. Liddy gulped. Her shield felt very meager against so many people, but Caroline tugged her onward. When she came within earshot, she heard Lady Sinclair's soft, musical voice. Even so, she was struck by the whispered strength, and Liddy felt warm reverence coil in her chest.

"I know you and my late husband's steward had previously discussed arrangements for shipments and supplies to be brought to the estate, but in the past months I've been dissatisfied with Mr. Kalin's management, and he's since been dismissed. I only wish to become better acquainted with the outstanding order we have and the details of our arrangement. It is something I should have taken a more active stand in long ago."

"Oh, I understand entirely, Lady Sinclair, and deeply admire such endeavors," Mr. Farrows said in an equally soft tone, stepping forward so Liddy could slide behind the counter. "Given an estate as large as Piedmont, it takes a great deal of effort to manage all the affairs. Were I in your place, I know the finances would be in complete shambles. Why, without Mr. Pike and Miss Lydia, I dare say the shop might spiral toward financial ruin, and I would be caught unawares. Forgive me, I do not think you have met my daughters." Mr. Farrows then gestured to Caroline and Liddy as they approached. "This is my eldest, Caroline, and my youngest, Lydia. Liddy, Caro, our esteemed patroness, Lady Sophia Sinclair of Piedmont Downs."

Both girls curtseyed while Lady Sinclair nodded her acknowledgement. From the corner of her eye, Liddy saw Mr. Farrows look between Caroline and Mr. Bennett, a subtle grin twitching around his eyes. "Caro, why don't you show Mr. Bennett around the shop?"

Caroline pursed her lips and gave a tight smile and led Mr. Bennett away. Liddy watched her sister go, but catching Lady Sinclair's eyes on her, she bowed her head. "I see you've since returned to Monroe's books," she said, noting the book Liddy had set on the counter. "I trust all the cases are still standing."

Blushing, Liddy answered. "Yes, ma'am. All Mr. Monroe's volumes remain intact and undisturbed."

A thousand better responses rang in her head, but Liddy's tongue already felt encumbered by the faint score of words. Feeling Lady Sinclair's eyes linger, Liddy swallowed hard and forced her gaze up to meet her eye.

"I hear that you have already met my brother, Mr. Bennett."

Liddy felt something strange pool in her gut, though she could not name the feeling. It made her wary of her answer. "Yes," she said. "He was kind enough to see if we were all right after he heard a cry."

Lady Sinclair's eyes did not falter, but something about the pull of her mouth reminded Liddy of a smirk. In that moment, Liddy did not know what to make of her ladyship's expression, and her own cheeks flushed. But as quickly as the look crossed her face, Lady Sinclair turned her attentions back to Mr. Farrows, and the pair delved into their business.

After a brief pause, Liddy squeezed past her father, quickly tied her apron about her waist, and moved down to where Robert stocked the selves and assembled an order. For several minutes, Robert did not acknowledge her arrival, his attention drawn to Caroline and Mr. Bennett. The gentleman stood at a respectful distance, the brim of his hat held at the small of his back and his fingers worked nervously along the felted garment. Mr. Bennett listened carefully as Caroline showed him piece by piece around the store. More than once, Caroline shot Liddy another imploring look, but Liddy angled her head as she worked so she might not see. From her side, she heard Robert sigh. "Everything all right, Robert?"

Robert looked at her for a moment and took the parcel of paper and lifted it to a high shelf. "As well as one can be, Miss Liddy."

Glancing between the smiling pair and Robert's drawn expression, Liddy felt her own heart ache in sympathy. "I think, perhaps, you underestimate yourself."

Robert did not follow her gaze, but instead retrieved the crate of goods he'd assembled and exited the shop, his brow fixed in a scowl. Liddy followed quickly despite the wall of heat which awaited her. "Had you thought to ask Caro, you would know her regard for you." Robert stopped quickly, and Liddy accidentally tumbled into his back. Righting herself, Liddy wrung her hands in her apron and continued. "You're a good man, Robert. You deserve happiness."

At once, Robert heaved the box onto an open space in the produce cart and the line of his shoulders sagged. Still, he did not turn back toward Liddy as he spoke. "Your sister will marry far above a shopkeeper's assistant. I would do her a great disservice to interfere." He drew an unsteady breath, his muscles tightening from the nape of his neck down to the tips of his fingers. "As for my own happiness, I will make do as I always have."

Liddy felt disquiet uncurl in her throat, yet she knew not what to say. Instinctively, she pressed forward and gently touched her hand to Robert's shoulder, but he flinched away as though it were an enemy's cold embrace. Without another word, he took up the box and swept off. Watching him go, Liddy ached to chase after him and talk some sense into him, but Robert would not easily let himself be persuaded. *The obstinate fool*, Liddy thought meanly. *Won't do a thing to please himself.*

At the sound of the shop door, Liddy started and spun about only to find Caroline and Mr. Bennett, each adorned by bonnet and hat respectively. "Liddy," Caroline said, quickly seizing her sister's hand in a firm grip, "Mrs. Pike bid us come for morning tea, and Mr. Bennett expressed a desire to see her garden even though the heat has deprived it of its springtime glory. Won't you join us?"

Liddy couldn't help the anxious smile that spread across her face. Though her sister looked every bit respectable, wisps of blond hair flew out at her temples and her eyes were too wide to be truly calm. Behind her, Mr. Bennett regarded the sisters with a polite smile, though he twitched onto the balls of his feet, eager to set off. Turning over her shoulder to Robert's rapidly retreating figure, Liddy said, "Caro, you'll have to go without me. Father will need my help until Robby gets back."

Caroline's mouth pinched into a tight smile, a look that made Liddy want to laugh and cower at once. But she had not lied; Mr. Farrows was never alone at the shop, and Caroline knew it. For a moment, Liddy's brow wrinkled in confusion. Caroline, being Caroline, had frequently brushed aside suitors without so much as batting an eyelash. If she did not want his attentions, why was she treading so delicately, like a wizard chasing pixies? And despite the silent aura of satisfaction radiating off Mr. Bennett, Liddy was certain he could only have good intentions toward Caroline. But before she could say anything, Caroline released her wrist and pushed her expression into something pleasing. "Please join us if you can, Liddy. I know Mrs. Pike enjoys your company."

Liddy swallowed the instinct to cackle. Mrs. Pike bore her company in the same way a chess master delighted correcting a novice's play. Instead of commenting, Liddy smiled and said, "As soon as I am able, Caro. Good day, Mr. Bennett. I hope you enjoy the garden."

Mr. Bennett bid her good day and offered Caroline his arm. Daintily, Caroline slipped her hand into the crook of his elbow and the pair pressed on into the bright heat. As they shuffled down the lane, Caroline in pale blue and Mr. Bennett in dove gray, Liddy couldn't help noticing the fine silhouette the pair made. They reminded her of a pair of dryads dancing off into the forest, heedless of whoever glimpsed their magic. In her heart, the urge to follow prickled and burned. What an adventure those two would have if Caroline gentled her wild heart, and if Mr. Bennett proved patient enough to wait for her.

Busying her hands by rearranging the produce to fill in holes in the display, Liddy let her mind wander farther. *Ripe from a long day's journey, she dismounted her steed and stomped through a grove of willows toward a secluded arm of the river. Thick underbrush and large boulders guarded the perimeter, and she could see clearly up and down the banks. Though far from defensible, the pool would do well enough for a bath. After unfastening her sword and shield and shucking her chainmail and breeches, she eased into the water. Her toes sank into the pool's silty bottom. One hand curled around the hilt of her dagger. Still, Liddy relaxed in the cool water, and sweat and stench sluiced from her skin. Under the peaceful canopy, her eyes drifted closed, and she listened to the songbird's melody.*

Some minutes later, a snapping twig startled Liddy from her slumber. She blinked awake to find a nymph standing at the far end of the pool. Her hair shone like spun silver, and her eyes were the deepest shade of blue Liddy had ever seen. Her hand coiled into a fist, but her knife had vanished. When she looked for her sword, the nymph sprang upon her, pressing her naked form against Liddy. Her breath caught at the tickle of fingers on her skin. The nymph's smile stretched wide to reveal rows of glistening teeth.

"I see your father keeps you busy, Miss Lydia."

Liddy jolted, full of fright, and her eyes snapped to Lady Sinclair standing under the shade of the awning, righting her gloves and straightening her hat. Liddy felt her hands clench around two tomatoes, and as her heart quieted, she released the fruit. Keeping her eyes down, she said, "Caroline and I do help as much as we can, though Caroline is often occupied by her mentor, Mrs. Pike."

"I have heard," Lady Sinclair replied, turning from Liddy toward the dusty lane where Caroline and Mr. Bennett stepped into Mrs. Pike's garden. "Dunnshire's resident matchmaker. An admiral's widow, I'm told. Quite odd of her to take such an interest in a shopkeeper's daughter."

Liddy looked from the empty gateway back to Lady Sinclair, and the warmth in her belly charred into blackened unease. Despite the sensation, she did not look away from the Lady's gaze. "Excuse my boldness your ladyship, but find you fault with Caroline?"

Lady Sinclair angled her head but made no move to leave the shade. "Is she then faultless in your eyes?"

Liddy shook her head. "No, but I have had almost seventeen years to study her while you've had scarcely as many minutes. Whatever her faults, Caroline is kind, honorable, and the most devoted sister anyone could ask for. Even you, your ladyship, would see that if you took the liberty to look."

For a moment, Liddy resumed her task until her words sunk through her thick skull. Her eyes widened and a flush colored her skin from cheeks to breast. Were Lady Sinclair not standing before her, her hands would have shot up to stop her mouth. But it would be too little too late. Liddy gulped around her embarrassment but forced herself to meet Lady Sinclair's gaze. The lady in question didn't so much as flinch, but the corner of her mouth perked into the same amused smirk she'd seen before. With a huff of polite laughter, Lady Sinclair said, "You are very bold, Miss Lydia. From your earlier demeanor, I would not have suspected such heart in one so young."

"Forgive me, your ladyship," Liddy whispered. "My mouth has run away with me, and I know not where it may lead."

"Nonsense," Lady Sinclair said, drawing closer with a quiet whoosh of silk. Her severe eyes seemed somehow more liquid and mirthful. "Do not hide from your opinions. Own them as you own every other aspect of yourself. And if it raises suspicion among the rabble," she continued, her voice dipping lower as she advanced, "let them talk. It is but hot air in the summer wind."

Liddy swallowed again and her gut twisted, pulling back and down as though her stomach wanted to squirm free. At the look in Lady Sinclair's eyes, Liddy felt over-warm and short of breath. No one had ever looked at her with anything more than polite regard or familial affection.

Before Liddy's spinning mind could settle, Lady Sinclair caught herself, her expression snapping shut behind an icy veneer. She broke her gaze and withdrew quickly, the faintest tinge of pink on her ladyship's cheeks. Before Liddy could ask if something ailed her, Lady Sinclair made for her carriage, a footman holding the door. She spoke to Liddy over her shoulder, her voice cold and flat compared to the music she'd previously heard. "Fare you well, Miss Lydia, and wish your sister well. I do not think we shall meet again for some time."

With that, the footman closed the carriage door, leaving Liddy alone and befuddled. What had brought about such an abrupt transformation? First, Lady Sinclair had been unreadable and amused, then open and willful, and finally withdrawn and cold. All in the space of a few minutes, too. It made her mind ache to riddle it out, but Liddy shook her head and let the fragments of unease and confusion flutter away. If the lady spoke truly, she would never have need of such knowledge. It would be far more prudent to cast aside such puzzles.

As quickly as she had settled on politely forgetting her ladyship, Mr. Farrows quietly opened the shop door and sidled up to his daughter with a conspiratorial grin. "Lady Sinclair and her brother do make a unique pair, don't you think, my darling?"

"I suppose so, father, though we've known neither long enough to form a fair judgment of character." Mr. Farrows nodded but his smile did not dissipate. Liddy furrowed her brow and set the last of the apples in order. "You suspect something contrary?"

"Well, while I am no expert on the minds of young noblemen, do not forget that I myself was a youth—"

"Were you?" Liddy said glibly. "Caro and I always assumed you burst into this world fully formed, like Athena from Zeus's head."

Mr. Farrows continued without acknowledging the interruption. "—and young men do not spend time with young women admiring flowers and shop goods unless they desire a deeper attachment."

Unsure of what to say, Liddy folded her hands and moved back toward the cool of the shop. "Lady Sinclair does not share your optimism," she said as she crossed the threshold, dusting her hands on her apron.

Mr. Farrows followed, his steps heavy on the floorboards. "She may not. I give her leave to her own opinions, but her sensibilities are not the same as ours. Anyone who marries a twice-widowed lord almost twice her age cannot be suspected of having the same sensibilities as you or I. Especially one with so dubious a reputation."

At the mention of Lord Sinclair, Liddy's stomach turned to goop. "You shouldn't say such things, father. Her reasons are her own."

"I make no judgment, Liddy." Mr. Farrows countered, his voice risen to the pitch he always reserved for Caroline. Liddy flinched instinctively. "These are observations. Nothing more."

From her father's tone, she could tell Mr. Farrows had no more to say on the subject. He quickly crossed to the back counter and continued his work in the ledger, his eyes scanning the page intently. Though Liddy felt rebuttal jumping in her throat, she bit the inside of her cheek to stop the urge and knotted her fingers in her apron's ties.

In her other world, Liddy heaved the nymph's watery corpse into the river and watched the current ferry away the body. Its transparent skin glittered under the sunlight, its silver blood seeping from the wound across its chest, fatal and dealt by a mortal hand. A small part of her mourned the loss of life, but her arms and neck bore bleeding bites and scratches from the fight. At the nape of her neck, she could feel a throbbing bruise blossoming. Sometimes sacrifice was a necessary and brutal fact of life.

~~*

In the weeks that followed, the village, and Liddy by proxy, saw little more of Lady Sinclair. Once, a footman from Piedmont Downs came into town to gather letters from the post, a parcel of books and other luxuries from the vendors. Even without setting foot off the estate,

Lady Sinclair set the village populace aswarm. Liddy did her best to politely abstain from all speculation regarding her new acquaintance. How she had never before noticed the level of speculation raised against the new warden of Piedmont, she could not say. Now, it seemed everywhere she turned, Liddy was ill-met with exasperation and disgust at Lady Sinclair's continued existence.

However, while her ladyship was more absent than ever before, her brother most certainly was not. Henry Bennett quickly and heartily ingratiated himself with the townsfolk. In his first afternoon, his kind demeanor and charming personality won over Mrs. Pike, who rapidly spread word to every family in the village proper. Overnight it seemed, Mr. Bennett became a newfound hero of the masses, though why Liddy couldn't tell. In the weeks since his arrival, she and Caroline scarcely went a day without encountering him. While Caroline remained so inscrutable as to her opinion of the gentleman, Liddy couldn't help hoping that her elder sister had warmed to the idea of marriage now that an eligible prospect had presented itself.

Far beyond the borders of Dunland, Liddy spurred her horse down a weary road through blue-flamed fields. In the north, three peaks rose, glossy as glass in the sunlight, shrouded in smoke. The dragon was close. She rode through a decrepit village, and villagers flocked out of ramshackle huts, their faces smeared with soot. A one-eyed elder with a feathered headdress and claw marks on her cheeks barred her path. "You cannot pass," said the elder, her voice shrill and her eyes hard. "To go into the mouth of the mountain will bring death on all of us."

Liddy looked from the lone woman in her path to the bystanders, each leaning forward, waiting for her decision. Her hand ran across the smooth pommel of her sword. The woman did not budge, her bare feet stuck in the ashy mud. Liddy narrowed her eyes, skimming over the villagers. She remembered her own village, awaiting her return with evidence of the dragon's demise. Unbidden, the image of her princess sprang to mind, her smile warm as summer wine and equally sweet, her hair soft and dark as the new moon and her eyes cutting yet secretly kind. The memory deepened her resolve.

"I cannot go back," she said. "I swore a vow I would not fail."

The woman drew a deep breath, her shoulders rolling back and holding steady. Her hands balled into fists at her sides. Her wrinkled expression tightened. "As have I."

A foreign voice echoed from beyond the skies, jovial and coy in her ears. "Well, you're as lost in the clouds as ever, Lid. I would have thought a year would have given you better sense."

Liddy started and her eyes swept up the figure standing before her as a wide smile burst on her cheeks. "Benji!"

Benjamin Pike, her childhood friend, laughed merrily and dropped his rucksack beside the counter while Liddy raced around and pulled him into a hug. In the year since he'd left for a position in the country as a tutor to Lord and Lady Stanley's wild brood, Benji's figure had filled out. Where before he'd been a skinny lad scarcely taller than herself, easily identified by his mop of red curls, now Benji bore himself better, shoulders back, chin held high, and brown eyes gleaming with mirth and mischief. Still, he hadn't grown into his ears which stuck out from his head like the handles of a chalice. She touched them for good measure and laughed. "We had no word you were coming in today," Liddy said. "Your mother kept your coming a secret."

Benjamin laughed and sidled closer to her. "Doubtless that is due to her own ignorance on the matter. Robby! Farrows!" he said, pausing to greet the two men when they came out of the store room to see to the commotion. "Good to see the pair of you. God Robby, you're getting old."

Robert shook his brother's offered hand with a look of amused annoyance. "And it would appear the years have not blessed you with another inch of height as you so hoped." To lend credence to his observation, Robert rolled his shoulders back into his full height. Benjamin *humph*ed cheerfully, and Robert grinned. "I'll always be taller than you, little brother. Never forget that."

"Now, now, boys," Mr. Farrows said, clapping each on the shoulder. "Back in the same county only minutes, and you're already at odds. Whatever would your mother say?"

"Nothing we haven't heard before," Benjamin quipped to Liddy. She chuckled under her breath but offered no further remark. It was only to be expected. As with Caroline, Benjamin was always the more verbose of their pair, and he accepted her quiet companionship.

The formalities seen to, Benjamin and Liddy stole away from the store, eager for a moment of privacy. Arm in arm, they snuck out of town, rushing past Mrs. Pike's gate. Their steps eager and their words merry, they crossed into the riverside wilderness north of town and nestled themselves in a grove of wild trees, branches heavy with summer peaches. Liddy breathed in the sweet scent of the fruit while Benjamin spoke. "The Stanleys have trees like that on their property," he said, plucking a long stem of grass and cleaning the dirt off with his fingertips. "In the afternoons, I take Max and Billy out exploring. Up and down hillocks. Over brambles. Into the woods. Those two love being out of doors. 'Two burgeoning sportsmen,' I've told Lord Stanley. Little Billy even says he wants to hunt a lion one day."

Liddy smiled and rubbed the fruit's skin as though it were a fortuneteller's orb. She could picture two young boys in huntsmen's garb tromping through the woods, one holding the stock of a musket, the other the barrel.

"Ernie thinks I should urge them toward more scholastic pursuits," Benjamin continued, a grin pulling at his mouth.

"The Stanley's eldest?" Liddy asked before taking a bite of fruit.

"Their ward, Ernest Smart. Lady Stanley's nephew. The Stanleys are pressing him toward the church. Ernie thinks he'd be happier as anything else. Says he'd rather live in the world than preach to its inhabitants." Benjamin shrugged, nibbling on the grass. "'Tis the downside for poor relations. They're all dependent on the whims of the rich."

"Is he staying at the estate while they summer in France?"

"No, the lucky rake is there with them," he said, his eyes narrowed jealously, but the smile pulled broader across his face. "I made him promise to bring back pictures of everything. Even bought him a sketch book as a going away present."

Liddy watched carefully as Benjamin's cheeks flushed and he nervously tugged at his curls, making the wild strands even more tangled. Her own smile was instinctual, but she knew better than to draw attention to it. Whatever she might suspect of Benji's inclinations, it would be impolite to speak of them. In her few short years, Liddy had only once come across the smallest suggestion of such proclivities in an old book Benji had been studying in the back of Monroe's bookshop. Her eyes went wide at the lithograph midway through the text, and she knew not what to make of two men embraced in such a manner. Since then, her opinions had softened, though clearly her society had not. Even now, she could not be open with her friend. The feeling unsettled her. "Some people are benefited by their society. Others are less fortunate."

"What of you, little Lid?" Benjamin asked, turning toward her with a conspiratorial grin. "How have you fared in my long absence?"

She opened her mouth to speak, but Benjamin continued without pause. "When I left, I remember you claimed you'd slay a thousand monsters to pass the hours. How high do your trophies number? One hundred? Five? Ten? All laid to waste by your valor?"

Liddy giggled. "Valor does not slay demons, Benji. But as you ask, I've kept Dunland safe in your absence. Excepting the dragon."

Benjamin tutted lightly. "A dragon, Liddy? However could you allow such a tragedy to befall us?"

"One knight is not an army, and it would take ten to slay a dragon. Not all of us can triumph over monsters simply by willing it."

He laughed. "Come now, Lid. There must be some mischief to report," said Benji, twirling the stalk of grass with a flourish. "An unspeakable *amour*? A mysterious death? A banishment? Anything?"

Liddy smiled and shook her head. "Mischief only follows you. As ever. Is Stratfield Gardens too boring for you?"

"Anywhere is interesting if you know where the secrets are buried."

"Then you've simply learned all of Dunnshire's. Whatever will you do to amuse yourself?"

"Invent some new secrets," Benjamin said, eyes bright with trouble.

Liddy chuckled. "Naturally. You'll have to start with Caroline."

"Ah, Caro. Isn't she ever a wonderful source! What adventure has befallen her this week?"

"A most persistent admirer," said Liddy between bites. At Benjamin's perked brow, Liddy explained the abrupt arrival and ingratiation of Mr. Bennett into Dunnshire society. "They'd make a fine pair if Caro could put some actual mirth into her smiles. Now she acts as though she's balancing upon a knife's point: each second agony, but to step off would be infinitely more frightful."

Benjamin shrugged. "Perhaps it is merely her partner that troubles her. What sort of beast is our Mr. Bennett? Traveling rogue or bumbling fool?"

"He's a gentleman of means, which pleases father, and a cultured young man, which pleases Mrs. Pike, and he's a determined will, which compels Caro to continue their association."

"And do you deem him worthy of Caroline?" Benjamin said. "Has he met with your challenge?"

Liddy looked down at the peach pit in her hand with tiny bits of flesh still clinging to it like sailors on a capsized ship. She remembered Mr. Bennett's offer to walk the groceries down to the widow, how he helped her put them away without a moment's hesitation or a backward glance to see if Caroline paid him any mind. And she remembered seeing him calling on the widow every few days, always bringing wildflowers with him, opening up her dusty old hovel with a touch of sunshine. She smiled. "He's kind-hearted. It's hard to disguise callousness or arrogance when a man spreads his time equally between the elderly, the infirm, and the gossip mongers, all the while assisting his sister with her estate."

"You paint our Mr. Bennett a saint, not some mere mortal," Benjamin teased, idly twirling the shoot of grass.

"You exaggerate," Liddy said calmly, tossing the pit of her peach into the river. "Mr. Bennett is a fine man, and if Caroline will have him, he will give every effort to make her happy."

Benjamin's easy grin subsided, and he turned back toward the river. Silence stretched between them. In the creases of his brow and the distant glaze of his eyes, Liddy read his heavy thoughts. Strange, levity usually radiated from Benji. She'd never known him to be burdened by anything. For a moment, Liddy wondered if he'd been set upon by some ancient curse, for Benjamin scarcely moved in the space of several minutes as though he'd been turned to stone. *To be a stone*, she thought, her head tilting to the side. *The world's silent witness. To be slowly worn away by wind, water, and time. To wear those scars like brands of courage.* It was a frightening thing, Liddy decided in the shade of the peach tree, to remain.

"Caro will make her own place in this world," Benjamin began, breaking Liddy from her thoughts. "Of that I'm certain."

In his pause, Liddy sensed the spirally question. "Of what, then, are you uncertain?"

"You."

Liddy turned toward Benjamin, one brow raised high, her spine rigid. "What of me?"

Benjamin shot her a knowing smirk. "Don't play coy, Lydia. You can scarcely expect anyone to believe you're content with the life of a shopkeeper's daughter. Least of all me."

Liddy knotted her hands in her lap. "There are worse livelihoods."

"But Liddy, surely you must thirst for adventures. To see the Nile or the Andes or even so far as the next county over. Given the complexity of your inner life, I refuse to believe you're happy to sit at home, grow into an old spinster and waste away."

Liddy looked at her old friend, at the openness of his expression and the genuine confusion playing across his eyes. She felt the urge to explain tickle at the back of her throat. Of everyone, Benji must be able to understand finding happiness within oneself. Surely. So what if the wide world looked on her with pity? Liddy knew the triumph of standing over a fallen enemy, the sorrow for fallen comrades, the regret of taking a life. She'd danced with dryads until dawn, swam with sea monsters and stared into the emerald eyes of a dragon. If no one else in a thousand years believed her, or could say they'd experienced the same, did it make her fantasies worth anything less?

Before she could devise an answer, a pair of horses galloped through the meadow across the river, one a tawny mare, the other a speckled gray. Astride them, Liddy noted Mr. Bennett in his customary gray coat and Lady Sinclair in a casual attitude: her curls half down, dressed in breeches, wearing a soft smile which she secreted away upon noticing the bystanders. Liddy gaped at the sight of the breeches, envious of both Lady Sinclair's daring attitude and her shapely legs. While her ladyship rode ahead, Mr. Bennett watered his horse, met with Liddy and introduced himself to Benjamin, not waiting for an introduction. Without hesitation, Benjamin dove into conversation, complimenting the mare's gait and coat.

They spoke amiably for several minutes until Lady Sinclair rode back, her eyes cold. Liddy flushed when Mr. Bennett beat her to Benjamin's introduction. Benji, for all his courtesy, gave a rakish smile and bow; in turn, Liddy nearly covered her face in embarrassment. Ever did Benji play the flirt.

Lady Sinclair nodded to the pair before turning to her brother. "Don't dally, Henry," she said. "Miss Lydia and her guest are enjoying the day." At the mention of her name, Lady Sinclair regarded Liddy, a faint smile glimmering at the corner of her eye. Liddy would gape to see such a sight if the grin had lasted longer than a moment. She watched as Lady Sinclair's eyes swept up Benjamin with a narrow-eyed look of dismay. Before she could make heads or tails of the look, Lady Sinclair turned to her brother. "Let the young couple alone to their *amour*."

Mr. Bennett blushed and bid their forgiveness. "Perhaps we may see you at Piedmont. The groves are ripe with berries, and we've no guests to pick them."

Lady Sinclair made no comment on the suggestion, only spurred her horse into the wood. Mr. Bennett looked between his retreating sister and the pair. Liddy felt her heart twist in sympathy, watching him scramble onto his horse. "So long as the weather remains fine, you may count on an invitation. You must excuse me!"

As the pair galloped away, Liddy felt a twinge of anxiety crawling in her belly. A day spent at Piedmont Downs sounded diverting, but spending so long in the contradictory company of Lady Sinclair knotted Liddy's stomach. But she'd have Benji to liven her befuddled mind.

"What a peculiar pair," Benjamin said abruptly, before Liddy's mind could stop spinning. "And they're siblings even. I see the resemblance in their eyes and carriage, but my, how differences abound. And did you catch the bit about '*amour*?' She makes it sound like I've absconded with your virtue."

"I'm sure she meant nothing of the sort," Liddy protested, though her already flushed cheeks darkened at the suggestion. "Lady Sinclair merely does not mince words."

Still, Benjamin glared in the direction of the riders. "I see now why she's such a favorite among the villagers. She could do with a lesson in tact."

Liddy chuckled at Benji's tone; she could imagine him reprimanding a youthful Lady Sinclair, but not making an inch of progress cutting through her cold facade. "Lady Sinclair has wealth and a title. She could behave like the patron saint of gossip mongers, and Dunnshire could still find fault with her existence."

"Regardless, she does herself no favors with such behavior." Then Benjamin chuckled. "If Caroline does find herself entwined with our Mr. Bennett, her ladyship will make a most fearsome in-law. Can you imagine it, Liddy?"

Liddy shook her head absently while her gaze lingered on the horse tracks across the brook. *In the dark of night, she followed down tracks weaving between geysers of fire and ash well out of sight of the village. When her horse reared and ran, she cursed herself under her breath. It would have been easier to take the village road into the mountain, but her own sense of honor would not let her uproot the elder. She would not undo the woman's vows even in the course of undertaking her own. Suddenly, a spurt of blue flames rose inches from her leg, catching her boot and breeches on fire. She screamed as her flesh singed and the smell uncoiled in the sizzling air.*

At the far edge of the fiery field, Liddy collapsed onto the forest floor, her leg already blistered. She chewed on bark to alleviate the pain, but it helped little. In the unending heat, she sighed and gave herself a brief respite. Tomorrow would be worse.

~~*

Truly enough, within a week both the Pike and Farrows families received invitations to picnic and take tea at Piedmont Downs, and both invitations were heartily accepted. So, the following Saturday, Mr. Farrows posted a succinct notice in the shop window, Liddy and Caroline put on their best day gowns and together with Robert, Benjamin, and Mrs. Pike, they set off a mile northward to the estate. While the party gossiped about the goings on in town—except Robert, who nodded distantly while admiring the roll of the landscape—Liddy took her position at the rear of the pack and let her mind wander.

Her booted footsteps crunched atop the sun-bleached bones of deceased heroes who had tried their hands against a demon and each failed. The smell of sulfur and decay withered in her throat. Her blistered flesh seized with each step. Twice she nearly retched. Regardless of the creeping unease in her spine Liddy persevered, her sword held at the ready. The closer she came to the dragon's keep, the more the air rippled and sizzled from its natural heat. Sweat beaded on her brow and dripped from the tip of her nose. She gulped, casting a cursory glance over her shoulder at the narrow valley, the walls long since melted into glass. Escape would not be easy should she fail to slay the beast. But before she could step into the jagged mouth of the cave, Caroline called her name as they arrived at the ancient gates of Piedmont Downs.

Walking up the overgrown lane, Liddy felt a hush fall over their party. She could imagine the park in wintertime, mists creeping through the underbrush, bare branches clawing at the sky, clambering for escape. How long had the grounds been left unkempt? Liddy could see the start of maintenance, where the hedgerows had been pruned into submission, and she could hear the buzz of bees lazing through the garden, drunk on the heat and nectar. At a row of once manicured poplars, the lane curved to the left and the manor house came into view. Built of heavy gray stone and jagged iron fixtures, the house struck Liddy as something medieval. She started at such an old style of house. Beside her, Benjamin said, "Positively gothic. No wonder she's forever dismissive. You must start to lose your head spending too much time in a house like that. Why ever hasn't she renovated it?"

Liddy's eyes moved from window to window, waiting to see a lady in waiting appear from the darkness. "Perhaps sentimental reasons," she offered, though she doubted it. Despite her own flights of fancy, she didn't think she could ever live in a castle; it struck her as a frightful, cold place.

Mr. Bennett and Lady Sinclair met the party, the former with a broad smile and pleasing demeanor, the latter decidedly less so. With the formalities observed, her ladyship absented herself from the picnic citing a splitting headache. Only Liddy felt burdened by this news, but then again, Lady Sinclair had barely acknowledged her existence beyond a cursory nod. Mr. Bennett gave his sister an imploring look, but she could not be swayed. And so the party made for the sweeping hill and descended upon a piece of wood bordered by a small brook. They opened their baskets and wandered along the brambles, gathering berries.

Liddy stayed near Benji as they foraged, laughing along to his stories as they wandered. Still, from the corner of her eyes she noted how Mr. Bennett floated around the group making easy conversation with all the members, though when he spoke to Caroline, something about the way he carried himself loosened. In contrast, Caroline remained tense and silent. When Mr. Farrows quietly observed Caroline's demure transformation to Mrs. Pike, Liddy too held her tongue when the latter suspected Caroline might finally have formed an attachment, and Mr. Bennett's four thousand pounds a year hardly hurt matters. Liddy sunk her nails into her palms with her effort to keep mum. Could no one else see unease drawn on Caroline's face?

By the time the sun rose high and the heat began to crest, Mr. Bennett led them back down the hill and to the manor house. Ahead of her, Mrs. Pike whispered, "Whatever *can* we expect walking into a dead man's house? Lord rest his soul."

Inside, the light was dim and the air still. Suits of armor lined the entry way, and dark stone covered the floors. Liddy suppressed a shiver at the cold atmosphere. A footman escorted them into a back parlor where tea was laid out. Mrs. Pike twittered about every detail, complimented each lavish furnishing as she went. Across the room, Benjamin rolled his eyes, which spurred a chuckle in Liddy.

As Mr. Bennett graciously accepted Mrs. Pike's praise, Liddy stopped, her eye drawn by a peculiar painting. The background was a rich green forest, tall trees, dark bushes tipped with red berries, and a brook weaving down a hillside. In the left mid-ground, a beautiful woman with golden curls and blood-smeared clothes wept. A fair young man in Grecian robes lay in her lap, a wound across his chest bleeding, his face pale with death. In the right foreground, a naked nymph stood, hands clasped before her, her head downturned and in profile, her eyes dark with tears. Liddy looked to the bottom of the frame and found an engraved title plate: *Oenone and her first love, Paris*. Something about the nymph's stricken expression moved Liddy, but she could not say what for sure. It was not open sorrow like the beautiful woman's, but instead a quieter melancholy, like slowly rising flood waters compared to a torrential deluge. It struck Liddy as a more poisonous kind of grief, slow and unending instead of sharp and readily borne.

Liddy blinked and turned to find the hall deserted, the only noise of her company the distant squeal of Mrs. Pike's shrill laughter. *In her mind, she pressed against the dark walls of the cave. She could hear the rumble of deep breath, and the sound echoed through the obsidian walls. She gritted her teeth against the throb in her leg, but still, she crept forward, sword poised at the ready, eyes sharp despite the thickening darkness. The deeper she went into the cave, the heavier the air hung with oppressive heat and the rancid scent of decomposition. She must be getting close.*

Suddenly, a clatter of stone rang out, like dice across a tabletop. Liddy froze. She'd trodden upon a pile of bones and knocked them to the ground. At once, the breathing stopped. Looking over her shoulder, she saw the mouth of the cave was not more than thirty feet away. If she must, she could still escape and try her luck in the canyon. But when she turned forward, she was met with an enormous pair of emerald eyes and the noxious scent of gas.

Liddy shook away the fantasy and took a half step toward her company when she heard a meek sob. She paused and turned back around. The hall led off into a series of closed doorways, the light too low for her to see the end. Her scalp prickled and her hands fisted nervously. It would be impolite to go down that hall. She might stumble upon the kitchens, or servant's quarters or even family rooms, and Liddy shuddered to think of what beasts might lurk there. But the cry came again, louder this time, sudden like a hiccup. It would be rude, yes, but Liddy only recalled that sound from one time before: when she was but a child and she'd come across Caroline quietly crying into her pillow on the morning of their mother's funeral.

Instantly her back stiffened, and her feet moved of their own accord, drawing her deeper into the corridor. At each door she paused and listened, until at the last one she heard the sound once more. Pressing her ear to the wood to be sure, Liddy heard a small, high voice muttering indiscernible words in between cries. Holding her breath, she turned the cold doorknob and peaked inside.

Liddy found a small nursery with a neat little table and chairs, a child's tea set laid out on it. The fine carpet was littered with books and blocks and sitting at the center was a fair-haired young girl in a bright green dress with blotchy, tearstained cheeks and a porcelain doll in her lap. Looking closer, though, Liddy saw that the doll's arm was raggedly broken. Liddy made a small gasp, and the girl started, her blue gaze shooting to Liddy, wide with horror. "Wh... what are you... doing?" the girl said meekly, drawing her knees up between her broken doll and the stranger.

Liddy opened the door wider but did not come inside. She looked down at the floor and swallowed her meager fright. Her own foolish curiosity had put her here; now she must endure. "Apologies, miss," she began. "I thought... I thought I heard someone calling... for a doctor."

The girl's brows screwed together in a twist of confusion. As she opened her mouth to reply, Liddy cocked her head to the side on impulse, raising an ear to better hear. "There it is again," she said, drawn farther into the room by the imagined voice. Though the girl tensed as she drew nearer, Liddy carefully knelt down a few feet away, smiling mildly and extending a hand, as she would if she were trying to coax a fairy from a hollow. "I think this is your doll. May I?"

Warily, the girl watched Liddy's outstretched palm. For a moment, her tiny hands clenched in the fabric of her doll's dress, holding her tightly to her chest. "Don't be afraid," Liddy said quietly. "I had a dolly of my own I couldn't part with when I was your age. I won't hurt her. You have my word."

The girls' mouth tightened, and she ducked her head low, but still she gingerly held the doll out toward Liddy. Rather than take the doll, Liddy scooted forward and listened carefully, considering the dolls words. "It was you I heard, Miss..." she looked to the girl. "What's her name?"

"Princess Charlotte of Piedmont."

"Apologies," Liddy said, curtseying deeply for the doll. "Princess Charlotte, however may I serve you?" She paused, listening and quietly noted the small smile slipping onto the girls face. "Your arm?" Liddy turned and studied the break. "Goodness me, this looks beyond my skills to heal. We may need a witch's balm to mend you, your highness." Then, looking to the girl, Liddy asked. "How may we find the housekeeper?"

The girl's grin faltered as her eyes flicked to the door. She withdrew. "I'm not allowed to go out while there are guests. Miss Sophia will be angry with me."

Liddy looked between the doorway and the girl before standing, dusting the crease out of her gown and offering her hand to the girl. "Well, if Miss Sophia is angry with you, we shall simply explain that we are on a mission of royal importance, and that any fault she may find will rest entirely on me."

The girl nibbled on her lower lip, still unsure. Liddy held firm, and smiled warmly. "Come. She'll mend faster if you show me the way."

With a sniff and a quick wipe of her eyes, the girl grabbed Liddy's thumb, leading her out of the room. Down winding corridors they went, both silent but for the click of their shoes on the floor. The girl knew the way and led quietly, but with each step, her shoulders seemed to ease, and she pulled Liddy a little less. In one of the lower halls, the girl stopped and meekly knocked on a door before ducking behind Liddy. A woman with dark skin and pale eyes opened the door, her brow furrowed, but looking between the doll in Liddy's hand and the child peeking out from behind Liddy's skirts, her eyes softened and she beckoned them in with a weary smile.

In a few short minutes, Princess Charlotte's arm was pasted and tied back in place, but the housekeeper gave the girl a stern warning to be more careful in the future. Liddy could see from the downward turn of the girl's head and her tight grip on the doll that she'd learned her lesson. However, just as they turned to return to the girl's room, Liddy heard the rustle of silk, and she looked down the hallway just in time to see Lady Sinclair freeze, her mouth dropped open in an expression of horror. Fast as a fury sent from hell, Lady Sinclair descended upon them, grabbed the girl's arm and pulled her away from Liddy and safely behind her own skirt. "Miss Lydia," she whispered, her voice sharp as a needle. "May I enquire as to how you are in the servant's quarters of my house?"

Liddy opened her mouth to speak, but the girl spoke up quickly. "She heard Princess Charlotte crying and came to help."

"Be silent, Penelope," Lady Sinclair snapped, her narrowed gaze falling on the child before turning to the housekeeper. "Please Ms. Smith, take her back to her rooms."

"Yes, milady," the housekeeper said before carefully taking Penelope's wrist and leading her away. As they walked, the girl looked over her shoulder, the start of tears clinging to her eyelashes. Liddy gave her a weak smile, but knew it would do little to mend her error.

Then she looked back to Lady Sinclair. Liddy's shoulders tensed and her mouth twisted into a grimace, anticipating the coming storm. Lady Sinclair was silent as she straightened herself into a long, taut line. "I hear it is most impolite in good society to snoop around another's home."

"Forgive me, your ladyship," Liddy said, the words automatically filling her throat.

"Why ever should I? In the time we've met, I've only seen a foolish, feather-brained girl, too lost in her head to pay mind to the world around her. Why do you deserve my forgiveness?"

Liddy would recoil from Lady Sinclair's cold venom, but she would not let herself be bullied into submission, not for so small a grievance. She dug her nails into her palms and held her head high. "Asking for forgiveness is custom, I'm told, when another party has been offended. But as I'm only some foolish child in your eyes, I suppose I cannot expect civil treatment. I acknowledge my fault in venturing away from the party, and for that I apologize. For any other fault, I ask no pardon. It is not in my nature to let a child crying go unattended. Now, please excuse me," Liddy said, pushing past Lady Sinclair. "I should return to the party."

On light steps, Liddy began down the corridor, careful to keep her back straight and her posture unaffected. Still, her heart pounded in her throat at the tiny victory. *She emerged from the dragon's keep weary but in triumph. Her armor was once more flecked with dragon's blood; she could feel it growing tacky on her skin and clumping in her hair. Sheathing her sword and hoisting the dragon's head in a sack upon her back,*

Liddy tromped down the mountainside, at last homeward bound. And soon, too, she'd be away from Lady Sinclair's harsh gaze and cruel words. The corner was not far; then she would be out of sight and could catch her breath and cheer at her own boldness.

"Miss Lydia."

She froze and circled slowly, forcing her face into a neutral expression as she faced a living dragon. In the darkness, Liddy saw Lady Sinclair standing in the same stiff posture as before, but her bright eyes seemed less hard and her mouth had softened. Liddy swallowed around the tangle of anxiety threatening to suffocate her.

"Take the stairs at the end of the corridor," Lady Sinclair said, her eyes darting from Liddy to just over her shoulder. "The footman at the top will take you to the drawing room."

Liddy felt all the breath rush out of her at such a mild response. Her eyes widened and her cheeks flushed, but still, she curtseyed briefly and called, "Thank you," before turning and taking the slow trek back to the party.

~~*

"Our hero," said her princess, dragging Liddy away from the banquet with a mouth on her neck and a hand at the small of her back. Liddy did not protest, feeling her princess's tapered waist and full hips beneath her fingertips. At her swelling warmth, she pushed the princess up against the wall, angling her head and slotting their mouths together once more. The princess giggled, already dragging Liddy's fine shirt out of her

breeches and working at the laces. "However shall we repay you for slaying such a ferocious beast?"

"Your highness," Liddy said, her voice high and breathless as a hand slipped into her breeches, venturing south. "Perhaps at the nearest bedchamber."

Her princess gave a wicked smile and leaned down to mouth at her ear. "Are you shy, my warrior?" she asked, circling Liddy's slit with soft fingertips.

"Only for your modesty."

Her princess hummed and raked her nails over Liddy's scarred flesh, palming Liddy's unbound breast and rolling her nipple. Liddy moaned at the new sensation just as her princess pressed two fingers upward into her center. Starting at the fullness, Liddy squirmed and ground down into the heel of her princess's hand. More pleasure coursed through her veins, making her warm and bold. Unbidden, she pulled her shirt over her head as her princess tugged her breeches down farther.

Quickly, the taller woman pushed off the wall and spun them. The cold stone on Liddy's back made her shiver. Slowly, the princess kissed down from her mouth to her breasts to her stomach. Dropping to her knees, the princess kissed Liddy's thighs, urging them open with her shoulders as she withdrew her fingers and licked Liddy's wetness from them. Liddy's mouth dropped open, her head tipped back, her eyes closed. Lips and warm breath whispered across her thighs. Gentle pressure on her slit. Probing circles. Liddy gasped. Her legs trembled at the mounting pleasure. One hand moved to her princess's curls, lightly touching the delicate strands. She willed her eyes to open. Her fingers tangled in long dark curls, and the eyes staring up at her were bright blue and filled with such rolling heat, her stomach quivered.

Liddy shot up in bed, her breath rushed, her cheeks flushed and her nightgown damp. Vividly, she remembered the sensation of a mouth on her... no, it was shameful to think, but her throat ran dry at the memory of those eyes. Only one person she knew had eyes that color. Without question, her princess now took the shape of Lady Sinclair.

The entire morning, Liddy was preoccupied by the dream. She could not shake the heat that flooded her core, no matter how many times she tried to focus on the shop's accounts. Every couple of lines, her mind would drift back to the darkened alcove, the sensation of breath on her skin, and the passion coursing in Lady Sinclair's eyes. Perhaps that was the worst part for Liddy. Were the subject of her unconscious fantasy anyone but her ladyship, she might have been able to disregard the dream; the undeniable fact that she could not troubled her greatly.

So great was her bemusement that she scarcely noticed as the shop door was closed with special care or when Caroline sidled up to her and rested her chin upon Liddy's shoulder. "Little sister, you are not yourself today."

Liddy sighed and rested her head against her sister's. Her quill pen flexed in her grip and Liddy settled the pen against the counter. She felt Caroline's arms pull round her waist. "Forgive me. I slept ill."

"Nothing to forgive, little Liddy. The summer wind will make fools of us all. Come," Caroline said, taking her sister's hand. "There's something I want to show you."

As Caroline dragged Liddy toward the back, Liddy said, "But I'm to mind the shop while father is out."

"Close your eyes."

"Caro!"

"Trust me," Caroline said, quickly stepping behind Liddy and covering her eyes with her hands. "A few minutes and you'll be back up front. The shop will keep itself for that long."

Liddy swallowed her protest and shuffled forward, worried she might trip in the cluttered hall that led from the shop to their small home. As they went, she smelled their evening soup bubbling on the coals and the musty scent of her father's books. There was something else though, sweet and zesty. Lemon. That was a rare smell in their house. Once when she was a child, their mother had saved to buy lemons from a vendor and baked thin slices into cakes for her and Caroline's birthdays. She could still taste the sweet at the back of her tongue.

At once, Caroline lifted her hands. Liddy was startled to find Robert, Benji, Mrs. Pike and Mr. Farrows standing around their table, two small wrapped parcels resting on its surface. Before Liddy could ask, the group called "Happy Birthday!"

Liddy's brow furrowed. "But my birthday is not until September."

"True," said Caroline, "but September is so dull. Always we are more concerned with gathering stock to last through spring than celebrating."

"And I was absent from your last birthday and will likely not make it to the next," said Benji. "In fact, the longer it goes the less chance we all have of keeping together."

"So, we've decided to celebrate now. While everyone may be present," explained Mr. Farrows.

At her father's words, Liddy felt Caroline stiffen beside her. She forced a grin onto her lips and squeezed

Caroline's hand. Robert cleared his throat and offered Liddy the first parcel. "This is from all of us, but we had help in selecting it."

With trembling fingers, Liddy opened the wrappings and found a book within, the grooves of the binding dusty and the pages scented with the salt of years. Across the cover in black letters it read *Metamorphosis*. Throat thick with rising glee, she cradled the book to her chest. "Thank you," she whispered, fighting the happy tears prickling along her eyelashes.

"And this, dear," said Mrs. Pike with a smile while pushing the second parcel forward. Gingerly, Liddy pulled at the string, too shocked to put down the book. As the wrappings fell away, the scent of lemon grew more vibrant, and she found a small tea cake within with a perfect circle of lemon atop it. "Miss Farrows told me how your mother made them when you were young. She and I found a recipe and persuaded Mr. Bunting, the baker, to whip up a batch. Unfortunately, he was only able to save one for us. You know how all the neighborhood goes mad when even the smallest delicacies become available. Come now, Miss Lydia. Eat it; it's all for you."

Liddy looked between Caroline and Mrs. Pike and bit her cheek in hopes of keeping her emotions in check. "No, I couldn't take the whole thing. You've all been so kind. A piece for everyone."

"Nonsense, Liddy," Mr. Farrows said. "It is yours. You must enjoy it."

Liddy was saved from further protest by a sharp rap upon the shop door. All heads snapped toward the shop, and Liddy, being closest, automatically moved back into the shop, setting her book on the counter and straightening her skirt before opening the door.

Standing in their stoop with a bouquet of wild flowers was Mr. Bennett, his brow tight in concentration, but he grinned on seeing her. "Good afternoon, Miss Lydia. I brought these to help brighten the shop," he said, offering the flowers.

Liddy took them with a smile and allowed him passage through the door. Finding a stoneware pitcher, she settled the flowers inside. Mr. Bennett removed his hat and drew breath to speak, but at the sound of heavy footsteps, he turned toward the hall to see Caroline emerge, her brow wrinkled with concern. Behind her, Liddy saw Mrs. Pike's long nose, Mr. Farrows's peering eyes, and Benji's broad ears. "Miss Farrows," Mr. Bennett said briskly, his voice hooking high at the end. "I had hoped I might have a word with you. Perhaps in private."

Liddy's eyes widened. The spray of flowers slipped from her grasp into the vase. Though Caroline's expression was nothing so obvious, Liddy saw the downward curve to her eyes, tension in her shoulders, and rigidity in her smile, and felt her own panic rise. Caroline bowed her head dutifully and asked if the garden would suffice. With a nod, Mr. Bennett followed her into the yard, his hands clenching on the brim of his hat.

As soon as the door shut behind them, Mrs. Pike twittered and flocked toward the window, sneaking a peak from the lower corner. Mr. Farrows did not say much himself, but he too took a position peering through the opposite corner, looking over his spectacles. Robert stomped toward the front of the shop, his back resolutely turned to the proceedings. Liddy tried not to notice how he angled his head toward the pair so he might hear what was whispered between the elders.

"I told you, didn't I, Mr. Farrows?" said Mrs. Pike. "'Any day now, Mr. Bennett could be seeking her hand.' That is what I said, is it not?"

Liddy's breath caught in her throat. From the side of her eye, she saw her book abandoned on the counter, the wildflowers now preoccupying her attention. How had she so easily forgotten the generous gift? And how had the party been thrown into such immediate disarray? Her heart sunk like lead in a puddle of mud. At once, she released the flowers, wiped her hands on her apron, and turned back into the house, her book in tow.

Swallowing, she half-gagged on the sweet scent of the cake. Caroline had been so thoughtful to suggest it to Mrs. Pike, but now it turned her stomach. Already, it felt like her world was slipping from her fingers. Before, Caroline had always balked notions of marriage; now it seemed she would shortly be gone. Liddy set her book on the mantle, gripped the wood with trembling fingers, and breathed in the bitter smoke, let the fumes clear her mind. If the flickering fire and glowing coals looked blurry, she merely bit her lip and wiped her eyes. *What use are tears? They won't make me any less forgettable.*

"Lid."

She nearly screamed as she spun and found Benjamin standing in the doorway, his brow furrowed in confusion and his eyes dark with worry. Absently, she raised her hand to catch a tear before it fell, all the while swallowing her hitching sobs. Benji's brow softened, and he fetched his handkerchief from the pocket of his waistcoat. He offered it to her with a weak smile, like a condolence. Without hesitation, Liddy took it and dried her eyes. All the while she felt Benjamin's eyes on her, but she couldn't bring herself to look. In a few minutes, she'd calm. It was useless, feeling poorly in such scenarios. Liddy had long ago accepted the fact that she would never belong to anyone, yet somehow the potential of Caro's future only worsened the sting. She shook her head and blotted her nose. What good would a husband be to her?

Liddy's gaze pulled to Benjamin. She could see his mind moving in the flash of his eyes. His hands tensed and relaxed at his sides, looking for something to hold. Folding the cloth back into its square and handing it back to him, she whispered, "Thank you."

Benji nodded. "It's a strange thing, who the heart is set upon. Erratic. Illogical. Completely beyond control."

Liddy's brow furrowed in confusion. "Benji, what—"

But she was interrupted by a high squeal from the shop. Without a second thought, she and Benji went to the kitchen window. In profile, she saw Mr. Bennett down on one knee, holding Caroline's hands in his own. His eyes were clear, his smile incandescent. Before him, Caroline nodded slowly, her own smile equally broad and her eyes watery. But Liddy's cheer caught in her chest.

At once, Mr. Farrows and Mrs. Pike swarmed out of the shop door, both cheering and crying gleefully. Caroline would be married. Caroline had tamed her wild heart. But as Benji led her back to the shop and into the garden to join the celebration, Liddy couldn't help thinking she'd never seen Caro look so terrified, so broken, like a fairy bound to single stone when the world moved mere inches away.

In the course of the following month, the entirety of Dunnshire was in an uproar. All involved parties agreed that a short engagement and a small country wedding suited best. Mrs. Pike was thrilled to help Caroline arrange everything. Invitations were sent. A dress was tailored. A cake was ordered. Mr. Bennett made arrangements with the parish priest. Everything came together so quickly and so seamlessly, Liddy could scarcely believe the good fortune. But every time she looked at her sister, Liddy saw the cracks in her happy gaze spreading farther.

One afternoon, Mrs. Pike, Caroline, and Liddy were called to Piedmont Downs to finalize more details of the wedding. The entire time Liddy stared at a spot on the far wall, determined not to let her mind wander into dangerous territory. Mrs. Pike and Mr. Bennett talked over one another, offering suggestions to which Caroline meekly conceded. Eventually, the effort of focusing through all the talk roused sharp pains behind Liddy's eyes, and she begged leave of the company.

With a sigh of relief, she stepped out into the oppressive heat, glad to be away from the noise. On the veranda, it was calm. The view overlooked a steep hill leading down to the wood where they'd picked berries. Now, the rolling green hills had yellowed in the weeks of drought. Soon, even fine estates would be turned to brown. Again Liddy was struck by a wave of ancient melancholy looking over Piedmont. Long ago it must have been a fine house, but today, it was some gothic relic, lost from its own time. Liddy felt a pang of sympathy with the old house. Closing her eyes, she swayed back and forth in time with the rhythmic rustle of leaves on the flagstone and the wind's ghostly melody.

When the wind shifted and carried in a clear strain of harp, Liddy started, her eyes snapping open. It came from the open set of French doors at the back of the house. Too intrigued to leave the melody be, Liddy crept toward the French doors, drawn forward by her ears. Peeking inside, she saw the room was brighter than any other she'd seen. The walls were a clear blue which reflected the soft light. The furnishings were delicate and modern. At the center of the room, Lady Sinclair sat before a grand harp, her dark curls hanging like a curtain between herself and the open doorway. Liddy watched, enraptured by her fingers plucking at the delicate strings, the tone of the music soft in volume yet overwhelming in timbre. Never before had she heard such music.

Eventually, Lady Sinclair reached the end of her refrain, her fingers hovering above the strings, letting the vibrations naturally end. With one sweeping motion, she pushed her long curls behind her ears and noticed the voyeur in her midst. Liddy flushed under her ladyship's abrupt gaze. She curtseyed politely and knotted her hands together before her. "Forgive my intrusion, your ladyship. I had never heard such music. I deeply apologize."

Lady Sinclair righted her harp and stood quietly, her hands clasping gently in front of her. Liddy watched as a half-smile graced her ladyship's face, crinkling at the corners of her eyes while her mouth barely moved. Though her blush held steady, she kept Lady Sinclair's gaze. "Do not fret, Miss Lydia. Your presence is a surprise, little more," said Lady Sinclair, her aura strangely warm compared to their last greeting. "I had actually hoped to speak with you, but I have not had the chance to call on you. I..." She paused, looking down at her entwined fingers before continuing quietly. "I had hoped to apologize actually." Liddy's brows shot up, and she drew forward into the parlor as Lady Sinclair continued. "My married life has been spent thirsting for discretion in a town that offers so little. I strive to remain respectable in the town's eyes for the sake of those under my protection."

"Penelope, you mean."

"Yes. When we met, you struck me as the type to discount such vicious lies. But on finding you in the rear corridors, I assumed the worst of you. For that and my foul temper, I ask your forgiveness. I should not have judged you so harshly."

Lady Sinclair looked up, her eyes soft with hope. Liddy's throat ran dry. She would never have guessed she would see Lady Sinclair so unguarded.

"Of course," Liddy said, struggling to regain her voice. "I had no intention of harm. I only—"

"I know," Lady Sinclair interrupted. "Penelope was most insistent when I went to see her that evening."

"How is she?"

"Quiet," said Lady Sinclair. "She's been most withdrawn since his lordship's passing. Though she took to you quite quickly. She asked if she might see you again."

Liddy smiled. "Your daughter is a very sweet girl. I'm sure you are proud of her."

Lady Sinclair stiffened, her shoulders going rigid and her eyes hardening. Quickly, she moved around Liddy, peeked both ways out the open French doors and pulled them closed. With the soft sound of nature shuttered out, the room was heavy with silence. Liddy watched the firm line of Lady Sinclair's back before her ladyship turned cautiously toward her. "I trust what I am about to divulge will remain in the strictest confidence."

Liddy nodded, her stomach twinging. Lady Sinclair moved to the chaise and gestured for Liddy to sit across from her. Liddy perched lightly on the edge of her chair, her curious heart thundering at being taken into such confidence.

"Lord Sinclair proposed to me when I was quite young, foolish and unaccustomed to the ways of the world. He was older than even my father's contemporaries, already twice married to more knowledgeable women than I, but when we were together, he was the kindest, most unselfish person I'd ever met. And of course, I'd only ever known the simple life of town, forever under my parent's thumb, bound always to their will. So a proposal from a rich man afforded me all the freedom I could hope for.

"Within three months, we were married and settled on his estate. Separated from my friends and family, I was miserable. I was still very much a child, you see, ill prepared to be anyone's wife, much less the mistress of a fine house. But James was good to me. Anything I requested, he saw to immediately. If I wanted to go riding, he procured the finest horses. If I desired apples, he'd plant an orchard. That was the sort of man he was. If he could make one person happy, no matter who, he'd be pleased. He was adored by everyone, the villagers and servants alike. The more time we spent together, the fonder I grew of him.

"About a year into our marriage, I was roused in the very early hours of the morning by the worst sound I'd ever heard: a screech of agony. At once, I went to find its source but with little luck. I went to James to see if he'd heard it when I saw light under his door. Looking through the keyhole, the sight shocked me. Within, I saw a woman lying on his bed, her stomach swollen with child. She'd once been beautiful, but hard times had fallen on her. Her blond hair was shorn, her skin was ruddy and chapped, and her howls were sickening. A graying man stood with her hand in his, mopping sweat from her brow. Our housekeeper knelt between her spread legs, calling words of wisdom to the woman. James stood to the side in his nightshirt and socks, ripping rags for the housekeeper. The woman cried out, her voice breaking under the strain, and gave one breath of sheer pain before she collapsed. At first, I did not understand what I was witnessing until I smelled blood in the air and heard a second, higher wail. James stepped forward at once, mussing at something with the housekeeper before he held up a blanket-wrapped babe. James offered the baby to the graying man, but the man cowered over the woman, touching her neck and wrist frantically before his expression drew thin and twisted in sorrow."

Lady Sinclair paused, biting her lips and staring into the carpet, no doubt reliving the memory. Liddy shook herself and quickly closed her gaping mouth, but she knew her eyes betrayed her shock. Sighing, her ladyship continued. "The man was gone by morning. James had the footmen dig a grave behind the house. And Penelope has been with us ever since."

Liddy felt her posture deflate. No wonder Lady Sinclair had shut the door. A story like that could scarcely be believed, yet from the soft words and honest timbre, Liddy did not doubt the events. But she knew she could never speak of it; such a story would forever damn the Sinclair name.

"Did you learn who they were?" Liddy whispered.

"At first, no," said Lady Sinclair. "James died shortly after, before I dared breathe a word of what I'd witnessed. To this day, I could only guess the woman's identity."

"And the man's?"

Lady Sinclair shook her head. "It would be disrespectful to say."

Though she yearned to know, Liddy nodded in understanding. Lady Sinclair was only trying to extend the same courtesy she desired. Liddy could find no fault with that.

Distantly, Liddy heard the hall clock chime three and started. She had been gone from Mrs. Pike and Caroline for almost twenty minutes. Rising, she said, "I should get back. I only intended to step out for a few minutes."

"Of course," Lady Sinclair said, also coming to her feet. Her voice still rang with the severity of her tale.

Liddy curtseyed. "Thank you, your ladyship. I promise, your trust will not be in vain."

Her ladyship nodded. As Liddy walked to the door, Lady Sinclair called her name. She turned.

"Do you suppose, Miss Lydia," said Lady Sinclair, her voice sharp and her hands tense, "that we might be... friends?"

A smile pulled across Liddy's face. "Of course."

~~*

A fortnight before the wedding day, Lady Sinclair opened the doors of her home to the residents of Dunnshire in celebration of her brother's engagement. The respectable half of the village received invitations to the private ball while the lower classes clung to the gates on the night in question, watching carriages and carts ferry their fellow men into the newly manicured grounds. As family of the bride, the Farrows were among the first to arrive and stood to welcome the guests. Liddy tried to smile, but already she felt her cheeks aching from the effort. Politely, she shook every gloved hand presented to her and curtseyed enough to make her dizzy. Mrs. Pike had pulled her corset strings too tight to show off her narrow figure, but in her lavender gown, she felt like a child playing pretend. In contrast, Caroline looked beautiful in a blue so pale it might as well be white. With her curls elegantly arranged and her arm safely tucked in Mr. Bennett's, she appeared a perfect young bride. Only Liddy saw the strain in her sister's smile and the rigidness in her carriage.

"I see they're keeping you busy, Miss Liddy," said Mr. Monroe as he arrived.

"Yes," Liddy answered, already strained by the proceedings, "apparently being sister of the bride means I am required to well-wish every person I find. And that I must accept all their congratulations. At least most are preoccupied by the strange splendor of Piedmont."

Mr. Monroe nodded and turned his eyes about the grand foyer. "The Sinclair's do know how to keep a house."

Liddy's brow furrowed. "You've been here before?"

"Oh, yes," he said, his eyes misted by memory. "Lord Sinclair was a dear friend from my youth. The only one who never gave up on me." He swallowed deeply, as if trying to dislodge a painful obtrusion. Looking to Liddy, he smiled weakly. "Forgive me, Miss Liddy. I have not been here since he died. Being in this house rouses some troubling memories. Excuse me. Enjoy your evening."

As more guests filed through the entryway, Liddy could not shake her exchange with Mr. Monroe. She was stricken by his expression, mouth drawn thin from sorrow, eyes far away. Still, at the back of her mind, an elusive memory prickled; try as she might, she could not recall it.

Eventually, the last of the guests had arrived and the festivities began. After supper, a troupe of musicians began a hearty melody. Caroline danced the first with her betrothed while Liddy stood by along the wall, her gloved hands entwined behind her back. While painted dancers waltzed beneath the lamplight, Liddy let her mind wander as she'd scarcely allowed herself in the recent weeks. In one blink, the ballroom melted away.

A hundred campfires burned through the darkness. She heard a distant chorus of roars, each grating as broken glass. Smoke and blood swirled in the air. She slumped against a tent post, feet sore and arms heavy from a day of fighting, but she would not shed her armor nor put away her sword. After all, her task remained incomplete. The beast had survived. It was no dragon, but instead a resilient hydra with two heads burst from its severed neck. In a fit of rage, it had descended from its mountain keep, cutting through the air like a living arrow, and razed the countryside in a gray-blue blaze, leaving a layer of toxic fumes in its wake.

Liddy hung her head, hoping to steal an hour of sleep before the battle resumed. Her strength already dwindled. She could not fathom how to defeat such a foe. Her eyes drifted shut. Victory seemed hopeless.

A hand trailed along her hip. A pair of blue eyes smoldered from between her thighs. A mouth like fire burned over her center.

Liddy started, fanning herself to cool her flushed face. Breath came short for the dreaded corset. How she wished to rip it off.

"Miss Liddy."

She turned to find Robert standing beside her, his shoes shined, his shirt freshly starched and buttoned to the neck, his hair combed within an inch of its life. "Hello, Robby. I see you've found me on the wall. I hadn't seen you or Benji arrive."

"Yes, Ben avails himself to Lady Sinclair as we speak," Robert said, nodding toward the head of the ballroom. Liddy turned to find her ladyship dressed in dark gray, her gaze cool but amused. Benjamin stood at her ear, his grin sly, his hands moving as he spoke, his red locks wild. At the sight, Liddy felt her heart unsettle, but she shook away the feeling.

"Benji does always make easy friends."

Robert chuckled. "I hardly think Lady Sinclair would call Benji a friend. More like an insufferable child."

Somehow, Robert's plain words warmed her. A small grin pulled at her mouth. "You are ever so kind to your little brother."

"An elder's birthright, I assure you."

The dance came to a close with a round of applause for the players. Robert clapped absently, looking between Liddy and the dance floor. Her eyes widened and her fanning sped. For a moment, she feared Robert might subject her to the horror of a dance. All her life, Liddy had been Caroline's practice partner, but she'd never had reason or incentive to learn. Seeing her wide eyes, Robert smiled and shook his head. "I would offer, but neither you nor I have cared for this particular pleasure."

Liddy heaved a sigh of relief and sank back against the wall. "Am I so transparent?"

Robert shook his head. "No, you are simply easy to understand. You don't want the world to notice you for fear of what they shall see."

"A spinster, you mean," she said meekly.

"Never."

Liddy was taken aback by Robert's contradiction. Her brow creased. Robert turned away from the dance floor, his eyes dark but filled with hope. "A warrior, perhaps. Waiting for the right person to find her in the darkness." His gaze turned back to the head of the room. Benji had taken Lady Sinclair's hand and politely kissed it, all the while holding her eyes with a look of roguish heat. Liddy looked away, to the dancers forming new lines of a quadrille. "I hope you see her, too."

At once, her heart stopped. Wide eyed, Liddy gaped for words to reply to Robert, but instead, he smiled kindly, bowed, and stepped off into the crowd. Even minutes after he'd gone, she had scarcely moved. Had Robert said...? How had he known? Her stomach rolled. Without thinking, Liddy moved into a dark corridor leading off the ballroom, her hand clutching at her chest as she struggled for breath. Around her, the air felt cooler and less cluttered. At the first window, she leaned forward on her palms, letting the rough stone scratch her skin. If Robert suspected her inclination, her reaction could only have confirmed it. But Robby bore her no malice. She was sure of that. Between the logic and the cool, her panic lessened.

A small hand settled between her shoulder blades. Liddy nearly flinched away from the soothing touch until she heard her sister's voice. "Little sister, are you ill?"

Liddy shook her head, heedless of how her curls loosened and fell from her bun. "Only a spell of dizziness," she whispered, throat dry and voice weak. Looking over her shoulder, she saw Caroline's brow knotted with concern, her face silhouetted against the light from the ballroom. "Did anyone else notice my departure?"

"Only Mr. Bennett, but he suspected you would prefer my presence to his."

Looking down at her arms, feeling them quiver under her weight, Liddy broke from the windowsill and settled with her back pressed to the wall. She closed her eyes and breathed deeply. "Mr. Bennett is a kind man."

Caroline's hand dropped from her shoulder. Liddy blinked and found her sister standing as she had before, but now her posture was drawn tight as a harp string. Caroline clasped her hands together, her knuckles white with strain. "Yes," she said, the words slipping out like a cat's hiss. "I suppose they say he is."

Liddy tilted her head to the side, curious as to her sister's phrasing. "Caro, has he harmed you?"

Caroline's eyes shot wide and her mouth tightened. She shook her head.

"Has he been cruel? Mistreated you in any way?"

Again, the elder shook her head, and her gaze drifted to the floor. "No, he hasn't."

Liddy pushed from the wall and stepped toward her sister. Seeing the doorway clear of prying eyes, Liddy whispered, "And yet the thought of marrying him turns your stomach."

Caroline sucked in her cheeks, likely biting them to hold her tongue. "Please, little Liddy," she said. "It is not so simple."

"It is always so simple," Liddy protested as she clasped her sister's hands. "He adores you, truly, but if you cannot bear to be his wife, marrying Mr. Bennett cannot be an option."

"It is my only option!" Caroline said, yanking free from Liddy. Caroline's lips trembled, but she held her emotions in check. With tears clinging to her lashes, Caroline looked to her little sister, her face pulled tight with sadness. "Not all of us can afford to live with our heads in another world. And what skills do I have? No talents. No extended family. No one but you and father. And if marrying Mr. Bennett ensures that we are all taken care of, I will. I must."

But Liddy read every broken hope on her sister's face, every failed dream in the unshed tears. Swallowing, Liddy stepped forward and embraced her sister. Never before had she suspected such selflessness from her sister, who always spoke of freedom and adventure above all else. To see her reduced to this wretched state broke Liddy's heart. "We'll always love you, Caro," she whispered. "No matter where your heart leads you. But do not sacrifice all that defines you for us. It will only lead to resentment and regret."

With that, Liddy pulled away and left Caroline to her thoughts. She returned to the ballroom, her mind uneasy from all that had transpired. Most ardently, Liddy wished the remaining hours might pass so she could return home to the simple comfort of her life, this brief adventure into the wider world forgotten in place of her reverie. For a moment, Liddy considered sneaking off to find Penelope, for she felt more ill fit the longer she spent in the adult world. But the clock had chimed ten some time ago; undoubtedly, Lady Sinclair's ward would be asleep.

Suddenly, an arm slid into the crook of hers. She started to find Benji sidled up against her. He gave her a roguish smile as they walked about the room, and Liddy felt something peculiar uncoil in her chest. "Where did you disappear to?" Benjamin asked, his grin coy and suspicious. "An actual flight into your magical world?"

"Regrettably, no," Liddy said quickly, craving silence when she knew she'd find only expectation. "I needed some air."

"Feeling faint amongst this lively party?"

"Ill." Liddy looked off at the dance floor. "The refreshment disagrees with me."

"Perhaps a dance to liven our heels," Benjamin suggested, giving Liddy a quick twirl. "Anything to put you in better spirits."

"Dancing would hardly help," Liddy said, pulling away from her friend. "You know that." At Benji's deflated look—his shoulders sagging and head hanging like a lost pup—Liddy continued. "Forgive me, Benji. The party puts me out of sorts. You know balls and I rarely agree."

"I think it more the company than the atmosphere," Benjamin said, turning pointedly toward the front of the hall. Following his gaze, Liddy found Mr. Bennett and Lady Sinclair engaged in a hushed argument, their brows knitted and their mouths drawn tight. Liddy nearly spoke when her eye caught Mr. Monroe approaching the pair, his head bowed and his expression sedate. Lady Sinclair regarded him with a gentle nod, her quarrel long forgotten as a look of sympathy bloomed in her eyes. In that moment, Liddy's jaw dropped. She remembered the afternoon a week earlier during their discussion of Lord Sinclair when the same expression crossed her ladyship's face. Now it was directed at Mr. Monroe. *"It would be disrespectful to say,"* she'd said. Liddy's respect would only matter in one circumstance: if she knew the graying man of whom Lady Sinclair spoke, and they had only one mutual acquaintance. He stood with Lady Sinclair now. But why would Mr. Monroe know such a woman as the one her ladyship described?

Before she could pursue that question, Benjamin snapped in front of her, drawing her back to the present. Instinctively, her eyes narrowed. "I'm not sure I understand," said Liddy.

Benjamin cocked his eyebrow. "There is little vagueness to it."

"Benji, I'm not one of your cohorts. You must speak plainly and believe truly that I cannot make out your implication." But Liddy could hear the tremor of her voice, the way the words ruffled as she spoke.

Quickly, Benjamin took her elbow and led her toward an alcove. In the brief silence, Liddy felt her heart hammer in her throat. Her eyes darted from face to face in search of an ally, but found none. Not even Benji as he leaned close, his words quiet and heavy, like stones from a slingshot. "Liddy, you're young but far from stupid. Do not pretend you've formed no attachment toward your sister's betrothed."

Liddy's jaw dropped. No. Surely Benji was playing another of his jokes. Surely he did not suspect her of such feelings. *You cannot be serious, Benji.* The thought rolled in her head but refused to cycle southward to her mouth. "How... how can you poss..."

"'He's a kind man,'" Benji quoted, eyes showing the firmness of his belief. "'Any man such as him is deserving of happiness.' Those are your words, little Liddy, but they will do you no good. And favoring him will only bring you heartache."

No, this was all a mistake. If she could only explain, he would see that. "No, Benji—"

"I saw how you reacted to the proposal," he interrupted. "You must have known what was coming. But you cannot persist, Liddy. He will soon be your brother."

Her vision swam against her will. Was Benji so blind? Her oldest friend had so misread her feelings. If she could find her voice, she could explain, but her voice remained cloistered away, pulled tight in her stomach to shield itself. The music roared in her ears. Voices chimed in and out in a discordant pulse. Her hands felt numb. Why couldn't she make him stop? Why couldn't she tell him he was wrong? But admitting it would be shameful.

"Oh Lid, don't cry," Benji cajoled, pulling her close and hiding her face in his chest. "I know. Love is painful. Just remember, your love for Caro will outweigh how you feel for anyone else. Hold on to that. It will keep you sane."

She couldn't breathe. She was drowning on dry land swaddled in fabric, held so tight her tears were wrung from her. She had to get away. Damn whoever saw. Damn whatever they thought. Sometimes retreat was the only option. Balling her fist in Benji's coat, Liddy pushed as hard as she could. His grip slid from her shoulder, and air rushed over her in a wave. In her weary gaze, she saw Benjamin step toward her, palms open, voice soft with concern. No, she would bear no comfort. Her hand flew, striking his cheek in a resonant crack. The jolt skittered up her arm. Benji's cheek flushed with the rise of blood, his mouth open and his eyes wide with shock.

"Liddy?" he whispered.

She swallowed hard, voice rising in her throat unbidden. "You're a cruel and foolish boy, Benjamin Pike. Every bit as bad as your mother."

Before she could note his reaction, Liddy turned and fled the ballroom to the first secluded alcove she found. At once, she sucked in cold air, letting her senses return to her. Panic left her sweat-slick and trembling. Turmoil left her ears ringing and the festivities a distant din of merriment. Embarrassment rendered her heart weak. How could Benji raise such foolish suspicions against her? How could he see her plainly but misinterpret every detail? And did others believe her besotted with Mr. Bennett? No, that could not be possible. Touching her chest, she felt her heart rumble like a newly roused giant, thunderous in its fury. With time and solitude, it would quiet. All too soon, she heard the heavy steps of heels down the corridor. Liddy's throat ran dry and her eyes turned toward the corner. She tried to push herself up to flee—where, she did not know—but her ankles wobbled. Then she heard a second set of footsteps drumming out of sync with the first.

"Mr. Pike," cut Lady Sinclair's voice like a frosty blade. "What are you doing away from the party?"

"I'm looking for Liddy. She's upset herself. I must find her," Benjamin replied. Her gut twisted and Liddy slid deeper into the shadows. *Please, no*, she wished, her eyes squeezing closed.

At once, the footsteps halted, the echo of their rhythm falling silent. Her breath caught in anticipation.

Why had Benji stopped? She could only imagine what Lady Sinclair had done to stop him.

"Haven't you done enough?" Lady Sinclair accused.

"I've done nothing."

"Were that the case, Miss Lydia would not have fled your presence." There came more silence. Liddy dug her nails into her palms. *Please, just a minute to compose myself.* That was all she needed. A minute's solitude to settle her mind. But she dared not utter the plea lest it draw Benjamin to her. "Now," Lady Sinclair continued, proper as ever, "see yourself back to the ballroom. I will find Miss Lydia and ensure she's taken care of."

Tension quivered in the air. *Please go, Ben,* she mouthed repeatedly, feeling new tears welling in her eyes. Just a moment alone. A moment and she'd be fine. Everything would be quiet. "What are you playing at, Lady Sinclair?" Benji asked, his voice dripping with flirtation, the floorboards squeaking as he shuffled toward the corner. Liddy fought against the swimming motion of her stomach.

"Unlike you, Mr. Pike, I do not see life as a game to be won or lost. I play at nothing. I will say again, return to the party, or I will have you removed for harassing my guest, a young woman soon to be my kin. You will find, Mr. Pike, that when family is concerned, I may be a most formidable enemy."

"Oh," Benjamin said, "all of Dunnshire knows how ardently you care for your family."

A slap rang out. Liddy gasped at the impact, her hands clamping around her mouth. She strained to hear Benji's sharp breath; she could almost see his other cheek swelling a vivid red. "Forgive me," he grunted.

"I shall not," Lady Sinclair said. "I only forgive they that deserve it. Now, get out of my house."

For a tense moment, there was only silence. Then Liddy heard the floorboards creek as Benjamin retreated, his departing footsteps faster than his coming. A small piece of her heart felt sorry for him, but she did not dwell on the feeling. Lady Sinclair had provided distraction from her turmoil. For that, Liddy would be eternally grateful. After a moment, the footsteps resumed, now slower and carefully measured. Lady Sinclair stopped at the corner and called, "Miss Lydia, are you close?"

Liddy swallowed and clenched her fist. She could run no more. "I am here, your ladyship."

Lady Sinclair's head instantly turned to her direction. Immediately, her shoulders loosened and she approached Liddy cautiously. As she came closer, Liddy noticed how soft her eyes were, like two lines of blue sky peeking through storm clouds. Though she pushed toward her feet, Liddy's knees buckled. Lady Sinclair made no mention of it; she simply stepped beside Liddy, and with an undue level of grace, sank to a seated position. Liddy focused on taking deep breaths, one long drag followed by one slow exhale. Then a flash of the evening crossed her mind, reopening the fresh wounds. She hiccupped and her choked sobs resumed. Her panic and shame spurred her tears harder. Try as she might, she could not stop.

Distantly, she felt warmth around her shoulders. Soft circles of pressure danced over her shoulder blades. Something smooth beneath her cheek. A low, melancholy sound waltzed in the air around her. A voice. A song. Liddy blinked past her tears. Lady Sinclair was soothing her back and singing a soft lullaby. Though her tears continued and her cheeks remained flushed, her sobbing eased. Absently, Liddy pressed her cheek into Lady Sinclair's silk clad shoulder and breathed in her light scent. Like lavender and rain, her ladyship smelled clean and regal, something inhuman and eternal. An angel, perhaps, but the texture of her gown beneath Liddy's fingertips proved her presence. Slowly, the song quieted, taking with it the budding warmth in Liddy's chest. In the silence, Liddy pulled away and blotted the tear stains from her rosy cheeks. Looking down at her skirt pooling over her lap, Liddy mumbled. "Forgive me, Lady Sinclair," she said, rising to her feet.

"There is noth—"

"I have not been myself for some weeks now," she said, smoothing her gown.

"No, no, I do not—,"

"I apologize for my uproar," Liddy said, curtseying on weak ankles. As she pushed forward, though, Lady Sinclair caught her hand in a tight grip. Liddy looked from the delicate hand curled around her glove, up the silk-clad arm, to Lady Sinclair's eyes, watery and full of uncertainty. Her heart beat stuttered. She blushed, instinctively ducking her head.

"No, don't," said Lady Sinclair, her left hand touching Liddy's chin and drawing her gaze. Liddy swallowed, her hands twitching in her gloves. Before she could dare mutter a word, Lady Sinclair cupped her cheek and leaned in.

The feeling of her ladyship's mouth on Liddy's was like nothing she'd ever experienced. At first, it was only a soft pressure, utterly unremarkable. Then Liddy felt the hot sweep of a tongue across her lips and coals popped in her belly, spurred by her own sharp gasp. Lady Sinclair pressed closer, her lips silken and plush. For a moment, Liddy considered closing her eyes and leaning into her ladyship, but a hot pulse of shame burned in her chest.

Wide-eyed, Liddy pulled away as though she'd been struck. Her fingers twitched for something to cling to in this strange reality. It must be some illusion standing before her, not a flesh and blood woman offering her... but was anything being offered? Liddy watched for any reaction from Lady Sinclair, but she stood perfectly still, her mouth stretched thin and her eyes bleak. Surely Lady Sinclair couldn't want some foolish girl, destined to live and die a spinster. Then her ladyship looked down, her neck, chest and cheeks flushed pink. Her hands twisted in the dark silk of her gloves, and she swallowed. "I will bid you good night now, Miss Lydia," Lady Sinclair said, avoiding even the slightest eye contact. "I do hope your evening brightens."

"Thank you, your ladyship," Liddy replied breathlessly. "It..." she continued as Lady Sinclair turned to leave. "It was none of your doing. It was only... men. Men are such fools."

Lady Sinclair stopped and turned her head partway, her jaw tense and sharp in silhouette. "So, too, are women," she said sadly. "Good night, Miss Lydia."

~~*

In the days that followed, despite all the commotion of ensuring the wedding ran smoothly, Liddy saw nothing of Lady Sinclair, though her ladyship was scarcely absent from Liddy's thought. Every free moment, it seemed, her mind flitted back to that darkened alcove, the heat of her ladyship's touch, and the lingering scent of lavender as she departed. Absently, Liddy would touch her lips, disbelieving that she'd actually been kissed. A small smile would curl her mouth, and she'd duck to hide her blush from anyone present.

Also, in those intervening days, Caroline's ire swelled. It seemed the elder sister could hardly go an hour without scowling, finding fault with every plan before swallowing her protests and letting tears well in her eyes. Every time, Liddy looked to her sister, hoping she might come to her senses. But Caroline would not bow her head, and every time she was in the company of Mr. Bennett, she played the devoted fiancée, giggling at the prospect of marriage. Only Liddy seemed to see the gaps in her performance; the other members of her entwined family did not notice. In fact, Mrs. Pike observed almost daily that she'd behaved similarly in the days leading to her own wedding. It took every ounce of Liddy's self-control not to shout that they were all being absolute fools.

Her battle against the hydra fared poorly. Fellow knights dropped left and right, poisoned by one head's toxic breath or charred by the other's fire. Even the boy bearing Dunland's banner had been slain. For every head they cleaved off, two more reared in its place, twice as vicious. Men and women cried around her, adding their voices to the bitter war song. She hid behind an outcropping of rock, heedless of the fresh corpses surrounding her. She scowled. Even if she could get close enough to strike the beast, the poison uncurled in her nose and throat, gagging her. She looked at one of the bodies as she caught her breath. The dead knight had a scrap of cloth tied over her nose and mouth. Dry, the cloth had done little to blot out the poison, evidenced by the knight's bulging purple flesh.

The image startled her awake the morning before the wedding.

Stretching, she looked to Caroline's side of the bed, only to find it empty, the blankets long cold. On the nightstand stood a folded note, her name written in Caroline's tidy script. Rubbing sleep from her eyes, Liddy leaned across the bed and snatched up the note. "*My dearest Liddy,*" the note read. *"You must forgive me, little sister, but I can endure this agony no more. You were right. Living a lie has been torture these past weeks; to endure a lifetime of false smiles and sentiment would set poison in my veins. I could not bear it.*

"By the time you've read this message, I will be long gone from the county. I know how this will pain you to read, but I do not think we shall meet again. If Papa does not disown me for my disobedience, society certainly will. Do not fret for me, Liddy. I will see the world as I always hoped. I only hope that you can find it in your heart to forgive me.

"Please pass on my apologies and well wishes to everyone, especially Mr. Bennett. You have always been right about him: he is a good man and would have endeavored to make me happy. Regrettably, as his wife, I never would have let him succeed. All my love, Caroline."

Liddy stared wide-eyed at the spaces between the words. Her eyes trained along the folds of the paper; they were heavily creased, as though folded and unfolded countless times. And the ink came out at different consistencies, as though Caroline had returned to the page over several days. Her heartbeat stuttered, and her fingers clenched on the paper. Sweeping her eyes over the room, Liddy saw the gaps where Caroline's possessions once stood: the ratty book of stories Mother read when they were children, an empty bottle of lilac scent, their mother's wedding ring, as well as Caroline's clothes and the tiny bundle of money her sister had saved under the mattress. It was all gone, like a spell seeping out of a wonderland, leaving a hollow ruin in its wake.

As she dressed, Liddy felt her mind swirling somewhere in the air beyond her form. She gave little thought to it as she buttoned her frock, but her eyes never left the paper. How could she tell them that Caroline had left? Her stomach curled around the empty sensation, but no sickness swam through her. She'd expected to feel more at the prospect of her sister's empty space in her life; instead, she felt a hollow fluttering in her chest, like a spark looking for tinder to ignite. What that meant, she could not say.

Three sharp bangs vibrated the floorboards, her father bounding on the ceiling to rally them to breakfast. "Liddy, Caro, the Pikes are already here. Come down."

Liddy swallowed the mounting panic and closed her eyes. She couldn't run away. It would be foolish to run from conflict. It only ever chased after her. *Her heart pounded in her ears like a war drum warning away any bystanders, but the drummers too fell against the hydra. Liddy blinked from the corpse but still took the cloth mask and wetted it with water from her canteen. Pressing it to her face, each breath felt cool and loose, no longer contaminated by the toxin. Relieved, Liddy peeked over the rock. The hydra laid down a blanket of fire and venom, but carefully kept its swarming heads above the toxic fumes. Was it, possibly, susceptible to its own venom? Could it be choked by the vapors? But how to ensnare the beast, she did not know. The hydra would be too smart to sink into the poisonous fog. Liddy looked left and right, and her eyes fell upon the upended banner, now soaked red by the bloody fields. It was a fool's errand, but they had no other option.*

Squaring her shoulders, Liddy took Caroline's note in her hands and breathed in the scent of earthy ink and dusty paper. She'd have no sword or lance in this battle, no shield to hide behind, only her mind and her voice.

Downstairs, Liddy found her father and Mrs. Pike engaged in a hushed conversation near the hearth, each holding cups of tea despite the mounting summer warmth. In the shop, she heard Robert setting up the till and preparing the few orders which were due about the village. Benji was nowhere to be seen, not that she felt a swell of surprise. Since the ball, Benji had absented himself from all wedding proceedings, and as the Farrows were occupied by little else, she saw none of him. While his absence was unusual, she couldn't blame him for such strange behavior. After all, it was almost a relief not to find his knowing smirk waiting for her.

The bottom stair creaked, and Mr. Farrows and Mrs. Pike turned toward her; if a look of disappointment deflated their faces, Liddy ignored it.

"Is Caroline not yet risen?" Mr. Farrows asked.

Liddy looked to the note. Her fingers didn't clench in the paper; instead she held the note with care, like a child treasuring her first doll. "I do not know," Liddy said, swallowing around her thickening anxiety.

"How can you not know, Miss Lydia?" said Mrs. Pike, her voice twittering higher than Liddy could imagine. "Were you not her bedfellow?"

"I..." Liddy rolled her shoulders and looked up to her father. "She's gone."

At once, the sound sucked out of the room: the coals popping, the clock ticking, even Robert shuffling about the shop. Liddy looked from Mrs. Pike's paling face to her father's wrinkled brow and narrowed eyes. And yet, Liddy felt air rush into her lungs. For the first time in months, the swirling in her stomach stopped. Speaking the words made them real. It was no spell, no trick. Not anymore.

Liddy offered them the letter. Mr. Farrows took it and read quietly, Mrs. Pike reading over his elbow, her expression unraveling at each word. Movement in the doorway drew her eye. It was Robert, head ducked to avoid the lintel, eyes tight and mouth opened in an unspoken question. 'Is she really?' Liddy almost heard. She nodded and watched his mouth tighten, his head bowed. Robert turned without a goodbye. His footsteps echoed through the store, and his slamming the door came with a crack. Only then did Mr. Farrows look up from the letter, his eyes distant with sorrow. Mrs. Pike took the letter from his limp fingers, but she resorted to folding it closed and open again. "We can send the boys," Mrs. Pike said hypnotically. "North and south. We can hire horses for them. She's only been gone a few hours. Eight at most. She can't have gone far."

"How could this happen?" Mr. Farrows sighed, dropping into his chair.

"She was so happy," Mrs. Pike commented.

Liddy looked between the two elders, her eyes narrowed and her mouth drawn open. "She hasn't been happy in weeks," she said quietly.

"Only wedding nerves," Mrs. Pike said with a flick of her wrist. "Every bride gets nerves before the big day. A marriage is a heavy change."

"How did I not predict this would happen?" said Mr. Farrows, staring through the wall, sightless. "She was always wild."

"Because the pair of you were convinced she'd reformed her unruly ways," Liddy blurted.

Mrs. Pike and her father turned to her, each momentarily thrust back into the waking world. "Miss Lydia," said Mrs. Pike, voice airy with shock. "Whatever has possessed you to say such things?"

"It is the truth. Caroline was positively miserable every moment of their engagement. The only reason she held out as long as she did was because she didn't want to be a disappointment to you two."

Mr. Farrows's eyes narrowed as he circled from Mrs. Pike to his remaining daughter. "That's quite enough, Liddy. Whatever her choices, Caroline is gone from us now. Within a fortnight, she'll have ruined herself," he said, words spat with disgust.

Liddy could not stop her outrage, no matter how hard she balled her hands into fists. "And you lay all blame on her?"

"Caroline thought only of herself. It is only the world's justice that she end up alone."

Liddy felt her cheeks flush with rage. *In Dunland, she sprinted for the banner, balled the fabric, and bolted toward the beast. While others shouted for her to retreat, she leapt bodies, weaved between lines of fire and sprang onto the hydra's back. Ducking low to avoid the heads snapping at her, Liddy scurried toward the nearest head, praying it wasn't a fire breather. The beast's scales chinked against her armor and cut through her breeches. Still, she did not stop, did not falter. Quickly, she unwound the bloody cloth, whipped it around the hydra's snout, and pulled tight. Even as it rose from the ground, wings flapping sporadically, heads thrashing in panic, Liddy held.* Against her father's censure, she held. Before today, she would have bowed her head and stood aside, a dutiful daughter. Before today, she would have looked on in silence, but now, Caroline was no more; she had no one left to balance, no hope of maintaining their place in society. No more.

"Had you not pushed her to believe her only choice was to marry, Caroline would be here now. Because of your unilateral decision, your elder daughter is lost irrevocably. And so am I."

Without another word, Liddy snatched the letter from Mrs. Pike, swept upstairs and packed her few things into a blanket and tied the ends. As she left the shop and her father's muted horror behind, the leaden weight in her chest lifted. One door was fastened tight with a heavy lock, forever barred. Only the road ahead remained.

~~*

For the rest of the summer, Liddy was always aware of the whispers. Though she never heard them, she could feel the empty space they vacated whenever she passed a couple in the street, could feel the change in air pressure as she came and went. What were they whispering about? Caroline's ruination, Mr. Farrows's dashed hopes, or her own disobedience? It was difficult to say, but she held her head high and soldiered on. In time, the gossip mongers would turn their eyes on the next scandal, and she would be free to return to the shadows she so treasured.

She turned off the main road and went up the newly tidied walk to Widow Jennings's home. Mrs. Jennings had been gracious enough to let her the room for extra help around the house and the company. Liddy paused at the front porch and shifted the wildflowers she'd gathered from one arm to the other. Mrs. Jennings had been so kind, kinder than she deserved, Liddy knew, but Liddy dared not seek a room with Mrs. Pike. And while her gut revolted to think of her father piddling around the shop, mouth tight to his own suffering, Liddy knew she could not go back; if she did, she would be forever at her father's mercy. She sighed and opened the door.

Inside, everything seemed covered in dust. Two chairs in the drawing room had the dust clothes drawn from them, though day by day new bits of furniture were revealed. While Liddy guessed she had never sneezed so much in her entire lifetime as she had in the past two weeks of helping Mrs. Jennings sort through her possessions, the work agreed with her. Touching old things, each imbued with a unique story, helped to settle her mind. Instead of the hydra in Dunland, Liddy delved into nearer history, the trials and misadventures of a simple country family and its fall from glory. With a sigh at the scent of freshly brewed tea, Liddy smiled. She grabbed a handful of flowers to replenish the vase in the front window, but was startled to find new flowers there, fresh with dew. Her heart stuttered. Only one person brought the widow wildflowers.

"Oh, Miss Liddy," came a voice from the hall. She turned to find Mr. Bennett frozen in the hallway, his eyes wide and his hands clenched before him. "Forgive me, I had not expected to meet you here. I thought you would be at the shop."

Liddy curtseyed, but her pulse stuttered at the statement. "You have not heard?"

Mr. Bennett's brow furrowed and shifted closer. "To what do you refer?"

Swallowing, Liddy set the bundle of wildflowers on a covered end table, a puff of dust unsettled by the action. "When Caro..." She paused, wincing at the train of thought and how foolishly she broached it to Mr. Bennett. "After... Mr. Farrows and I disagreed concerning Caroline. And, feeling we could not reach an accord, I..." She bit her lip, looking down at the spray of cornflowers, rubbing the petal like a shaman summoning power from the blooms.

"You left as well," Mr. Bennett said quietly, the words coming out like gasps of air.

Liddy nodded shyly before looking back to Mr. Bennett. His eyes seemed wider and he leaned against the wall, one hand raking through his hair, his hat deposited on the nearest surface. For a moment, Liddy started toward him, but instead knotted her hands together and looked down at the dusty floorboards, waiting for a response.

"Good God," said Mr. Bennett after some minutes of silence. "I never thought... I never dreamed it would come to this. Miss Liddy, can you ever forgive me for the damage I've done to your family?"

Liddy felt her mouth drop open, and she stepped forward immediately, taking Mr. Bennett's loose hand in both of hers. "Mr. Bennett, you cannot blame yourself for what has transpired."

"If I had not persisted, your sister would still be with you."

"We've no way to know," Liddy insisted. "Caroline has always been an untamable force. And in the months before your coming, the pressure on her to marry had only mounted. Whether it had been you or the butcher's boy or a travelling dignitary from some far off realm, Caroline was pressured to say 'yes' and would have remained increasingly unhappy. If any is to be blamed, lay it on me. I saw her turmoil and I did nothing. I thought her sensible enough to seek help if she required it. If anything, Mr. Bennett, I assure you her going was likely the brightest moment of her life, regardless of how society will now see her. Caroline, for once, entirely free." The thought drew a smile to Liddy's face, however short-lived. "What she will make of her freedom remains to be seen. We can only hope the best for her now."

Mr. Bennett looked from Liddy's hands to her face. His eyes no longer seemed panicked, but his jaw remained tight as though focusing his entire form on remaining calm and composed. Liddy gave his hand a quick squeeze before releasing it and holding her own hands before her. Slowly, Mr. Bennett nodded with a sigh. "You are remarkably thoughtful for one so young, Miss Liddy."

"When you live so long in your own head, such things come naturally, I'm afraid. The surest path to wisdom is loneliness."

"I'm sure that's what philosophers make of it. Even so, I thank you, Miss Liddy, though it grieves me that I must soon leave this county."

Liddy felt her face flush. "I'm sure Lady Sinclair will miss you most ardently."

Mr. Bennett shook his head and made toward the front door. "For a short while, perhaps, but we will be reunited soon enough. From what she told me, Lady Sinclair intends to away to London with all possible dispatch."

Even as Mr. Bennett spoke, bowed, and kissed the back of her hand in adieu, Liddy barely heard him, but her limbs moved reflexively in response. However, once the front door closed behind him, Liddy collapsed against the door as though physically struck. Her eyes grew wide. Her mouth dropped open. Her breath ran shallow. The whole while her attention focused on one vital fact: Lady Sinclair was leaving.

~~*

The body of the fallen hydra had been picked clean by vultures, the black bones slowly bleaching silver in the sunlight. Liddy bowed her head in reverence of the field where so many gave their lives against so foul a monster. Next year, the fields would grow tall from the fallen bodies, but she did not want to think of far off days. All she wanted was to rest with the knowledge that Dunland was safe.

A knock at the door startled Liddy from her reverie. She set down the dusting cloth and tugged the scarf from her head as she answered Mrs. Jennings's door. On the porch, Benji rocked on the balls of his feet, his hands clasped behind his back, his hair unruly as ever. Liddy nearly froze at the sight of her old friend, but she swallowed quickly and nodded. "Good afternoon."

Benjamin nibbled on his lower lip and nodded in turn. The skin around his eyes was darker than she remembered, and his face looked thinner. Before he could speak, she continued, "You look awful."

Rather than feign offense, Benjamin chuckled, the sound quiet and self-deprecating compared to his usual snark. "Yes, well, no rest for the wicked, as they say."

At the subdued hurt in his eyes, Liddy swallowed and wringed her hands. "Benji, I—"

"Oh, no," said Benjamin, instantly attentive to her shift in attitude. "Don't you dare say you're sorry, Lid."

"But I was—"

"Entirely correct," Benji said quickly, looking down at his feet. "I'm not half as clever as I'd like to be, nor half as sensible."

Liddy's brow rose and she stepped outside, closing the door behind her.

"I know," Benji continued. "Never expected I'd apologize for my behavior either. But after Caro left and Rob followed—"

"Robert went after her?" she interrupted, her voice high as she led the way to a small bench.

"At once, actually." Benjamin sat beside Liddy and leaned forward onto his knees. "Though I don't expect he'll have luck finding her."

Liddy nodded. Without any indication of where Caroline had gone, tracking her would be a Herculean labor. "If anyone can," she said hopefully, "it will be your brother."

"Indeed, the poor sod's as lost on her as ever. He would have been a better fit than our Mr. Bennett."

Liddy chuckled at the name, no longer weary of how events had transpired. Still, her eyebrow rose as she turned to Benji. "Did you really think I'd fallen for him?"

Benjamin sighed and shrugged. "It seemed the most likely option. After all, you were behaving so differently, I assumed the only explanation was an attachment. But now, you seem even more transformed. Lighter."

She did feel lighter ever since she'd moved out of the shop. Still, Liddy shook her head, grinning at her friend's simple confusion. Her smile diminished when she recalled Lady Sinclair's imminent departure. She did not let her shoulders sink. "Well, you were close," she conceded.

Benji sat back quickly, his brow twisted as he turned toward Liddy. She giggled at the strained expression and the goings on behind his eyes. Twice he opened and shut his mouth before shaking away some thought. Finally, he leaned toward her and whispered, "Her ladyship?"

Liddy flushed but nodded. Her chest swelled in undue glee at how quickly Benji's eyes widened and how he laughed nervously. "No, you cannot be serious," he said, nearly breathless from giggling.

"Were you so blind?" she asked.

Quieting himself, Benji shook his head and looked down at his toes. He drew a deep breath and said meaningfully, "Perhaps merely hopeful that one of us might possess a shred of respectability." Before Liddy could comment, he chuckled once more. "Liddy Farrows, a skirt chaser."

In mock offense, she slapped his arm while smiling. "No one will ever believe you."

But her threat turned to mutual laughter, and the pair was merry once more.

~~*

With Benji's departure for Stratfield Gardens at the close of August, the winds turned cool in Dunnshire. Liddy watched from Mrs. Jennings's window as carts laden with the last summer produce rolled through town. Once a week, hired deliverers brought Mrs. Jennings groceries, but Liddy took the delivery silently. With it cooler out, Liddy and Mrs. Jennings spent longer periods out of doors, sitting on the porch, watching townsfolk pass. Liddy read aloud from old books, fictions and nonfictions alike, and Mrs. Jennings closed her eyes to better hear the words. In the afternoons, they continued to work clearing the clutter from the house until the drawing room, at least, was fit to take visitors. As they gathered together a parcel of old books to take to Mr. Monroe's, Mrs. Jennings observed, "This winter's sure to be a cold one."

Liddy nodded. "Each year they grow colder, it seems."

"I should hate to think of you on your own when the snows come," said Mrs. Jennings, her eyes clear and her smile warm. "There will always be room here for you. Goodness knows, I could do with the company."

Liddy smiled sadly and turned back to the work. Silence stretched as they fitted books into a box. Occasionally Liddy would set aside a title she wished to read before sending it to Mr. Monroe. On more than one occasion, Mrs. Jennings urged her to keep a few for herself, but Liddy would not further encroach on the old widow's kindness. She knew before too long she'd need to find gainful employment and loath as she was to leave Mrs. Jennings's side, it was unlikely she'd find anything of worth in Dunnshire.

"Mr. Monroe will be glad of the new stock," Liddy commented.

"New, I think, is not how one would describe these," said Mrs. Jennings, wiping a layer of dust from one volume. "But I think he shall be glad just the same. Timothy Monroe always cared for old things, even when he was a boy."

"What was he like?"

"Shorter," Mrs. Jennings quipped with a wrinkled grin, "and perhaps a might bit forward. Made no effort to keep the friends he found. I imagine if the business with Miss Eliza had gone differently, he and your father would not have broken."

Liddy's brow perked at the information. "Mr. Monroe and my father were friends?"

"Thick as thieves, ever since they were boys. If Miss Eliza hadn't run off with that vagabond, everyone expected she and Mr. Monroe would be wed. The fact they did not was perhaps most shocking to your father. Not long after, the pair quarreled and have not spoken since."

"What did they quarrel over?" Liddy asked, her curiosity once more getting the better of her.

"Well, no one truly knows, but the noise on the wind always claimed it was because Timothy let poor Eliza go without a fight. I don't think your father could handle knowing Timothy allowed his only sister to be ruined to good society. But that's neither here nor there, as they say," said Mrs. Jennings, adding one last book to the crate. "If you're so curious, ask him when you take these to the shop."

Liddy swallowed her questions and nodded. All the way to the bookshop, her mind swam in circles about this information. Mr. Monroe had loved Eliza before she'd left, so much so that he did not stop her. And twenty years later, he had brought a woman of low repute to Piedmont and aided in the birth of her child. True, it could be coincidence, but what if Mr. Monroe's love had never ceased? It would explain his stricken expression upon returning to Piedmont. And what if the once beautiful woman had been her lost aunt, Eliza? The possibilities set an ache in Liddy's skull.

At the sight of the black carriage in front of Mr. Monroe's bookshop, Liddy's heart nearly stopped. In the past weeks, she'd scarcely allowed herself to think of Lady Sinclair. In fact, she'd suspected that her ladyship had long since departed given the absence of her mention in the town gossip. Liddy's cheeks flushed though not from exertion; her breath sped for reasons other than the heavy crate in her arms. As much as the urge to run lightened her heels, Liddy felt something warm and sweet form in her belly. Looking over her shoulder, she wondered if she could live with herself, giving up her only chance to say goodbye to her ladyship. Shifting the crate into a more manageable position, Liddy swallowed her anticipation and strode into the bookshop.

At the sound of the bell, Mr. Monroe looked up from behind the counter and gave her an amiable nod. Lady Sinclair, today dressed in dark plum, turned toward the door. A shy smile rose on her ladyship's face, eyes warm despite their shuttered nature. Liddy ducked her head as her gut pulsed and her cheeks darkened. Still, she crossed the squeaky floorboards and settled her crate upon the counter. She found her hands together in front of her and waited for Mr. Monroe to finish his business with Lady Sinclair.

Lady Sinclair opened her pocket book and slid a broad paper note across the counter. "You do me a great service, Mr. Monroe. I do not expect to return to Piedmont for some time and already the library needs attention. If you encounter any problems, you may contact me through my steward."

"Of course, your ladyship. I am honored to see to such a collection," said Mr. Monroe with a bow. Then he strode down the counter to Liddy. "Another box from Mrs. Jennings?"

"Indeed," Liddy said, her eyes not quite meeting Mr. Monroe's.

"I should stop sending for books from London," he said with a smile, taking the first book from the pile. "At the rate Mrs. Jennings is finding books, I shan't have a shelf to spare. Anything for you today, Liddy?"

"Sadly, no," she said, feeling Lady Sinclair's gaze on her. She curtseyed. "Good day, your ladyship."

Lady Sinclair inclined her head as well. "Miss Lydia, I had hoped to find you. Before he left, Henry said you were letting a room from the Widow Jennings."

"Yes, ma'am. I've been helping her about the house. Of late, she's been going through her old possessions she no longer needs." Liddy paused, unsure of what to say. "It is good to see you."

"And you as well," said Lady Sinclair, her voice resonant with the same warmth that fluttered in Liddy's stomach. "I wonder if I might have a word."

Liddy looked from Lady Sinclair to the crate of books and finally to Mr. Monroe. He looked up from the spine of the first book and said, "Sorting through these will take some time. I will call on Mrs. Jennings when I've completed my assessment. May I assist you with anything else?"

Liddy shook her head. "Thank you. Good day, Mr. Monroe."

"And you Liddy, Lady Sinclair."

Lady Sinclair nodded and offered Liddy her arm. "Shall we walk?"

Liddy blushed and coiled her arm with Lady Sinclair's, so close she could feel body heat radiating from her ladyship's side. Outside, they turned and strolled down the lane. At first, they were silent, their footsteps quiet and in sync. For a while, Liddy's heart battered against her throat, but she swallowed and willed her breathing to slow. Then Lady Sinclair began: "I wanted to offer you my sincerest condolences regarding Caroline's flight. I know it would be difficult were I to lose Henry. I depend upon him dearly. But I cannot fathom the intimacy you had with your sister. It must be unbearable."

"Thank you," Liddy replied quietly. "At times, it is like she's never gone, like I'll turn and find her returning from some adventure through the countryside. Other times, it's like she was never here at all."

"You are lucky to have found a place with Mrs. Jennings."

"It is only temporary," said Liddy. "Already I feel like a burden to her. She insists I am not, but I know soon I shall be leaving myself."

Lady Sinclair turned toward her, startled by the answer. "Where will you go?"

"I haven't the slightest idea," Liddy answered honestly. "Somewhere. I know sums and figures, and my penmanship is fair. I know I can find work with those skills."

Lady Sinclair nodded, her brow creased in thought and her jaw tensed and relaxed at odd intervals. She looked to Liddy and asked, "Have you any thoughts of going to town?"

"Perhaps, but I've no connections and nowhere to stay."

"I ask," Lady Sinclair said, pausing to consider her words, "because Penelope will shortly be in need of a governess. Since James passed, she has been nonresponsive to most persons she's met. Except, of course, you. She took to you quite quickly. I know governess is a most taxing position on a young woman, especially one without experience, but should you like it, the position is yours."

Liddy stopped, her eyes wide with disbelief. Here, Lady Sinclair offered her food, shelter, an occupation, and escape from this too-familiar town which held too many memories. It was almost too good to be sure, but looking at the open plea in Lady Sinclair's gaze, Liddy did not doubt the sincerity of her offer. Still, the memory of their kiss jolted Liddy's stomach. Could she be deserving of a second chance? She did not know, yet her heart fluttered hopefully.

"When would I be needed in London?"

"As soon as you are able. Penelope has already left with Henry. I am to follow tomorrow."

"And what would my duties be?"

"Tending to Penelope. Instructing her basic education, nurturing her to read and explore if she so desires, helping her to adjust to her new position in society until she's old enough to have a companion of her own age."

"And then?"

"Whatever you wish," Lady Sinclair said simply.

Liddy drew her hand from her ladyship's arm, her cheeks flushing at the prospect. She did not think herself bold enough to ask. However, Lady Sinclair always awoke something brave inside her soul, the warrior she always dreamed of being. The words welled on her tongue, waiting to be spoken.

"Would you have me?"

Beside her, Lady Sinclair startled. Liddy could tell from the sharp swish of her gown on the cobbles. "Miss Lydia?"

"My lady," she repeated, looking up at Lady Sinclair's stricken expression, unable to restrain the hopeful turn of her mouth. "Would you have me?"

Without pause, Lady Sinclair stepped close to Liddy. With soft eyes and a smile, her ladyship wound their hands together. "Whole-heartedly."

Liddy's hand clenched tight around Lady Sinclair's, happy tears pooling in her eye.

And later, when she'd bid her adieu to Mrs. Jennings and thanked her for her kindness and the carriage had been called, Liddy could not stop her smile as she kissed her lady.

LIVING IN SIN

ANASTASIA VITSKY

CHAPTER ONE

By evening she was back in love again,
though not so wholly but throughout the night
she woke sometimes to feel the daylight coming
like a relentless milkman up the stairs.
Adrienne Rich, "Living in Sin"[1]

Audra slides her hand over my collarbone, slipping the satin pink bra strap over my shoulder. I bat her hand away and adjust my bra.

"Ouch," she says, withdrawing to her end of the couch. "I did take a shower this morning." She picks up her neon pink coffee mug and takes a sip.

"I love you." I scan my pile of papers, frantic to finish my report before the deadline. "I'm just..."

"Busy," Audra offers. She takes another sip, watching me.

"I've got to finish before Grandma's birthday party."

At the silence, I realize my mistake. "Look, I'm sorry. I know you want to go, but it'll be tapioca pudding and cake with dull conversation."

Two patches of pink appear on Audra's cheeks, and she clinks her cup onto the ceramic mosaic coaster. We

---

chose the set together when she first moved in. "You act like you're ashamed of me."

I groan. "We've gone through this a thousand times. That's not how my family works."

"Huh." Audra stands up and carries her mug to the kitchen sink. "Thought I was part of your family." She returns to the living room and sits in the chair furthest away from me.

I pound away for five full minutes until I give in. Audra has silent treatment down to a science. I can apologize, but it won't change anything. "I need some space," I plead.

"That can be arranged." She stalks out of the room and slams our bedroom door.

~~*

"Sorry I'm late." An hour later, I lay my silver-wrapped package on the divider next to my parents' entryway. "I had to finish some work."

Dad gives a grunt as he carries an enormous box fan to set up in the hallway. Company means more body heat, and this spring is warmer than usual. "Everyone else is in Grandma's room."

My aunt and uncle must have arrived earlier than usual. I wonder if Mom is upset at my tardiness, but I head down the hallway before I can think.

"Ciara!" My mom senses my entrance even though she seems preoccupied with helping Grandma sit up. Grandma's white hair waves around her face, a testament to Mom's skill in rolling the multicolored curlers. Pink for smaller curls on the top, blue for larger ones toward the back, and green at the bottom for a hint of curl.

"Hi, Grandma," I say, and I hug her in between her oxygen tubes. I'm glad they keep her alive, but I hate how they've turned my grandmother into a frail old woman. "Happy birthday."

"Adele," she replies, and everyone avoids looking at my mother. I'm her twin, everyone says, and Grandma gets confused. Today must be one of her bad days. "What are you doing out of school? Tell Dad to come home early."

"Okay," I answer, and I kiss her cheek. What good would it do to correct her? I'd only make her upset, and she wouldn't believe me. I turn to hug the others. "How're you, Uncle Ted? Auntie Marge, how's your knee?"

Auntie Marge smells like lilacs, the way she always does, but she has a new cane. "Can't complain," she says, tapping the four-pronged tips against the floor. "You missed church last week. Pastor Janice gave a good sermon, too. She set all the biddies abuzz by talking about that so-called homosexual marriage. Such a shock to everyone. Evelyn gave her pacemaker a workout. You're looking tired. Don't you get any rest?"

Not much, but I don't say the words aloud. Today's fatigue reflects conflict with Audra rather than lack of sleep. "My roommate kept me up." It's a handy tactic, telling the truth in order to deceive.

"You should bring her over," Uncle Ted says, leaning back in his upholstered armchair and folding his hands across his ample stomach. "Nice girl."

I made the mistake of bringing Audra to a family picnic when we first met, and everyone loved her. She hates the same football team as Uncle Ted, which made her a favorite for life. Then Audra and I became more than friends, and everything changed. I couldn't risk having her in the same room as my family.

"Don't bother her poor roommate. If Ciara brings anyone over, it should be a nice young man. You never called the last one back, did you? You should give Scott a call," Auntie Marge scolds. "He's got a co-worker who would be perfect for you. If you're too picky, you'll find yourself an old maid. Don't laugh at me! You'd think I don't know anything about life." She tugs at the lightweight shawl she insists on wearing no matter how hot the weather.

Maybe I should mind her words more, but I grin. Auntie Marge means, *I badgered my son until he picked a random person for a blind date.* I probably would care if Scott and I didn't have an understanding. I go on the "dates" he sets up, to make his mom happy, but he warns the guys I only want a friendly, one-time outing. In exchange for keeping his mom off his back, Scott drops by now and then to help with maintenance tasks around the house. Come to think of it, the air conditioner has been wheezing lately. It could use some of Scott's tender loving care.

Before I can ask about Scott's absence, Mom fusses with Grandma's oxygen tube. "You can wear my good necklace if you want."

"No!" I exclaim, before I can stop myself. With Mom's pearls and their gold clasp, Scott's co-worker will wonder whether I'm fifty years old. If I don't stop her now, she'll insist on styling my hair as well. "They're worth a fortune." The truth does come in handy, doesn't it? "I'd never forgive myself if something happened to them." Such as taking off the necklace, stowing it underneath the table in the restaurant, and forgetting it there.

Mom nods, placated. "Don't fight him if he wants to pay."

I won't let anyone pay my way, especially if the charade is solely to please my family, but I agree. I won't fight; I'll calmly explain that I want to go out as friends. It's an odd set-up, but it works. Today, however, I feel guilty despite the initial humor. Looking at Auntie Marge's tidily painted nails and palette-perfect eye shadow and blush chosen according to the Mary Kay catalog, I remember Audra's words. She wants to sit in this room as a tangible sign of her status as family member. She came out to her family in high school, and her parents were relieved her nonconformity had a name. My family, on the other hand, wouldn't understand. They like Audra, but they like her as my friend. What would I accomplish by bringing Audra here? She would take offense at Auntie Marge's suggestions, and she'd insist I reject the matchmaking offers. We've had the argument more times than I can count.

"I'm out and I'm proud, and who cares? It's no big deal."

"It's no big deal for you! My family isn't like yours."

"You've got to start living your own life instead of tiptoeing around, afraid of making them mad."

I've never told Audra, but sometimes I have to tiptoe around her more than my family. She doesn't understand that I can't make my family into different people, and I don't want to.

"I'm your family!"

She is. But she's not. Has she been right all along? Am I wrong to keep her away from my family? Should I tell Auntie Marge why none of her matchmaking efforts will succeed?

Grandma mumbles something we can't hear, and Mom leans forward. "What did you say, Mother?"

Grandma ignores Mom and focuses on me. "Adele," she repeats, and Mom gives an unhappy twitch. I play along, trying to respect two generations of women at the same time.

"Yes, Grandma?"

"You know the answer," Grandma chides me.

I'm not as good as Mom at hiding my surprise. Caught interlocking my fingers on top of my crossed legs, I miss and kick the foot lever hanging from the side rail of the hospital bed. I don't dare look at anyone else in the room as I persuade myself that Grandma must be thinking back to when she gave Mom advice. Probably, she thinks she's telling Mom which boy to date or how to style her hair.

Auntie Marge shoots Mom a sympathetic look. I wonder how I will feel when Mom confuses me with others in her old age.

"Have some water, Mother." Mom pushes a small bottle toward Grandma. We're lucky Mom served on the hospice board for years. Unlike other families that panicked, viewing hospice as a death sentence, Mom used her insider knowledge for Grandma's benefit. Once Grandma needed care, Mom knew all the right people to call and papers to fill out. She got Grandma the best equipment, the nicest nurses, and an extra weekly visit. I feel sorry for the man who tried to tell Mom "no" to approving the hospital bed. She threatened to call the state health board and report him. I hope he still has a job.

I wish Mom didn't have to retire early to become Grandma's full-time caregiver, but no one could talk her out of it. She said she was tired of the politics dealing with her school's administration, but still. I hope she won't regret her decision after Grandma dies. It's a horrible thought, but I can't help wondering.

"Don't be scared," Grandma says, and Mom's hand trembles as she puts the water bottle onto the end table. Grandma seems to have forgotten Mom, though, and reaches for me. I grasp her papery hand lined with faint blue veins, and she moves her mouth as if to speak. She loses steam halfway through and leans back into her pillows. She reaches for an imaginary cigarette, forgetting the doctor has forbidden them for years.

Before I can ask Grandma what she knows, she closes her eyes. I want to kick myself. She can't stay alert for too long at a time, and I should have given her my gift right away. I chose the most hideous sweater I could find out of season, with a vomit-green Christmas tree and stoned Rudolph. Grandma won't make it to Christmas to wear the sweater, but she loves receiving clothes as a gift. "Dead people don't need new clothes," she says, and every gift of clothing affirms her life. I've made it a game to find the worst possible clothing gifts and remind her to be grateful. Hideous new clothes are only given to people who are alive. Even though her dresser drawers are full of brand-new sweaters, tops, and pants she can't wear, she asks us to take them out for her every now and then. Before, when she wasn't as weak, she would put them on. Now, she holds clothes against her shrunken body and poses for photos. I hate doing it, but for Grandma, we would do a lot more.

While Grandma rests, we eat a quiet dinner of roasted chicken and potatoes. She awakens for a few moments afterward, but not long enough to unwrap gifts or take photos. Instead, she tells me to bend next to her. She takes out a smooth lavender stone and urges me to put it into my pocket. "Don't lose it," she says, and I promise. I'm too old for hopscotch or rock collecting, but my agreement makes her worry lines relax. "You're a good girl," she says, and I hold my breath waiting for her to call me by my mother's name again. Instead, she waves for me to give her something to drink.

Before I leave, Dad pulls me aside. "Don't tell your mother." He winks as he slips a roll of bills into the pocket of my jeans. I glimpse Benjamin Franklin's picture and gasp.

"Dad," I protest. "I'm fine, really." Mom has to keep track of Dad's paycheck, or he would give it to anyone who asks and a few who don't. I give the wad back to him, but he shrugs.

"Buy yourself a treat," he says. "You haven't paid off those car repairs yet, have you?"

I feel like the worst daughter ever, taking money as an adult child, but his eyes crinkle. He might be offering a secret chocolate ice cream cone before dinner or taking me to the movie Mom decreed too violent for an eight-year-old. I can use the money, but more than that, I like having a dad who wants to take care of me. Something tells me he likes taking care of me, too. I kiss his stubbly cheek and pocket the money. "You spoil me."

"What are dads for?"

Mom appears with a grocery bag full of leftovers packed into individual food storage containers. "Don't work so hard," she scolds, hooking the bag under my thumb.

"You're one to talk." Despite fighting for Grandma to receive extra home visits from the nurse, Mom manages to make it more work rather than less. She insists on cleaning before the nurse arrives and baking a fresh treat. "Grandma hasn't been sleeping, has she?" If Grandma doesn't sleep, neither does Mom.

Mom fusses with the containers. "No, but she's already on so much medication. I hate to add anything to help her sleep. Nothing tastes good to her now, and that would only make it worse."

"What Grandma needs is wine and a cigarette." We laugh. Except Mom laughs too late, and her face crumples at the end. "She's had a long life," I remind us.

"I know." Mom's chin trembles. "But she's still my mother."

Dad puts his arm around her shoulder, and I back toward the door. I want to comfort her, too, but this is Dad's territory. Watching him stand tall next to her makes me wish Audra were here to do the same to me. Where will we be when we are Mom and Dad's age? I hope, whatever happens, that I will fit into her arms the way Mom nestles against Dad. I wish I could bring her to my family, but I can't spoil what I have. Why can't she understand?

I let myself out, and Dad's voice rumbles behind me. Before I'm quite out of earshot, Mom's voice rises. "*How* much did you give her?"

I smile and load the food into my car. Mom must feel better already.

CHAPTER TWO

"I'm home!" I fish the container of lemon meringue pie out of the grocery bag. "Mom made something special for you."

I come to an abrupt stop. Spread on the kitchen counter is a cardboard pizza box and an empty wine bottle. Audra's taken one piece and left the rest to grow cold. I should have told her I'd bring food from the party. Then I scoff at myself. Why should she wait several hours to eat leftovers from a party she couldn't attend? I stuff the food into the fridge and walk into our bedroom. I draw back. Audra sits on our bed, her suitcase propped against the wall. She crosses her arms, and I want to take her hands in mine. I stammer, but she waves away my trite apologies.

"I'm not mad."

That's not the first lie of the night, nor will it be her last.

"I was going to leave without a good-bye, but we've been together too long for that. It's over, Ciara."

I slump against the door, putting my hands to my cheeks. "Grandma's dying," I protest, and I cough to get the words out. Remembering Mom's crumpled face cuts my breath, and Audra's pinched lips cut off my hearing. Her mouth moves, saying words that don't reach my brain. I shake my head to clear my ears, but her next words make me wish I hadn't.

"She's always dying," Audra snaps. "She's been dying ever since I met you. What excuse will you come up with after she finally does it?"

I gape at her. "That's horrible." The Audra who went to five different pharmacies to find anti-nausea medicine for me would never throw a dying grandmother in my face. The Audra who texted me song lyrics every morning for our first three weeks together could not dream of using words to hurt.

"You keep me away from your family, and you call me horrible?" She heaves herself off the bed.

"Grandma dying isn't a lie!" I flinch as she approaches me, but she moves to the dresser instead. My perfume bottles and jewelry lie in their usual heap, while she has wiped her half clean. She's torn a photo of us in half, with a jagged edge to show where she used to stand next to me.

"It's convenient." Audra picks up her hairbrush from our dresser. My dresser now, I guess. "Every time, you tell me to wait a little longer. Then your grandma has a turn for the worse. Or you go on another damn date. How long since I moved in? I'll tell you. Nine months, three weeks, and four days. The first time you excluded me from your family, I gave you a pass. For almost ten months, I let you treat me like a mistress who shamed you."

"That's not how it is." I think of all the times I took phone calls on the sly or pretended I had to work late. All because I didn't want a fight with Audra about spending time with my family... without her. She's right, but she's wrong. I can't let myself think about it, so I counterattack. "I never asked to meet your family. I'll stop going with you to visit them."

She stares at me. "Do you think that would make us even?" Her chin quivers, Audra who never cries.

"Yes," I say because I don't know. The 'wrong answer' buzzer goes off in my head, even before she scowls.

"Are you hearing anything I'm saying?"

I rub my eyes. I want her to think I have dust in my eyes, not tears. "You don't understand my family," I plead. I hate myself for begging, but I can't let her leave. I need her arms around me, reassuring me we will grow old together.

"How could I, when you hide me from them?" She stares down at me, and a wisp of hair falls across her face. I want to brush it away, and my arm aches from holding back. "I'm done." Before I can ask, she clarifies. "You tell your family about us, or I leave."

She's given the order many times before, but not over a packed suitcase.

"Now," she insists. "Right this minute, or I'm out the door."

"But it's late!" Mom and Dad must have gone to bed already, though that's not the issue. Audra knows it.

"Yes," she snaps. "It's far too late." She stands up and picks up her suitcase. The emerald ribbon flutters from the handle.

"Audra." She pauses, and I want to take her hand. I want to remind her of our first day as a couple, sneaking kisses in between giggles as we pretended to discuss serious business matters. "I love you."

"Not enough."

But she pauses, and she sets the suitcase next to me. The edge of the ribbon caresses my kneecap. Irrationally, I want to tackle her, as if physical restraint can change her mind where words have failed. "How can you say that?"

"Not enough to accept me for who I am." She spits the words out, and her eyes glitter with unshed tears.

Tears sting my eyes, too. We're crying in sympathy, but we can't have empathy for each other. "You won't accept me for who I am, either. I can't tell my family about you. Not won't, can't."

She bites her lip. "Have a nice life, Ciara. Do the world a favor, and don't date anyone else. You're not ready to be in a relationship until you get over your issues."

I gape at her. "Don't go," I whisper.

"You've got some messed-up crap, and I should have seen it before. You want me to stay? Call your parents. Say they'll have a new daughter-in-law as soon as marriage is legal."

I stand, unable to move or speak, watching a split-screen movie in my head. On the one side stands Audra, the only woman I've ever loved. On the other side are Grandma, Auntie Marge, Uncle Ted, Mom, and Dad. "Okay," I whisper, praying Grandma will find a way to forgive me.

"See, I told you... What?" Audra stares at me. "Okay, I should go?"

"Okay," I say, trembling. "Tomorrow. I can't do it tonight. I can't."

She keeps staring at me, trying to speak. Finally she gives an odd sort of nod. "I'll sleep on the couch. I need some space."

I shiver, rubbing my goose-fleshed arms. The mockery of my own words reduces me to silence. I want her to come toward me, the way Dad moved toward

Mom, but I wonder if I'm Dad in this moment. I close my eyes, picturing the scene.

I move toward Audra, and she allows me to brush her hair back and kiss her on the lips. I close my eyes, holding onto her for balance. "Don't leave me," I beg. "Stay here."

And for reasons she never will tell me, she allows me to lead her to our bed. I undress her, tenderly, and I kiss the side of her neck. She shivers but allows me to hold her, and I squeeze her tight. I don't want to think of a lifetime without her. A lifetime alone.

"You're in my way."

I jerk awake from my daydream to find her standing in front of me, hands on her hips. I imagined caressing her, and my throat tightens at the reminder the dream can never become reality.

"I don't..."

"My pajamas are in my suitcase." She brushes me aside and yanks the ribbon-encircled handle. My heart thuds as I reach toward her sweet-scented skin. She spins on her heel, and she leaves me alone in the room we have shared for the past nine months, three weeks, and four days.

CHAPTER THREE

Later that night, after I fall asleep in an exhausted stupor, something taps against my arm. I frown, sleepily opening my eyes. I'm still in my day clothes, and I never turned out the light. Above me stands someone who looks like Mom, but younger and with longer hair. "Huh?"

"Wake up," she says. "Give me the stone."

I bat at her as if she is a mosquito and try to go back to sleep, but she taps me again. Not a proper tap from a full-bodied arm, but a light whisper. I shiver from the cold and shrug her off.

"The lavender stone," she repeats. "It's in your pocket."

"What?" More to humor her than out of any belief, I slide my hand into my jeans pocket. Sure enough, below Dad's roll of money lies Grandma's stone. I hold it out uncertainly. "This?"

"Yes," she nods. "You'll need it to come with me. Hold it tight."

I get up, grumbling, and she places her not-quite-there finger on my lips. "Shh."

I should know better than to follow a random apparition, but curiosity gets the better of me. "Where are we going?"

Instead of answering me, she wafts through the wall in a noiseless motion. I stare at the framed copy of

Monet's bridge over a pond of water lilies until her translucent head appears instead of the painting.

"Come on," she urges. She snaps her fingers that appear through the blank wall. "I forgot you don't know how. Hold my hand." She reaches for my right hand, the one closed around the stone.

I obey, closing my eyes in terror as the white painted plaster hurtles toward my soft, vulnerable body. When I open them, the woman appears more substantial. Instead of a sheen around the edges of her body, her skin stands out in sharp relief against the background. A pianist plays the blues while a few brass players join in, and my escort crooks her finger at the bartender. A good-looking man, he winks while polishing the counter with a white cloth. Rows of bottles peek from behind glass doors edged in a pale wooden trellis. A stuffed alligator perches on top of the cabinet, watching while the bartender reaches for a martini glass and mixes a drink. Streaks of orange and yellow form before he asks as an afterthought.

"Your usual, Muriel?"

"Best gin and sin in town." She seats herself at the bar, tipping a cigarette out of its gilt-edged carrier. She places the cigarette into a long, narrow black-and-brown holder ringed with gold at the top and bottom, flaring out ever so slightly in between. She swings a sequin-tipped toe toward the barstool next to her. "Sit down," she tells me. "Horace will get you something."

I need something stiff, all right. I hang back, confused by the impossible reality in front of me. Muriel is my grandmother's name, but this woman can't be more than twenty or twenty-five. Grandma wears orthopedic lace-up shoes, or least she did when she could still walk. This Muriel's feet peek out of crisscrossed black leather straps attached to far higher heels than I've seen anyone wear. Instead of pink polyester wrinkle-free pants, a gray circle skirt settles over a sleeveless black body suit and leggings. On one side, her skirt gathers into a fabric rosette over a large pocket. Her chic red hat tilts backward, and carefully made-up eyelashes blink at me from over her cigarette holder.

My grandmother is hot, I'm a sick woman, and I'm going to hell for more reasons than one.

"Grandma?" I ask in disbelief. Horace sets a glass in front of me.

"Drink up," he says. "You need this more than she does. Want some gator bites, on the house?"

I shudder a "No, thank you" and lift the cup to my lips, hoping I won't shrink to nine inches and drown in my tears. I take a tentative sip, and the pungent gin sets my tongue tingling. Pomegranate, orange, and another fruit swirl in my mouth, creating an unfamiliar but pleasant mixture of sweet and strong. Fortified, I glance at Grandma, who drains her glass. Horace hands her another and takes the empty glass away without being asked.

"You're good to me," Grandma says, tapping the end of her cigarette against the ashtray.

He hands her a new napkin. "You kept us in business all those years."

"What..." My voice trails off.

"Sit down."

I sit. Yesterday's slept-in jeans and polo shirt feel grubby and frumpy next to her ensemble. I never thought I would be out-dressed by my grandmother.

A horrible thought occurs to me. "Am I dead? Are you... Is this why...?"

Anastasia Vitsky

Grandma reaches over and holds out her hand. Uncomprehending, I wait until she takes the light-colored stone and sets it on the counter. She pets the rounded top with her fingertip, breathing in and blowing out a puff of gray. "First good smoke I've had in years. Your mother and the doctors fuss all the time. Oxygen, my lungs. What's the point of living in misery?"

Chills prickle my skin. Is this good-bye? She looks at me and gives a laugh.

"You're not dead," she says. "Nor am I. You need a story."

I need a lot more than a story, but the alcohol has done me good. "What kind?"

"Choose," Grandma answers.

I have to lean forward to hear her over the wailing of the trumpet, and I cough on the smoky air. "Choose," she says, the way Audra told me to choose. Forlorn, I twist the barstool from side to side. I can't ask my newly young grandmother if I should choose between my girlfriend and family, when she would faint with horror if she knew I had the girlfriend. Except that sitting in this bar, this backward leap in time, has taken the gray out of Grandma's hair and restored the original dark sheen. This grandmother looks less like a frail old woman and more like someone who lives life to the fullest.

"You need a story," she repeats, and she is right. I could be four years old again, scared of monsters under my bed while she soothes me to sleep.

"What if someone you loved asked for something you couldn't give?" I take another sip to avoid giving myself away. She doesn't have to know which loved person I mean.

"What kind of thing? Money? Time?"

I struggle to explain. "They expect you to do something you can't."

"Can't or won't?"

"Can't," I say with irritation. After all, she is part of the reason I can't. "If I could, I would."

"Would you?"

Whenever I told Grandma about fights with my parents or school friends, she took their side. At least it felt like it, the way she told me to think of their perspective. "I want a story," I say, falling into her trap. "Of when you gave to someone you loved something you couldn't give."

Grandma, or Muriel as perhaps I should call this younger version, stubs the end of her cigarette into the ashes. She sets down her holder and drinks a generous amount of cocktail. "I wanted to be a singer," she says.

I blink. This is new to me. She stands up and drifts toward the piano. The musicians are in the middle of something mournful, but she sits on the edge of the piano bench with her shoulder rubbing against that of the pianist. She hums along, then lets loose with the most powerful contralto voice I've ever heard. My jaw drops, and she morphs the warm-up arpeggio into a counterpoint to the other instruments' melody. Where their notes droop with the weight of the world, she adds another layer using syncopated rhythms. She doesn't change anything they play, but her voice adds a new quality to the music. Something, perhaps I dare to call it hopeful. As if their grief were waiting for her to enter, to add light, and to deepen their mournfulness into a richness impossible with her voice alone. Without amplification, her voice carries over the combined piano and brass.

Anastasia Vitsky

How could I have come from such talent? Years of music lessons have taught me theory and little else.

Breathless, Muriel flushes as everyone in the club applauds her.

"That's some sweet singing," the trumpet player says, slapping her a high-five. "You should come around more often."

She stands and gives him a kiss, one so chaste and yet full of love that my eyes sting with tears. I should look away, but I have never seen such passion before. She caresses the trumpet player's cheek and pats it. "You know I can't," she says, and the edges of her mouth tighten. I hold my breath as she comes back toward me, emptying the rest of her drink.

"Why didn't you tell anyone you could sing?" I demand. Not so much as a lullaby, not a sing-along to the endless repetitions of my favorite Disney movie, not even a hum with the radio. Only during church would she sing, soft and low. She sang as if ashamed, and I assumed she didn't like her voice.

"Jimmy didn't want me to sing," she answers, and I stare at her. Grandpa, who opened doors for her, carried her packages, and refused to let get her hands dirty on anything but household chores? Grandma never drove a car, never took care of the yard, and never so much as lifted a hammer to hang a picture.

"Why not?" But I know the answer. It was in the explosion of her lips on the trumpet player's cheek, in the lingering gaze into his eyes before she stepped out of the performing circle. It was the light in her eyes as she sang, when she leaned against the piano player but had eyes only for the trumpeter. "Why?" I ask instead, feeling lonely. My grandfather couldn't read music. She never sang with him.

"Ciara..."

"You gave up singing for him." My voice comes out flat, angry. How could she? She could have been a concert singer, a professional musician, or at the very least a music teacher. Instead she baked cookies and mended Grandpa's socks until he died. I feel as if she has taken her singing away from me, personally. I could have been the granddaughter of a famous singer. "How could you?"

She rolls the creamy stone in her palm, as if it is a die to cast. "I couldn't give up my singing." She pauses and tosses the colored chip into the air. It tumbles onto the counter in a clatter, skittering and bumbling next to her empty glass before landing with the smooth side down. I couldn't give up my singing if I sang as well as Grandma, either. As Muriel. I'm confused, trying to understand these dual selves.

"If you couldn't, you—"

She brushes the folds of her skirt, looking at me with pity. "When you love someone, you give up what you cannot."

CHAPTER FOUR

Muriel, or Grandma, escorts me back to the three-bedroom apartment I share with the woman I love and hurt more than anyone in the world. So focused am I on finding Audra that I give Grandma a cursory wave before stumbling into the living room. The stone lies in my pocket, consecrated by our excursion. Audra lies huddled on the couch, knees to her chest and arms wrapped around her legs. She looks so miserable, even in sleep, that I tiptoe toward her. I reach toward the lock of hair falling across her face, but I draw back. Her vicious comments from last night echo in my ears. I'm a liar, I use Grandma as an excuse, I hide her. They're true, aren't they? But they are also words from a woman who lashes out in hurt.

If Audra had to choose between me and her family, whom would she choose?

In that moment, I know. She would choose me.

Self-talk or no, I'm terrified to touch her. Sleeping, I can watch her chest rise and fall. She moans, scratching the back of her neck and clasping her legs. The double-jointed pinky flares against her leg, alone amongst her other single-jointed fingers. I used to tease her, walking her fingers across my chest and bending to kiss the inside of her wrist.

Most couples have a cute or meaningful meeting story, but Audra and I have none. I worked with a friend of hers who liked to host dinner parties, and we met each other there. We neither liked nor disliked each other at first sight, but instead made polite conversation while squished in between hordes of other people trying to do the same thing. She didn't make me laugh, I didn't hate her guts, and she didn't woo me with flowers and chocolates. The closest we got to romance was paying for each other's dinner when we went out. Purely dinner, mind. I didn't know I liked women, and she was afraid to spook me.

I reach out and take Audra's hand in mine, remembering the first time she did that to me. She reached across the dinner table, pretending she wanted the check. Her fingernails brushed the back of my hand, and her eyes met mine. Before I could say anything, she picked up the check and took out her wallet. I trace the faint blue veins radiating from her wrist to her knuckles. If she and I marry, her wedding ring would rest above the third knuckle, next to the vein connecting to her heart.

I should be shocked at the thoughts I've never allowed myself to entertain, but I run my fingers across the baby-fine hair on her hand. Soft and nearly invisible, the hair reminds of earlier times when our ancestors needed protection against the cold. As we learned to enclose ourselves within temperature-controlled climates, the protective covering fell away, leaving behind a trace.

I want her to wake up, but I continue touching her. The minuscule scar across her first knuckle, invisible to anyone but the two of us who know it's there, is a faint reminder of when I tried to take the paring knife out of her hand and she moved before I could take away the blade. Such a lot of blood, and now she bears only a small, white, cut-shaped mark. She bled so much I thought I'd have to take her to the hospital, but she healed on her own.

I lift her hand and kiss the scar, protective fine hair, and thread-like blue lines leading to her heart. She stirs, and as if by muscle memory, she unravels to bring me closer to her.

"Audra," I whisper. I am a wildlife photographer creeping toward a rare bird that will fly away at any moment. Her slightly crooked pinky, bent from its years of double-jointed flaring, curls like a translucent sea anemone into its shell. Her close-cut nails tuck against the pad next to her thumb. The morning sunlight shines in the reflection of those buffed nails, glossy and perfect. I didn't realize I could love a woman until Audra put her hand into mine. The female body contains zones far more erogenous than the hand, but its touch made me see her as a woman for the first time.

"Ciara," she mumbles, and the memory of her anger washes across her sleepy face. She jerks her hand, but I hold fast. This is the hand that taught me how to love; it has become part of me.

"You need a story," I say, fast instead of grand the way Grandma said it.

"Leggo of me..."

"Do you know, every scar on this hand, I've seen you get? Cutting the tomatoes." I tug the skin on her knuckle, just enough to show the faint white line. "This burn." A tiny small circle an inch above the rounded bone on the outside of her wrist. She got too close to a radiator during a night of not-so-chaste kissing. She said it didn't hurt, but I held an ice cube in my mouth and glided it across her skin until she swore for real that it no longer hurt. "The knife." The faint line on the inside of her thumb where an X-Acto knife jumped from linoleum tile to her flesh. She'd needed two stitches for that one, and I cried more than she did.

She watches me, wary and foreboding, but she loosens her hand to rest in mine.

"This is my story, too," I say, because it is. "You can't take away the marks of our time together."

She jumps up and flings her hand to her chest. "Do you think I don't know that?" She pushes against me, but I hold her arms. Then her elbows when she shrinks away.

"Audra," I say, and the words come before I can think them through. "I was selfish. Please forgive me." So was she, but I have hurt her enough. Her eyes widen at my words, and she relaxes. I think of Grandma, mending socks for the man who took away her music. No, not 'took away'. Grandma made her own choices. I try to speak, but Audra cups my chin when the tears form.

"I was so angry," she says. "I didn't know I could hate you that much."

I lower my arms, reeling as if she slapped me. The gentleness of her tone makes the words burn all the more.

"What happened to you?" She bends forward, her hair swinging in its sleep-tousled curtain. "You're softer. Different."

So is she. Or is she different because I have changed? Has she stayed the same while I transformed, or have we flipped an unspoken switch to restore us to an earlier set point? No, not earlier. We still carry the weight of irreconcilable difference. I am different and she is different, but we still have our difference.

"Why did you apologize?"

Because last night I listened to the most beautiful voice I've ever heard, and that voice never got a chance to shine. Because my grandmother is Muriel Rodnier, a woman who raised four children and buried two. Because I understand, at last, the power I have inside of me. I can't change my family, but I can cause the woman I love most to spend a night shivering on the couch, so lonely that she hugs her knees to her chest.

Because apologizing isn't about being wrong; apologizing means Audra is right for me. Because I'd rather have Audra than be right. We can both be wrong, but we can't both be right.

"I hurt you," I say, because it's true. And, strangely enough, the admission makes her relax more. I'd have thought telling Audra she is right would make her more strident in her anger, but she softens like a too-full helium balloon hissing as it lets out air. She holds my hands in hers, and every cell of her skin against mine brings back a flood of memories. Catching snowflakes on our tongues, or pretending to. Riding the city bus late at night, just to say we did it. Watching *Up* together and dropping pennies into our own glass jar. We planned a dozen trips a week, bringing home travel brochures and printing quotes from online travel planning sites. Quoting *The Matrix* and *The Princess Bride* at random intervals least likely to make sense. We'd spout them while slipping into the shower or popping into the room without warning.

For nine months, three weeks, and five days, Audra has been my life partner. How could I relegate her as an afterthought, the recipient of Mom's leftovers?

Audra kisses me, a sweet girlish meeting of the lips. The night away from her has made me long for her, and

I straddle her while she sits on the couch. Her sleepyhead hair snags in my fingers.

"Stop trying to hit me and hit me," she says, and I laugh. I smack her hip, just for show, and wrap my arms around her. I squeeze extra tight, until she gives a breathless gasp. "You hogged the bed last night."

I'm too focused on taking off her shirt to defend myself. "Stop talking," I moan.

"Only fair I get some bed time now, right?" She slides out from underneath me and stands up, walking toward the hallway.

I stare at her. Could she mean what I think she means? I fall back onto the couch until she pokes her head back into the room.

"What, I've got to do all the work? Are you coming or not?"

I jump off the couch, and we never make it to the bed. Our clothes hit various points on the wall and the carpet.

CHAPTER FIVE

"Hey." Audra shakes my jeans before throwing them into the washing machine. "What's this?" A light purple stone falls onto the floor.

I pick it up and tuck the stone into my pocket. "Just something," I evade. "What do you want for dinner?"

The phone rings. "It's me," says Scott. "Jake's friend has a brother, Damien. How about going out with him on Saturday afternoon? There's a jazz festival at the Fez."

I glance at Audra, whose face turns red. She knows how these calls work. I shake my head at her. "Thanks, Scott, but actually I want to go with Audra." She stops sorting clothes and listens to my end of the conversation. "Maybe another time?" I want to be polite, but Audra won't see it that way. "I mean, thanks, but I don't want to go on any dates."

"What, my friends' brothers aren't good enough for you?" Scott laughs. He couldn't care less whether I go on dates he sets up, but he knows the price we will both pay if I refuse.

Because bigamy is illegal, I want to say. I stand behind Audra and massage her neck with my free hand. "I may have found someone," I admit. Audra leans her head against my stomach.

"That's great! You should tell everyone."

Yeah, I should tell everyone I want to disown me. If only Scott knew what he was suggesting. "Not yet."

"Bring him to the barbecue on Saturday."
And that explains why I can't.

~~*

Over a dinner of tomato basil soup, grilled cheese sandwiches, and raspberry iced tea, Audra makes careful conversation.

"We should get some house plants," she says. "Lots of plants would freshen the air, and aloe would be useful to have on hand."

I dunk the crust of my sandwich into my soup. "I kill plants," I explain. "It would be plant abuse." I should be glad she wants to make a purchase together, but something holds me back. Her suitcase remains packed, an elephant in the room despite the days and nights we have spent together since then.

"Or a spider plant," she says. "I don't think you could kill it. What if we got an African violet and I did all of the tending?" She refills my glass of iced tea. "Philodendrons are hardy, too."

"Where would we put them?" I don't want plants in our home to remain after she leaves.

Patiently, she refrains from pointing out empty corners and our clutter-free balcony. "What's wrong, Ciara?"

A few days ago, I threw myself at her with pleas to stay. Today, I want her to leave and get it over with, if she's not going to promise to stay. "The soup's cold," I complain.

She sighs and takes my bowl. "What do you expect when you take twenty minutes to eat?" She jabs microwave buttons until the plate spins on the rotating circle. Those beautiful hands of hers, both delicate and strong, never stop moving. They wring out a dishrag, clean up the counter, put away dry dishes, and flip her hair over her shoulder. They set the bowl of soup in front of me, half-empty but steaming and bubbling.

"How was work?" I ask, because it's the only thing I can say without sounding churlish.

"Not a single bite," she admits. She works as an independent realtor, and the sales pitch lifestyle wears on her. "I brought in this family to look at a two-story perfect for them, and they wanted a bigger yard. They hate yard work and maintenance, but they want more lawn than a baseball diamond."

"Come with me," I blurt out.

"To the baseball diamond?" She folds and refolds her yellow cloth napkin. Mom made them for me when I moved out.

"My parents are having a barbecue this Saturday," I say, but Audra bursts into tears as soon as I say 'my parents'. My gut spasms with regret that comes a split-second too late, but her noisy, unrestrained sobs are the first I've ever seen her cry in almost as long as we've been together. "I'm sorry. You don't have to come." *Please don't come*, I think to myself, and I'm ashamed.

"No," she says, covering her face with the napkin. "You don't mean it. You don't really want me to go."

I don't, but how can I tell her that? "I do," I lie. "Come to the barbecue." What am I doing? My brain shrieks at me to hit 'undo' on the past three minutes of conversation, but Audra beams at me with tear-swollen eyes.

"Let's go shopping," she says. "I need a new dress."

"It'll be pretty informal," I object, but she waves my words away.

"And flowers for your mom. What does she like? Don't complain, grouch," she chirps. "I'll get you some, too. Can I call your parents by their first names, or would they want me to say Mr. and Mrs. Lessou?"

The sickness in my stomach settles, and all I can see is her shining eyes. I've never seen her so happy, not at Christmas or her birthday or celebrating our anniversary. How can I take that away from her? "Yellow roses," I say at last. "New ones, before they've really opened. She likes those because they last longer."

"Come on!" Audra grabs me, heedless of the dirty dishes she normally would insist on clearing before doing anything else. "If we leave right now, I bet we can find dresses for both of us. There's a sale at Macy's."

~~*

On Saturday morning, Audra pounds on the bathroom door. "I need my curling iron!"

Silently, I unlock the door long enough to pass her the iron. Before she can say anything else, I shut the door and resume kneeling over the toilet.

"Hey!" The pounding continues. I never close the door to her, but I can't let her see me this way. "And my gel. Open up!"

"In a minute!" I shout back, retching. I turn on the fan to hide the sound of my dry heaving. I can almost feel the sides of my stomach touching as my insides churn in an endless, agonizing dance. "Your hair looks fine, anyway!"

If I've hidden my sexuality from my family for more than twenty years, I can hide my misery from my girlfriend for a few hours. I brace myself against the outer ridges of the toilet seat, convulsing with efforts to bring up the contents of my empty stomach. I've made two trips to the bathroom in the past four hours, and a foolish attempt to have toast and tea for breakfast resulted in this latest Technicolor display.

At last, I cup my hand underneath the faucet, swish the water around my mouth, spit out, and give my teeth a quick brushing. I open the door, and Audra stands in the hallway touching up the ends of her hair. She stands in her nylons, and her new sundress of lime green and white stripes shows up perfectly against her tanned skin. She turns off the iron and gathers her hair into a half ponytail. Because I love when she does her nails, she's given herself a French manicure with a shimmer of lightest green. Her hands shine with the softness of a paraffin wax dip.

"Wait," she says. She grabs a pair of scissors from the dresser in our bedroom and snips off a tag from the hem of my skirt. Despite my protests, she bought me a flared hot pink skirt with matching top. The white sandals buckle underneath a hot pink jewel on the outside of each ankle. Mom will wonder why I'm overdressed for a casual grilling of steaks, but Dad will tell me I am beautiful.

It's the last thought that forces me to get my act together. "Audra," I say. "You know our new dresses will come home smelling of smoke, right?"

She switches off the curling iron and picks up her white purse and bouquet of yellow roses peeking from around wisps of baby's breath. Happiness radiates from every part of her body, from the curve of her elbow to the instep of her arch. "I don't care," she says. "I won't let you down."

In the car, Audra chatters about everything from charcoal briquettes to cuts of steak. I grip the handle of my door, fighting back waves of nausea. "Stop," I moan. "Stop the car."

"What?"

I point to the next driveway leading into a fast-food restaurant. "Pull in there." Audra turns the wheel and shifts the car into park. I unbuckle my seat belt, open my door, and lean out to christen the parking lot with spectacular chunks of green and yellow vomit. Shocked, Audra passes me wet wipes and a bottle of water. I rinse out my mouth and spit, and she gives me a peppermint. I put it in my mouth, shaking as I close the door.

"Ciara, if you're sick we can go home."

Yes! I want to shout. How easy to blame everything on illness. She would take care of me, we would miss the get-together, and I wouldn't have to explain. But we have come too far to continue the lies. Grandma told me love means giving up what I can't, but she couldn't have meant this. Even in her years of self-sacrifice, she couldn't have meant to make herself sick.

"Ciara?"

"I can't," I say. I keep my eyes on the candy wrapper to avoid seeing her disappointment. If I tell my family, I will hear how I will go to hell for living an unnatural life, or that I could like boys if I tried hard enough. I can't say Grandma is dying, or Mom will cry and Dad will threaten to find and kill whatever boy 'ruined' me for men, or Auntie Marge will faint and blame my parents. I've said it before, and it makes her angry. It makes me angry, too. I shouldn't have to hide who I am, but Mom shouldn't have had to give up her career and Grandma shouldn't have had to give up what made her happy. In a perfect world, Audra would be right. In this world, we do the best we can.

Audra's tense voice shatters the silence. "I should have known," she snaps. She did know, I realize. She already knew.

"We'll have one tense and awful afternoon with them today, if they don't throw us out, and nothing will be the same again. Why don't we find work somewhere else, Audra? Realtors can get a job anywhere. If we move away, it won't matter that my family won't talk to me anymore. I can stop seeing them, if you want me to." At my last words, I understand Grandma's advice. "Giving up" doesn't mean telling my family; it means putting Audra first.

Instead of the anger I expect, Audra's response warms with surprise. "You would give up your family?"

"Yeah." Grandma did that for Grandpa, didn't she? She didn't want to become a professional singer, with nothing but records and awards in her empty house. "You're my family, too."

Audra says nothing for several minutes. "It's not because of me?"

I look up at her. "What?"

"It's not because I didn't finish college? Or I'm not smart enough? Or my family is too weird?" She slides the seatbelt back and forth in her hands. A green jewel glitters in the sun.

My heart twists. I'd been too busy being angry at her pressuring me to tell my family that I hadn't seen the obvious.

"It's not me?"

"I've been a jerk," I say in a rush. "I'm sorry I never realized you thought that. No, you could be Maya Angelou and Adrienne Rich rolled into one, and my family would react the same way."

"But you would stop seeing them, so you could be with me?"

At last, I know the right answer. "Not stop seeing them altogether. But if we move away, it won't be as much of an issue. They won't be ten minutes away, and I won't run over there every other day." *Grandma's dying,* I think to myself, and I stop. Muriel would understand.

For so long I think Audra has forgotten I'm in the car, she stares across the steering wheel at the snake of cars wriggling through speakerphones and pickup windows of the drive-through. "Your grandma's dying," she says. This time, without the contempt she usually adds to the words.

"She is," I agree. "But you're alive, and so am I." Never have I felt so strong, and never have I felt this sure of myself. "There's only one Audra, and I'm not losing you."

She releases the wheel, and she takes my hand in hers. "There's only one Ciara, and I'm not losing you, either. You're also not going to lose your family over me. Come on, I'll drop you off at your parents."

"But..."

"I'll bring my gorgeous new dress to the gay bar, and I'll flirt with everyone there. You'll be sorry." She laughs, though, and she squeezes my hand. "I'll come home with a fistful of phone numbers and new plants. You don't get a veto."

I give a startled laugh. "That's it? New plants?"

"I'll find something."

The insides of my stomach settle, and for the first time in days I feel hungry. "You're amazing," I say.

"I know." She reaches over to fasten my seat belt for me, and she pulls out of the parking lot. When we arrive at my parents' house, I open the car door and hesitate.

"Come on," I say. "Walk me to the door before you leave."

Her eyes light up, and she reaches for the flowers in the back seat.

Chapter Six

"Grandma." I enter her bedroom in a waft of charcoal smoke and grilled steak. Her eyes are closed, but fingers tap twice against the bed sheets. That's her sign she is listening, even if she can't keep her eyes open. I am so grateful to find her still alive after our adventure that I'll take any sign of life. I pull up a chair and sit next to her bed. "You sly devil, hiding your talents from us all these years. Did anyone ever find out about your singing?"

Her eyes flutter open, and a hint of a smile plays across her face.

"You could have sung a little," I chide. "No one would have suspected if you sang a solo now and then at church, or with us grandkids."

Her lips part, and a wisp of a laugh emerges.

"Was Horace a real person?"

She tries to respond, but a coughing fit paralyzes her. Alarmed, I give her the cup with its plastic straw. She wheezes, and Mom rushes in.

"What's wrong?"

"Nothing." I take out the lavender stone and hold it out. "Thank you," I say. Grandma shakes her head and pushes the stone toward me. "Are you sure? You don't need it?"

"What's going on?" Mom flits across the room, checking monitors and oxygen and medication.

"It's yours," Grandma says, and I take the stone back with relief. Her face contorts, and Mom jumps to her side. I wanted to ask if I'll see Muriel again, but Mom is too busy checking Grandma's readings and asking if she needs something for the pain. Grandma gives a curt nod, too breathless to speak.

"Hey," I say to Mom as she draws the morphine into a syringe and screws it into the IV cap. As sad as it is to have Grandma on hospice, they allow her as much pain medication as she needs. Still, I can't think about the reality while standing next to her. "Have you ever heard of gin and sin?"

Mom crooks an eyebrow. "How did you know about that?"

"Why?" It's not the most famous of drinks, but it's not obscure, either.

"It was Mom's favorite drink."

"I know." At her curious look, I explain. "Grandma told me once." No need to say when.

Mom finishes giving the medication and adjusts Grandma's blanket. Despite the early warmth this year, Grandma hates air conditioning and complains of chill. Mom fusses at her to eat more to get extra insulation, but no one tells Grandma what to do.

"Hey, Mom?" I speak before I can lose my nerve. "I don't want Auntie Marge to have Scott set up dates for me anymore."

She's not really paying attention. "Why not, hon?"

In a perfect world, I'd tell her why. In a Lifetime television movie, I'd blurt out the truth and we'd cry over the revelation. We'd grow in understanding of each other. Audra's LGBT rights activist friends would force a confrontation and lecture about the real meaning of parental love. They would say Mom and Dad should accept me as I am. They would preach about courage and authenticity. What they wouldn't understand is that courage comes in many forms. Love means giving up what I cannot, and for me Audra gave up a relationship with what should be her family-in-law. Maybe I'm not a good girlfriend, but I'm good enough for Audra to still want me. In the real world, we find love the way we can.

"Mom?" I wait until she gives me her full attention. "I don't think I want to get married." At least not the way she thinks about marriage.

She pauses. "Don't you think you should tell Marge that?" She doesn't scold me about future grandchildren or Dad walking me down the aisle. They've been saving for my wedding since I was born, but she doesn't remind me.

"Okay." I blink back. Was it this simple all along? "Do you think she'll be upset?"

"Yes." Mom laughs. "But that's life."

I want to hug her, but she wouldn't understand. Instead, I change the subject. "Do you mind if I leave early? Audra and I wanted to go to the Fez."

"Sure," Mom says after a beat. "Why don't we all go, too? Your dad loves jazz."

"Mom," I protest.

"It's not like you kids invented jazz, you know. We won't bug you. We can sit at different tables so we won't embarrass you."

I want to stick my tongue out at her deliberate 'Mom' voice, the one that always seems to know best. Then I think it through. If the Fez is like other music festivals, we'll sit outside sipping various mixed drinks while soaking in the music. People will chatter now and then, but not about anything serious. If I had to pick the least emotionally fraught place for my parents to meet Audra again, this would be it.

"Okay," I say. I pick up my phone and dial. "Can you pick me up early? We all want to go to the Fez."

"We?" Audra's voice cracks in surprise.

"Yeah. Mom promises not to embarrass us. Do you mind?"

"No," Audra says, and she makes her 'no' into the most joyous affirmation I've ever heard. "No. But are you sure?"

I glance at Grandma who sleeps peacefully, and Mom whose hair has begun to show gray from underneath her careful home dye jobs.

"Yes," I say. "Hurry."

But no matter how long she takes, the relentless milkman will never climb our stairs again.

OPEN

WATERS

VALERIE MORES

The wind wrapped around Jane, salty and cold, caressing her like a lover and teasing her wild, golden, curly mane. She closed her eyes, allowing herself to indulge in its comfort and wash away the memories that dared whisper against her consciousness. The past was the past. All that mattered right now was the present and the future. And what a glorious future she imagined it would be.

With a smirk, she opened her eyes and barked, "Coll: speed?!"

"Steady at seven and a half knots, Captain," the man's voice sounded from port side, rising above the crash of the waves.

Jane took another look through her spyglass at the large galleon cruising beyond the bow of the *Tantibus*, hovering just below the horizon. She frowned. They hadn't bridged the gap much since they started trailing the ship and the news was worrying. Considering the speed the *Tantibus* was traveling, she should have made excellent ground.

"Worth," she called out, into the organized chaos of sweaty bodies below on the main deck. A well-built man, skin tanned by the sun, with a mop of dirty, brown hair, broke apart from the others, taking just three leaps up the stairs before settling in his place at her side. "Take a look," she commanded, handing over the spyglass to her first mate and nodding her head toward the merchant ship. "Would you say she's riding low?"

Worth took the device and brought it up to his right eye, pointing it toward their prize. "No, she doesn't appear to be," he stated after a minute, scowling. He handed her back the spyglass.

Silence fell over them, with only the constant slap of the sea against the hull and the steady clamor of her crew ensuring the ship stayed on course and afloat filling in the background. She hummed in consideration and took another glance through the spyglass to ensure she wasn't completely imagining things. Finally, with a sigh, she was forced to admit that yes, her suspicions were entirely correct, as usual. Why couldn't she be wrong just this once?

Jane spun on her heel, facing the main deck. "Pull in the sails!" she shouted, gesturing to the men below, who paused and gazed up in confusion. "Bring her back around! North!"

"But Captain," a voice—Coll—sounded from amidst the men about the main deck, "what about the galleon? The loot?"

"She's not carrying. Nothing but a decoy," she stated coldly.

There were several groans of annoyance equal from amongst the crew. It meant extending their days at sea for another week or so as they chased down the true merchant ship and delivered the stolen goods back to their cache, and her men were already restless. They had been at sea for only a few days, but she had promised them a quick plunder, as the last port they'd docked at only housed them for a few hours. Not enough time for them to drink their fill or have a decent lay. Jane knew what her men needed and took great care to fulfill their desires, lest they decide having a woman as captain wasn't worth it.

She'd sailed with at least half these men going on ten years now, through her first couple of years aboard the *Tantibus* and as she climbed her way through the ranks, and these last few years as she captained. There had been a rough patch in the transition, when the captain at the time had suddenly decided he didn't much approve of her growing popularity and strove to throw her overboard on the standard notion that it was bad luck to have a woman aboard, despite the fact that she had been aboard his ship for years and he had displayed no concern towards her presence before. But she remembered that day fondly, as the crew turned on the then-captain, throwing their loyalties towards her instead. And once the man had been properly mutinied, the rest of the crew had argued over who should be his replacement. That was when Worth had spoken up, his voice booming out over the rest and nominated her. Yes, there had been some objections, but a majority seemed open enough to the idea that the notion passed. So, she'd found herself the newly-instated captain of the *Tantibus* and had been ever since.

Jane smiled at the memory. It hadn't been easy, that was for sure, but Worth had been there to help her out every step of the way. He had been her first real friend aboard the ship—despite his intimidating size, he was in truth, kind-hearted, at least to her—and one of the few who hadn't at one point or another, tried to proposition her like a whore. Of course, they all soon found that she wasn't one they wanted to mess with. Worth, she trusted, but she knew if his goals ever swayed from her own, she wouldn't hesitate to let him go. This was not a profession one could afford to be merciful and caring in. For now, though, they were aligned perfectly.

So really, it had been no contest who she'd wanted as her first mate. Jane glanced over at Worth, watching him berate a fellow crew member on his poor ability to adjust the main sheet. She knew she could probably have come to love him if they had met under different circumstances.

In another life, perhaps. But as it was, she had never been truly able to get past Thomas and the loss she had suffered.

Sorrow washed over Jane like the waves that surrounded her as the memories came unhindered now, despite her attempts to keep them back. They had grown up together, she and Thomas Avery, known each other since she could hardly walk. Being just a few years apart had never really mattered to them; he was the one who taught her how to fight with a blade at a very tender age, running over to teach her all he learned that day from his father. And later, he'd showed her how to fire a pistol. He had been the one to show her what it was like to be free, to live outside the rules of her household, to stand up for herself despite her gender, to be bold and daring, and later, to love. She couldn't remember the day she knew, the day she could feel their relationship change into something more. It had just happened. She came to realize she loved him, and had always loved him.

And she couldn't have been happier.

"Lost, Captain?" Worth questioned with a grin. The humor behind the question failed to bring a smile to her face as she continued to unconsciously stroke the charred wedding ring that hung on a silver chain around her neck. Worth must have seen the lack of reaction from her, as a beat later, he asked seriously, "Everything alright?"

He didn't know of her past. None of them did. And Jane had no desire to remedy that.

She grunted, her lips quirking as she leaned heavily on the railing. "Just don't like being played a fool. Nor the Navy's poor excuse for an attempt at it," she lied. Nevertheless, she mused, it *was* true, just not the reason for her current mood.

Worth let out a hearty chuckle at that. "Aye, but only you would call such a ruse a poor excuse." He gazed beyond the stern back toward the now slowly-disappearing dot that was the Royal Navy's decoy galleon. "I'm sure they'll try harder next time."

Jane allowed a small smile to cross her features. "Hopefully there won't be a next time," she said, giving Worth a sidelong glance.

The Royal Navy thought her a fool, she knew, but truly, this was just insulting. No matter, they would find she wasn't one they should strive to insult eventually.

Jane huffed at the thought. She really must be mad. Normally, she tried to avoid the Royal Navy at all costs. Their warships were something to behold and definitely not a force to be trifled with. Though, she knew some captains and their crew living under the piracy name that made it their life goal to bugger the Royal Navy, sinking crew down along with the ship without offering them a position under their flag. Jane however, had never felt the desire to stoop so low. The Royal Navy had never done her any wrong, save for attempting to prevent her from pillaging as she pleased, but that was more of a nuisance than an actual danger. She was indifferent to them, but if pressed, she would say she didn't enjoy their antipiracy laws and tactics. That just encouraged her to steer clear of their damned ships.

That is, until now.

Just a few weeks ago, while restocking in Port Nempth, Jane had gotten wind through her illustrious network that a merchant ship was departing from Port Farray to Port Hempsey to deliver fifty-six casks of gunpowder, a good number of 12-pounders, and various ammunition to the Royal Navy. And that just wouldn't do. There had also been rumors going around the taverns and whorehouses that the Royal Navy was amassing an armada big enough to hunt down and take out every pirate ship in British waters. It was a daunting thought, that her way of life could be threatened so easily. Again.

And she'd be damned if she didn't do anything about it this time.

Pillaging the armed merchant ship was the first step she and her crew were to take in what was bound to be a bloody battle between the Royal Navy and the various pirating vessels across the sea. She had no doubt that despite the united front some pirate captains put out, these were still pirates, and pirates usually lived by an every-man-for-himself rule. She garnered it wouldn't hurt to get a head start stockpiling for the war to come. Besides, she could use the ammunition. The better armed the *Tantibus* was, the better chance she had at surviving the upcoming war.

"What now, Captain?" Worth asked.

Jane remained silent as she continued to stare out at the vast expanse of ocean before her, fingers tracing the cracks and mars of the ring around her neck unconsciously. "There was another ship at port," she said after a beat. "The *Liberty*—dreadful name for a ship, honestly—she's the one we're after."

Worth hesitated for a moment. Jane could see his mind calculating, whirling like the wind around them. Soon enough, he was nodding in agreement. "But we've no idea where she's heading. Clearly, Landry's information was wrong, so she may not even be heading to Port Hempsey."

"No, she's definitely not, else we would have spotted her by now," Jane remarked assuredly. Her mind was calculating now, putting all the pieces into place, trying to stay a step ahead of her prize, even as she found herself a few steps behind. No matter, she'd make sure they caught up in no time.

"Then where? Kingsley?" Worth asked.

"Precisely," she confirmed with a nod. "It houses the only other Royal Navy stronghold close enough to Port Farray. That's where she'll be heading."

Worth gave another nod as he, too, gazed out at the sea before them. "She's got a head start. Leagues away by now."

"Aye," Jane agreed, her smirk growing into a knowing grin, "but she's weighed down by fifty-six casks. We'll catch up in a day or two. Long before she reaches port."

~~*

A day and a half was all it took.

By just a day's mark, Newby's call echoed down from the crow's nest to Jane and the crew on the main deck. All eyes cast about, quickly finding the pearl white sails of the Liberty highlighted against the cerulean horizon.

The merchant galleon was sure a sight to behold. Larger than the *Tantibus*—which was a sixth-rate frigate with only twenty cannons aboard, but had the advantage of speed and ease of maneuverability in the waters—with multiple decks, each of them housing several cannons, including two chasers on the main deck. In all, Jane concluded there were at least thirty aboard, plus seventy to eighty crewmen aboard with who knew what kind of combat training. In firepower, they were almost equal, but in crewmen, the *Liberty* outnumbered them two to one—if Jane's assumptions were correct, that is. And they almost always were. The boarding of the ship alone would be a challenge, but the fight to keep it would be even greater. She knew the risk, and had known from the beginning. Her men were more than capable of taking the galleon.

She just had to make sure they agreed to her insane plan.

"Gentlemen!" Jane crowed, as her men donned their weapons and loaded themselves up for the battle ahead. Metal screeched as swords were sharpened, ropes creaked as they were tightened around the cannons, and the click of pistols being loaded and cocked reverberated around the main deck. "Gather about."

A circle formed around her, men shuffling, their boots scraping the deck as all eyes looked to her for direction. This was when the thrill of the fight ahead and the adrenaline pumping through her veins began, filling her up and making her feel well and truly alive. She lived for these moments. It was at times like these that she could see the trust and loyalty these men had in her, in what she could do and what she could give them. She could see it in their eyes. They would follow her to the edge of the world and back again if she so demanded it.

For now, she'd just settle for capturing the *Liberty*.

"We all know the prestige of royal galleons. Outfitted with the best guns and cannons, made to withstand attacks and continue on to port like nothing happened. But we have the advantage here. She may be bigger and better at most things, but she doesn't have the speed and agility of the *Tantibus*. We've faced worse odds before and look, we're still here. And stronger than ever!" Cries of agreement rose up from the crew as Jane's words riled them up. Good. The more riled they were, the more unpredictable they would be once the fight began. Unpredictable meant victory.

Jane took a breath, and shifted her weight, restless with the thrum of excitement and continued, "If we can damage her rigging with a few shots from the bow chaser, we'll be able to get the *Tantibus* close enough to board and the *Liberty* won't be going anywhere. She's a newer model, so she's lacking the stern-chasers and won't be able to return fire without a turn. Which, with the disabled rigging, will not be possible. With her incapacitated, we get to choose the side of attack. She's strongest portside, so we'll match her starboard side. Despite this, she'll still think she can rake us through in just a few shots. What she won't be expecting is a boarding mid-pass."

Several voices rose in complaint, but Jane quickly shut them down with a raised hand.

"Yes, I know it's a gamble and those that take on that task are at risk of being picked off. But I believe it will catch them enough off-guard that we can get at least a dozen men aboard to start taking their crew out. Most of her men will be below deck, manning the cannons, so just taking out those above will leave fewer cannons to be loosed as men come above to take their places."

She watched as some heads nodded in agreement, and others looked about trying to gauge their fellow crewmembers' opinions.

Soon enough, Cooksley spoke up, his arrogant voice rising above the murmur of the other men, "Aye, but there's only so many men a man can take on before he's downed. It's suicide, Captain. It'll never work and I, for one, don't fancy losing my life over something as half-brained as that." He looked about him, trying to gauge the reaction of his statements in the rest of the crew. Jane almost laughed out loud. Being malicious and ruthless had gained him little support amongst the crew. Besides, the last attempt at mutiny back when Jane had been newly captained hadn't gone too well. Those involved still lay at the bottom of the ocean somewhere. Cooksley may desire her position but the odds of obtaining it were not in his favor.

Jane held up a finger. "Not with Coll, Newby, and myself picking them off from here."

The crew was silent, digesting the plan with furrowed brows and hard lines. But Jane just smiled confidently. Making a pass at the *Liberty* with her full strength would leave the *Tantibus* vulnerable to significant damage. Sliding into the *Liberty*'s wake and firing their cannons at her stern would make a smaller target and delay boarding to its fullest. Jane knew from experience that the longer she waited to board, the more the crew was prepared for it and could fight them off. Quick and easy, that was the trick. Her plan was a new one, but they had never taken on a full-fledged merchant galleon before. A galleon warship would have been another matter and most likely impossible for the *Tantibus* and her crew, but as a merchant ship, the *Liberty* had to lower the amount of defenses in order to make room for more goods. And although the Liberty was carrying powder and ammunition of all sorts, she was not equipped to fight with most of it.

And it played out better than she would have thought possible.

Worth had volunteered—as Jane knew he would—to be one of the first men to board and he amounted to most of their success. The man was a fighter, parrying, blocking, and jabbing his sword in expertly-practiced maneuvers. Jane barked a laugh as she watched him twist his body and disarm his opponent with a flick of his wrist. She had taught him the move.

This was what she lived for, what she loved: the fight, the battle, watching her tactical plans play out before her, even if she wasn't down there in the fray of it all. The weight of the gun was enough, the smell of the gunpowder, and the quick, deft movements of her hands as she loaded another shot, downing the *Liberty's* crewmen one by one as they got in her crew's way.

"Secure!" Worth shouted from the *Liberty's* deck.

Jane got to her feet leisurely, striding over and swinging aboard the *Liberty*. Her boots thudded against the wooden deck as she landed gracefully, looking about the main deck. The *Liberty's* twelve remaining crew members were now kneeling, bloodied and beaten, before five of her own, guns and swords alike trained upon their bowed heads. The stench of sweat and blood hung in the air, only swept away occasionally by the sweet, salty breeze that washed over the sea.

"Ship's ours, Captain," Newby stated with a smug look. Jane smiled as she performed an exaggerated bow to the men—both hers and their new captives—before striding over to the hatch in the middle of the deck and ascending the steep stairs toward the hold. She felt the giddiness that usually preceded a successful mission take over the further she descended. It didn't matter how many ships she took nor what treasures they held aboard, a successful mission never failed give her a rush of pride and accomplishment, to make her feel like this life she led was what she truly wanted, what she was *good* at. That this was enough, had to be enough, *needed* to be enough.

"What have we got, lads?" Jane crowed to her men scattered about the hold.

Coll stepped forward, his eyes roaming over the sheet of paper in his hands. "Fifty-two casks of powder, two thousand rounds of shot, eighteen twelve-pounders, and one hundred and fifty new guns."

Jane hummed in mock discontent. "Four casks short. How disappointing."

The answering laughter brought a smile back to Jane's face. She ventured further into the space, inspecting the various casks and goods about the hold.

"We can't take the twelve-pounders. Those will have to stay, unfortunately," she stated sadly and a grumble of disappointed agreement rose from the men around her, "but we can use the shot and the casks—"

"She'll be weighed down heavily, Captain," Coll stated matter-of-factly.

Jane nodded, brushing her fingers over one of the casks. "Aye, I am well aware. But if we are indeed heading for a war, these casks will be invaluable to us. More so than they will be at the bottom of the ocean."

Coll paused for a beat. "Aye."

Jane nodded to him, running her hand lazily over another cask before striding back through the hold toward the ladder. When she reached it, she turned back and addressed the men below, "Any food or supplies that are found may be brought aboard at the approval of Coll. Let's load her up, boys, and get the hell off this bloody Navy ship!"

A cheer of "Aye, Captain!" followed Jane as she made her way back up to the main deck. Coll, as the quartermaster going on ten years now, knew everything that went on about the *Tantibus*, including what goods they had and could carry without sinking the ship. He was in charge of getting everything aboard and then ensuring the *Liberty* sank to the bottom of the ocean, along with the goods they would be unable to take. And he was damn good at it.

"Captain!" Worth's call echoed down the hatch, the tone not so much urgent, but certainly hinting at a necessity that mustn't be ignored. It was a tone Jane knew quite well now, one that told her that whatever it was, it was a nuisance, but still required her attention in order for it to be resolved. Jane ran a hand through her hair with a sigh. Everything had been going so well.

She quickly ascended the stairs, the thud of her boots drumming out an ominous beat. But everything on the main deck was as she remembered, give or take a handful of captive crew, and the addition of Worth from god knows where.

She looked at him expectantly.

Worth gave her an annoyed look, aimed not at her, but at whatever had given him cause to call her. "Captain's quarters," he said with a jerk of his head toward the stern, where the mentioned quarters lay. "Their captain wishes to speak with you."

Jane's eyebrows rose incredulously. "And why must I be made to go to him? It is he who should be out here with the rest of his bloody crew," she said, gesturing to the men still kneeling on deck.

"It's..." Worth paused, "complicated, Captain. There's a matter of leverage."

"Ah," Jane nodded, making her way over to the captain's quarters, "of course there is. I knew this had gone too smoothly."

Worth let out a huff of amusement as he followed behind her, "Don't even try to deny it, you love surprises. Smooth was never to your liking."

Jane waved a hand flippantly in the air. "I will neither confirm nor deny this," she answered with a smile, a glint of mischief in her eye. When things went perfectly according to plan, the element of surprise for her was removed. No shock, no spike in adrenaline, no skip of the heart. If there wasn't at least one unexpected person vying for your heart on the end of their blade, where was the fun in that?

"Gentlemen," Jane announced with an air of aloofness, coupled with arrogance, as she strode leisurely through the open doors to the Captain's quarters. "What seems to be the problem?"

Millett, one of the older, shorter, but no less equipped, men of her crew, stood off to the side, his pistol aimed at what appeared to be nothing more than standard hostage situation in the middle of the room. The first was a man, grey-bearded and stocky, his belly rivaling that of a pregnant woman. But it was the other that mostly obscured this man that caught Jane by surprise—and a little off-guard, she admitted somewhat reluctantly—causing her to pause for a second to ensure that no, she wasn't imagining things. For there, held at knifepoint at the throat—and being used as a human shield—by what had to have been the captain of the galleon, was a common whore.

Well, maybe "common" was too harsh of a word. She was indeed very beautiful. Though, Jane mused, that was the standard for whores, was it not? They needed to entice future clients with their, uh, coveted features and whatnot. So, the skin-baring dress that displayed her occupation with the utmost certainty, exhibiting a delectable helping of cleavage, peeking ankles, and forearms, came as no surprise to Jane. She was lean, but no doubt well-endowed where it mattered to her clientele, with a full head of dark brown tresses that were falling out of the hastily-woven knot secured to the back of her head. But it was the whore's eyes, a soft, light brown with a spark of fire running through them that really caught Jane's attention. Thinly-veiled defiance, that's what it was. She was no fan of her situation any more than Jane was. But outwardly, the whore seemed bored and annoyed more than fearful. It was intriguing to say the least.

What shocked Jane, though, was the fact that the whore was here aboard the ship at all. It was bad luck to have a woman aboard; every sailor knew that, and—her strangely lenient crew aside—most believed wholeheartedly in such nonsense. Jane tried not to roll her eyes every time she heard men speak of the absurd superstition, because her time at sea was clear evidence to disprove it. Granted, despite seeing her in passing or being boarded and attacked by her and her crew, her gender still remained but a rumor at most. Most captains and crewmen believed the notorious pirate Captain Avery was not the woman few claimed her to be, but was, in fact, a man. No woman could ever be a captain, let alone a successful one.

"What is—who the fuck is this?!" The man snarled in Jane's direction. "I asked for your captain, you rats, not some fucking cunt!" he spat at Worth and Millett. Then he turned his attention back toward Jane as she gazed back at him with cool indifference. "Bring me the captain this instant or I'll slit her pretty little throat." The man brought the knife closer to the whore's bared throat, emphasizing his absurdly futile point.

A beat passed in the cabin before all three pirates burst out laughing.

"You think I care about the life of some whore?" Jane asked incredulously, once she had calmed. "You believe I'm going to just leave you alone, spare your fucking life, because of some misguided morals or good conscience that you think I have? Have you no idea what has become of your crew?" She gestured out toward the bow of the galleon, where the remaining crew of the Liberty still knelt, awaiting judgment from her. She let out another bark of a laugh. "Believe me, I have no conscience and my morals are not in your favor."

The man didn't even miss a beat as he sneered back at her. "Why should I care what some wench believes?! Fetch your captain so that we may talk man-to-man instead of him hiding behind some woman!"

Jane cocked an eyebrow, gesturing to the man and his current predicament. "Isn't that what you're doing? Hiding behind some woman?"

Silence fell over the room for a moment as the portly man digested the accusation. But soon enough, his face morphed once again into a sneer and he held tighter to the whore, her skin almost white with the strength in which he grasped her. But her bored look only turned to one of disgust just as the air of annoyance remained ever-present. "Just get your captain, you cunt, or I spill her blood right here."

A cocky smirk expanded across Jane's face. She leaned forward ever-so-slightly toward the galleon's captain, and tipped her hat down further in what she hoped was construed as an insulting mock salute. "I *am* the captain, mate."

Jane watched with amusement as various emotions flashed across the man's face in quick succession, from calculating to confusion to disbelief, before finally settling on hard anger.

In the next moment, he snarled and shoved the knife he was holding closer to the whore, nicking the skin on her neck in the process. Jane rolled her eyes. She could see that the man wouldn't kill the only hostage he had, the only thing that he believed, however foolishly, was his ticket out of here with his life still intact. He was but a greedy merchant sailor playing at a Navy ship captain. There was no way he would be able to kill her. He didn't have the stomach for it.

"The way I see it, you have two choices," Jane sighed, stepping back and folding her arms across her chest. "One: you release the whore and join your fellow sailors out on the main deck for a little... chat, where you may just get out of this alive. That remains to be determined, as you have now not only offended and annoyed me, but also delayed my voyage. Or two: you could continue to stand there, naively thinking I'm going to let you go simply because I wish to spare the life of this woman—whom I do not know or care about—and know that your life is forfeit. Your choice, sailor. But at the moment, the whore has a better chance of living than you do, and she currently has a knife to her throat."

The captain's eyes flickered between Jane, Worth, and Millett uncertainly, his face a mix of hatred and disbelief. A moment passed, then two, in this fashion until Jane was at the end of her patience.

"I don't have time for this," she huffed in annoyance. Before the galleon captain could even register Jane's words, she pulled her pistol from her belt, aimed, and shot the man in the head in one fluid motion, the bullet missing the whore's temple by a hair's breadth.

The knife clattered to the floor, the sound ominous after the great reverberation of the pistol as the captain's body followed with a thud. The smell of gunpowder filled the room.

"Right then," Millett proclaimed, looking slightly shocked, but masking it well enough. Jane just shrugged and stashed her pistol back into her belt.

Movement by the body caught all three pirates' eyes and glanced over toward where the whore still stood. The woman straightened from her forced hunch, brushing her revealing dress out and then stepped over the outstretched arm of the now-dead captain. She could see Worth and Millett staring at the whore with equal measures of shock and confusion.

Jane just snorted in amusement.

The whore glanced up, her eyes displaying her continued boredom even as she took note of the three pirates currently staring at her. "Wha'?" she asked, a slight accent in her voice. She crossed her arms over her chest as her eyes flitted over each of them in turn.

Worth was the first to react, brow pinched. "Well, I was expecting more of a reaction, to be honest."

The whore just cocked an eyebrow, shifting her weight suggestively. "Sorry ta disappoint, love," she responded coolly, voice low and sultry. "I can put on quite a performance, though, if ya'd rather." A mask of pure seduction dropped over her features in an instant, her body language following not far behind.

Jane found herself staring at the whore with wonder. The way she seemed unfazed by the threat on her life, how she showed very little interest in the danger she was in, or the sort of people surrounding her, was surprising. And yes, very impressive, for lack of a better word. Any other person—any other *woman*—

would have shown at least an ounce of fear or horror at what had just occurred. Instead, the whore just slipped back into her promiscuous persona, hooding her eyes and canting her hips and inviting all with her voluptuous bosom.

Jane shook her head, clearing her thoughts. That wasn't the point. The point was this whore went about like nothing had happened, like a man didn't just die right beside her. She was just a *whore.* Jane was immediately wary, and made a mental note to keep an eye on the seductive woman.

But a part of her couldn't help but see the parallels of their two very different lives, and wondered if the whore too had unknowingly entered her profession. And she pitied the poor creature before her.

Well, not that much."

Enough," Jane commanded. They had wasted more than their allotted time already. Every second they wasted aboard this ship was another second added to their travels and another second they risked getting apprehended by the Royal Navy. Jane looked over the whore once more before making a split-second decision. "She's coming with us. Bring her out." With that, Jane left the captain's quarters, not bothering to glance back to ensure her orders were followed. She knew they would be.

The remaining crew of the galleon were still kneeling where Jane had seen them last, though there were now only nine captive men instead of the twelve that were there previously. That didn't concern her much, nor surprise her, upon seeing that Cooksley was one of the guards, a wicked smile playing over his face as he caressed one of the men with the blade of his sword.

"I'm sure you lot know how this goes," Jane spoke to the kneeling men, letting a bit of arrogance slip into her tone. "You can either join up with my crew, or take a little swim, like a few of your mates have already experienced, I assume." She looked pointedly at Cooksley.

Cooksley just flashed her a smirk. "They were being... troublesome."

"Yes, I'm sure they were."

Suddenly, the smirk upon Cooksley's face morphed, becoming more hostile, more... predatory, she realized, as his eyes locked onto something just over Jane's shoulder. A chill ran down her spine at that look. It was the same look the man had gotten when he had first laid eyes on her, when he had tried to coerce her into... unsavory acts. A wave of protective anger washed over Jane so strongly that it took her by surprise. It was a feeling she hadn't felt in years, a feeling she hadn't *let* herself feel. But this one had come on much stronger than ever before. She pushed it back forcefully, burying it under a layer of indifference, logic, and tactic. But Jane knew immediately the reason behind it, a reason that now stood next to her, held firmly, but not roughly, in Worth's grasp. The whore.

"Well, now, what do we have here?" Cooksley purred, his eyes glinting with desire as they roved over the newest arrival. He took a step closer. Anger built up in Jane again and she had to forcefully restrain herself from stepping between Cooksley and the woman. She was just a whore. Why should Jane care?

Ignoring the way Cooksley kept staring at the whore—and with a quick glance, Jane noticed the whore displaying the same disgust she had toward the Liberty's captain—Jane strode up to the first man in the line, a thin, lean thing with a mop of deep black hair and a cut upon his forehead that was bleeding profusely. "Name?" she demanded.

"Isaac Demply," the wisp of a man responded with a sneer as he stared at her with steel in his eyes. Jane just raised her eyebrows.

"Well, what'll it be, Mr. Demply?" Jane asked haughtily. Though from the man's cold answer of his name, she could gather what his response would be already. It was the usual with most of the crew they captured. Most, even if they were not completely averse to switching sides, were neither too keen on sailing with nor taking orders from a woman. Most would rather take their chances in the cold waters below and hope for a passing ship or uncharted island. It was absurd, really. Like she would let them go that easily.

Unsurprisingly, Demply spat at her feet. "You can go to hell."

Jane sighed, glancing over at Mundy and upon catching his eye, jerking her head toward the open sea. She watched as Mundy hauled the thin man to his feet and dragged him over to the edge. She turned back to the rest of the captured crew and, hearing the sound of steel slicing through flesh and a splash off to the side a second later, flashed them all a smile.

"Anyone else?"

As it turned out, indeed, four others opted to join their fellow crew member overboard—whether it was truly their choice or not—rather than subject themselves to a woman's leadership and a life of pirating, while the remaining four swore their loyalty. Jane doubted they meant it. Most who did would try to escape the second the *Tantibus* docked ashore. And most who attempted such a thing were killed not long afterwards. Her crew was observant and knew when a new member was itching to flee. They took care of traitors quickly. She had taught them well.

"Captain," a voice sounded behind her and she turned to face the new arrival. Coll stood before her, slightly out of breath, his hair plastered to his forehead with sweat. "The last of the goods are being loaded as we speak. She's set."

"Brilliant. Poke some holes in her hull before you leave," she grinned at him. Coll nodded and disappeared back below the Liberty's deck as Jane turned away, addressing the men around her at large. "Let's go home, boys!"

A cheer answered her announcement and the crew, including the newest members, made their way back aboard the *Tantibus*. Jane watched with a frown as Cooksley's eyes wandered over the whore, having never left her striking form once since she had emerged on deck. It caused another wave of rage to build up in Jane's gut, which she tried unsuccessfully to ignore. What the hell was wrong with her?

Worth guided the whore before him across the plank between the two ships, keeping hold of her arm as both a stabilizer and a prevention technique. They still didn't know the whore or her intentions. For all they knew, she was just as spiteful as the other recruited crew members and just managed to mask it well. What made Jane spare her life, she herself didn't even know. She hadn't even offered the woman a choice.

Jane frowned, stroking her ring absentmindedly as she stared after the woman. What was it about this whore that made Jane act so irrationally? Innocent life or not, Jane never extended them the same treatment she did the other members of the captured ship's crew. Was it perhaps the fact that she was a woman? That must have been it, for what else could it be? Until they made it to the next port, she would just have to ignore the whore's gender and treat her like the prisoner she now was.

That thought however flew out of Jane's mind as, once she reached the *Tantibus*, the whore was pulled from Worth's grasp by Cooksley, that predatory glint in his eye once more.

"What a pretty little thing you are," Jane heard Cooksley growl, as he pulled her flush against him "What's your name, sweetheart?"

The whore glared up at him, the fire of defiance ablaze in her eyes. "None of ya concern, ya rat." She growled.

"It's Cecily, and she is a feisty one, I tell ya," spoke a short, pudgy man from the new recruits, the grin on his face telling all he knew this fact firsthand. The crew laughed, the sound making Jane's blood boil and with hurried steps, she closed the gap and gracefully leaped down upon the deck of her ship.

"Cecily," Cooksley hummed, running his hands along her hips in an exceedingly inappropriate manner.

And for the first time, the whore—Cecily, the man had said her name was—displayed the defiance that Jane had thought she had seen bubbling just under the surface when they were in the captain's quarters. She slapped Cooksley's hands away with anger, no longer trying to mask her disgust. But whether it was disgust for Cooksley himself or for being brought aboard the *Tantibus* against her will, Jane didn't know. She didn't much care, either, for she was feeling that overwhelming anger and protectiveness at the former.

Her hand automatically strayed to the hilt of her sword as she planted her feet in a clear challenge a few paces away from where Cooksley was petting and smirking down at a struggling Cecily. The slither of metal against leather brought silence down upon the crew and all eyes found Jane as she leveled her sword toward Cooksley. "Unhand her immediately or I shall slit your throat and wash the deck in your blood."

"Captain..." Worth warned, and she saw him glance at her uncertainly in her periphery. She could only imagine how it must look, the captain threatening the life of one of her own crew over the well-being of some whore. He must think her mad, they all must. Jane just wished she would allow herself to give a fuck.

"Aw, come on, Captain," Cooksley purred, brushing Cecily's hair aside to get to her neck. Cecily tried to pull away again, a look of loathing on her face. But there was nowhere to go, not with a meaty arm wrapped across her chest. She only managed to flinch away, which just bared her neck further. "We've been at sea for weeks now. And we have so graciously saved this woman's life. I think she owes us."

"I don't owe ya anythin'," Cecily spat. Then she rammed her elbow hard into Cooksley's stomach. The breath left him in a forceful exhale, but he didn't release his hold on her, even as she squirmed in his arms, practically growling in her frustration.

Jane just squared her shoulders and glared hard at Cooksley. "Do not make me repeat myself, Cooksley," she threatened, her voice low and cold: a warning. One that all her men knew was foolish to challenge. She had never lost one, not yet, and she damn well didn't plan to start now.

There was a moment, just a moment where Jane was sure he was going to continue on and do something rash all in the name of defiance. But then he relaxed, shoving Cecily away from him with a shrug and a flippant gesture, as though he couldn't care less about some whore. Like she wasn't worth it. Just that gesture alone almost caused Jane to run him through right then and there, damn the consequences.

"Take her to my quarters," she ordered Worth, without taking her eyes off of Cooksley. When Worth, with Cecily now safely in his grasp, had been swallowed up in the throng of crew, Jane relaxed her stance and sheathed her sword. She looked about, glaring at her men with all the authority she could muster. "As for the rest of you, this woman is not to be harmed in anyway whilst aboard this ship. Is that understood?"

Nods and "ayes" sounded in answer from the men before her, but she took note that Cooksley did neither and his features remained coolly detached. He was going to continue to be a problem, she could tell. "If any of you so much as touch her, you will be taking a little trip down to Davy Jones for a permanent stay."

And without waiting for any other replies or protests, Jane strode toward her quarters, the line of crew parting respectfully to let her pass.

As she approached, Worth exited the quarters, his face neutral, despite the strange way his captain was acting. Or at least she assumed he thought it strange. She certainly did and she was the one who was acting as such. Frankly, it scared her.

"Order the men to disengage from the *Liberty* and set sail for the island immediately," Jane ordered in a tone perhaps a little too harsh for talking to the first mate who had shown her no ill will. "I want to unload this lot before the Navy even realizes one of her ships has disappeared."

"Aye, Captain," Worth answered with a nod before looking over at the slowly-sinking galleon. His brow was furrowed and she could tell he was contemplating something, but was hesitant to speak.

She sighed, pausing to turn and face him. "What is it, Worth? Spit it out."

His light azure eyes found hers as he crossed his arms over his chest and jerked his head toward her quarters. "What do you plan to do with her?" Jane noticed he failed to add her title, but it bothered her little.

She was more focused on finding an answer to his question, for she hadn't the slightest idea. She had acted on instinct: an instinct that hadn't arisen in her in years. An instinct she had thought she had gotten over and moved past so she could live, breathe, and not have to deal with loss, pain, and heartache. Clearly, that wasn't the case. There was something about Cecily, something that sparked a... feeling—no, that wasn't it. She really couldn't place it, to be honest. But it was there, and it made her act in ways she normally wouldn't have.

But she needed to tell Worth something, needed to assure him that his Captain was still here and still in her right mind, even if she felt far from it.

"I plan to drop her off at the next port and be done with her. But I refuse to listen to the men fight over her until that can be done," she stated, hoping it came off nonchalant.

Worth stared at her for a second longer, his eyes searching her for who knew what. She kept her face impassive and her body relaxed, slipping back into her arrogant persona with ease. And Worth seemed to accept it, for with another nod, he turned and started relaying her orders to the men.

Jane stared after him, wondering what sort of gossip she may have just incited before deciding she didn't much care and strode into her chambers, closing the door behind her.

~~*

"So, ya are the Captain?" a silky voice drawled from the depths of her quarters. Jane turned around, unbuttoning her coat, expecting to find Cecily standing in the center, awaiting her. But the whore was not there, and Jane cocked an eyebrow at finding the woman lounging in her chair at the table littered with maps and notes. She almost laughed out loud at the sight, but quickly composed her expression into one of annoyance.

"I would have thought that obvious by now, *my lady*," Jane retorted, sarcasm dripping from the title as she hung her coat by the door.

Cecily just picked up the compass from the table, twirling it idly between long, lithe fingers and chuckled, "I am no lady."

Jane huffed. "Yes, that much is clear."

Ignoring her, Jane approached the other side of the table and glanced down at the map, running her fingers across its surface. They were a great distance from their cache island, one that lay almost on the far side of the mainland and past a few ports that, if not given a wide berth, could prove problematic. But they had done longer and more risky trips before, and she knew that they could make it in a few weeks with minimal stops.

One, of course, would be to drop off the strange creature now sprawled in her chair, seeming to not have a care in the world for her predicament.

"Do ya have a name?" Cecily probed, breaking the silence. Jane continued staring at the map, hoping to maintain the precious quiet. But it seemed Cecily had never learned that silence was a virtue. "Or shall I just call ya 'Cap'ain'?" she finished, and Jane could feel the whore's eyes upon her, scrutinizing her. She tried once again to ignore it, but couldn't help the miniscule shiver that ran down her spine.

Jane sighed, not even having to try very hard to sound exasperated. "Have we not just established that I am indeed the captain? There is no need to call me anything but."

The creak of the chair followed her proclamation as Cecily got up. Jane stole a quick glance up to see the woman straighten out her dress before once again focusing on the map before her. "If tha' is wha' ya wish... Cap'ain," she stated in a sultry voice, the words like a caress, silky and warm as they flowed through the room.

A tantalizingly sweet smell assaulted Jane's nose seconds before arms wrapped around her chest, fingers finding the buttons on her outer corset and managing to undo one. Jane whirled and slapped the hands away in one fluid motion, shock having wiped away her arrogance in a flash, and she scrambled to replace it with annoyance and insult, even as she felt her cheeks flush.

"What *are* you doing?" Jane demanded as she glared at Cecily, appalled and unable to rid her airways of the sweet smell that surrounded Cecily. Or whatever it was that she carried to make her smell so sweet. It was, Jane had to admit, not all that unpleasant. "I am not one of your clients."

Cecily just stared back, heat in her eyes, causing Jane's cheeks to flare up once again. She wished Cecily would stop, truly she did, but at the same time felt that spark inside her alight, stronger than before. She squashed it forcefully. And despite not understanding what was happening to her right now, Jane knew that whatever it was, it made her vulnerable, and she would not have that. She needed to regain control now.

Cecily took a step forward and Jane took one back in response, making her pause and stay her ground. A quick flash of hurt crossed Cecily's face before being replaced once more with a confident, sultry look. It happened so fast that Jane was sure she had imagined it. "Why else would ya have taken me ta ya quarters?" Cecily asked.

"Would you rather be out there?" Jane inquired, gesturing toward the doors and the main deck beyond. "I cannot stop them from taking what they will from you, *my lady*, if they are so inclined to do so."

"I was under the impression tha' it was ya who desired somethin' from me." Cecily shifted her stance to one more inviting, one that begged for attention, and Jane had no doubt it was successful at getting it, seeing as she herself had to try hard to ignore it.

But she managed, crossing her arms defensively. "A very poor impression, I can assure you."

Cecily cocked her eyebrow, disbelief evident upon her face. "Everyone wants a little somethin', even ya."

Jane shook her head. "Nothing but to drop you off at the nearest port and be on my way."

"Then why even take me at'll?" Cecily asked, disbelief morphing into confusion as the seductive act dropped to reveal a hint of the woman beneath.

"Would you have rather stayed?" Jane questioned.

A frown creased Cecily's face as she defended, "At least there, I was earnin' my keep."

That statement took Jane by surprise. She knew how these sorts of things worked, how a whore earned her living and how they were hired. But normally that was ashore and in a whorehouse, where they were allowed to live and earn their keep. Not aboard a ship. But she'd never claimed to know the inner workings of the sex trade.

"Earning your keep?" Jane asked with a raise of her eyebrows. "Is that what you want?"

Silence met Jane's inquiry as Cecily looked down at the floor, brow furrowed in anger. But again, whether it was due to her current predicament or to the nature of her previous one, Jane didn't know.

"Because from the way you acted," Jane continued, seeing she wasn't about to receive an answer, "I was under the impression that you had not chosen to be aboard that ship at all. Am I correct?"

Cecily's head snapped up, and glared at Jane. "I owed them a debt," she stated defensively.

Ah, that was more like it. Jane wondered what she had done to wind up in such a position. It must have been some debt to be taken aboard a ship that, for all she knew, could be at sea for months.

Jane nodded at Cecily. "One that you won't have to pay off anymore."

The chuckle that escaped Cecily's lips was not what Jane had expected in response. "So wha', now I owe ya?"

"Not at all," Jane snorted, with a shake of her head. "I do not take from whores."

Cecily just quirked an eyebrow at Jane, a smile playing at her lips, and crossed her arms over her half-bared chest. "Yes, tha' much is clear."

A chuckle escaped Jane's lips before she could stop it. Cecily was now parroting her own words back at her, the little cheeky whore. She was like no whore Jane had ever met before, and she had met plenty in her lifetime. Most, however, left the sass behind when soliciting, as it tended to not bode well for business. Men didn't like a fuck that talked back to them. And here this one had blatantly refused and been disgusted by Cooksley's antics, a potential client, and yet had come on to Worth without invitation. What her game was, Jane had yet to discover. Her body language invited, while her cheek dissuaded. It was intriguing, to say the least, and Jane found herself taking a step toward Cecily unconsciously before she halted her movement.

She had no more time to mull over this fact, as the ship gave a sudden lurch and Jane was forced to grab the edge of the table behind her to keep from toppling over. She cursed, feeling the ship level out again and strode out of her quarters in order to determine what on earth her crew was attempting to pull off. Cecily made to follow, but Jane slammed the door in her face, locking it with the key around her neck. Annoyed cries of protest sounded from the room beyond, but Jane ignored them, facing the main deck as she started shouting at the men running about, trying in vain to forget the intriguing woman now locked safely in her quarters.

~~*

"Why do ya continue ta treat me as a—"

"Prisoner?" Jane interrupted, knowing exactly what Cecily was referring to before she had even finished. It wasn't hard to guess. She had become more and more anxious as the days had passed with her cooped up in the captain's quarters. "That's because you are one. Just because you fail to accept it doesn't make it any less true," she finished, not even bothering to look up from the notes she was currently reading. But though she couldn't see Cecily, she could still smell the now-familiar, sweet scent she exuded and which seemed to now fill every corner of the room.

Jane could also feel the unamused glare Cecily shot her and heard the slide of skin and the rustle of fabric as she crossed her arms over her chest.

"The sooner you do accept your fate, the sooner we can move on," Jane continued, when Cecily didn't answer. "For in case you were unable to conclude, resisting would be unpleasant."

Cecily let out a breathy laugh. "I'm not the one resistin', love. Ya are."

Jane wasn't quite sure they were talking about the same thing anymore.

It had been a couple of days since the raid on the galleon, since Cecily had come aboard the ship and started making a nuisance of herself. The first day hadn't been too troublesome. But that had more to do with Jane avoiding her quarters and less to do with Cecily herself. That was, until night fell, and Jane turned in for the night. She had walked into her quarters to find a very underdressed—although still covered, however poorly—Cecily sprawled tantalizingly on her bed. Jane could feel the flush staining her cheeks that had nothing to do with the anger she outwardly displayed. In fact, her mouth had gone dry and her heart had sped up, but there was no way in hell she would ever admit it. Cecily was beautiful, Jane could at least admit to herself, but she couldn't afford to get attached, couldn't afford to let down her guard, especially for some good-for-nothing whore.

And to make matters worse, Cecily had refused to move, even when Jane threatened to throw her overboard. She had just called her bluff and snuggled deeper into the bed sheets, stretching her body like a cat and effectively wiping all thought from Jane's mind. Jane repaid the favor by pulling out her pistol and aiming at Cecily's head until, with a pout, she dragged herself and the topmost sheet from the bed and flopped down on the floor in the corner of the room.

Jane got very little sleep that night, going over and over in her head all the different responses her body and instincts had to this woman, and trying to decide what on earth it all meant. But as morning arose, chasing the three hours of sleep she had managed to get away, Jane still didn't have a clue. It was frustrating her to no end, and it took all her effort to not display and take out her frustration on her crew.

Although Cecily hadn't attempted that performance again, it didn't mean she let up. The flirting, even days later, was at an all-time high and the innuendoes never seemed to cease. Jane wasn't sure what Cecily was playing at, why she continued to pester Jane, even when she had both displayed and stated her disinterest. Whores usually moved on to the next available clientele once the disinterest had been duly noted. But then again, as she had very early on realized, Cecily was not an average whore.

In fact, the longer Jane spent around her, the more she came to realize that despite her skill at invitation and displaying herself, she was an awful whore—well, on the aspects Jane was able to judge her by, that was. She was persistent to the point of annoying, mouthy, and, as Jane found out one night, picky.

"It's about control, isn't it?" Cecily had asked on the third night, having blurted out the confession after Worth had left the quarters with Jane's orders ringing in his ears.

Jane looked over at Cecily lounging on her bed once more—fully clothed this time—to find her staring back at her with knowing eyes. "What?"

"Tha's wha' ya desire, wha' ya need in life," Cecily explained, looking up at the wooden paneling above her, as though she was a child gazing up at the stars. "Ya need control and the respect and loyalty of your crew is how ya gain it. It's wha' ya have ta retain every day."

"That does not concern you," Jane stated, her tone warning. She didn't mind talking to Cecily: the probing questions, the inane chatter, and the snarky comments. In fact, she secretly enjoyed it, but this time she did not like where this conversation was going. It was tip-toeing the line of her past, and she had never disclosed that information to anyone, and was sure as hell not going to start now.

"It's wha' I strive for," Cecily continued, ignoring Jane's comment, "even in the smallest quantities."

Jane glanced over then, Cecily's words having intrigued her. A whore in control, that was unheard of. They were women who did as they were told and nothing more. They were owned by those who used them, completely and without question. But from the way Cecily spoke, Jane could tell she was talking about keeping a hold of the control she currently had and not gaining control. Curiosity sparked in Jane, causing her to throw her fear of the conversation out the window in order to learn more about this strange woman. "How so?"

Cecily sighed. "It makes me feel like I have a choice, like I'm not completely at the mercy of others. I choose who I flaunt myself for, I choose who gets ta have me for the night." The memory of Cecily shoving at Cooksley flashed across Jane's mind. She hadn't chosen him and had therefore refused his advances, unlike Worth, whom she had made advances toward. "It makes it feel like I chose this life, instead of the other way aroun'."

"Didn't you?"

"No, not really. I ran away from home a week before I turned of age. My father had arranged for me ta get married ta this wretched man twenty years my senior and well, tha' wasn't my idea of a good match," Cecily stated with a shrug, like that was the most logical thing in the world, a woman with a mind of her own. "So I left."

And suddenly, without having been told, Jane knew exactly how Cecily had ended up in the profession she was in. It was a story that was all too familiar, all too close to home.

Cecily sighed into the silence before continuing, "Not much else for a woman with no money ta her name nor husband ta speak of, besides," she paused, gesturing at herself, "this."

Jane nodded in understanding. "If I hadn't found the *Tantibus*, we might have met a bit earlier," she stated, before she could change her mind. It was the first time she had ever given away a hint of her past to anyone. "But fate led me down a different path." She glanced around her quarters, her mind journeying to the past, and when she had first been brought to this very room, a day after she had stowed away and minutes after being found in the cargo hold. Little did she know then that this very ship, this very room, was to become her home.

"Ya?" And the sound of laughter soon filled the chambers. Jane frowned.

"I'm sorry," Cecily apologized when she had calmed down somewhat, wiping tears from her eyes. "I just can't see ya in my position, bossin' the men aroun' and slappin' their hands away as ya threaten ta 'wash the floor in their blood' if they so much as touch ya where ya don't desire."

And Jane, too, found herself laughing at the mental image, despite the dark humor and rawness of it.

"Obviously, I was unable to see myself in that position either," Jane stated, the smile slowly falling from her face as she realized what she had just said.

"Ya... ya've never laid with anyone?"

"No," Jane cut her off a little too harshly, coming to her senses and stopping the conversation before it could venture further down that path. Her hand automatically reached for the ring still nestled against her breast. Yes, she had hinted at her past to Cecily, opened up more to someone who she had known for only a few days than she had to any she had known for years, but that didn't mean she was ready to rip open that painful and bloody wound she called her past. And she might never be ready.

"But tha' ring?" Cecily continued, and Jane immediately tensed. "The one ya always wear aroun' ya neck—"

"Is none of your business," Jane snapped, effectively halting the conversation.

Cecily fell silent there, sensing Jane's refusal to speak more on the topic. After a moment, she extracted herself from the bed and padded over to her corner, lying down amidst the nest of sheets and pillows she had collected over the days and shut her eyes.

Jane released a breath she hadn't realized she had been holding and followed suit, stripping off her outer layers and crawling under the covers.

But her mind refused to let her sleep until it had had the last word. This woman had gotten under her skin and left her mark, despite Jane's resistance and barriers to keep her out.

Just her luck.

~~*

After their conversation on control, Jane let up on her tight rein on Cecily. The following day, she left the door open, a clear invitation for her to wander about and explore the ship. Though she had warned Cecily that despite her threats and warnings to her crew, some may still try to proposition her or force her. Cecily had just shrugged it off.

And now Jane understood why.

A week had passed since Cecily had come aboard, four days since she had been free to move about the deck, and she—although annoyingly curious about the workings and every aspect the ship and life at sea—had yet to leave Jane's sight. And Jane wasn't stupid to think she was doing it without purpose.

For every time Cecily caught Jane looking at her, her promiscuous persona would come back full force. Her hips would sway and her posture would straighten, inviting all who gazed upon her to look their fill. And the way Jane's men stared at her, like she was a feast and they were all starving, made Jane want to lock her back up so no other could look at her in such a way. And she hated it, hated the way Cecily made her feel, even though she still didn't quite understand what these emotions and feelings meant. All she knew is that they were tearing down her walls and leaving her vulnerable.

"Ya do realize he wants ya gone?" Cecily questioned on the eighth day, coming up beside Jane after a particularly tiresome argument with Cooksley. The man, it seemed, was becoming more and more troublesome ever since the raid, arguing with her over every decision and growling about her inability to run a ship when he thought she wasn't listening.

Jane nodded, as she watched Cooksley berate one of the new recruits on his ability to swab the deck. "Yes, I know."

"And yet, ya do nothin' about it?"

"What can I do?" Jane questioned, not taking her eyes off the belligerent man. "Maroon him? On what grounds? I can't just leave one of my men to die without probable cause." Jane saw Cecily open her mouth, no doubt to argue that point, but she quickly beat her to it. "And 'being an ass' is not a good enough reason."

"He's no ass." Cecily chuckled. "Asses are helpful and hardworkin' and do as they are told. Tha' man's a pinch-faced shabbaroon."

Jane let out a bark of a laugh. "A shabbaroon?"

Cecily furrowed her brow in consideration before shrugging. "Not sure wha' it means, ta be honest. Mr. Hadley used that word ta describe his business partner the couple of times he came ta see me." Cecily paused there, as though lost in thought. "But based off the relations of those two, I feel tha' word best describes Mr. Cooksley there."

The smile that brought to Jane's face returned every time she laid eyes on Cooksley the rest of the day.

~~*

"How old are ya?" Cecily asked that night, as she idly played with one of the many navigation instruments laid out upon the table. It wasn't a strange question, if Jane was to be honest. Cecily had been getting bolder and bolder with her questions, sometimes getting so personal that Jane would snap at her and the room would fall into uncomfortable silence. By now, she no doubt knew Jane's limit and how much she was willing to answer, and yet, she still constantly pushed. As much as it made Jane angry, she could also feel it slowly pushing her limit further back.

"Just about twenty-six now," she answered from where she was lying atop the bed. It dawned on her then that they had switched positions. It was usually Cecily who laid claim to the bed in the hours before sleep overruled Jane's duties and she kicked her out. She found herself missing it, knowing that as she fell asleep tonight, the impression and warmth usually left on the other side of the bed would not be present.

Jane heard Cecily mumble something, bringing her back to the conversation. "What did you say?"

"Nothin'," Cecily sighed, but Jane could hear the smile in her voice. "Just talkin' ta myself."

"Be careful with that, or I may just have to lock you up on charges of insanity," Jane cautioned with false warning. "Or witchcraft. I heard that's a popular one nowadays."

Cecily chuckled, glancing at Jane and wiggling her fingers at her in what she took to be a magical gesture. Jane just snorted.

Her amusement soon turned into a yawn, though.

"I guess tha's my cue then," Cecily said before trailing off into a yawn herself as she got up from the chair. Jane closed her eyes, listening to the comforting sound of Cecily's soft footsteps as she padded across the chambers.

She had never thought that after all that had happened to her, all that she had gone through and all that she had lost, that she would be able to let another in. And yet, she found herself helpless to resist Cecily. Cecily had wormed her way into her heart and made a home there. It was frightening, and yes, Jane knew it made her vulnerable, but she couldn't help it. She had tried so hard to deny what she felt for her, to remain detached and unemotional, but it had been a losing battle from the second Jane had laid eyes on her. Not that it would matter. The day after tomorrow, they would reach Port Galtry and Cecily would disappear from her life as though she had never been there. Just like her family, like Thomas.

Jane was broken out of her musing as the footsteps switched direction and approached the bed. The sweet smell that was solely Cecily became slightly more pungent as the footsteps paused by the edge of the bed. Jane cracked open her eyes, barely catching a glimpse of Cecily's cocky smile before warm, soft lips met her own. Jane tensed, eyes going wide, completely caught off-guard. She didn't move, didn't even breathe, the shock holding her in place. But then, it was over before her brain worked out what had happened.

"Goodnight, *Cap'ain*," Cecily purred in her ear, the tone of the title sounding strange and foreign coming from the woman's lips, even though it was laced with her usual sarcasm. Then Cecily turned toward her corner of the room, hips swaying confidently.

Jane wasn't sure what made her do it, was probably not even in her right mind. Her hand shot out before Cecily could get far, grasping her wrist lightly, but with intent.

"Stay," was all she said.

And Cecily did.

~~*

Suffice to say they did not, in fact, stop at Port Galtry. Cecily had downright refused to be dropped off like last week's garbage upon the deck and would argue with Jane every time she brought it up.

"The sea is no place for you," Jane stated as Cecily glared daggers at her, the cool, salty wind ruffling her hair as they faced off on the quarter deck. "Just being aboard, you are putting your life at risk."

Cecily raised her eyebrows at that, crossing her arms in anger. "Oh, and whose fault is tha'? I wouldn't even be on board if it weren't for ya!"

A chuckle sounded from behind her, the owner trying to stifle the sound, but ultimately being unsuccessful. She didn't even have to turn around to know who it was. She had seen Worth's amusement at their antics toward one another as the days passed.

"No, you'd be at the bottom of the sea," Jane said, ignoring Worth.

"Where ya could very well be not a day from now," Cecily quickly countered. "I'm. Not. Leavin'."

A handful of heated words later, Jane had reluctantly relented. And if she was to be honest with herself, she was relieved. Jane had grown quite fond of Cecily. More than fond, as Cecily liked to say, but that was a matter of opinion.

"I am not," Jane denied a day later, when Cecily brought up her fondness of her again. They were sprawled on Jane's bed, Cecily's head pillowed on her chest, her fingers idly running down Jane's arm, leaving goose bumps in their wake. It wasn't until after the first night, letting Cecily sleep beside her and in her arms, getting drunk off her scent, that Jane realized how completely starved for touch she was. She felt like a fish that had been without water and finally dumped back into the ocean. And even though all they had done was sleep, it was more than Jane had ever hoped for.

"Ya are, and I ya."

Jane grunted at the proclamation, but didn't make any move to deny it. It was true, after all. She had finally come to realize that. All these years she had spent traveling the ocean, trying to find the next thing, the next adventure and treasure that would fill the hole in her. But perhaps she had been, and still was, chasing the wrong thing. Perhaps all those years she had closed herself off, bottled herself up, and built a wall around her heart in order to prevent ever feeling loss again, when all she needed to do was let one person in and let herself open up and be opened up by someone.

Or perhaps, just this someone.

"Like a lion, ya are," Cecily continued, tilting her head up and looking at Jane. She reached a hand up, running her fingers through Jane's sun-ripened hair, letting the unruly curls wash over the digits. "Golden mane and all."

Jane snorted with amusement, wondering where on earth Cecily came up with these ridiculous thoughts. "I am no lion."

Cecily frowned in disapproval. "No, ya are right," she conceded, and Jane raised her eyebrows at the unexpected agreement, but Cecily just ignored her and continued on. "Lions are lazy, overbearin', and well, male. Ya are much more than tha'. Fierce, strong, protective. A lioness. My lioness."

Jane let out a laugh to cover up the swelling of emotion she felt in her chest and the heat that was no doubt coloring her cheeks. Despite the little time they had known each other, Jane had discovered that it wasn't often that Cecily got endearing and sentimental, and that she was to enjoy it when it did.

But she wasn't able to enjoy it for long.

"Also arrogant and demandin'," Cecily continued with a sly grin, "but tha's wha' ya have me for: ta make sure tha' head of yas remains a decent size."

Jane just rolled her eyes, dipping her head down to place a sweet kiss on top of Cecily's dark brown hair. She would be lying if she said she didn't enjoy the compliments and sentiments. But she would also be lying if she said she didn't enjoy the sass that followed.

~~*

"SAIL!" a call sounded from above, drawing all heads up to where Newby was perched precariously in the crow's nest. He pointed directly off the stern and all eyes on the main deck followed his line, trying in vain to catch a glimpse of the claimed pursuer.

"There's another ship?" Cecily asked, moving forward to stand beside Jane on the quarterdeck. Jane hummed in affirmation and pulled out her spyglass. She could barely make out the advancing ship, but there was one thing that was for certain: it was heading straight for them.

"That horizon has been bare since we passed port," Jane remarked with a scowl, fingers tracing the ring around her neck.

"Well, that fact remains true no longer," Worth stated from her right. Jane steadied the spy glass, hoping to catch sight of a flag or some mark or evidence of what sort was following them. But after a while, she dropped the spy glass from her eye and handed it over to Worth.

"I can't make out her allegiance, not from this distance." Jane paused before addressing Worth, who was currently looking his fill at the advancing ship. "Keep her going steady," she commanded.

Worth handed her back the spy glass with a nod. "Captain, if she's a member of the Navy—"

"Then she'll catch us whether we attempt to run or not," Jane finished, resigned, but still determined. She would just have to hope that it wouldn't come to that. A firefight was not an option, not against the Royal Navy. That was one fight Jane knew they would not win, extra powder and shot or not. "If that is a Navy ship, we'll slow down in order to not arouse suspicions. Until then, keep her pace steady."

"Aye, Captain."

It was not a situation she had hoped to be in. They hadn't seen hide or tail of another ship for a week now, and all of a sudden, just a day after passing Port Galtry, a sail is spotted on the horizon. And not just a glimpse of one sailing off to another port, no. This ship was matching them, gaining on them, actually, seeing as with the extra weight, they had only been able to reach a top speed of four knots. She was set on the same course as the *Tantibus*, a fact that did not bode well for their future.

"No… wait," Jane stopped Worth as he made to descend to the main deck, her hand automatically reaching for her ring as her mind whirled. If they stayed on course, their pursuers would determine their destination, and they could not and would not give up the location of their cache if their true intention for sailing out in the open waters was made known. They needed to veer, however slightly, off course. And for that, they need a bit more speed.

"Raise the topsail!" Jane shouted as she whirled around to face her crew. "Both main and mizzen! We need all the speed she can muster!"

The men below her scrambled to obey, pulling ropes and tying knots in order to release the sails at the topmost part of both the main and mizzen masts.

"Captain," Coll shouted from down on the main deck beside the main mast, his eyes riddled with worry, "the mast won't hold!"

"She'll hold," Jane assured him. It was a risky maneuver she was pulling here, one that could very well split the main mast and leave them crippled, but she was confident that the mast would hold. It was her ship, after all, and although Coll knew her inside and out, nobody understood her like Jane. *Tantibus* could take it.

Jane felt Cecily's eyes on her and she looked to her side, catching the warm, brown eyes. There was a sense of awe in them she had never seen before. That look was all it took to inflate the ego Cecily constantly teased her about, causing Jane to flash her a confident smirk before dropping down to the main deck to watch over the proceedings.

The top sail of the mizzen unfurled and took wind, quickly followed by the main's. Groans and creaks emanated from the main mast, but she held, just as Jane had predicted. She allowed the grin to spread across her face again as cheers from the crew arose around her.

But she wasn't finished yet.

"Bring her up into it!" She ordered, making a sweeping gesture with her arm.

Dover, who was at the wheel, obeyed, turning it just so the sails caught the wind more effectively, but Jane quickly took over once she saw his hesitation to go any further. She held onto the wheel with effort, more groans and creaks sounding from the mast and even the deck, but slowly, the ship performed to her bidding.

"Here," she commanded Dover, sliding to the side and allowing him to take a hold of the wheel. "Hold her there!"

Dover nodded, holding the wheel steady as Jane returned to Cecily's side. She glanced over for a second, long enough for Cecily to raise her eyebrows in a poor attempt at playing unimpressed and Jane to flash her another arrogant smile, before taking another look through her spyglass. The ship was only slightly closer than before, but still not enough for her to make out any markings of allegiance. But she could see her turn, so her bow was once again aimed straight at the *Tantibus's* stern. There was no doubt anymore that the ship intended to run them down. And with the distances it had traveled in the short time between glimpses through the spyglass, Jane was sure it would happen sooner rather than later.

As if reading her mind, Cecily sidled closer to her and asked in a low voice, "How long 'til she's at us?"

Jane took a second to calculate. "A day, maybe less. But no more than that," she replied with a sigh.

"Wha' do ya plan ta do?"

Jane shrugged. "I'm not sure yet. Depends who's at her helm."

"And if it's the Navy?"

"Then we better hope the new recruits can play their parts and keep their gobs shut. It's going to take some damn good acting if it's the Navy that decides to board."

Silence fell between them, the only sound being the slap of the sea and the orders being relayed amongst the crew on the main deck.

"You don't seem worried," Jane remarked after a moment, noticing the relaxed look on Cecily's face: the same look she had worn when Jane had first met her, knife to her throat, life on the line, but still relaxed and bored.

"Oh, I'm not," Cecily assured her, without taking her eyes off the horizon and the ship sailing upon it. "As long as ya in control, my lioness, I have nothin' ta fear."

Jane just nodded. "As it should be."

"Well," Cecily began, and Jane felt a smile creep upon her face, knowing the usual insult was coming and looking forward to it. "Except bein' squashed by ya enormous ego. It's takin' up all the space aboard this ship. I'm afraid, for the good of the crew and myself, it'll have ta go."

~~*

Jane gazed through the spyglass for a long while, trying to keep it steady and hoping her eyes were playing tricks on her.

But after another minute, she was forced to concede that they weren't.

"She's a member of the Royal Navy," she said without emotion, handing the spyglass over to Worth. The Navy flag had been as clear as day at the top of the main mast, waving at her tauntingly.

Worth made to grab the spy glass from Jane, but it was snatched out of her hand before he could grab it. Cecily, spyglass in hand, strode forward a pace in order to be out of reach and have time to look upon the ship. Worth caught Jane's eye and Jane just shook her head, trying to keep the fond smile that threatened to break forth off her face. This was not the time to show any display of affection.

"We can fight her off," a voice sounded from behind Jane. She knew who it was without even turning around, having heard his argumentative tone often enough in the past two weeks, let alone the last seven years he had been aboard, to recognize it anywhere. "Done it before," Cooksley finished.

Jane just shook her head. "Not weighed down as we are. Won't stand a chance."

"With all that powder and shot, they won't be able to keep up," Cooksley countered, his voice rising in anticipation and confidence.

"Yes, but that there is war ship," Jane growled, her anger getting the best of her. She took a deep breath to calm herself and continued. "Fourth-rate, sixty cannons easily, and if they are prepared, eighty men aboard, all ready to fight until their last breath. She'll sink us before we even get to use any of the extra powder. No, its best we play off at being a simple merchant ship."

"You don't want to admit you're scared of the Navy. Well, I'm not, and let me tell you—"

"You will hold your tongue!" Jane shouted, whirling around to face Cooksley. She was at her wits' end with him, and could tell by the way his jaw clenched in anger, that he could see the threat in her eyes and would, for the time being, leave it be. She wondered how long that would truly last. He'd probably be at her in another hour, at the very least.

"If they are so inclined to board, then we shall let them," Jane ordered, not breaking the staring contest with Cooksley that she suddenly found herself in. "We are not to engage unless absolutely necessary, and I shall be the judge of that. Do I make myself clear?"

Cooksley looked like he would like nothing more than to argue or run her through. Perhaps both.

"Yes, *Captain*," he sneered. It didn't matter. She still had the upper hand and, until she could find a clean and reasonable excuse to toss him out, it would remain that way. The crew was loyal to her, first and foremost. He couldn't even compete.

"Good," she nodded, turning her back on the man in a clear dismissal.

As Cooksley's footsteps faded, Cecily once again sidled up beside her, having finally relented and handed the spyglass over to Worth. "Now what?" she asked, giving Jane a sidelong glance.

Jane leaned on the railing, staring over the crashing waves toward the fast approaching Navy ship, determination and anticipation filling her up with confidence. "Now, we wait."

~~*

Her estimation was off by a handful of hours. The Navy ship, it seemed, was faster than she had anticipated, or the *Tantibus* was more weighted than she had originally thought. No matter, their extra speed had done nothing to lengthen their time, but she was comforted to know that the slight veer off-course would at least allow them to fabricate a new destination to one of the ports off the distant coast, should they be questioned. And she had no doubt they would be.

But she was ready. All except for one thing.

"Go, wait in my quarters until this whole business has been sorted," Jane commanded to Cecily, lying a comforting, but firm, hand upon her slim shoulder.

"I will not hide away like some scullery maid," Cecily refused, stepping out of the touch and turning to face Jane fully with defiance in her eyes. "I can handle myself."

"Of that, I have no doubt." Jane closed the distance between them again and placed both her hands on Cecily's shoulders, smiling at her reassuringly. "But it would arouse suspicion if not one, but two women were to be seen in opposing states of dress upon a simple merchant ship. You in that... garment," she stated, her eyes roving over Cecily, not sure whether her dress could indeed be construed as one. There was far too much skin showing for it to be compared to a lady's everyday garb. Definitely would arouse suspicion... and interest, which Jane wished to avoid that at all costs, especially the latter.

Cecily searched Jane's eyes, piercing browns diving deep into her own blues, gazing into her soul. After a few beats, she seemed to find what she was looking for.

"Fine," Cecily relented, though her eyes still betrayed her indignation. Jane knew Cecily wouldn't be happy with her decision from the second she came to it, but truly it was for the best. If not the crew's own safety, then at least for Cecily's own.

And when Jane had started thinking more of everyone else's safety—especially Cecily's—and less of her own, she didn't know. She used to not give a rat's ass about anyone but herself, despite her outward appearance of otherwise. Now, it was like she couldn't give a damn if she lived or died, as long as Cecily's life was spared.

Jane shoved those thoughts to the back of her head, forcing herself to focus on the here and now. She had commanded her crew to stow away all incriminating evidence, including several pieces of garb certain members wore and—as they were seen as more of a liability than not—the new recruits from the *Liberty*. She didn't want to take the chance that those men would say anything condemnatory, damning them all to a fight they were bound to lose. No, they all needed to play their parts and pass themselves off as nothing more than simple merchant sailors, and that very well couldn't be done with those men free to walk about and talk to whomever they pleased.

"Nearly there," Jane muttered to herself, watching as the Navy warship maneuvered alongside the *Tantibus*. She had conversed shortly with a crewmember aboard the Navy ship as they had approached, and agreed to allow them aboard—he had said it was on orders of the king that they check every merchant ship, so she really didn't have a choice in the matter. It was an impressive ship, she would say that, even though it was not by far the most impressive she had seen.

The sound of the Navy ship's planks being thrown against the rail and various nets and hooks securing the two ships together announced the boarding. Jane straightened. She stepped out into the middle of the main deck, Worth at her side and the rest of her crew scattered about her, awaiting the appearance of the Navy's own.

But she felt calm, relaxed even, and confident that her and her crew's true intentions and reasons for being about were well hidden.

Booted footsteps were heard seconds before a man with greasy brown hair, partially hidden under a black tricorne, and an equally-unwashed, scruffy jaw jumped down onto the main deck. A very familiar and extremely deceitful man.

Immediately Jane's calm and relaxed feeling disappeared and she tensed, inwardly cursing her own stupidity for not seeing it sooner. She had thought it odd that a Navy ship would have orders to board any and every ship, even if there was rumored to be a war coming. It was usually a few words exchanged in passing, and then the Navy would let the ship be on their way, unless something seemed off. And yes, the disappearance of the *Liberty* could have been discovered by now, but the nearest Navy port or ship was hundreds of miles away. There should not be one in this area, and that was why she had chosen this route. Of course, this was no war ship of the Royal Navy.

But before she could do anything more, forty men jumped over the railing behind their captain and pistols were leveled at her and her crew.

Her men, though, seemed to understand the change in situation and, despite her orders to not engage without her signal, began firing.

It was a bloody mess, and while they were equally numbered, the other men seemed more prepared for a fight, with the element of surprise on their side. Jane managed to down two of them before she found herself eye-to-eye with the muzzle of a pistol.

"Drop your weapons or the wench eats my shot," the scruffy man shouted to her remaining crew. Scuffles ceased, quickly followed by the damning sound of pistols and swords clattering on the deck as they were dropped. The man nodded to his men over her shoulder before once again focusing on her.

For a split second, Jane feared the man knew exactly who she was. But she soon threw that thought out the window. Of course he didn't. Very few outside her crew did. He probably just saw her as the woman she was, and she decided to play toward a man's instinct to protect. He probably didn't know just how lucky he had got with his choice in leverage.

"Captain Lock," Jane drawled, attempting to hide her growing apprehension—for a whole different, clearly-evident reason—behind a mask of despise and disinterest.

"Sorry, do I know you?" the scruffy man—Lock—asked, his tone mocking as his eyes roved over Jane's form hungrily.

"Not in the slightest, but I sure know you." And she was glad she did, but not so glad that he was the one that had boarded her ship. He had a rather nasty reputation.

She had come across him once at Port Demply a year ago while they were docked and gathering up supplies for their next raid. Well, she hadn't personally met him, but Worth had pointed him out to her. She had sent Worth to go meet with some of the other pirate captains, who had been discussing the newly-spreading rumors about the Navy amassing an armada to take out the pirates. And from what Worth had said, Jane had immediately disliked this man she had never met, and continued to do so, even now that she had.

"Glad to hear my reputation precedes me," Lock smirked, his eyes glinting with cruel amusement as his crew laughed behind him.

"Not particularly, *Captain*," Jane spat sarcastically.

Lock cocked an eyebrow at her. She could tell he was trying to remember, trying to spark a memory that would tell him how she knew him and he did not. She watched as he scowled, evidently coming up with nothing before his eyes swept toward Worth standing at gunpoint a few paces beside her, in search for answers. And it was there that he seemed to find them, for his eyes alit with recognition and immediately focused on her again.

"Well, well, it seems the rumors are true."

Jane just tilted her head up in answer, letting the man think whatever he wanted. But she understood his conclusion. Worth had no doubt had to claim who he was, and under whom he served, when he had met Captain Lock. But despise the rumors that surrounded her and the questions he had been asked, Jane had ordered him to not divulge anything.

"You know, I didn't believe it when I first heard," Lock stated, lowering his weapon as he laughed. Confidence oozed from him as he began to pace in front of Jane, the rest of his crew keeping their pistols at the ready, trained on her and her crew. Jane purposefully kept her eyes on him, not wanting to see the bodies that now littered the deck around her. "The infamous Captain Avery, a woman, captaining her own ship. Thought it... farfetched. Had to see it for myself."

A few seconds passed before he was standing before her once again. He took a step closer, much to Jane's displeasure and swept the muzzle of his pistol through her hair, brushing a lock of it behind her shoulder.

Jane batted the pistol aside, but it seemed Lock had anticipated the move. A rough, calloused hand clamped around her wrist and she was jerked forward, only to be stopped by the sweaty, rank body of Lock himself.

"And it is a sweet sight to behold," he purred, gazing at her predatorily as he wrapped one arm around her torso and comfortably settled the other on her shoulder, so the muzzle of his pistol brushed against her temple. His crew laughed behind him, but whether it was at his proclamation or her obvious displeasure, Jane didn't care.

She stood still, refusing to let Lock intimidate her, even as his hold on her wrist tightened painfully. Instead, she asked coldly, "What do you want?"

"Many things, my sweet," he cooed, leaning down to sniff at her hair and neck. She pulled away sharply, as far as she could. He retreated, but didn't release his hold on her.

"But for now, I'll start with the return of my goods that are currently stashed in your hold." The predatory glint in his eye was back.

Jane just chuckled. "We have nothing of yours."

"Oh, yes, you do. That ship you sank a few weeks ago? That was my merchant. Need to be prepared for this war I've been hearing so much about. And I do enjoy a good rouse, especially if it makes the Royal Navy look like fools." He gazed back toward his idled ship and the Navy flag still waving innocently at the top, before looking back down at Jane and flashing a grin. "But I'm sure you know that by now."

"Yes, I certainly do. And how cowardly you are, hiding behind a flag."

Jane watched as Lock grit his teeth. Obviously, he wasn't too fond of being called cowardly. But he reined back his cool and sneered at her. "Ah, but it works. Makes fools of you all, enemy and brethren alike."

"There is only one fool here, and it is not I."

"We shall see about that." Lock promised in a low whisper. Then he straightened, his voice louder so those surrounding them could overhear, "But I'm afraid I'll be needing recompense for the goods that are now rusting at the bottom of the ocean. Those twelve-pounders were hard to come by."

"Then you might as well learn to swim, *Captain*," Jane said matter-of-factly. "The ocean floor is a long way down."

Chuckles of laughter sounded from her captive crew, a few noises of scuffles, and the sound of flesh hitting flesh as her crew got out of hand and fought back. But they were soon subdued once more, and Lock narrowed his eyes at her. A brief flash of anger marred his face before his confident façade once again took up residence.

Before she could even blink, a stinging pain emanated from her cheek and her head was thrown to the side from the force of the blow. "Like I said," Jane said casually, straightening back up and staring back into Lock's eyes, "Cowardly. Slapping a fellow pirate instead of challenging them." She clicked her tongue a few times, shaking her head at his antics.

"I don't need to challenge you. I have already won."

"If that's what you believe."

This time it was the butt of the gun that made contact with the side of her head. The blow was hard, causing her knees to buckle slightly, but not enough to render her unconscious. But damn it, it sure hurt like hell.

She could hear shouts of insults and more scuffles behind her as her crew reacted to the abuse, but the ringing in her head made it all sound far away.

"Fuck you," Jane spat out as she straightened up once more, briefly letting her own anger get the best of her. She bit it back immediately, knowing that displaying such an emotion could break the hold she had on Lock. She was angering him: that much was evident. And anger caused mistakes. She just hoped hers didn't cost her before his cost him.

But his next words drove all those thoughts from her head in an instant.

"No, my dear, it is I that shall be doing the fucking."

Despite her calm exterior, Jane couldn't help the fear that spiked through her, her veins turning to ice. No, he couldn't possibly. That was the lowest of the low, the worst sort of degradation. But what else could he have meant? From the short time Jane had been in his presence, and from what she had heard about him, she knew exactly what he had in mind.

"You see," Lock continued, oblivious to the panic now running through Jane's mind, "I don't quite believe these so-called rumors that surround you. On the outside, yes, they appear to be true, but I'm afraid I'm going to need a little bit more... evidence to satisfy my growing curiosity."

There was no doubt now what he meant, but Jane was sure as hell not going to give up without a fight. What was left of her dignity and respect was at stake. Not to mention her virginity.

"You won't get anything from me."

"We shall see about that," he said. He nodded to the men nearest to him, and before Jane could react, Lock had released her into the grasp of two burly men, who began to drag her toward her captain's quarters.

Toward the quarters where Cecily was currently hiding.

Jane could hear the sounds of her crew once more protesting and fighting their captors, guns going off and grunts of pain and shouts of anger. But that was all background noise to her, barely decipherable as horror shot through her anew. This was the very last thing Jane wanted right now. A year ago, it would have been all about her and her own, but now, she was more fearful for Cecily's safety than her own.

Immediately, she fell limp in her captors' hands, playing as though she had given up and forcing the two men holding her to adjust their grips. That's when she struck. With a few well-placed jabs and a twist of her body—she sent up a silent thank you to Thomas, wherever he resided, for those skills—she managed to step out of the two men's grasp, and pulled out the knife in her boot. She brandished it, showing the two men the business end as she placed herself between them and her quarters.

A hearty laugh rose above the sound of the continued fighting behind the two men. "What, may I ask, do you plan to do with that little thing, love?"

Lock.

"Why don't you come over here and find out," Jane beckoned, hoping the invitation was enough an incentive for him to do just that. She couldn't wait to stick him with her knife. Any object would suffice, really, as long as he wasn't breathing when she was done.

Lock tutted, clearly unimpressed with her bait. "You won't get far. Be dead before you can make a dent in our numbers."

"Rather dead than rotten," Jane spat out, intending to fight her way through as many as she could before they felled her. She would die, she had no doubt about that, but by god if she didn't plan to take as many of his men down with her as she could.

The sound of a door slamming back on wooden walls broke the tension of the stand-off. All eyes whipped around toward the captain's quarters, and Jane's heart sunk. No, no, no, not now, why couldn't she have just once done as she had been told?

So caught up in Cecily, Jane barely had time to notice the two men spring into action before they were on her. She was able to hold off against them for a few seconds nonetheless. But another hard blow to the back of her head and the knife was knocked from her hands all too soon. She stumbled slightly, righting herself with a wave of dizziness, but not before the men had once again restrained her.

She had been right: Cecily was really going to be the death of her.

"Bloody pieces of—!" Cecily bellowed, stalking out of the quarters fuming, skirts flying as she raged. "I have had it with ya wretched lot! This—oh!"

She broke off, seeming to notice the atmosphere and scene before her for the first time. The anger that had previously been bursting out of her before disappeared in an instant, replaced by confusion. A confusion that matched Jane's own. What on earth was Cecily doing? The woman clearly had a death wish to come bursting out here, unarmed and unprepared for what was occurring. Fear clamped around Jane's heart cold and restricting, her head ringing with more than just the effects of the blow.

"Stay where you are," Lock commanded, stalking forward. He had his pistol at the ready, aimed directly at Cecily's head. Seemed the man wasn't taking any more chances with the surprises on this ship. As he damn well should.

But Cecily didn't appear to be fearful or even shocked anymore. Instead, her eyes found Lock and it was like her whole persona had changed completely. Her eyes drank in his toned body and greasy hair like he was something she had been waiting for. Then she tilted her head slightly, a heated, sultry look washing over her face as she adjusted her body to play up her attributes the way Jane had seen her do before when trying to garner the attention of a potential client. The way she had done multiple times for Jane herself.

Jane's heart sank even further.

"Well, if ya say so, love," Cecily stated, giving Lock a wicked smile. She ignored Jane completely, not once glancing over at her. Was this a game? Was it a trick, a rouse? Jane wished the woman would give her a sign, anything to dispel her fears. But Cecily refused to take her eyes off Lock and dread and fear warred for dominance in Jane's heart.

"And who might you be, missy?" Lock asked, licking his lips as his eyes roamed unashamed up and down Cecily's scantily-clad body.

"Their fuckin' whore. Not tha' I ever got anythin' for it," she spat, glaring daggers at Jane. And Jane's heart broke. There was no hint of the love or humor that her eyes normally possessed. Only anger and disgust. The Cecily that Jane knew was gone and the whore they had originally thought her to be was all she was.

It had all been a lie.

Jane opened her mouth to call out, but hesitated, still hoping and praying that what she was seeing wasn't true, that she hadn't been played for a fool. An act, that's what it was. Cecily was just acting. She had to be.

But nothing changed in Cecily's eyes, no spark of mischief or defiance or even a semblance of regret. There was only utter disgust as she grimaced at Jane before focusing once more on Lock.

An act, that's all it was. Just an act. It had to be.

"Ya don't want her," Cecily purred, sauntering up to Lock and pulling herself flush against him, running a finger down his chest teasingly. "She's not good for nothin', except bein' a fuckin' bitch. Put up one hell of a fight, she will, and after the day you've had, wha' with takin' this here screechin' board of a ship, it's sure ta be more of a pain than pleasure. But me, I'll take care of ya. Ya can just lie back and let me do all the work." She gazed up at him from beneath her eyelashes, flirting, teasing, giving.

Just an act, just an act, just an act.

Lock grinned down at Cecily, completely taken by her. Jane couldn't blame him. Cecily knew exactly how to make herself desirable.

"That's quite an offer you're making there." Lock stated. His eyes hardened and his hand snatched Cecily's wrist tight. For her part, Cecily barely winced, just resumed looking at him with sultry eyes.

It was then that Jane's conviction that Cecily was acting was renewed. The woman she knew would never have taken such abuse from anyone, not without a sarcastic comment or an insult to their person.

But there was still a sliver of doubt in Jane, one she tried desperately to squash, but was having very little success.

"But I'm familiar with ruses," Lock continued, "and know one when I see it."

Cecily's smile just heated further. "Then ya should know my offer is genuine, Cap'ain."

Lock paused at that, seeming to contemplate Cecily's subtle challenge. Doubt flickered across his face briefly before his arrogance won out once more and he grinned predatorily at her.

"The following night, you will watch as your so-called *Captain* is ravaged to prove your intentions are, in fact, genuine. Until then, you shall not be let out of my sight."

Cecily glanced over at Jane, her eyes full of hatred and a wicked grin on her face. "It would be my pleasure."

Lock nodded in satisfaction. Without taking his eyes or his hands off Cecily, he addressed his crew, "Lock 'em in the brig!"

She glanced up, seeing that her crew—no more than fifteen strong with the addition of the new recruits, who had been found and dragged up on deck—remained at gunpoint, all their weapons thrown into a pile on the port side of the main deck. All except Cooksley and his two supporters, who, when offered to join Lock's crew, had accepted readily and were now standing amongst them looking happier than they had even been under her command.

"Traitorous bastards," Jane muttered under her breath.

But she couldn't help feel a bit of warmth and pride seeping back into her soul. Most of her crew had stayed loyal to her, had refused to join Lock's crew, even knowing they wouldn't live to see another sunrise should they choose to do so. She didn't delude herself into thinking that in any way gave her an advantage, but it did give her some comfort and strength. Jane shifted in the grip of the two men, earning her a growl and a painful squeeze to her upper arm from the one on her right.

"Aye, Captain," one of Lock's men guarding Jane's crew stated, his tone betraying his confusion at the order, but his loyalty making him follow it nonetheless. Jane understood his confusion. Once offered a place in the victorious pirate's crew, the remaining members were killed and thrown overboard, or left to sink with the ship. For all intents and purposes, the brig should be emptying at this point, not filling.

Lock tore his eyes from Cecily, who continued to pet him adoringly, and grinned at his men. "It's a long, arduous journey back home, and I think we've found our entertainment!"

Cheers of "aye" answered Lock's proclamation, Cooksley and his mates the loudest of them all. And they began herding her crew toward the hatch and the brig below.

Jane herself was propelled forward, the men restraining her walking her forward to join her crew in the hold.

But Lock's voice rang out once more, stopping the three of them in their tracks. "Not that one," he commanded, his gaze glinting at Jane, as Cecily ignored her from his side. "She's coming with me."

~~*

Jane kicked at the floor with her heel in frustration. Of course, he would keep her in her own quarters. Because being humiliated, degraded, having her purity threatened, crew taken, and title stripped were not enough. No, she had to be locked up in her own quarters, too.

Lock had produced shackles from somewhere—she'd be surprised if they weren't the ones she kept on board the *Tantibus,* because that just seemed fitting right about now—and secured her wrists to the bedpost of her own bed. It was done in such a way that she could neither stand properly nor get atop the bed, having to instead awkwardly sit on the floor, chained up like an animal. Just another cut to her pride and dignity.

"Comfortable, *Captain*?" Lock sneered, crouching down in front of her, devoid of both his coat and hat, making himself at home in her quarters, the bilge rat.

Jane spat at him, not daring to look at Cecily standing behind him, running her fingers through his hair. Though she still told herself it had to be an act, couldn't be anything but an act, it still hurt. It still tore at her heart to see the woman she cared about, the woman she thought cared for her, clamoring all over another as if Jane had never even mattered.

Lock stood up, face set in a sneer as he wiped the spit from his cheek. The only thing she received for it was a hard kick to the ribs.

Jane grunted, the air leaving her lungs in a swift exhalation as pain lanced up her side. She gasped for breath, feeling like there wasn't enough air in the room.

Gasping, she glared up at Lock, refusing to let him think he had gotten the best of her, would ever get the best of her. Whether she died or lived through this whole ordeal, she would never let him win.

Cecily stepped forward, sliding herself in front of Lock with the ease and grace of practice, her back to Jane. "Let me take care of ya, Cap'ain," she purred, capturing the man's attention immediately as she flaunted her breasts. "Let me make ya feel good."

Lock slid his hands up her sides possessively, a feral grin spreading across his face. His gaze swept up momentarily and, noticing Jane watching, addressed her even as he continued to fondle Cecily. "Don't worry love," he mock-soothed her, "you'll get your turn tomorrow." If this was an act—an assumption that Jane was thinking was not true anymore, what with the current event—Cecily was being damn convincing. Jane didn't think that she would take it this far. And yet, here they were.

Jane averted her eyes, ignoring Lock's comment and knowing exactly to where the event unfolding before her would lead, and having no desire to be any more a witness to it than she was already forced to be.

But try as she might, she couldn't shut out the sounds.

The rustle of clothing pushed aside, followed by strings of compliments and ribald comments hissed out between breathy pants. The squelch of lips and spit on skin was punctuated by moans or grunts until those took over entirely, filling up the room with their imagery and obvious manner as the bed frame rocked and bumped, taking Jane's iron-clamped wrists for a ride. Her head filled with scenarios without her consent, taunting and teasing her with what she and Cecily could have had, what they could have been, but might be no more, if the space between them was filled with lies and betrayal. Try as she might, Jane felt her heart ache as she was forced to bear witness, sitting there chained like a dog, listening to the reason why her world may very well shatter to pieces again. And it continued to shatter, over and over again, until she felt like she couldn't breathe, couldn't even draw a single breath, as tears slipped down her face unhindered and unwanted, but whether from anger or misery, she no longer knew.

She sat there, hearing the sounds of their coupling replay over and over in her head even after they had smoothed out into even breaths and soft snores. Even after the sunlight had disappeared from beyond the window and darkness had taken its place.

But though the sounds were on replay, Jane's mind was whirling, thinking, planning, going through scenarios and ways she could turn the tide in her favor. She would come out of this no less the woman she was, with her life intact or not.

~~*

"Rise and shine, poppet!"

Jane awoke with a start, jumping as hands appeared in front of her, grabbing and hauling her to her feet, pawing at her unnecessarily as they unshackled her wrists. She didn't even remember that important detail occurring, but then again, such a rude awakening left little for her sleep-addled brain to digest.

She was all but dragged from the captain's quarters—her own bloody quarters for fuck's sake—and out onto the main deck. The sun's rays pierced her eyes like daggers, forcing her to blink to allow her sight to adjust. By then, she and her unscheduled entourage had come to halt and she was finally able to take in her surroundings.

The members of Lock's crew stood surrounding their captain on the main deck, all with various degrees of malignant anticipation and vengeful glee upon their faces. Jane could feel the rocking of the ship beneath her feet, so used to the movement that she hadn't noticed it before. They must have gotten underway sometime yesterday—Lock, obviously too lazy to unload his goods from her ship and onto his own, decided to just sail them both onward—while she was... indisposed. Jane forcefully pushed the memories from the day before from her mind, knowing that she needed a clear head today if she was to live to see tomorrow.

She did, however, notice that Cecily seemed to be absent from what she could see of the crowd. A pang of worry shot through her before she could stop it, wondering for a second if Cecily was hurt, or worse. Lock had said that she was to remain in his sight at all times. But there were too many sweaty bodies around for Jane to get a good look, and she had more pressing matters to focus on at the moment.

"Ah, there she is! The infamous Captain Avery," Lock crowed, spreading his arms wide. His attention on her drew that of his surrounding crew as well, all eyes finding her and the anticipation seeming to grow within the circle. It did not look promising.

"I think the dear Captain here should show us her skills," Lock pressed on, striding toward her leisurely, arms still out in what could be construed as a friendly gesture, if not for the feral grin on his face. "Show us her worth and how she earned her title. What do ya say, boys?"

A resounding "Aye!" sounded from the crew around her.

Lock threw an arm around her shoulders, then the men who had brought her out released her into his care as he forcefully steered her forward and toward the middle of the circle of men.

"You know, we've heard a lot about you," he intoned, lowering his voice in an exaggerated whisper. "About your aptitude with a sword, how you can kill a man dead with a single shot from a hundred yards away, about your tactics and inventive strategies that usually end with you and your crew victorious."

He stopped just at the last row of men, a pathway still open for him to continue on down, but he ignored it. Instead, he leaned in close until she could feel his breath on her ear.

"Let's see if those other rumors are true," he sneered, before roughly shoving her into the center of the ring.

The gap closed behind her as she stumbled on the deck. A clatter of metal followed close behind her, and she glanced toward the sound, noticing the sword at her feet just before she registered movement of someone else being thrown into the ring across from her.

Dread filled her, knowing now exactly what she was being forced to do.

"It's a fight to the death," Lock announced. "If either of you refuse, you will not only lose your life, but cause another of your crew to take your place sooner than they would otherwise. The reward for coming out victorious is a little more time with what remains of your life."

Looking up, Jane immediately recognized the man who she was going to have to fight. A tall, willowy man—more of a boy, really, which was a shame—a sword held deftly, but not overly skillfully, in his hand. He had been amongst those who had been recruited from the *Liberty*. For a split second, Jane wondered if this boy was loyal to Lock. After all, the new recruits had been off a ship that had been carrying Lock's goods. But she dismissed the thought almost as soon as it came up. A merchant sailor was just that: a merchant. This boy was not loyal to Lock.

But the fact still remained that the lad was just that. Jane would estimate he was no older than seventeen, eighteen at the most. Not uncommonly young to be aboard a ship, but still young. Not someone whose life should be taken away so frivolously.

"Begin!" Lock shouted, breaking the silence that had settled over the deck.

With a cry, the boy immediately launched toward Jane, sword poised to swipe at her middle. A poor first move, in her opinion. He was at her in a second, but it wasn't until he began sweeping the sword arm across to gut her that she moved.

Jane dropped on the deck with her legs spread in a half-crouch as her right hand snatched up the sword at her feet. The boy's swipe flew over her head, missing her completely. She immediately shifted her body and weight to her outstretched foot, coming up from her crouch onto the boy's right side, his current weak side.

She wasted no time at all in stepping in behind him, placing her sword at his throat. He instantly stilled.

"I do not want to kill you," she whispered in his ear, hoping he understood.

"Good, then it shall make my job a whole lot easier," he grunted out. She felt his weight begin to shift once more, this time in order to help him swipe back at her.

She pressed her sword closer, tightening her grip and forcing the boy to be still once more.

"Listen to me. You think they are going to let you live if you win? They'll kill you, too, eventually." The boy gave a grunt, but whether it was in affirmation or disbelief, Jane didn't know.

"Just kill him already!" A voice sounded from the surrounding men. A chorus of agreement and insults followed the outburst and Jane knew her time was running out.

"Just play dead," she whispered hurriedly. Then, before the boy gave any sign of understanding, Jane dropped her sword, put both hands on the side of his head, and twisted sharply. She pulled her strength with the act, so not to hurt the boy, but for all intents and purposes, it looked like she had just snapped his neck.

The boy flopped on the deck, limp. Apparently, Jane's plan had looked good enough to him after all.

"Impressive, *Captain*," Lock congratulated, with a sarcastic undertone as Jane looked up. "But that was over much too quick." He strode toward her lazily, stopping next to the boy and glancing down at his prone form.

"Shame," he stated, nudging the boy with the toe of his boot. Then he turned, seeming to lose interest, and Jane released the breath she hadn't even realized she had been holding.

But the next second, Lock whirled back around, unsheathing his sword in the process, and stabbed the boy where he lay. The boy jerked, eyes springing open in shock and pain. Jane flinched in surprise.

Lock tutted, staring down at the boy before extracting his sword from his chest with a sharp jerk. The boy gasped in pain, jerked, and gurgled for a few seconds, before he finally laid still, blood pooling around him.

Lock wiped his sword on a clean section of the boy's shirt before leveling it at Jane. "You try that again, and I'll kill your entire crew right now and slit the whore's throat for good measure."

With that, he strode away, a cruel smile once again alighting his features, as though he hadn't just killed a boy in cold blood.

He must have signaled one of his men, for the line before her suddenly parted and another crewmember was shoved into the center, huffing indignantly at the rough handling, but managing to stay on his feet easily enough. Jane's heart pained as she recognized him. Michael Jeffries, a man who had been a valued member of her crew for almost five years now. His dexterity with a blade was renowned amongst her crew, if not others as well. He was truly one of the finest on the *Tantibus,* if not the finest. This was not a fight she would win easily, but she knew she could. She had to.

No more ruses, no more plans. This was kill or be killed, with not just her own life on the line. And she had no choice but to follow the rules.

"Begin!"

~~*

Thankfully—although in some cases remorsefully— she had so far managed to emerge victorious in every one of the fights. Four of the seven, however, had been members of her own crew—including the first boy and Jeffries—and she had taken no pleasure in ending their lives. The rest of her opponents had been volunteer men from Lock's own crew, accusing her own men of going easy on her because really, how hard could it be to best a woman? Jane was sure the evidence spoke for itself, and yet, Lock's men continued to step forward into the executioner's ring, falling before her blade one after the other.

But she was tiring to the point of exhaustion. The last few fights had been hard-won, from which she had received several bruises, knocks to the head—which did not help her coordination in the slightest—along with multiple cuts and slashes to her torso and extremities. Her strength and ability to continue on was waning, and she wasn't sure how much longer she could last. But nor did she know how long Lock would let this go on. At this rate, she would be dead in another few rounds, and he wouldn't be able to make good on his threat from yesterday.

Jane paused at that thought. Maybe her current state had been his plan from the start. Wear her out so that when he did bed her, it wasn't as much of a struggle.

Lock's call of, "Who's next?" rose above the chatter that had arisen after her latest feat, and the body of the man currently being dragged toward the railing and tossed overboard without a care. There was to be no honorable send off for anyone aboard, even for those of Lock's own crew. Honestly, the man was an insult to pirates everywhere, which was a feat in and of itself.

"It would be my pleasure," a familiar cocky voice sounded from her left. She glanced toward the man now emerging from the crowd, sword in hand, for once feeling gleeful anticipation for the next fight.

"This I shall enjoy," Cooksley taunted.

Jane just flashed him a vicious grin and growled, "That makes two of us."

Cooksley charged immediately, not bothering to wait for Lock's permission. The clash of metal on metal reverberated across the deck as their swords met. Jane, although taken by surprise with his sudden attack, was able to bring her sword up in time to meet his blow. Metal hissed as the blades slid along each other, breaking apart only to collide together again and again in quick succession, as each opponent tried to sneak under the other's guard. Cooksley very nearly succeeded, one of his strikes missing Jane by a hair's breadth. But she gave as good as she got, nearly gutting him before he just managed to step out of range.

"This is what you were waiting for, was it not? A chance to gut me and take command? Too bad there isn't much left to command," Jane said with false sympathy. Her breath was coming in short pants now, sweat coating her forehead and plastering flyaway hairs to her face. Cooksley was definitely faring better, barely breaking a sweat, but he hadn't been at it for what felt like hours. He had the advantage, but she was nothing if not a survivor.

"Yes, a pity, it truly is," Cooksley responded, making a jab at her torso which she effectively parried, but with more effort than should have been necessary. "Guess I'll just settle for the former then."

He almost was able to gut her on more than one occasion, but in the end, it was his bravado which gave her the opening she needed. He fell to his knees gasping and grimacing in agony, her sword protruding from his chest. Blood ran down Jane's sword arm, pouring from a deep slice on her bicep, a token from the man dying before her. But as much as Jane despised the man, especially during the last few weeks, she didn't feel he deserved to suffer. So with a final swipe, she slit his throat, leaving his body to fall lifeless onto the deck.

And yet, she felt no weight lifted from her shoulders with his death, no relief, no joy. He had made his choice, had willingly joined Lock's crew, and volunteered for this fight. So why didn't she feel any better about his death than she did her own loyal crew? She should feel something, but she was just too exhausted, her brain unable to give the energy it took to create emotion for this man. Just as well, she supposed.

"I think you've had enough for one day," Lock remarked from his perch by the main mast. He motioned toward her flippantly and several crew members immediately stepped forward. She made a stand, leveling the sword toward the advancing men, but she was barely able to nick them before they wrestled the weapon out of her hands and restrained her. Exhausted, she gave little fight as they half-led, half-dragged her away.

But as they neared her quarters, the thought of what was to come jolted through her. A new surge of adrenaline—small in comparison, but still present nonetheless—coursed through her body. She couldn't let this happen, couldn't just give up, no matter how drained she felt or how hopeless it seemed.

She pulled back, taking the men leading her by surprise and scrambling out of their hold. She had no weapon anymore, no way to fight the twenty-something men that still occupied her ship and had taken everything from her. But in her weary brain, none of this registered. All Jane could comprehend was her need to get away.

She fought with all her might, striking out at the man who held her and those that came to take his place. And she felt she was winning, succeeding despite her fatigue and lack of options for escape. It didn't matter though, for she wasn't as adept as she usually was. The next thing she felt was a pain in the side of her skull just before the whole world tilted on its side and darkness enveloped her. She didn't even remember hitting the deck.

~~*

Waking with a pounding headache was not something Jane particularly enjoyed. Truly it was, well, a pain in both the literal and figurative forms. Worse than any hangover she'd ever experienced.

But this pain by far outshined them all. Not only did she have to deal with the headache, but also sore and paining muscles and injuries from the fights earlier that day—or had it been the day before? Her internal clock was a little off at the moment, so it was quite difficult to be sure. Though upon quick inspection, she was glad to see that her open wounds had been decently wrapped and—she assumed—somewhat treated, so she wouldn't be dying of infection any time soon. If she was lucky, that is. Not that it mattered, as she was sure there were worse ways that she would be dying when the time came.

As her mind became more aware, so did her extremities, and she attempted to sit up. That proved to be harder than she originally thought as she found herself shackled wrist-to-wrist to not only to the bedpost on the side as before, but to a hook, now decoratively set in the wall above the head of the bed.

Fear shot through Jane, thinking that the deed had already been done and that the fight that had occurred actually had very little to do with the soreness of her muscles. She only calmed a bit when another mental inspection of her body immediately dismissed that thought. And the fact that she was still fully-clothed, except her boots and socks for some odd reason, helped calm her slightly. But only slightly.

It was a deed that she had no doubt was going to come to pass. And soon, if her current position was anything to go by.

Lock was nowhere to be found in the room, which was also odd, but thankfully it seemed the man had no intention of taking her whilst she was unconscious. How noble. But not knowing when he might return gave her an uncertain amount of time to devise a plan.

That thought was what drove Jane to begin a frantic search for anything and everything that could be used in her defense and escape. Jane maneuvered her body just so, moving her foot off the bed to brush the underside where she usually kept a knife stashed. No knife.

Lock had more brains than she thought. He was apparently not taking the chance of underestimating her again. Not a single scrap of anything remotely helpful was within reach.

Jane could feel her frustration spiraling while she desperately started pulling and struggling with the manacles, hoping, praying, pleading to any deity that would listen, to just let her strength be enough to break them. But nothing came of it except a few new bruises.

She sank back, her breath coming in short pants from the exertion. There was nothing she could do, nothing at all but to wait for Lock to return and hope she could somehow overpower him and... and... then what?

It would be all for nothing. She would have over two dozen pirates to get through, and despite her confidence in her prowess, she knew that even she couldn't best them all and survive. She would be overpowered and then end up dead or right back here again. This was truly not a situation that bode well for her.

Jane didn't know how much time passed as she lay there, lost in her own thoughts and drowning in the despair that ebbed and flowed like the tide. Hope and determination filled her, only to wane as the gravity of it all washed over her once more. She could feel a few tears slip down her face, but she was otherwise completely unaware of her surroundings. Maybe it was better that way.

But after a time, she was sure she could hear voices, familiar and soothing, but it was unclear whether they were in her head or not. She couldn't make out what they were saying, nor did her mind connect who exactly it was that was speaking, friend or foe. And she couldn't seem to acquire the energy to find out.

However, her brain decided that it did want to discover who on earth was making such a fuss, especially when hands enclosed her wrists and began fiddling with the manacles surrounding them. But only bits and pieces made their way through the fog that had covered her mind.

" ... 'ain... time to... the ship... "

" ... wrong... what did... her... "

Then a voice, soft and silky and so achingly familiar, swept the fog aside altogether, slamming her back into the present with jarring force.

"Lioness? Come on, talk ta me," it pleaded.

Cecily.

Jane blinked, needing to know if the woman who she thought she cared for, may even love, was really here, or if it was just a figment of her own imagination and desire.

But it wasn't. As her vision cleared, Cecily's concerned face came into focus, just as beautiful as she remembered. And she felt her heart swell with the fondness she felt for the woman.

It had been an act after all.

Though the memories of her supposed betrayal, the hate and disgust that had been so clear in Cecily's eyes as she had glared at Jane still burned through her mind, she forced herself to disregard them. It hadn't been real. Cecily was here and she hadn't betrayed her.

"How did you—?" Jane babbled out, but Cecily shushed her quickly.

"Come on, love, there's no time for tha'," Cecily stated with a shake of her head, cupping Jane's face in her soft hands. "Ya've got a ship ta take back."

It was then that Jane became aware of her freedom as she reached out to take ahold of Cecily's hands—to stop her or just to hold her, Jane didn't know yet. Her wrists were red and raw, the skin broken in places but they were no longer shackled. She was free, she had been freed.

And Cecily, encouraging Jane to get up to take her ship back, was here, by her side once more. Not the Cecily that had made an appearance when Lock had taken the ship, but the Cecily she knew and... loved. Yes, she loved her. After all that had happened, admitting that seemed like nothing in comparison.

She was here, the Cecily who did what she wanted and took orders from no one. Who insulted and cut down Jane in order to keep her ego a normal size, and yet whispered endearments and sweet nothings to soothe the ache. The one who desired control, but was happy to give most of it up to Jane. That Cecily was hovering over her, concern hidden behind a smile that was now slowly forming on her face as Jane stared up at her.

It was clear to Jane that she had been the one to release her.

Jane stared back at Cecily, searching her eyes for... something, anything that would convince her without a doubt that she wasn't just fabricating lies based off her own hopes and desires. That Cecily, the Cecily she knew, had been the only Cecily the whole time, just hidden behind a mask, instead of the other way around. That she had been hers and only hers and still remained hers.

"My lioness," Cecily said, smiling down wickedly at Jane before bending down and sliding her lips against Jane's. And Jane knew immediately that Cecily was hers and had always been hers. She leaned up into the kiss, deepening it and feeling Cecily respond enthusiastically.

But the moment broke all too fast for Jane's liking as Cecily pulled back.

"Later, I promise," she said with a small smile. "But for now, let's take ya ship back."

Jane nodded before tensing as she became aware of a shuffling movement by the door of another person in the room.

Her head shot over, expecting Lock or one of his crewmen to be standing there, leering at her. But the sight that greeted her was a better one. The tall form of Worth, slightly bruised, roughed up, and just a bit uncomfortable at the display of affection he had no doubt just witnessed, but otherwise unhurt.

He cleared his throat upon noticing her focus on him. "Captain," he greeted with a dip of his head.

Jane could feel her face fall at the title and she looked down, ashamed. She had killed her own men, those loyal to her, just to spare her own life. "I am not worthy of that title."

"According to us, you are," Worth corrected, looking quite adamant and determined.

Jane got up from the bed, wincing slightly as her sore muscles stretched and strained before walking over to Worth and clasping him on the shoulder. She tried to convey all her thanks to him, not just for today, but for all the years he had stood by her and helped her and helped her.

Worth just nodded back in understanding.

"We really ought to move along now," he whispered with a glance back toward the door as though he expected it to open any second. "I'm not sure how long the rest of the crew can stay hidden before their absence from the brig is discovered."

"What?" Jane asked, surprised. But really it should have occurred to her earlier, seeing as how Worth had so obviously gotten out. "How'd you all get out?"

Worth just nodded toward Cecily in answer.

Cecil shrugged in response, like helping condemned men escape the brig was easy. "I managed ta flitch Lock's keys while he was uhhh... sleepin', and unlock the brig. I told them ta wait for an opportune moment, and well, tha' seems ta be now, so we best be movin' along."

"But where's Lock?" Jane asked in confusion. He was supposed to be keeping an eye on Cecily, and if she was here...

"Drinkin' with his crew," Cecily spat, scrunching her nose in disgust. But Jane couldn't help how adorable the look was, despite the nature of it. "They're spread out all over the ship, so gettin' here was a little tricky, but Worth was able ta cut down their numbers on our way here, so tha' should be beneficial."

"And noticeable," Jane commented, and Worth gave a nod. They really needed to get moving.

Jane strode quietly over to the door, Worth and Cecily behind her.

"I estimate no more than thirty now remain aboard," Worth stated, with just a hint of smugness. Jane grinned, knowing he was the reason for their drop in numbers. There are eleven of us, including you, so I think the odds are decent enough."

"Aye."

"Here," Worth said, offering a sword, "you best take this."

"You know about my stash." It wasn't a question, merely an amused statement as Jane recognized the sword in her hands. She kept a secret stash of various weapons in these quarters, well-hidden and hard to find, unless you knew where to look.

"Yes, of course, I'm your first mate. I feel it's my duty to know."

Jane just grumbled half-heartedly as Worth slowly opened the door, checking to make sure the way was clear. She was incredibly grateful that he had come to help her, that he hadn't given up on her, and still saw her as his captain, despite all that had happened. She just hoped the rest of the men felt the same.

"Looks like the crew got a little impatient," Worth announced, throwing open the door wide as a few of Lock's men approached, swords at the ready and murder in their eyes. The sound of metal clanging and shouts could be heard from beyond, proving Worth's theory.

"Coll probably put them up to it," Jane accused, stepping forward to meet one of the men head-on. She feigned to the right, only to slice the man clean across his torso as she shifted direction at the last second. He dropped at her feet with a pained cry. "That man is too damn persuasive for his own good."

"Yes, well then, let's hope he did a fine job of it!" Worth called from ahead, cutting his way across the deck.

"Aye!"

Jane turned around then, about to order Cecily to stay in her quarters, only to find the woman behind her, a pistol in her hand. She stared at her in shock.

"Wha'?" Cecily asked innocently, and Jane was immediately reminded of their first meeting in the captain's quarters of the *Liberty*.

Suddenly, something behind Jane caught Cecily's attention, and she shifted her weight in order to turn around. But before she could face the threat, Cecily had raised the pistol and fired, the shot brushing past Jane's head, the air from it moving her hair. She finally turned fully, watching as the man that had been sneaking up behind her toppled over lifeless, a hole in his head.

Jane looked back at Cecily in shock, mouth agape comically, if Cecily's bark of laughter was anything to go by.

"I may not know my way aroun' a blade, but a pistol is pretty damn easy," she explained, hurrying past Jane toward the downed man. "Just aim and shoot."

"You've used your one shot."

"Don't worry," Cecily appeased, reaching down and snatching up the dead man's pistol at his waist. She checked it over and finding it loaded, nodded in approval. "I'll be collectin' them along the way."

Jane laughed, not knowing if it was due to the absurdity of Cecily knowing her way around a pistol, or to cover up the flush of her cheeks at the arousal it spurred in her. But it was soon wiped from her face as a man to her left gave a cry of outrage, charging, and she was slammed right back into the fight.

~~*

Jane would love to say that the battle had been clean and neat. That she and her crew had taken back the *Tantibus* with ease and little loss or injury. That everything had gone off without a hitch.

But that would be a lie.

It had been bloody and gruesome, men lying on the deck, bleeding, their innards on display for all to see, limbs severed and blood, so much blood, staining the wood. It would take ages to get it out, if it was even possible

Jane had done the best she could, taking down men right and left, shouting orders to her crew as she spotted them, hoping that they all shared Worth's resolve that she was still a worthy captain.

They did, following her without question and grouping behind her, so their strength grew with their numbers. She led them with confidence, Cecily by her side. The woman was a force to be reckoned with when determined enough, taking down men with any pistol she could get her hands on, and when there were none, bludgeoning her opponents with the empty gun.

Jane had to remind herself on multiple occasions to focus on the fight occurring around her, as she got distracted watching Cecily fight, and wondering how on earth this woman was hers. She loved her, truly and wholeheartedly, and hoped Cecily knew that.

Well, if they made out of this alive, she would just have to show her.

When they finally did take back the *Tantibus*, it was by forcing the remaining six of Lock's crew members—not including Lock himself, as Jane had personally slit his throat in a very anticlimactic fight seconds before—to surrender to her and her crew. Despite her hate for these men, she decide that they were needed and offered them the usual choice, join her or die. Needless to say, her offer was taken up by all but one of the men, her prowess from earlier most likely still remembered.

With that, she ordered all able hands aboard the ship to turn her about in order to fire upon Lock's warship still following not far behind. By some miracle, they managed to knock half its cannons out of commission with the first round, enabling them to win a firefight that would have otherwise been suicide, with minimal damage.

Several of her crew had lost their lives in the initial battle, and a couple more in the following firefight, including Coll. He had been more a man of words than weapons, so it came as little surprise that he had died, but it still weighed her heart. Especially when the rest of her crew confirmed that he had been the one to persuade them to begin the fight early. It had most likely been the reason they had come out victorious. A few minutes later, and the element of surprise would have been lost.

Most of her crew, however, came out of the battle with few wounds and bruises, including herself. But Jane didn't care much. She was once again manning her ship, steering her toward their cache island to repair and regroup. The battle had been won.

"Come on *Cap'ain*, let's tend ta those wounds," a silky voice demanded to her right, followed by a sweet, intoxicating smell that caressed her senses. A pair of arms wrapped around her shoulders, a hand covering her own lovingly, where she had been stroking the ring about her neck. She winced, several of the wounds twinging with the contact.

Jane glanced over at Cecily, her heart nearly bursting with the sight. Warm, brown eyes shone with adoration, full lips parted slightly in a coy grin as fingers danced lightly over her shoulders. Cecily would never know the effect she had on Jane, for there were no words she could use to describe it. Love would never be able to fully explain it, but it was the closest word she had.

Cecily seemed to read it all in Jane's eyes, though, for her smile turned into a more serious expression as she stated, "I know." Then her smile was back the next instant, teasing. "But if we don't get those wounds wrapped, ya won't be aroun' for me to show ya just how /feel."

Jane grinned, despite the pit of nervousness that had opened up in her stomach, trying to swallow her excitement whole. But she ignored it, glancing away to see Worth approaching to take the helm in her place. She nodded her thanks to him, and he, in turn, cocked an eyebrow and smirked knowingly as Cecily took her hand and led her away.

Toward her quarters.

Toward a new life.

Toward the rest of their lives.

SKY

KNIGHTS

ALEX POWELL

ONE

"We're approaching the coordinates."

Dounia hand-signalled back and concentrated on the landscape below them, a forest dotted with snow and ice. Somewhere down there, below the tree line, was the German front line. Dounia's ear twitched and she grinned into the mirror spell that Ira had set up, and saw Ira's return smile reflected back at her from the cockpit behind hers.

"It's time to cut the engines."

"I hate this part the most," Meow said from his position wrapped around Dounia's shoulders.

"Cutting engines," Ira said, her voice muffled by the telephone spell that projected her voice into Dounia's cockpit.

The plane dipped, and Dounia's stomach plunged as they descended. The engines stilled and quieted, leaving the three of them alone in the air, with only the whirling of the wind to accompany them. Meow's ears flattened against his skull, and he curled up closer around Dounia's shoulders. His claws scraped against her skin, even through her leather bomber jacket.

"Cat's aren't made for flying," Meow complained against her ear.

"And yet you always insist on coming."

"I can't just let you two get yourselves killed without me, can I?"

"Hey, quit your jabbering, you two," Ira said. She winked through the lens of her goggles. "Are we in formation?"

Dounia checked Ira's other mirror spells that had been set up outside the plane to reflect what was behind them and reported back. "In formation. Going in."

Dounia watched the two planes behind her in the mirror spell and waited. Any moment, the two of them were going to put on a burst of speed and distract the German anti-aircraft gunners so that she and Ira could go in for the bombing run.

"And they're off," Ira said. "Bombs primed, coordinates approaching at two hundred fifty meters."

Dounia smiled. "Get ready, we're going to have to do this fast."

"Every single time, you tell me this," Ira said. "We're used to it by now, surely."

"I will never be used to this," Meow said, digging his claws in tighter.

"Two hundred meters." Dounia got ready, muscles coiled and ready for action. She flashed another grin at Ira in the mirror spell, feeling the adrenaline thrumming through her veins, skin practically bursting with it. Meow could complain all he liked; this was the best feeling in the world.

"One hundred fifty meters."

There was no sound of engines, just the wind whistling past—and if Dounia strained her ears, the sound of anticipating snow. Dounia hoped they'd return before the blizzard started. Their formation had been pushing it with the weather like this. But if it meant surprising the German lines, it was a risk the squadron had been willing to take.

"One hundred meters. Seventy-five. Fifty and closing," Ira said. "Get ready. Bombs away. Go!"

Meow yowled in her ear as Dounia leapt into action, jumping up and out of her seat in the cockpit and edging her way carefully out across the wing of the biplane as Ira mirrored her on the other side. Below her, the tops of the trees flew past in a blur, but Dounia ignored it. She wouldn't fall, and she was fearless. The wind pulled at her, fighting to drag her off her perch on the wing, but Dounia, air veteran extraordinaire, knew how to keep her feet. As soon as Dounia was in position, she signalled to Ira.

"This is sheer madness," Meow muttered, tail lashing against the collar of her jacket.

Dounia restarted her propeller, hands steady as she pulled the engine back into action by hand. The propeller roared to life, and she and Ira scrambled back into their seats. Meow shivered against her neck and growled unhappily. Dounia raised her hand and stroked his back, soothing him back into compliance.

Dounia steered the plane back up and around. A few stray bursts of anti-aircraft gun rounds fired off around them, but Dounia escaped them easily. It was a shot in the dark, and Dounia grinned fiercely, the thrill of flight still running through her veins.

"Reform, we're going in for another run, maybe two."

The other two planes in their small formation regrouped with them in midair. This time around, Dounia and Ira would be distracting the enemy so that their comrade could bomb them.

"Is everyone still alright?" Dounia asked.

"Looks like," Ira replied. "Our formation comrades are both still intact, at least."

Meow growled again, low in his throat, and Dounia caressed the spot between his ears. "Steady, my brother," she said.

"Why can't you just blast them with a fireball?" Meow whined, scrunched up around her neck.

"I might catch our wooden plane on fire," Dounia replied dryly. "And give away our position."

Just as they fell in line behind their comrade, the first few flakes of snow began to fall. The huge, fat flakes, fluffy and soft, drifted gently down to earth. However, Dounia was certain that the snowfall would soon intensify. Before they knew it, they'd be snared in the midst of a white-out snowstorm. Dounia didn't want to land their plane in the middle of a blizzard, but they still had two runs to go.

"We'd better make this quick," Ira said. "We can make it."

"Are you sure?" Dounia asked.

"We can make it," Ira repeated, and Dounia didn't argue. Somehow, Ira always knew.

"Coming back around on coordinates," Ira said, and Dounia focused again.

It was almost time, and Dounia was ready. This part was just as difficult as flying low over the German lines and dropping their load. They might not be cutting their engines this time around, but they'd have to court the fire of the anti-aircraft guns. It was just as dangerous and just as exhilarating as their previous run.

"They've launched Messerschmitts," Ira reported. "Stay on target."

The bar had been raised, but Messerschmitts had a stalling speed of less than their Po-2's highest speed, so while a Messerschmitt could strafe them on a fly-by, tailing a Po-2 would stall their craft. A German plane roared by overhead, the sound of their engines drowning out all other noise, until the spatter of machine gun fire punctured the air.

"We're fine," Ira said. "It missed us."

Ira said so to soothe Meow's ruffled feathers, as a growl rumbled up from his throat at the threat.

Luck had failed one of their stalwart comrades. The strafing run by the German planes had damaged them beyond help, and they spiralled down, yawing wildly through the frigid, snow-filled air. Dounia watched them go. The downed plane flailed like a flake on the wind, to its resting place in a frost-coated strand of trees.

"They might still be alive," Dounia said, straining to see if there was any movement below.

"Stay on target," Ira repeated. "Our other comrade is still aloft and still needs to drop their bombs. Approaching coordinates, put on speed... now!"

They shot ahead, and a moment later, a spotlight discovered them. Dounia dragged at her controls, dodging the ray of light that illuminated them and made them a target. The anti-aircraft guns started firing. They were close enough that Dounia saw the puffs of smoke below as the guns emptied their ire into the night.

"At least we know we've found the German lines," Dounia said, grinning.

"Messerschmitt!" Meow screamed, claws digging in painfully.

Backlit against the night sky, they tempted the guns to target them. This time, the strafing run damaged their plane. Dounia ducked her head as bullets cascaded all around her, digging into the frame of their craft and blasting chunks out of it.

When Dounia raised her head again, they remained aloft, if not completely intact.

"Everyone okay?" Dounia asked.

"No thanks to anything you did," Meow grumbled against her ear, and his fur bristled against her cheek.

"Fine," Ira said, but her voice was tight with tension.

Dounia focused her eyes back on her fellow aviator, and her heart leapt in her chest at the sight of blood, dark against the sleeve of Ira's jacket.

"You're hit," she said.

"Yes, it's a scratch," Ira replied. "Nothing to worry about. I'm fine."

"You're not fine!" Dounia said, baring her teeth.

There was nothing to be done up here, in their cockpits thousands of feet above the ground. They needed to return to base. Their craft was damaged, and one of their pilots injured. Surely, they could turn back at this point.

"We can turn back," Ira said, somehow realizing what Dounia was thinking. "Our last plane was taken down, bombs and all, and the blizzard is picking up. We got in five runs tonight anyway."

Without thinking or replying, Dounia turned them around, heart thrumming in rage and worry. Now that she could concentrate, she smelled it, the hot, metallic tang of Ira's blood as it permeated the cockpit.

"You're going to be fine," Dounia said.

"Of course," Ira replied. "Of course."

The rest of the squadron clearly had the same idea, and they rose into the sky, up above the first layer of clouds, away from the brewing snowstorm. Now that they were safe, Meow crawled off of Dounia's shoulders and scrambled over to Ira to check her injury. Of course,

Meow couldn't actually help, but he hated Ira being hurt as much as Dounia did.

Dounia could barely concentrate on landing the plane she was so worried about Ira, but she forced herself to pay attention. Landing in a crosswind while it was snowing out was no easy matter, and the snowfall threatened to turn into a full-on blizzard very soon.

A shockingly cold burst of wetness against her cheek startled Dounia and she looked up, although the shield spell on her cockpit was invisible to her eye. Ira had shielded their cockpits with spells to block the elements from entering, but the spells were failing. Ira usually renewed them when they did, but she was more occupied with tying a tourniquet around her arm.

They would be fine. They were nearly back to their base, and then Ira could get medical treatment. Meow was being more of a nuisance than help, nudging at Ira's arm and stalking back and forth across her lap, bristling and twitching in agitation. Ira allowed him, smiling slightly, and not seeming to mind the inconvenience.

The plane in front of them dipped down, and Dounia followed their lead. She kept the plane steady, even as they broke through the clouds and re-emerged into the beginnings of a raging snowstorm. More snowflakes were breaking past the shield spell, floating down to hit Dounia's face. Her goggles protected her from getting any in her eyes.

Ira finished tying off the tourniquet and studied the instrument panel in front of her. As the navigator, she was supposed to lead them back to base. Dounia was following the other planes in their formation, but it was better if Ira guided them.

"Adjust our course by two degrees," Ira said. "We're almost there, fifteen point two kilos out. Start your decent now."

Dounia followed her instructions, but cast a worried glance at Meow as he returned to her shoulders.

"She's losing quite a lot of blood," Meow whispered. "I'd say just over a pint."

"Did it hit a major blood vessel?" Dounia asked.

"It took a chunk out of her arm," Meow reported rapidly. "Upper arm. I don't think it hit a major vessel, but we need to get her to the surgeons as soon as we land."

"I can hear you worrying over there," Ira called, sounding amused. "I'm fine."

"A pint of blood is no laughing manner," Dounia returned. "Your body only has five to lose!"

"Are you paying attention to our altitude? I know I am," Ira said. "And we need to adjust again because while you were distracted, we drifted off course."

Dounia clenched her teeth, but returned to the controls, forcing herself to concentrate on flying the plane rather than on her wounded comrade. If she crashed the plane, it wouldn't matter if Ira was bleeding, because neither of them had parachutes.

"Coming in, adjust your heading by fifteen degrees on my mark... now," Ira said, and Dounia could make out the snowy runway ahead of them in the dark, the lights of the ground crew glowing like fireflies, beacons in the night.

"I was lying, I hate this part more," Meow said darkly, ears flat against his skull.

The ground rose up in front of them, and Meow clenched his eyes shut as they came in for their landing. The controls jarred in Dounia's hands, but the plane stayed steady, slowing down in spite of the ice that was building up on the runway.

"Are we down?" Meow asked plaintively.

"We're down," Dounia said, taxiing their plane off the runway and finding her berth through the rising storm.

The ground crew came to strap their plane down, and Dounia climbed out of the front cockpit. She walked carefully across the wing to the back cockpit where Ira struggled to climb out while using only one arm. Dounia rushed to help her, and Ira let her with a fond smile.

"Come on, we need to get to the medical bay," Dounia urged, getting an arm under Ira's uninjured arm.

"I got blood on my map," Ira complained. "Do you think supply will let me have a new one?"

"I wouldn't count on it," Dounia sighed and shook her head.

When they the best pilots received second-hand male uniforms that didn't fit properly and open-cockpit planes, getting a new map was probably out of the question. Speaking of their plane... Dounia checked their *kukuruznik* over for damage. The thing was held together with bits of Ira's constructive magic and determination. It was a few more bullet holes the worse for wear, but still mostly in one piece. Their little planes were tough, for all they were old and made of wood and canvas.

Ira removed her bomber hat, and her thick, brown hair fluffed up as it was freed from its confines. Dounia and Ira had met the day when all the women in the regiment were ordered to cut their hair to military regulations. It had grown a bit since then, but when it had been sheared off by the military barbers, it had been long enough for Ira to sit on.

Dounia hadn't cared when her hair had been cut, and had actually enjoyed the freedom of movement it gave her. She kept it cropped short, like the male aviators. Ira, on the other hand, had been upset for the entire week after her hair had been cut. However, a haircut was a small price to pay in exchange for being allowed to fight for their homeland.

There was a line-up for the surgery when they arrived. Ira wasn't the only one to come away scored from the battle.

"Look, mine's not so bad," Ira pointed out cheerfully.

"I would prefer it if your face remained unmarred by bullet shrapnel," Dounia replied dryly.

"At least I can still use this arm," Ira said, laughing.

Dounia didn't think that any of their comrades being injured was a laughing matter, especially not Ira, and stiffened silently. Ira noticed immediately and grasped Dounia's upper arm in a tight grip.

"Dounia, dear one, I'm fine. The doctor will see me soon."

Before either of them could speak, another pilot, Svetlana Romanovna, popped her head in and said, "Dounia, you'll never guess who's here!"

Dounia looked and raised her eyebrows questioningly. She was in no mood for guessing right now.

Sveta sighed and said, "Tanya is here."

Dounia thought she'd been on edge before, but her stomach lurched at the words and then her gut tied itself into a knot. Tanya wasn't supposed to be here. Tanya was supposed to be back in Moscow, where it was safe.

Torn, Dounia looked back and forth between Sveta and Ira.

"Go," Ira said. "You need to see her. Meow will look after me, won't you?"

Meow answered by uncurling from around Dounia's shoulders and jumping across to Ira's.

That was all Dounia needed to hear. She rushed after Sveta, out into the growing storm, shoulders tight with tension and stomach churning.

One Tsareva sister was enough of a sacrifice to the motherland. Why was Tanya here?

~~*

Ira watched Dounia stride out of the tent and smiled to herself. Dounia always wanted to take care of everybody so much, and although most people found her vigilance stifling, Ira found it comforting. Somebody had to look after everyone, after all.

"Ira, you're up next," the girl behind her said.

Ira looked over her shoulder and said, "Oh, Zina, are you sure? That looks broken."

Zina shook her head. "It's my own fault. I jumped out of my plane and slipped on the ice. I wasn't injured in battle. This was just me being clumsy! You keep your place in line."

Ira was about to protest, but now that she was paying attention, she felt slightly light-headed from blood loss. Meow noticed her slightly off-balance stance and growled low in his throat in worry.

"Lieutenant Sverzhenskaya, you're up," one of the nurses said, pursing her lip.

Ira sat down and waited for the doctor to come see her. It didn't take long, and in a moment her sleeve was cut away, her wound was rinsed out with vodka, and the doctor was stitching her up. Ira stayed as still as possible, wincing with each pass of the needle.

"I can't look," Meow said, shoving his head behind her ear, tail twitching in agitation.

Ira put a hand up to stroke his head soothingly.

"If you had just become a doctor, you wouldn't have to put up with this," the doctor said unsympathetically.

"Doctor Glazova, I'll kindly thank you not to question my choices," Ira said flatly, feeling the prick of Meow's claws as he bristled defensively.

"Your constructive magic is wasted on planes! Just think of the lives you could save with the proper training. You could just knit your own flesh back together in a moment, and poor Lieutenant Kuzmina's wrist would be fixed up in a heartbeat."

Ira smiled tightly. "Thank you for your work, doctor."

She left the tent quickly. Every single time she came into the medical tent, it was the same thing. Somehow, Ira always had the bad luck of running into Doctor Glazova whenever she was there. It was as if the woman was constantly working! She was glad Dounia hadn't been there. The last time this had happened, Dounia had almost gotten into a yelling match with the doctor.

Ira knew that she could have gone to university. They accepted very few women, but a woman with constructive magic could be a doctor. She was smart, and dedicated, and any university would have been happy to take her. Instead, she'd gone and joined a flying club and become a flying instructor and a part-time plane mechanic.

"She's just afraid of flying," Meow hissed, curling up around her shoulders again.

Ira didn't point out that Meow was also afraid of flying. Their valiant comrade insisted on coming up every single bombing run anyway, terror notwithstanding.

The storm was raging as she left the medical bay and went to look for Dounia. If she knew anything, it was that aviators always ended up at the mess tent, so that's where she headed first. She poked her head in, and there was a group already assembled. Ira smiled. Dounia was talking heatedly with a young woman that bore a striking resemblance to herself, and in her ardour, had completely forgotten to take off her bomber cap.

"Dounia, sweet one, take off your cap," she called as she entered.

Dounia looked up and came over, pushing the others aside to get to Ira. Meow jumped back across to Dounia's shoulders when they were in reach.

"Is your arm alright?" Dounia asked in concern.

"Nothing a few stitches couldn't fix," Ira said firmly, and then reached up to remove Dounia's cap.

As soon as the cap was off, Dounia shook her head, and two large triangular shapes sprung up as they were set free from the cap's confines. Dounia flexed her ears, a matching pair to Meow's, and groaned.

"They always feel funny after being stuffed under my hat like that," Dounia complained.

"I don't think I'll ever get used to that," a new voice joined them. Tanya, Dounia's younger sister, came up beside them, staring at her sister's cat-like ears. "I haven't told mama about them, and I assume you haven't either."

"I've been busy," Dounia said defensively.

"What's wrong with her ears?" Meow asked, sitting up straight on Dounia's shoulder. "I can tell you right now they are far superior to human ears."

"He's just saying that because you shared his blood," Tanya huffed.

"And what noble blood it is," Ira said. "When did you get here, Tanya?"

Tanya bounced on the balls of her feet and answered, "I just got here an hour ago, but all of you were still up in the air. I was worried about you, you know. I saw that there was a storm coming in, and I thought it might be dangerous, but I know that Dounia's the best pilot, so obviously you would be fine. I was still worried though. Did you get hurt, Ira? You know Dounia always gets really grumpy and snappish when you're hurt."

She babbled the words out so fast that Ira could hardly process what she was saying.

Dounia, no doubt used to the barrage of words replied first. "You've met Ira all of three times. That doesn't count as 'always.'"

"It does when she's been injured all three times that I met her!" Tanya trilled, still bouncing up on her toes. "And you've been grumpy all three times, too."

Ira tried to recount in her head these three times. The first week after they'd been assigned to a team, they'd met Tanya because she'd come to try and apply to the air force, like Dounia. She'd been rejected because her eyesight was bad and she had to wear glasses. Ira had managed to accidentally temporarily blind herself with a mirror spell that she hadn't perfected yet. How was she supposed to know that the angle of the sun and the angle of the mirror spell would align like that?

The second time, it was just after Dounia had volunteered for the experimental magic operation that had given her perfect night vision, cat ears, and Meow. Perfect night vision had been what they were going for, and the scientists had decided that the ears were a side effect that wasn't really worth the perks of being able to see at night. Ira had a sprained ankle, because Meow used to have a bad habit of pacing around when he was anxious and Ira had tripped on him.

The third time was right now.

"She's right, I was injured," Ira reported. "All three times."

"That makes it sound like you're always injured," Dounia grumbled. "Which is completely untrue; you've only been injured when Tanya was here. Tanya, you're bad luck. Go back to Moscow, and then we'll all be safe."

"That can't be true," Tanya protested. "People get hurt all the time."

"Not so much as a stubbed toe any other time," Ira smiled. "I've only been injured when you're around."

"That does make me sound like bad luck!" Tanya said, sounding thrilled at the idea. "Anyway, I came to tell Dounia my good news."

"You're going back to Moscow tonight," Dounia said.

"No, don't make fun of me, Dounia!" Tanya finally stopped bouncing on the spot. "You know how I wrote and said I was training to be a radio officer? Well, I finally got a placement."

"Back in Moscow."

"No, near the front," Tanya said. "I'm very good under pressure, they said. That's why I was given such a useful position."

"Useful."

Oh, dear, Ira recognized that tone of voice. It usually led to an hours-long argument that was carried out at roughly the volume of a Messerschmitt taking off. She braced herself and waited for the inevitable.

"Yes, useful," Tanya said, a hint of hardness entering her voice. Evidently she also recognized Dounia's tone, and was aware of what usually ensued. "They offered me the position and I accepted."

"Didn't you think of what our parents would want? You'll be in danger that close to the front!" Dounia's voice was already rising.

"You didn't care what our parents said," Tanya said. "You just signed up, and I know it's a lot more dangerous than sitting behind the lines and radioing out bombing targets."

"We can't both be in danger!"

"Our whole country is in danger. That's the whole point of this war," Tanya snapped back in reply.

"I don't think you understand."

"No, I don't think *you* understand!"

The two of them faced off, nose to nose. They were both short, stocky women, and the image was a funny one. Generally, Ira liked watching Dounia argue with someone, for this reason alone. But the conversation topic did not bode well for the future.

"You can't go to the front. You said you were going to ask to be stationed here! Or Moscow! Did you lie to me?"

"You can't tell me what to do anymore, Dounia. We're both adults now."

"Fine!" Dounia snapped, shaking with anger. "Do what you like. But I'm not going to support you on this, because I don't agree. You said you'd stay away from the front lines."

"I only said that so that mama and pap wouldn't try and stop me," Tanya said. The *and you* part of the statement was left silent and implied.

"I refuse to argue with someone who lies to get her way!" Dounia yelled and stormed out of the mess tent.

Tanya watched her go sadly.

"Was I a fool to hope that she'd be happy for me?" Tanya asked.

Ira patted her shoulder. "I'll try and talk her around, but she is very hard to convince once she has an opinion. As you know already, I'm guessing. How long will you be here?"

Tanya looked at the ground. "Only long enough for everybody else assigned to the front to report in, and then we all have to move. Probably a few days."

"I'll see what I can do," Ira said, but she wasn't sure that Dounia would come around anytime soon, not when it came to her baby sister being in danger.

Dounia and Ira shared sleeping quarters, and Dounia was already curled up and pretending to be asleep when Ira got back. Ira pretended she didn't realize Dounia was pretending and undressed as quietly as possible, before slipping into bed behind her. She fit her longer body up behind Dounia's short frame snuggly.

Ira smiled as she felt Dounia shift back into the cradle of Ira's body and slung an arm around her waist, tangling their legs together. She placed a soft kiss right at the nape of her neck and nuzzled her head into the back of her shoulder.

Dounia shifted in her arms, turning her head slightly so that Ira could kiss behind her ear and the side of her face. Ira leaned up onto her elbow to give herself some leverage so that she could finally press her mouth against Dounia's.

"If you're going to do *that*, I'm leaving," Meow grumbled from where he'd settled in the corner, and he disappeared quickly.

Ira ignored him in favour of moving around to get herself positioned on top of Dounia. Dounia was warm from being under the covers, and Ira tried to get closer. Dounia finally helped by turning onto her back and pulling Ira on top of her. Ira settled onto her and leaned down to kiss her again.

"We shouldn't be doing this now, too many people are still awake," Dounia murmured, but didn't pull away.

"There's a storm. No one else is out in this weather, even if they are awake."

Dounia argued no further, getting her arms up around Ira's back and tilting her head up to deepen the kiss that Ira had started. Dounia's mouth was warm and soft and Ira hummed happily into the kiss. She was in no hurry to get anywhere tonight.

Dounia had other plans, apparently, spreading her legs so that she could wrap them around Ira's hips, pushing up against her and demanding attention.

"Something you wanted, dearest?" Ira asked, laughing softly.

"You know what I want," Dounia said, huffing and arching her hips up again.

Dounia was already slick and open with desire, and two of Ira's long fingers breached her opening easily. Dounia squirmed underneath her, urging her deeper. Ira nuzzled at Dounia's neck, tilting it to the side so she could lick and nip at the soft skin. Dounia threw her head back and shoved a hand over her mouth to keep quiet.

Ira grinned and curled her fingers against her warm inner wall, pushing up at her swollen nub with her thumb. Dounia's hips shuddered up against Ira's hand, and her teeth bit into her own hand in an effort to keep the noises inside. Dounia moaned low in her throat, a rough, needy sound barely contained.

Ira pressed herself up against Dounia, and Dounia helpfully pushed her knee up between Ira's legs, giving her a warm surface to writhe against.

Panting and covered in sweat, the two of them collapsed together in a sated pile, with barely enough energy to settle themselves in for sleep.

"I'm tired," Dounia said, and she sounded drained.

Ira had been trying to distract her from the argument that Dounia had just had with Tanya, but it looked like Dounia was still worried about it.

"Maybe things will be different tomorrow," Ira offered.

"I doubt it."

"Sleep, *kotyonok*," Ira said softly.

Dounia relaxed into their embrace and her breath soon evened out, slow and deep. Ira pressed her face into Dounia's hair and breathed, Dounia's scent calming her. Dounia wasn't the only one who worried about her loved ones.

Two

Dounia saw a flash of familiar black hair and heavy-lensed frames and immediately hid behind the corner. She was somewhat ashamed of how she was avoiding Tanya, but she didn't know what to say anymore. Things were complicated.

"Are you hiding again?" Meow asked grumpily from around her neck. "This is getting to be annoying, Dounia. You need to talk to her."

"You sound like Ira," grumbled Dounia, shoulders stiffening.

"Ira is right," Meow said. "You do need to talk to her. She leaves in the morning."

Dounia hadn't known that.

"To the front?" she asked in a whisper.

"Where else? She hasn't changed her mind just because you won't talk to her."

Dounia bit hard on her lip and didn't say anything else. She didn't want to tell Meow that she'd very childishly been hoping that Tanya would feel guilty about Dounia avoiding her and do exactly that. Apparently Tanya was made of sterner stuff than she'd thought and wasn't backing down. Dounia should have realized she wouldn't. If she wouldn't listen to their parents, there was no way that she would listen to Dounia.

Meow made a sharp noise and jumped down off her shoulder. "If you're going to be this silly, I'm going to find Ira."

Dounia was avoiding Ira as well. Not as much as Tanya, but only because she had to work with Ira still. But outside of practicing manoeuvres and doing more nightly bombing raids, she wasn't talking much to Ira either. Ira kept trying to talk her into making up with Tanya, and Dounia just didn't want to do it. Nor did she want to talk about it or why she didn't want to talk about it. Or anything to do with feelings, really.

Dounia knew she was bad at explaining feelings, and didn't like talking about them in general. It was causing problems now, and had in the past as well. It was not her most endearing quality.

The best part about the whole situation was that Dounia knew she had this problem and was still adamantly refusing to try and fix it. Never mind that Tanya was the younger of the two; Dounia was the one being childish.

Dounia peeked around the corner again and sighed. Tanya was sprawled on the ground with several of the other pilots and navigators of the regiment, one of whom was Ira. Ira and Tanya were sitting together and chatting.

"So are you going to go talk to them yet?"

Dounia stifled a yelp and jumped back, glaring down at Meow, who had snuck up behind her. Meow flicked his tail and regarded her with a flat, unwavering stare, as only cats can.

"I can't talk to them," Dounia hissed. "It's not as if Tanya would listen to me anyway. She's already made up her mind to go."

"So you're not going to say goodbye to your sister just because she's not doing as you say?" Meow asked. "What was the last thing you said to her? Do you want those to be your final words before she has to go into dangerous territory?"

"Now you're really sounding like Ira," Dounia growled. "Why is she taking Tanya's side in this? Ira's *my* lover, not hers."

"Yes, and Tanya's *your* sister. Everybody is yours and because they are yours, they are only allowed to do what you want. Also, you might want to keep your voice down, someone might hear you."

"I'm pretty sure they already know," Dounia grumbled.

"Assuming something and hearing it said aloud are two different things," Meow said. "No one can accuse you based on an assumption. But if you say it, then you've just admitted it, and an admission can be court marshalled."

"See? You're worried about me, right?" Dounia asked, making a sharp gesture with both hands. "I'm worried about Tanya. She could get hurt! She doesn't know what she's getting into."

"Neither did you when you first joined up," Meow pointed out.

Dounia heaved a heavy breath and looked at the ground. "Who could have ever expected this when we volunteered to fight? Nothing could have prepared us for the sights we have seen or the things that we have done in the name of the motherland."

"And you do not want Tanya to have her eyes opened to this," Meow finished.

"No, these eyes have seen too much, and I want her to be spared," Dounia said, peering back around the corner to watch Tanya talk to her fellow aviators. "Look at them all, they're congratulating her. How could they? She is going straight into the mouth of hell. It looks bad enough from the air."

"She is not a child. It is her own choice, as it was yours. She's the same age now as you were when you first joined."

Dounia didn't say anything, because Meow was right. She had no right to keep her sister from doing exactly as she herself had done when women were first admitted to the Soviet forces.

"I want to know what they are saying," Dounia said. "Will you let me listen, brother?"

Meow flattened his ears, but agreed begrudgingly. "I should not be enabling you in your avoidance manoeuvres, but maybe if you could hear what they were saying, you would cease to act so foolishly. It is a good thing I love you, *solnyshko*, or I would refuse to put up with this tiptoeing around."

Meow padded off, and Dounia sat down and leaned back against the wall behind her, closing her eyes and concentrating. Or, rather, not concentrating. She had to let her mind free, set it loose to wander and it would be drawn to Meow's head like a moth to flame.

She and Meow shared blood, after all.

Sometimes they could see or hear through each other's senses. She'd gotten Meow's night vision and his ears. Meow had gotten her vocal chords and colour vision. No one who had taken part in the experiment had thought their blood would mingle so much, and it was agreed that they wouldn't try again on a human subject until they were sure it would work as planned.

It was a good thing that Meow was a witch familiar. Who knows what would have happened if they'd used an ordinary cat. What if their brains had been switched? A familiar had similar intelligence to humans and sometimes formed empathic connections with their chosen witch. Meow was the only proof ever uncovered that familiars actually understood the human language.

Meow's mind glowed green and violet in her mind's eye, and she followed it until they connected. Each time Meow blinked, the scene around him came more into focus and sound filtered in slowly. She was next to Ira's feet, encased in over-large combat boots worn out from numerous night missions.

"I've tried everything, Ira, and nothing is working. Any time I get close to her, she runs away and hides."

That was Tanya's voice from somewhere above them.

"You have to be patient. She likes to be chased you know. But if you pull away from her, then she'll come to you," Ira said.

"Is that how you got Dounia, in the end?" Tanya asked curiously.

"Of course. All the chasing around in the world, and my Dounia was reticent as ever. As soon as I turn away and start ignoring her, she comes to ask why I'm not interested anymore. Of course, I never stopped being interested. And you still want to talk to her, but you must let her come to you."

"If she would just come back, I would tell her that if she really wanted, I would ask to be reassigned," Tanya said with a sigh and shake of her head. "But she must ask me, I am not just going to do it because I know she wants me to!"

"Both so stubborn," Ira shrugged. "I have done what I could, but now Dounia is avoiding me as well."

"And me," Meow grumbled, and his voice sounded very loud in her head.

"She can't avoid us forever. This part of the camp isn't that big!" Ira pointed out. "She will run into one of us eventually."

It sounded like everyone was against her, then. Fine! Did they not think she could find a way to avoid them? She could do a lot better than that. Even Meow would have trouble finding her if she left the camp.

Getting stiffly to her feet, Dounia marched hurriedly in the other direction, towards the edge of their camp. Their regiment was staying in one place, but they were still a part of the 4th Air Army, which included several other squadrons. The air base itself was huge, and if they thought she couldn't avoid them among all that, then they were very much mistaken.

It took her only a minute to remember why she never went outside the camp.

First of all: she had cat ears. The rest of her regiment had heard the stories and were used to seeing her with them. Her ears were very difficult to hide in normal circumstances, as they tended to move by themselves. The story had been kept as quiet as possible, and although there had been rumours, nothing had ever been confirmed.

Second: there were only two other all-female regiments, and the rest were all men. The majority of them had the tendency of making unsavoury remarks about their female comrades, even though they were on the same side.

Dounia put her hood up to hide her ears, but nothing would hide how short she was. Rebellion burning in her belly, Dounia refused to turn back and kept on her way, marching past supply tents and other various semi-permanent structures. It had snowed in the night, and everything was dusted in a fine layer of white.

Mostly, the men were ignoring her. Dounia was short, and kept having to walk around people, not wanting to draw attention to herself by refusing to move out of the way. Somewhere in all this hubbub were two other female regiments, and wouldn't care if another woman was wandering among them.

"Ah, what have we here? A little mouse?"

Apparently it was too much to ask to simply be left alone. Dounia had been solely among female crewmembers for so long that she had forgotten what men were like. Some liked altercations and humiliating other people just because they could, and many of them picked fights or disparaged their female counterparts.

"Leave me alone," Dounia said flatly, ducking her head further into the hood. "I am on an errand. I do not want any trouble."

Someone grasped the back of her hood and pulled hard.

"Oh, a little kitten! My mistake!"

There were three of them, all leaning on each other and laughing. She saw it in their eyes. They had been looking for a target, and here she had presented them with the perfect one. They were all wearing bomber jackets similar to hers, although theirs fit better, having been sized properly.

One of them reached out and grabbed one of her ears, saying, "Oh, do you need these—"

Dounia grabbed his hand and twisted.

"Ow, there's no need for violence, little cat," one of the pilots said.

"You were going to pull on my ear!" Dounia snarled, backing away.

"It's just a bit of fun," his fellow continued. "If you didn't want to play, you shouldn't have worn them!"

Oh dear. These idiots thought that they were fake and not actually attached to her head. That pull had hurt! Dounia rubbed her ear and glared.

"A black cat. You must be one of the witches."

Well, no matter what derogatory name they wanted to call them, Dounia was a part of the night bomber regiment, and they did some damn good flying if you asked her.

"So I am. What do you want?" Dounia demanded, ears flattening.

"I want you to go home to your mama. War is no place for little girls."

"This 'little girl' is worth an Iron Cross to the Germans. How about you?" Dounia retorted, bristling.

"It just means you're annoying," one of the men said.

"It means the Germans want to pin a medal on anyone who can put women back in their place," another added.

"It means," a new voice added, "that the women are better flyers than you and the Germans know it. Stop harassing this lady and get back to work. You're going back up in half an hour, and if you could land half as well as the girls, maybe you would all come back in one piece."

The men slunk away and Dounia watched them go, only turning to face this newest person once they were out of her line of sight.

"Commander Shikov at your service," the new man introduced himself, offering his hand.

He was almost as short as Dounia.

Dounia took his hand and said, "Lieutenant Tsareva, 46th Taman Guards."

"A pleasure," Commander Shikov said. "My apologies for my men. They have been told many times already to respect their female comrades, but the lesson does not seem to stick."

Dounia didn't want to tell him it was fine, because it wasn't fine at all. She was a soldier, same as the rest of them, and she served her country and risked death alongside them. He seemed to be a nice man, however. Would he still be a nice man if she managed to offend him?

"I'm glad you are not like them," Dounia said finally.

"You are rather far from home, Lt. Tsareva," Commander Shikov commented, looking at her ears strangely. Had he realized they were real?

"No farther than anyone else," Dounia said sharply.

"Oh, I meant from your end of camp. What brings you to this end of the 4th Air Army?"

She wasn't about to tell him she was avoiding her younger sister. Female soldiers were called names like 'little girl' all the time. She couldn't make it seem like they all did childish things like that.

"I wanted to see what it was like," Dounia said haltingly. "We never go outside our area."

"Oh, in that case, let me show you around."

Dounia was extremely suspicious of his motives, but it wasn't exactly as if she could tell him that she preferred the company of women. Also, she had no sense of direction on the ground, and having a guide would be nice. Besides, if she were with the Commander, he served the dual purpose of giving her an excuse not to return to camp and keeping away the men who would otherwise harass her.

"Lead on," she said, gesturing.

To his merit, he did not try and offer her his arm.

~~*

Ira and Meow swept the camp one last time before returning to the mess where everyone had agreed to meet up.

"Any luck?" Sveta asked, upon their return.

Ira shook her head solemnly. "No sign at all."

"What if she comes back and wants to talk?" Tanya fretted, pacing frantically back and forth. "I can't leave before she returns!"

Ira sighed sadly. Tanya might have to do just that. They'd received the news just hours ago: Tanya and all of her fellow radio officers were being sent to the front tonight. If Dounia didn't return soon, then Tanya would have to leave without even saying goodbye.

"I'm sure she'll be back soon," Ira said, but internally, she had a weight in her stomach that wouldn't go away.

"I can't not go," Tanya said. "They need us at the front!"

"Lieutenant Tsareva, you are needed. Come."

Tanya's superiors were here looking for her already. Tanya looked between the officers and Ira in anguish, hands clutched together. Her lip trembled, and she bit down on it and took several deep breaths.

"Coming," Tanya said, turning to go with them, voice oddly flat.

Ira watched as she left, the urge to go after Tanya or find Dounia struggling within her. But there was nothing to be done, because Tanya was gone and Dounia wasn't here. How could she possibly tell Dounia that her little sister had been taken off to the front without her even saying goodbye?

The atmosphere in the mess tent after that was subdued. No one liked having to see family separated. Most of them had siblings or cousins who were also a part of the war effort.

When Dounia finally returned, she was talking animatedly to a strange male officer and stopped short when she noticed the unhappy mood in the air.

"What's going on?" she asked, voice suddenly afraid.

"Dounia, it's Tanya," Ira said, feeling the tightness in her throat that meant she was going to do something embarrassing, like cry. "The last radio officer arrived early. Their orders have been expedited. Tanya is already on her way to the front."

For a second, Dounia was completely expressionless, and then her face crumpled.

"And you let her go?" Dounia cried, her voice thick and angry.

"There was no choice! We couldn't find you!" Ira tried to explain, holding up her hands.

Dounia hunched over, face in her hands and she shook, a fine tremor running through her body, making her shoulders heave. "How could you let her go?"

"We couldn't do anything!" Ira said, and to her surprise, her face was wet and streaked with tears.

"She can't be gone," Dounia moaned, low and terrible into her hands. "She was supposed to stay here where she would be safe!"

Ira finally managed to stumble forward, just in time to catch Dounia's figure as she collapsed to her knees on the frozen ground.

"She'll be okay," Ira said, clutching Dounia's shivering form to her. "She'll be okay."

Her words sounded so empty.

~~*

Ira and Dounia sprinted across the tarmac towards their plane, the lights of the airfield glaring and bright, obscuring the night beyond their reach. Other aviators were also running on their way to their planes, dashing amongst the ground crew, who were hard at work getting them ready to fly.

Ira had taken time earlier to come by and put all the necessary spells on their little *kukuruznik*, repairing the shrapnel damage from their last run as best she could. Sometimes, she thought that magic was all that kept the hardy planes together.

Dounia climbed the wing and vaulted into the front cockpit. Without a word, she strapped herself in and pulled her goggles down over her eyes.

Dounia hadn't been talking to anyone lately. She had been avoiding Ira and Meow, answering their queries in a monosyllabic monotone. She wasn't eating either, picking at her food and leaving most of it untouched. Ira suspected that she wasn't sleeping well either, tossing and turning restlessly, and scooting away whenever Ira tried to approach her.

Tanya had sent a letter from the front as soon as she had arrived. Dounia hadn't opened it, and it was tucked away among her meagre possessions still sealed.

Ira climbed more carefully into her own cockpit behind Dounia's, settling in and raising a hand to make sure that Meow was still comfortable around her shoulders.

Ira checked their bombing coordinates and was about to relay them to Dounia when a runner suddenly dashed up to the plane and jumped up on their wing to speak to Ira. Frowning, Ira leaned forward so that the girl could speak into her ear. The airfield was loud with the buzz of propellers coming alive, and she couldn't miss this message.

"Change of coordinates," the runner said. "The Germans have launched a night time raid and have overrun our lines."

"New coordinates?" Ira demanded.

The girl told her, and Ira's insides clenched up with icy dread. Both Meow and Dounia were watching the exchange, and Dounia's brows drew in at the expression on her face.

She repeated the coordinates back to the girl, just to be absolutely sure, but they were the correct ones.

Tanya had sent Ira a message too, nothing like a full letter, but something. That message contained only one piece of information—Tanya's current location, coordinates and all. Those coordinates matched the coordinates of their target perfectly.

Ira told Dounia the new coordinates numbly, and although Dounia could obviously tell something was very wrong, she didn't know what it was. Which meant that Dounia didn't know that her sister's current position was overrun with enemy troops and they were about to drop bombs on them, enemy and ally alike.

Dounia didn't ask, just got their props going and started taxiing to the runway for take-off.

Ira's throat felt frozen. She had to tell Dounia right now, but she couldn't find the words, locked behind her teeth and crystallized in her lungs. She'd promised. She'd *promised* Dounia that Tanya would be okay.

They were just over halfway there when Dounia finally asked, "Ira, where are we going?"

For a moment, Ira trembled in her seat and couldn't say a word.

"Ira?" Dounia asked, and Ira knew that Dounia knew and just needed it confirmed.

"The new coordinates," Ira said, voice ragged. "Dounia, we have to turn around. The coordinates are the same as the ones your sister told me is her current position. We can't... we can't drop explosives on your sister!"

Meow's claws dug through Ira's bomber jacket and into her shoulder.

Dounia was silent, but their little bomber's course held steady. Ira's breathing was wavering and short, a few moments from going into hyperventilation. Her heart was pounding so hard against her ribcage that it hurt to be alive.

"Who called down the bombing run?" Dounia asked softly.

"It had to have been the radio officer on duty," Ira answered. "It could have been Tanya. I don't know; they have duty shifts, and Tanya didn't tell me which one she was."

Dounia didn't turn around. They kept in formation with the two bombers on either side of them, flying low over the treetops as they approached the front lines. The Germans wouldn't expect them to bomb their own coordinates, which meant they wouldn't be ready with their spotlights and shrapnel.

"We have to carry out the mission," Dounia said, voice brittle. "It is better that Tanya and our fellow soldiers die by our fire than fall into the hands of the Germans."

Ira knew that. The Germans hated that they were being defied by women and did particularly horrific things to those enemy women that did become their prisoners. Soviet soldiers didn't stay prisoners for very long before they were executed. Dounia was right, it was better this way.

Some of them might escape. That was the only hope they had, that their own troops withdrew far enough that they weren't caught in the bomb blasts.

Up ahead of them, another night bomber regiment had already started bombing their lines, and the tree line ahead of them was aflame, vermillion smoke curling up into the blue of the winter sky. They were already on their way back to base for another load of bombs. Their three-plane formation advanced into the light of the fires unchallenged, and they could all release their loads as one, without the need of manoeuvring and distraction tactics.

In the mirror spell set up to guard their rear, Ira saw pillars of fire shoot into the air like geysers, sending sparks high into the sky to fall back down as ash when it cooled.

There would be nothing left of the site by morning.

Bombs delivered, they turned to go back to base to get fitted up with another round. The night was far from over, and they would continue to ferry back and forth with more explosives.

The night stretched out endlessly, and Ira lost count of how many runs they made. It was all a blur, carried out on automatic. None of them spoke the entire night, not Dounia to exalt in the delight of flying, not Meow to complain, and not Ira to admonish them both.

When they finally landed for the night, dawn was only an hour off. The ground crew tied their aircrafts down and aircraft mechanics moved in to check them over for malfunctions.

None of the aviators retired to their bunks, as exhausted as they were. They all knew that they'd just bombed their own lines, and waited fitfully to find out if there were any survivors. The faces around them were grim and taciturn. Dounia's eyes were hollow, and she looked so diminished it was if she were a wraith.

"What's wrong with Dounia?" Zina asked, coming up on Ira's other side.

"Tanya was there," Ira said shortly and didn't say anything else.

Ira didn't tell anyone else, but she could tell the terrible news had circulated around the room as a careful space opened up around them. Everyone wanted to offer condolences, but Dounia's shut-off expression made it hard to approach her.

Ira didn't dare to move any closer to Dounia, knowing that when Dounia was upset she pulled away from those trying to offer comfort. She liked to pretend that she didn't need it.

"She could have survived. There are people starting to arrive right now from the front," Zina said, coming back to Ira's side.

Normally after a successful run, they celebrated, chatting and talking and linking arms in their exuberance, still fired up on adrenaline and danger. This was the most terrible atmosphere Ira had ever experienced. They hadn't had to drop bombs on their own lines often, and the fact that Tanya had been there made it all the worse. Ira felt guilt tearing up her insides, and she could barely imagine what Dounia must be feeling. How was one supposed to tell their parents that their baby girl might be dead, and that they had had a hand in it?

They waited in a tense, uncomfortable mood, drinking bad coffee to stay awake. The sun was rising before they heard any news from the front.

Another runner came to tell them that most of the survivors had arrived and were being treated for injuries and being processed.

"There might be some stragglers, but we have most of the survivors now," she said.

"Do you know the name of the radio officer who called down the bombing run?" Dounia demanded, some of the fight returning to her voice.

The runner searched her face carefully, then looked down at her clipboard. "A Lieutenant Tatiana Ivanovna Tsareva was the one who called the bombing run on her own coordinates."

"It was her," Dounia said and seemed to sigh and curl in on herself.

Ira finally gathered the courage to shift closer to Dounia and wrapped a tentative arm around her shoulder. Dounia collapsed against her, and Ira held onto her tightly and waited.

There was a list of the survivors, and another for the missing and the dead.

The rest of their comrades stayed back, waiting for Dounia to check first, although many of them had friends who had also been on the front.

"I don't know if I can look," Dounia said, looking around at all those assembled. "What do I do if she's not on the right list?"

"You won't know till you look," Sveta said gently. "What if she's a survivor, and is somewhere in the hospital ward? Wouldn't you want to know so that you can go and find her?"

"How did you deal with this? Not knowing?" Dounia asked Ira, squeezing her hand hard.

They never talked about this, about Ira's older brother Pavel who had been killed in action early on in the war. Back when the Treaty of Non-Aggression was supposed to keep him safe, when the Germans had broken their promise and invaded their homeland.

"It was different," Ira whispered back. "I knew that he hadn't survived, even while no one could confirm his death. Even if he survived the initial attack, our own army burned everything to the ground behind them. He would have died long before he could have found his way back to our lines."

Ira didn't blame their own forces for what they had done, because it was what had to happen to hinder the advance of the enemy. She blamed the Germans. They were the enemy, the ones that had promised not to attack them, and who had gone back against their pact. What kind of deal was it, when one made a promise with those who had no honour?

"My Pasha had no chance at all," Ira finished, swallowing hard.

They stepped up to the list together, and Ira began reading the list of survivors. It was in no particular order, and Ira assumed that it had been written up as people came in, all in a jumble of confusion. Ira didn't know whether to have hope or cry in frustration while she searched the names. If it had been in alphabetical order, they would have known immediately, or if it had least been sorted by sex or section.

But no, Ira had to read every single name to try and find Tanya's. Ira hated the feeling of hope she got whenever she saw the word "Tsareva" or "Tatiana" anywhere on the list. But the names didn't coincide on her first run through of the list.

Her stomach dropped as she returned to the top, looking again. She must have missed it. She had to have missed it. She was frantically running the tip of her finger down the list, each name so large in her head as she skimmed over it that it was driving her mad.

Eventually, Dounia grabbed her elbow and shook her head, pulling them over to the other list, the list that they dreaded to find Tanya on.

The rest of the aviators wilted behind them as they realized what had happened. They crowded to the list behind them, voices subdued. Even those who found who they were looking for didn't exclaim in excitement as they usually would have.

"If I see her name on this list, it's all over."

"The runner said there could be stragglers," Ira said.

"That's a very slim chance and a false hope if there ever was one," Dounia said.

They looked, and it seemed like cruel fate that they both found it almost immediately, the name jumping off the page at them.

Lieutenant Tatiana Ivanovna Tsareva, Missing in Action, presumed dead.

Dounia held onto Ira's hand tightly, and Meow let out an anguished howl. It was the only sound to be heard for miles, as the rest of the 4th Air Army silently mourned the loss of their fallen comrades.

THREE

Dounia lay on her stomach on her cot, unmoving and silent except for her even breathing. It was the middle of the afternoon, but she couldn't bring herself to move. She listened to her own heartbeat and closed her eyes against the world. Breathing seemed like too much effort and Dounia wondered if she should just stop.

There was a rustle of movement as Ira poked her head into their quarters behind her, checking in on her. Ira hovered, uncertain whether or not disturbing Dounia would do any good in her current state.

"Have you eaten?" Ira finally asked.

Dounia sighed and didn't reply. She hadn't eaten anything all day, now that she bothered to think about it. Getting up, getting dressed and going all the way to the mess was beyond her capabilities at the moment.

Her stomach was numb. Sometime in the past several hours, it had ceased to bother her with demands for sustenance and she could ignore it.

"Come on, get up," Ira said, coming to stand near her head.

Ira poked and prodded at her until she finally groaned and started shifting herself into a sitting position, taking the path of least resistance. Her entire body felt heavy, and it took all of Dounia's effort just to get herself upright. She looked at Ira dully, noting her worried expression and dismissing it.

"Come on, don't make me do it for you," Ira said, finding a clean uniform and presenting it to Dounia in a neat pile.

Slowly, and with effort, Dounia pulled the shirt she'd slept in over her head and dragged the new one on, lingering over the buttons at the collar. Ira waited patiently for her to finish and then put Dounia's boots down in front of her.

While she dressed, Meow came in and jumped up on the bed to watch her anxiously, sitting beside her and curling and re-curling his tail around himself.

She could protest. She used to be good at protesting. She couldn't remember how to do it right now, not without giving away how much she really didn't care about anything at the moment.

She followed them to the mess, and her head spun for a moment. Ira steadied her against her light-headedness and sat her down at one of the tables. Meow stood guard while Ira went to get them something to eat.

There were other aviators around her, talking quietly. She could feel their gazes pricking at her, and although they didn't approach, she knew they remained curious.

"How long has it been?"

"Two weeks."

"She doesn't look like she's doing that great."

"Would you?"

Dounia stopped listening. She already knew what had happened; she didn't need to hear it rehashed over and over again. She did that enough in her own head.

A heavy clunk as Ira set down two sets of food and sat down across from her. Dounia looked at the plate of indiscernible mush in front of her unenthusiastically.

She gave it a half-hearted poke with her spoon and sighed.

"Come on, love, eat up. We have a mission tonight."

Dounia raised her head and obediently took a bite, then another. If they were flying tonight, she needed the energy. Bombing the Nazis was the only thing she seemed to have any motivation for anymore.

Dounia readied herself in silence, pulling on her heavy bomber jacket over her uniform and sliding her hands firmly and deliberately into her gloves. She had never really appreciated what it meant to fight for her country until she had failed. She could not fail again.

Ira and Meow were talking quietly outside the tent, perhaps thinking in her current state, Dounia wouldn't bother with listening in on them.

"Are you sure she's okay to fly?"

"She has to be," Ira responded, steel in her tone. "We are still the ones that guard our country and we cannot afford to be weak."

At least Ira understood what she was going through. Dounia hadn't met Ira yet when Ira's brother Pavel had been killed, but she did know that his death was her reason for joining.

It was a clear night, and the cloud cover was minimal. German radar had a hard time picking up their wood and canvas *kukuruznik*, but backlit by the moon, they would be silhouetted against the night sky. Dounia knew that she should be worried about this, but couldn't bring herself to care. She couldn't do anything about the weather anyway, and their side's only weather witch was with a different army.

"We'll be flying low tonight," Ira noted as they all clambered aboard the plane.

"Great," Meow said. "I love being able to see the ground going by underneath me to remind me I'm mortal."

"Shhh," Ira said, picking him up in her arms. "You'll be fine."

As instructed, Dounia flew low over the treetops to avoid being seen. They would have to rise higher once they got nearer to the front lines so that the bomb blasts wouldn't destroy them.

"Messerschmitts!" Meow screamed.

"What?" Dounia strained her ears. "I can't hear them."

"Why have they launched planes?" Ira asked, scanning the sky ahead of them.

"They must realize that on such a clear night they'll be able to see us more easily," Dounia said, and then, she could hear the low thrum of their engines.

"Our planes don't have guns," Ira said grimly.

"I have a pistol."

"Because that's going to do any good in a moving aircraft," Meow said sarcastically, ears flattening.

"We're going in first, so gain some altitude, will you?" Ira commanded sharply.

"The German pilots will see us," Dounia hissed in return.

"We're going to have to risk it."

Dounia pulled up slightly, but not as far as Ira wanted her to. The Messerschmitt's stalling speed only worked in their favour in close-quarter dog fighting. Ira told her the coordinates tersely, but didn't order her to rise any higher.

"Are they waiting for us?" Meow asked, green eyes glinting in the moonlight.

"You know, I think they might be," Ira said in a low voice. "I don't like this."

The enemy planes appeared ahead of them, and anticipation tightened in Dounia's stomach as she got ready for some intense manoeuvring. Ira snapped out their closing distance, and Dounia dared to bring them up and into the line of sight of their enemies.

Suddenly, the spotlights came up, highlighting all their planes and exposing them to enemy fire.

Dounia blinked hard against the abrupt glare, and then jerked her controls automatically at the staccato firing of the machine guns. The Germans had spotted them and were coming in fast and hard. Dounia zigzagged across the sky, trying to shake the spotlight following her.

"Fifty meters and closing," Ira said urgently. "Dounia, we don't have enough altitude. We'll have to circle back around."

Circling back around would expose them to more enemy fire. Dounia clenched her teeth hard and swooped in, aligning their aircraft with the target below.

"Dounia!" Ira screamed and Meow yowled in unison.

They weren't high enough, and the Messerschmitts were swinging back around. They were lit up from below by the spotlights, and puffs of smoke burst all around as the anti-aircraft guns fired away at them.

Heart pounding, Dounia hit the release button for the bombs they carried and they dropped away. A moment later, shrapnel ripped through the wings of their plane as the anti-aircraft guns found their mark. The roar of engines ahead of them intensified and the Messerschmitts came back around, firing in point blank range, doing as much damage as possible to their forces.

More bullets tore through their craft. The sound of tearing wood and canvas was extremely loud in her ears.

Suddenly, an explosion rocked the plane, the concussive blast throwing them violently off-course. The plane shuddered violently, and the frame, already weakened by the machine gun fire, started breaking apart in midair.

Ira was screaming, and they were descending far too rapidly. The trees rushed up at them and Dounia tried futilely to pull up. The aircraft was unresponsive beneath her hands and dipped uncontrollably towards the forest below.

"We're going to crash!" Meow yelled.

There was no time to tell him about the obviousness of this statement, because within moments they crashed into the tops of the trees. The wings crunched dreadfully as they hit the resistance of the branches around them. For a second, the branches were breaking with a high-pitched snapping noise, but then the plane shuddered again and groaned painfully, right before the wings tore straight off.

All the spells that were holding the plane together shattered all at once. The last glimpse Dounia got of Ira was of her clutching Meow tight to her chest and bracing herself against her control panel. Then, something flew at her sideways and struck her across the forehead.

When Dounia next opened her eyes, the plane had stopped moving, and something warm and sticky dripped into her eyes. Dounia wiped at it with her arm, and her sleeve came away dark with blood. She probed at the wound and winced as she found the gash across her forehead. A branch must have hit her after the shield spell around the cockpit failed.

She looked around. Their plane was wedged tight in the trees. Their descent had been halted by the thickness of the branches holding them. The body of their plane was still intact, if barely. She twisted in her seat to look behind her.

"Ira," she said urgently, trying to move around the crumpled sections of the plane. "Ira, are you there?"

A groan answered her, and she struggled out of her cockpit. Ira and Meow remained in their cockpit, and Ira was moving sluggishly.

"Are you okay?" Dounia asked desperately.

"I can't move my arm," Ira said groggily as she freed Meow from the cage of her arms and felt around for the edge of the cockpit.

Ira heaved herself up by one arm, holding the other awkwardly against her body. Dounia reached in to help her out, and together they leaned over the side of the plane and looked down.

"The ground has to be twenty feet down," Dounia said.

"Good thing there's branches then," Ira responded.

"How can you climb with only one arm?" Dounia demanded, realizing their predicament and starting to panic.

"I'll have to. We are behind the German lines, and soon they will send out a party to find us," Ira said. "We cannot be here when they arrive."

"Behind... we're behind the lines?" Dounia asked, freezing with fear.

"Yes. You were not keeping track, but I was. We're definitely behind the lines, and we're only about ten kilometers away from their nearest camp."

"Not good odds," Dounia said bleakly.

"But they are not quite impossible odds, so let's go. First, we have to get out of this tree!"

Dounia went first, climbing below Ira in the hope that if she fell, at least Dounia could try to catch her. Meow rode down on her shoulders in wide-eyed silence, having not said a single word since the crash. Ira's foot slipped once while they were climbing down, and she aborted a cry of pain.

"Are you okay?" Dounia asked.

"My arm," Ira said. "I'll have to see when we get down, but I don't think it's good."

They all made it down, surprisingly, and Dounia watched anxiously as Ira tried to move her arm, noting that it was the same one she'd been shot in previously. She was sure it had healed since then. Ira whimpered and immediately stopped trying to move it.

"It's broken," Ira said in a voice tight with pain.

"Come on," Meow said, breaking his silence. "We can't stay here. We'll figure out what to do once we get further away."

They struggled through the deep snow, Ira moving the snow around behind them with her magic to cover their obvious footprints. It was slow going, and Dounia hoped very hard that the Germans did not have skis, which would give them advantage in mobility.

After what seemed like hours, Meow's ears pricked up, and he growled in warning.

"I can hear them," Meow said in a low voice. "They're in the woods."

Dounia reached up and removed her cap, freeing her ears and listening. Yes, there it was, far off and echoing through the trees. There were voices in the woods, although it was hard to tell their position.

"They'll know we weren't in the plane," Dounia whispered. "They'll come looking for us."

"We need to find a place to hide for now," Ira said. "On a night like this, if they get close enough, they'll be able to see our shadows moving. We can't risk them seeing us!"

They found a tiny little cave, barely big enough to fit them, but at least it got them out of sight. Dounia helped Ira sit down and then knelt beside her.

"I don't know if we should take off your jacket," Dounia said. "It's cold out, and there's no shelter here if you get a chill."

"I don't have to look at it," Ira said. "I can tell it's broken."

"What do we do?" Dounia asked. "We don't have a medical kit or even any water or food."

"I can try to heal it," Ira said. "It can't be that much harder than fixing a plane."

Meow snorted. "Do carpenters ever perform surgery? No, they do not, because building a house and fixing a living body are two different things. Don't even try it. There's no telling what harm you could accidentally do to your body."

"You can make a splint," Dounia offered. "At least it is better than nothing."

Furtively, Dounia set out a little ways from the cave to try and find something sturdy that might help Ira build something. If only they had thought of this earlier when they were surrounded by broken wood! After a few minutes, she found some dead branches and brought them back.

"This will have to do," Ira said grimly, and set to work.

~~*

It finally started snowing in the early hours of the morning and the three of them could move from their hiding place. Dounia was in the lead, saying that the person with the broken arm shouldn't face the Nazis first.

Ira looked down at her crude arm splint and tried to move her fingertips again. Once again, that simple movement sent shocks of pain up her arm and into her shoulder and she breathed in deeply several times to keep from throwing up. She'd never had a large injury like this, and she was especially disconcerted that an entire quadrant of her body was immobilized.

For once in her life, Ira wished she actually had become a doctor.

"If I was a doctor, I could fix this," Ira said as they walked through the snow drifts that were beginning to pile up more as it snowed.

"If you were a doctor, you wouldn't be here at all," Dounia pointed out.

"My construction spells didn't do us much good, so I don't see why I should be here," Ira growled, flinching as the tense of her shoulder made her arm ache.

"You know, if the wings had stayed on, we would be dead, right?" Meow said.

"It was my fault," Dounia said, looking back over her shoulder. "You know it is. I shouldn't have released the bombs while we were flying so low."

"I think that we would have ended up shot down anyway," Meow said. "There were too many spotlights and planes flying around. I bet we weren't even the only ones to be shot down."

"At least we might have made it back to our lines," Dounia argued.

Ira sighed and stopped herself from snapping at them. The pain was making her less patient than she usually was. It was very distracting. Every second thought she had was surprise at how much having a broken arm *hurt*.

She blinked dark spots out of her vision and shook her head. She couldn't afford to pass out now, with the enemy hot on their tail.

"Let's just get out of here," she panted, an acrid taste filling her mouth.

Then she threw up, coughing and gagging as the additional movement jarred her arm again, sending spikes of white-hot agony up and down the limb. Dounia rushed to steady her, and Ira wiped off her mouth shakily.

"Let's go," Ira said again, and they set off in silence.

They'd been walking a long time, and apart from the angry throbbing of her arm, Ira was battling the foggy embrace of sleep. They'd been up all night, not daring to grab a quick nap with the enemy still close behind them. Light was filtering through the trees as dawn approached, and at its familiar appearance, Ira's body was insisting that she lie down and sleep.

She yawned, and Dounia turned back toward her in concern.

"I'm just sleepy," she said, a tad grumpily. They'd just been shot out of the sky, her arm had been broken and they were behind enemy lines. She felt she had good reason to be tetchy.

"We can't sleep now," Dounia said.

"I know," Ira replied, rolling her eyes. "Sorry for disturbing your concentration with my unnecessary bodily functions. Next time I'll keep my yawning bottled up."

"There's no need to snap at me."

"You started it!"

"Shhh!" Meow hissed, ears flat to his skull. "There's someone here."

And the woods around them erupted in gunfire.

Ira threw herself to the ground, heedless of her injury and kept the scream struggling to tear out of her throat behind her teeth. She couldn't give away where she'd landed. She heaved in ragged breaths and tried to concentrate on the wet, grainy feeling of snow melting against her cheek.

Dounia was crouched behind a tree in front of her, exchanging fire with the squad that had finally caught up with them. Meow picked his way across the snow and nudged at her face. Ira's ears were ringing again, and her stomach rolled with nausea.

Ira struggled to crawl her way up to Dounia's side, hiding behind the cover of a tree and a thick bush that might still provide cover even though winter had stripped it of its leaves.

"There has to be at least fifteen of them over there," Dounia reported. "I don't have many shots left—definitely not enough for all of them."

"Why don't they just swarm us?" Ira asked.

"If they wait for me to run out of ammo, they can capture us without risking getting shot," Dounia replied, keeping her eyes on their enemy.

"But don't they know you're a witch?" Meow asked, crawling up onto Dounia's shoulder. "They must suspect at least."

"There are very few combat mages in the world," Dounia replied with a sharp smile. "Most of us don't have the power necessary to actually do any harm."

"Or they think that we have non-combative magic, like mine," Ira said. "You can't really fix someone to death."

"So what you're really saying is that they're underestimating you," Meow said, tail twitching.

"Yes."

"I think it's about the time to disabuse them of that notion," Ira said.

"I might catch the forest on fire."

"It's enemy territory. Let it burn."

Dounia stepped out of her hiding place, and for a moment, Ira was terrified that they would shoot her before she could begin. Dounia carelessly removed her gloves and dropped them on the ground. She raised her hands, and then turned over her shoulder to look at Ira.

"You might want to get behind something more solid than that."

Ira rolled to her feet and ran several yards, throwing herself down into the dip behind a nearby boulder. She really needed stop moving so much, her arm was broken enough as it was without additional help. She heard a whoosh behind her, and chanced a peek around the boulder to see the fate of their enemies.

The woods in front of Dounia were on fire, and Dounia was standing there, arms raised to shoulder level, simply watching. The soldiers that had been taking refuge behind the trees started screaming and the woods erupted in flame. Ira watched passively as they all burned, screams eventually dying down and stopping.

After a few minutes, Dounia lowered her arms and the flames extinguished completely, not even the residual heat of the fire remaining. Everything was cold ash, as if the fire's dregs were hours old and not minutes.

When Ira stepped out, she could smell charred flesh on the air and gagged, backing away from the scene and covering her face with her undamaged arm.

Dounia turned and retrieved her gloves, sliding them on over ordinary-looking hands.

"And to think that I mostly use my craft to start campfires and keep my tea warm," Dounia said, smile empty.

"The enemy will have probably seen the smoke," Ira said. "We should get out of here."

"I should have kept some of them from burning so that we could take their uniforms," Dounia said, sighing and shaking her head.

"We'll get another chance for that," Ira replied wryly. "That's one thing we won't run out of on this side of the lines, and that's Germans."

Meow crept down from Dounia's shoulders and into her arms, fur standing on end and tail lashing wildly. Dounia stroked his head, and he growled in the back of his throat.

"We would have died," Ira said. "If you hadn't burned them."

"This is why I'm a pilot," Dounia said, voice still flat. "The fire is farther away from you."

Dounia warmed up Ira's tea when it grew cold.

"I'm not a combat mage," Dounia said, and Ira could see her hands were shaking. "I make tea and toast."

Ira moved up beside her and grasped her shoulder, squeezing it reassuringly.

"This is war," Meow said, from his perch on Dounia's other shoulder. "Tea and toast doesn't win battles."

"One day, will we look back at this and wonder why we did these things? I wonder how I'll live with them," Dounia said, but reached up and curled her fingers through Meow's fur.

As they walked away, the smell of smoke and charred remains cleared from the air, and Ira could breathe again.

"I never knew I had that much power," Dounia said eventually.

Ira hadn't either. She'd never seen anybody with the power to light the entire forest on fire. Healing and fixing things didn't come in levels that high. She couldn't take something too badly damaged and make it whole again. Eventually its structural integrity would collapse and she'd be left with nothing. And healers couldn't make a dying person live if they were past a certain point.

"I could have killed them all with a small spark," Dounia continued. "Just a little fire, like the ones I start back at base for boiling water. Their clothes would have caught, and there would be nothing they could do to put it out again."

"Why didn't you?" Ira asked, in spite of herself. She didn't like the way Dounia was talking right now, but what did one do in these situations? Every soldier had fractures in their heads that one didn't examine too carefully.

"I wanted it to be over quickly," Dounia said in a small voice.

"They make our people suffer," Ira pointed out.

"I am not them," Dounia replied.

There was silence for a while, as they heaved their legs up and out of the deep snow, only to plunge them back in again, time and time again. The hard work of walking kept Ira's mind off her arm, which was giving off a low background hum of pain in her head.

"I wonder if Tanya died this way," Dounia said, sounding bleak.

Ira didn't know what to say to that either, because Tanya probably had. The fire from the bombs they dropped wasn't much different from Dounia's fire, after all. Ira looked over at Meow, who stared back at her unblinkingly. One of them had to say something now, but it looked as if neither of them had the words.

Ira was almost relieved to hear the low rumble of an aircraft engine heading their way until she remembered that it meant the enemy was making a serious effort to find them. Which meant the Germans suspected they were still alive.

"Get down!" Ira said, grabbing Dounia's arm and rushing them under the cover of the nearest clump of evergreens.

"How far do you think we are from the burn site?" Dounia whispered, even though there was no way for the enemy to hear them from all the way up there.

"Not far enough," Meow growled, bristling. "And we haven't covered our trail at all since then."

Ira winced. She hadn't been wiping away their footprints since they stopped at the small cave after they crashed. That, and making the splint for her arm, had drained all her energy, and it was all that she could do just to stay on her feet. Pure exhaustion threatened to drag her down with every step, but they had to put distance between them and the patrol they'd killed.

"Can't," Ira said, and even getting enough breath in her lungs to talk was draining. "I'm just about done right now, and if I covered our trail, you'd be carrying me right now."

"I wouldn't mind," Dounia said.

"You need your hands free in case we run into another patrol," Ira said. "We can rest later."

"I just wish we knew how far the front lines were," Dounia said.

"It can't be that far, we've been walking all night," Ira replied, trying to calculate where they might be.

"We haven't been going very fast, what with your arm and the snow," Dounia pointed out. "I know you're the navigator, but it's pretty hard to do anything without a compass, or even a map."

"Not that I can see anything above the trees anyway," Ira said glumly. "If I could just make out some landmarks I might be able to triangulate our position, but I can't see a thing from here."

The plane above them started flying back and forth in an obvious search pattern, and the three of them huddled together, very still under the cover of their patch of trees. Eventually, it flew off, and Ira peered out from under the branches to watch it go. Its flight path was very close to the one that Ira and Dounia were walking.

"We must be going the right way," Ira said, looking around.

"Must be," Dounia repeated, and they all came out from under the trees and continued their trek across enemy territory.

It didn't feel like enemy territory until they came to the edge of the forest and looked out upon a burnt and blackened landscape, dusted neatly with a layer of snow. The jagged, black ends of what had once been trees thrust up through the snow, the only remains of what had once been a dense forest.

There was a long, black-on-white corridor of destruction, grown cold now, but Ira could imagine what it looked like all aflame. She'd seen it herself from the cockpit of her plane.

"This was the front line," Dounia said, scanning the horizon with her eyes. "They've advanced even further than I thought."

"Do we have to cross that?" Meow asked anxiously. "It's very out in the open. If that plane flies over again while we're crossing it, they'll see us right away."

"And anyone on the other side would see us coming," Ira said grimly. "But the fact stands that we have to cross. We've bombed the hell out of this area, and going around would take us days."

"We don't have days," Dounia said, shaking her head.

"We have no food or water," Meow said. "Or any survival equipment."

"I can't even start a fire," Dounia said. "Not if the enemy might see the smoke."

They all looked across the vast, empty space in front of them, littered with the remains of the destruction they'd rained down only weeks ago.

"If we cross it in the dark, they might not see us," Ira said, squinting across to try and see if she could see the other side. It was all just trees, with no sign of where the enemy could be.

"True," Meow said. "I really don't like the idea of us crossing in the daylight. Too many people could see us and kill us from a long way off."

One German sniper or one scout plane was all it would take, and none of them would have a chance, not without a place to hide or take cover.

They made themselves as comfortable as possible at the edge of the forest to wait for nightfall. They had several hours before it began to get dark, even this deep in winter, when night came early. Dounia cleared them a space by melting the snow off a small patch of ground. At least they would be dry while they waited.

Ira tried to make a better splint for her arm, and she wondered again if maybe she would be able to fix the break herself. Dounia must have known what she was considering, because she gave her a sharp look. Ira sighed, but knew that if she did it wrong, she could do enough damage that the shock could kill her.

A little while later, Dounia melted them some snow to drink. Ira's stomach gurgled and the water she'd gulped down swished around inside. She was so hungry, but there was nothing out here to eat.

"Sleep," Dounia told her. "I'll keep watch for a bit."

"I'll take the next shift," Ira said, already yawning and settling down, uncaring that the ground was so hard and lumpy.

"No, Meow will take the next shift."

She heard Meow protest, but the rest was lost in a darkening haze as she surrendered to sleep, unable to keep her eyes open once she'd given her body permission to rest.

FOUR

Night came swiftly, and across the empty expanse in front of them, a string of lights illuminated the forest where the German front lines were setting up for the night. Maybe from above, their camps were blacked out, to keep the night bombers from seeing their position. But from the ground, Dounia could see them perfectly.

"Do you think they're keeping up watch on the other side?" Ira asked, coming up beside her, Meow curled over her good shoulder.

"Most likely they're watching the sky for our sisters," Dounia said. "Or looking toward our lines. No one looks for enemies from behind."

"Do you think that they are still searching for us?" Ira asked. "I haven't heard a thing since that plane, but you two are the ones with the hearing."

"Not a sound," Dounia shook her head. "Not anything at all."

She hadn't heard any birds in the trees or animals in the woods the entire time they'd been here. It made sense that no animals wanted to live near an active warzone, but it was still eerie, the lack of life here. Just them and snow-covered trees.

"Let's cross. We have to hurry; we can't still be in sight once the sun rises again," Ira said, but paused, looking at Dounia. "Is it just me, or does it feel wrong to step across this burnt earth?"

"I don't want to cross either," Dounia admitted, a crawling feeling beginning in her belly at the thought of being out in the open. "But we must."

"It's a different feeling," Meow said, eyes glinting in the night. "This was where our front lines were a few weeks ago."

"We'll retake it," Ira said, voice steel-hard and determined. "They thought they had us beaten once, but we forced them back from the gates of Moscow. They will never win."

"Never," Dounia agreed, and took Ira's hand in hers.

Together, they stepped out into the vast corridor, feet crunching on the new snow. The bombing had wiped away all the snow that had fallen previously, and it was less deep than the snow in the forest. Dounia walked as fast as she dared, making sure that Ira kept her footing in the rough, uneven landscape.

"What a dead empty place," Ira said, and the sound echoed in the barren, snow-coated landscape.

"Shhh," Meow hissed, ears flattening. "Your voices will carry over the snow."

"Do you think anyone heard that?" Dounia asked in a whisper.

"Can't say," Meow replied, ears pricking forward to listen. "I can't hear anything."

They continued, and Dounia guided Ira as best she could. Dounia and Meow could both see the ground just fine in the dark, but Ira was almost blind. It was a cloudy night, and it might yet start snowing again, so there was no moon to light the way. But it also meant there was no light to see them by, so Dounia was thankful for that. She just had to make sure that Ira didn't twist an ankle on the uneven terrain.

It was slow going, but Dounia dared not rush Ira any faster. If she injured a leg, that was it for them. Dounia could try and carry Ira all the way to their front lines, but it would put their chances of success at almost zero. The odds weren't that great as it was.

That's when she heard it, the rattling, whistling sound of wood and canvas wings on the air.

"Do you hear it?" she whispered to Meow.

"Yes," Meow said, eyes to the sky. "They're coming."

It wasn't long until up ahead of them, spouts of fire shot into the air and the earth rumbled as the night bombers dropped their loads on the front lines. Soon, parts of the enemy line ahead of them blazed scarlet, and the Germans shouted commands as they tried to bring the fires under control.

"At least we know where we're headed," Ira said, smiling grimly as the bombardment of the Germans continued.

"It almost looks pretty from here," Dounia said.

"Yes, look at those sparks, thrown so high into the air," Ira said, pointing at a particularly large fire. "Huge embers flying up and up, like a signal for us to follow."

The spotlights came on, sweeping over the night sky, searching for their tormentors that rained death and fire down on them from the air. Sometimes they would catch a flicker of movement, the edge of a wing or the flash of a tail, but there was hardly any sound to give them away. Just a whoosh, as if there were giant birds swooping in from above, giant birds of prey.

"It sounds so strange, like a demon in the night," Dounia whispered. "I had no idea that we sounded like that when we came diving in. It's scary."

"If I didn't know that it was our very own comrades up there defying death in their little wooden planes, I would almost say that we were something, some sort of magical being in the air," Ira replied.

"No wonder they hate us so much," Dounia said. "We're some terrifying thing that comes in the night that no one can kill, or even see."

"I can see why shooting us down is worth an Iron Cross now," Ira said. "I always thought it was so funny, that the Germans feared us enough to offer such a reward for our deaths."

"And here I thought we were just little girls in flying wooden crates." Dounia stifled a laugh in the crook of her arm. "Or so our men would have us believe."

"We're not girls at all. We're dragons."

"They are right to fear you," Meow said, baring his teeth. "Do they not know our history and all of those armies that have tried to invade our homeland in centuries past? The women of Russia have always been dragons."

Their courage bolstered, the three of them walked with certainty, twice as determined to reach their destination with their comrades flying overhead.

The wide swath of destruction had looked so vast from where they had been, but crossing it took less time than Dounia had imagined it would. Soon, they were almost on the other side, near to the camps, and she slowed down to a crawl. From where they were, the sound of men talking was loud and Dounia could make out the shape of tents in their camp.

That's when she heard it, and grabbed Ira's arm to stop her from going any further.

There was a sentry up ahead of them, and he said something to his companion, laughing and looking up at the sky. They hadn't seen Dounia or Ira, but it was a close thing.

Dounia spoke absolutely no German at all. She knew the word for "yes" because it was so close to their own word for "yes," but that was it. Ira knew a little, having made a point of learning once the war had started.

She leaned in close to Ira's ear and breathed, "What are they saying?"

"They are wondering if the bombing will continue," Ira whispered back, so softly that a human ear wouldn't have been able to hear it.

It would continue, that Dounia was sure of. Maybe something had delayed them, but another round of bombing would undoubtedly start up soon. It was a good night for it. There was cloud cover, and it wasn't snowing. It wasn't even windy. An ideal night for flying, if Dounia did say so herself. Without wind, the bombers had a much higher chance of hitting their targets.

"They have uniforms," Meow pointed out.

"That they do," Dounia replied, grinning. "And we have a nice distraction in the form of our own people bombing the German lines."

"A bomb might hit us," Ira said.

"Or it might not. It's our best chance to cross without being seen, when everyone is distracted."

Ira nodded, and as Dounia predicted, another round of bombing began soon after that. Under the cover of the explosions, no one heard a pistol fire twice. Everyone in the enemy camp was so busy with their spotlights and anti-aircraft guns that no one thought to go check on the sentries. No one saw two women and one black cat stripping the Germans of their uniforms and putting them on over their bomber jackets.

"This is so awkward," Ira complained, trying to fit the sleeve of the German jacket over both her bomber jacket and her splint.

"At least we look more bulky and less likely to look like women," Dounia replied. "The German army doesn't recruit women, you know."

"And short hair as well," Ira said, patting at her hair that she's braided back and hidden underneath the German helmet.

"How am I supposed to hide my ears?" Dounia complained. "This helmet feels horrible digging in and flattening them."

"You can't wear your bomber cap, people will notice!" Ira hissed back, looking at her critically. "It's no good, I can still see the tips of your ears."

"It will have to do," Dounia growled, trying to fit the helmet down further. "My ears can only be compacted down so far."

"Let's hope that everyone is too busy to notice," Meow said. "We have to go now, while everyone is distracted!"

Dounia dragged the bodies of the two German soldiers out further into the empty landscape and hid them in a bomb crater. Ira tried to help, but the strain on her arm made her pale with pain, so Dounia made her stop.

"Okay, now we can go," Dounia said, and they set off toward the camp.

Dounia's heart pounded harshly, becoming louder and louder the closer they got to the camp. The sounds of bombs exploding and the rapid fire of anti-aircraft guns nearby grew louder as well, until her head was a mess of noise. It was different. In the air, everything was quiet, and even the explosions seemed distant. If the edges of the helmet weren't digging into her ears so much, she'd be thankful for the way it dulled her hearing.

No one noticed their approach, too busy focusing on the gentle swooshing noise of the bombers coming in for another run. There were swarms of people everywhere, manning the guns and the spotlights, or simply putting out fires as they spread.

"I think we can hurry," Ira said into her ear, careful not to let them be overheard speaking Russian, although with all the bombs going off, no one could hear them anyway.

Dounia picked up her pace, trying to look like they were rushing with a purpose, like everybody else. She could hardly believe where she was right now, right in the middle of the enemy camp while their comrades flew by overhead.

The Germans were all very loud, Dounia thought. Or maybe they only seemed so loud because she couldn't understand what they were all shouting about. They looked very different from Russian men, or maybe it was her imagination. They all looked similar to her. Or maybe she was just scared, and they all looked the same to her because they were all the enemy, and any one of them would kill her without a second thought if they knew who she was.

They kept saying some word, over and over.

"*Nachthexen!*"

"What does it mean?" she asked Ira.

"Night witches," Ira said, grinning. "That's their name for us. The night witches."

They ran until Ira had a stitch in her side, and they stopped behind a tent, hidden in the shadows, panting. The cold winter air burned Dounia's lungs from the inside out, and her throat was raw all the way down. She hardly ever needed to run, and she never had to run after a full day of walking. She'd thought she was fit enough just jumping in and out of her plane, but this was exhausting.

"Where do we need to go to get to our lines?" Dounia asked, trying to calm her breathing and her racing heart, which was pounding so hard that her ribs ached.

"The same way we're going already," Ira gasped, doubled over and kneading her side. "That's not the thing I'm most worried about. Everyone is facing that direction, so if we try and slip out that way, we'll probably be noticed."

"Not to mention that the people manning our lines won't know it's us. They might think we're the enemy and shoot us," Meow pointed out.

"Are you telling me that we're stuck in this camp until we figure out how to get past them all without being noticed?" Dounia asked, far too tired to go off on a rant. She closed her eyes and leaned her forehead against the tent pole.

"It's not as if we had time to think up a plan with the Germans hard on our tail," Ira said. "We have to keep moving. I'm just glad we managed to get this far without being killed."

"Well, do you have a plan now?" Dounia asked.

"No," Ira snapped back. "Sorry if I can't think right now, but I'm mostly running on adrenaline and that floaty feeling you get when you're in pain. And I am in quite a lot of pain because my arm is broken!"

Meow's ears flattened, and he hissed, "Careful, your voices are too high to be mistaken for men's, and if you shout any louder someone is going to notice us."

"So what are we going to do?" Dounia asked, wracking her brain for a plan, but coming up blank.

"If I just knew how a German camp functioned, this would be a lot easier," Ira said irritably. "If it's anything like ours though, then someone is always on watch towards the enemy lines."

There was a sudden shout from behind them and Dounia turned on her heel sharply to face whoever had come up behind them.

It was a German officer, and although he looked a little worse for wear, his eyesight was just fine. He yelled at them in German for about half a minute and then stopped mid-sentence. His eyes went first to Meow, who arched his back and hissed at him. Then he looked at their faces and took a step back in surprise.

He said something else in German, sounding shocked, and Dounia was starting to get really annoyed with not being able to understand anything that was being said.

"How much trouble are we in?" she asked Ira.

"He's about to add it all up, so I suggest we run," Ira said.

"Okay," Dounia said.

Without warning, Meow launched himself off Ira's shoulder and landed claws-first on the officer's face, yowling furiously. When Dounia moved to help, Ira grabbed her arm and pulled. They fled, and behind them the officer started screaming angry invectives in German.

There was nothing Dounia could do but run.

~~*

Ira couldn't remember the last time she'd run this fast, but it was all she could think of to do with the screams of the German officer were fading from her ears. Overhead, she heard the characteristic swoosh of her comrades coming in for another bombing run. It was an ideal distraction, except for the fact that any of those bombs could drop right on top of her.

Meow tore up alongside her yowling, "Go! Go! Go!"

Ira had no breath left to say anything, and kept running. Everyone else around them was scurrying back and forth too, so their mad dash through the enemy camp went largely unnoticed.

Bombs started going off around them, sending shockwaves rumbling through the earth, shaking the ground beneath their feet. Everything smelled of ash and smoke, and it stung her eyes. It was chaos, and all she could hear was her own heartbeat pounding in her ears. Every other sound was lost in screams and explosions.

They slowed down eventually, and Ira pulled Dounia around the corner of an anti-aircraft gun turret and waited to see if the German officer was still following them. The explosions rocked the encampment, and a bomb dropped on the other side of the turret, throwing snow and earth up into the air in a wet spray.

"*Hey you*!" someone yelled, and it took Ira a moment to realize this yell was being directed at them.

She turned, hoping that Dounia's ears weren't too noticeable in the dark, and that Meow was staying out of sight. Another officer, not the same one, thankfully, was coming toward them.

He squinted at them through a pair of glasses that had lost one lens and said, "*You're very young to be on the front, lad. Where are you two off to in such a hurry?*"

"*We...*" Ira said, but couldn't think of anything.

"*Running from the Witches, aren't you,*" the officer continued. "*You can't have been here long then. They're* no different than any other enemy, for all that they are women. They're not mythical or anything like that, just ordinary soldiers. Their terror tactics work well, I'll grant you that. Come on, then, no more running. We have to help put out some of those fires."

Ira looked at Dounia helplessly before remembering that Dounia didn't even know what the man was saying. There wasn't much choice but to follow the man, however, and she beckoned for Dounia to come with her.

The German officer recruited a few more troops that didn't have any tasks, and got them to form a chain. Ira couldn't believe that they were going to waste precious water on fires when she realized that the bucket she'd been handed was full of snow.

"*Hurry, pass it down*," the officer instructed them, and Ira complied as fast as she could.

Dounia didn't ask anything out loud, but her eyes were wide and questioning. Obviously she couldn't say anything, just in case someone in the line overheard her speaking Russian.

Ira's arm throbbed in reminder that she couldn't use it, and Ira lifted the buckets with only one arm while pretending she was actually lifting with two. She bit her lip at the strain, and her good arm started burning in protest. Her arm muscles started shaking, and lancing pain began shooting up her broken arm with all the movement.

Just when she thought she would drop the next bucket, the officer raised his arm and brought their operation to a halt.

"*Good work, boys*," the officer said, dismissing them all.

Just as Ira thought that maybe they could finally sneak away, he turned to them and said to Ira, "*I noticed that your arm was injured. I must insist you go to the medical tent. I will escort you.*"

"*Sir,*" Ira said, trying to make her voice as low as possible. She had a low voice for a woman, but for a man it was still somewhat high. "*My friend...*"

She hurriedly checked the name on Dounia's breast pocket.

"*My friend Cpl. Weiss will take me there,*" Ira said slowly, making sure not to pronounce her German with an accent.

Hopefully the officer would think she was just trying to be heard over the yelling and explosions going on around them. She didn't think she was speaking with a noticeable Russian accent, but she'd never actually spoken with a native German speaker, so it was possible her pronunciation was off.

Ira had never thought that she would end up in a situation where she had to speak German convincingly enough to sneak through enemy lines, and now she wished she'd studied harder when she'd had the chance.

She waited, hardly daring to breathe.

"*I will escort you to the tent, and Weiss can stay with you,*" the officer pronounced. "*Now don't think you can get out of manning the lines like this every time. You might just be lads, but we must all do our part.*"

Ira didn't argue, following the man to the medical tent. Dounia grabbed onto her arm and shot her another look, eyebrows furrowed, but Ira could only shake her head and gesture for them to follow. There was no time to explain, and Ira hoped desperately that the officer wouldn't look too closely at them. For now, he thought that she and Dounia were a pair of young soldiers, but any moment now he could get a better look at them and figure it out. But he would figure it out a lot faster if Ira tried to disobey orders.

Unfortunately, the tent they were taken to was well lit, and Ira ducked her head to try and hide the roundness of her face. Dounia's face was sharper and less feminine than hers, but she also had cat ears, which were more noticeable than she would like. Dounia was right, the helmet she was wearing really didn't cover them up that well.

Thankfully, the German officer was still half blind, so maybe he would think the roundness of her face was just his blurry vision.

"*Doctor!*" the officer said loudly, causing half the occupants of the tent to look up.

The patients all lost interest and went back to waiting for their turn.

A young man, probably not yet thirty despite the premature grey streak, rapidly came over and waited for the officer to continue, face attentive and amiable. He had a streak of blood under one eye, and his hair was starting to get a little long in the front, pushed back off his face and plastered there with sweat. He had a mild, pleasant expression as he greeted them.

"*Can I help you, sir?*" he asked, smiling.

"*This lad here has an injured arm. See to him, will you?*" the officer said, and then marched right back out of the tent without a word.

Ira could tell he was the type of officer that expected to have his needs seen to right away, and that he probably thought that Ira would have her arm looked at as soon as he left. Ira looked over the rest of the tent and saw that there were still four other soldiers in between her and getting seen to.

"*Doctor, I apologize*," she said, realizing she was speaking too formally but didn't know how German soldiers spoke to each other. "*I am happy to wait my turn.*"

The doctor looked at her sharply, and an unusual look entered his eyes. The light was too bright, and his eyes too quick. He knew she wasn't a German soldier, she could tell. The look he had was one of a man piecing things together. She waited, ready to knock him over and run again, and tensed up in preparation.

"*Oh, no, my lad, no need to be frightened*," he said gently.

He knew she wasn't a native German speaker and was speaking slowly, enunciating for her so that she could understand him better. Ira felt like her heart would beat itself to death on her ribcage as it quaked with fear in her chest. He knew.

"*You and your friend wait here*," he said, still speaking slowly and softly, as if he were trying to tame a wild animal. "*I will look at your arm when I'm finished.*"

Should she run? What if he was calming her down so that he could go and get somebody else to capture them? Her heart was beating too fast and she wasn't breathing. All of a sudden, her vision swam and her legs felt watery and weak.

"*Oh, oh,*" she heard the doctor say, and suddenly there was an arm around her back steadying her and lowering her down to the ground. "*You've been through a lot, haven't you, my poor boy. I'll get you some water.*"

Ira breathed, and the doctor crossed the tent to get a canteen, handing it to Dounia. He leaned over very close and instructed her "little sips." In Russian. No one else in the tent was even paying attention, but Dounia's eyes were wide and dilated in panic.

"*Shhh, there's a lad*," the doctor said, switching back to German, and then leaving them leaning against the tent wall to go attend his other patients.

Dounia helped Ira drink some of the water from the canteen and then took a swig herself, panting.

"He knows we're Russian," Dounia whispered in Ira's ear.

"Yes, I could tell," Ira whispered back.

"What do we do?" Dounia hissed.

"I'm not sure we can do anything about that," Ira said. "He hasn't tried to hurt us yet."

"*Yet*," Dounia said darkly. "Doesn't mean he *won't*."

"Well, I think that we shouldn't try to do anything unless he actually tries to hurt us, or alert anyone else to our presence," Ira said. "I'm too exhausted to run anymore, and my arm hurts. My entire side feels like it's on fire."

Dounia flinched, and Ira realized what she'd said.

"Sorry," Ira whispered. Bad choice of words.

"Where's Meow?" asked Dounia. "I lost him after that officer grabbed us."

"I don't know," Ira said. "I'm sure he's fine. He's a smart cat, and I'm sure he knows how to stay out of trouble. Or at least out of the line of fire."

They quieted after that, waiting for the doctor to do whatever it was he was going to do. There was something else, Ira was certain of that. He wasn't just going to fix her arm, that was for sure. Ira didn't even know if he was going to try and help her at all. They were an enemy to his country, and Ira couldn't trust his motives.

Slowly, the tent emptied. They were the last ones inside the tent, and there were no new patients to contend with. Ira could still hear bombs going off, but far away down the line. It seemed that the bombardment of this section was over.

"*Now, let's look at your arm.*"

The doctor spoke accented but recognizable Russian, probably more fluently than she spoke German. Ira eyed him warily, but complied, trying to struggle out of the German uniform. Dounia helped her, and the doctor waited patiently.

"*Nachthexen,*" he said, eyes widening when her bomber jacket underneath was revealed.

"*Yes,*" Ira replied shortly, releasing the makeshift splint she'd had keeping her arm in place.

"*I knew that you were Russian,*" the doctor continued. "*I thought you were just stragglers from the bombing. You're the pilots of the plane that was downed yesterday.*"

Ira ignored him piecing together their story and focused on getting her bomber jacket off over her injured arm. Dounia helped, and soon it was just her uniform covering her arm up.

"*I'm sorry,*" the doctor said and cut her sleeve away with a pair of scissors.

Ira couldn't watch after that, although she heard Dounia hiss in concern as the injury was finally revealed. As Ira was looking away, there was a movement at the edge of the tent and Meow slipped inside, coming to her side immediately. Ira reached out and stroked his head, trying to distract herself.

"*Oh? And where did you come from, small one?*" the doctor asked.

"*I've been here since the start,*" Meow said, swishing his tail.

The doctor dropped the scissors and stared at Meow in shock.

"*You can talk,*" he said. "*You're a cat.*"

"*Do cats not talk where you come from?*" Meow asked, and Ira shot him a quelling look.

"*No, they don't talk where he's from, Meow.*"

"*How was I supposed to know it was a secret?*" Meow asked and twitched his tail.

"*Nachthexen,*" the doctor muttered under his breath again, and then returned to Ira's arm.

Ira distracted herself from the pain by stroking Meow's fur, and the doctor reset her arm carefully, splinted it and then made a sling for her.

"*There, it is set properly now and will heal in the right position,*" the doctor said, stepping back to survey his work.

"*Thank you, doctor...?*" Ira said, realizing that they hadn't gotten the doctor's name.

"*Engel,*" he said, washing his hands.

"Why are you helping us?" Dounia asked, eyes narrowed in suspicion.

"Ah, I almost forgot," Doctor Engel said. "But it's not the type of thing that I can tell you, you must see it to believe it yourself. Put your uniform jacket back on, we must cross the camp to the hospital. It is not far from here."

"This is not the hospital?" Ira asked, looking around at the narrow cot and medical tools around the small tent.

"No, it is just a medical bay. The soldiers who have long-term injuries are in a bigger tent. Now come," Doctor Engel beckoned for them to follow him. "The night is not over, and we may be able to get you out of here yet."

"What if it's a trap?" Dounia whispered as Ira clumsily pulled her jacket back over her shoulders.

"If it's a trap, then set him on fire," Ira said. "But for now, it looks as if he is helping us. He set my arm properly. Why would he do that if he just wanted to kill or capture us?"

"Wasting time?" Dounia suggested sceptically.

"I want to see what he has to show us," Ira said firmly, and they followed the doctor back out into the night where the soldiers on the front line were settling back into their routines.

Ira and Dounia kept their heads down, and Ira hid Meow inside her jacket. A few distant explosions could be heard a long way off, but it appeared the bombardment of this section of the lines was over.

Doctor Engel brought them inside the tent and turned the lights on. There were only two, and they were dim and flickering, barely lighting up the space inside the tent. There were several forms asleep on the cots, and they didn't stir at the intrusion. Doctor Engel passed them by and went directly to the last cot.

"Here she is. I've been wondering how I was going to get her out of here, but now that you're here, you can all go together."

"What?" Ira asked.

Doctor Engel gently rocked the sleeping form until she began to stir, drawing back the fabric that kept her face hidden.

"Tanya," Dounia breathed into the quiet of the night air.

FIVE

Her sister was alive.

Dounia couldn't believe her eyes, but there in front of her was Tanya's face in the most impossible of places, lying there on a cot in a German field hospital. Hesitantly, fearing that if she touched the visage in front of her, it wouldn't be real, Dounia reached out.

Her skin was cool, but soft and very, very real against the pads of Dounia's fingers.

"Tanya," she said again, and Tanya's eyes blinked open slowly.

"Who's there? Am I dreaming again?" she asked sleepily. "Because I thought for sure that I heard the voice of my sister, Dounia."

"It's me," Dounia said. "I'm here, it's really me. You're not dreaming."

Tanya smiled and squinted up at Dounia's face. "How can you be here?"

"It's a long story," Dounia said. "But I'm here, and Ira, and Meow, too. Doctor Engel brought us to you. I should have known we would find you. Ira's injured again."

"And you're grumpy," Tanya said.

"You saved my sister?" Dounia asked Doctor Engel.

Doctor Engel blinked in surprise, but nodded.

Dounia threw her arms around him and squeezed as hard as she could. "Thank you," she said. "Thank you. Thank you."

Eventually, she had to let him go, and she moved back to Tanya's side. Tanya slowly got her hands free from the tangle of blankets and grasped at Dounia's. They were covered in thick bandages, and Dounia was careful as she let Tanya take her hands.

"Is she hurt?" Ira asked, looking at the bandages that went up most of Tanya's arm.

"It's not as bad as it looks," Doctor Engel said. "She did sustain some burns and a concussion from hitting her head. The concussion cleared up in a few days. The burns are all second and first degree, but I've told my superiors they're third degree."

"What, why?" Ira asked, and Dounia turned to hear his answer.

"The officers want to interrogate her. If they knew she was in better health than I've told them, they would take her away."

"So you've been lying to them to keep her safe," Dounia said.

"Yes, but even with the deception, they weren't going to be put off for long. It's a miracle that you two have shown up. I've been trying to think of a way to get her out of the camp for days now."

"We might not be all you hoped," Ira said grimly.

"She's right. We haven't figured out how to get out of the camp yet," Dounia said, shaking her head. "We have been trying to make a plan, but everything here is so chaotic."

"Oh, that's easy," Doctor Engel waved his hand. "I already had a plan to get her out, but it required me to have an accomplice. Tanya told me she doesn't know how to drive, not to mention her injuries, so that was out. Until you two showed up."

"Why would she need to know how to drive?" asked Dounia, frowning.

"There is a vehicle bay not far from here where jeeps are stationed in between supply runs," Doctor Engel said. "We need to get you one of those jeeps and you will drive out of here."

"They'll start shooting at us," Dounia pointed out dryly.

"Not immediately," Doctor Engel replied cheerfully. "All of our guns are pointed at the sky. Why would they suspect that their vehicle had just been hijacked by the enemy on the ground?"

"I'm sure they would notice when we start driving toward enemy territory," Meow said, jumping onto Tanya's cot and nudging at her hand.

"I was not going to ask, but... why can your cat talk?" Doctor Engel peered down at Meow curiously.

"I am a familiar," Meow said, throwing his nose into the air. "We are different from normal cats."

"I see. So you really are witches," Doctor Engel turned back to Dounia and Ira. "You don't look like witches to me."

"What do witches look like?" Ira asked with a small smile.

"But where do you come from?" Doctor Engel scrubbed at his messy hair with one hand. "Why does Germany not have witches? Or any other place, for that matter."

"Finland has witches," Dounia said, thinking hard. "And Sweden and Norway, too. I can't say if there are any farther away than that. We are northern creatures, as far as I can tell."

Doctor Engel stared hard at her. "I can't help but notice that you have..."

Dounia sighed and removed her helmet.

"That's much better," Dounia said, and her ears sprung up and forward.

"Cat ears," Doctor Engel said. "Should I ask?"

"Better not to," Dounia said, and when she smiled, she let the tips of her canines flash for just an instant.

Doctor Engel found warm clothes that would fit Tanya and helped Dounia to dress her. Tanya herself wasn't much help, sleepily shifting this way and that as they got the clothes on her. Although Tanya wasn't as badly hurt as Doctor Engel would have his superiors believe, she was still injured and dosed with as much morphine as her body could handle. Second-degree burns were extremely painful, and they covered a large amount of Tanya's body.

"I am worried about infection," Doctor Engel told them as he wrapped yet another layer around Tanya's body. "She would do much better to be in a proper hospital far from the front lines, but obviously no one cared how well an enemy was treated."

"Except you," Dounia said.

"Except me," Doctor Engel said. "Come, help me get her up. We need to carry her without making anyone else suspicious. I will wrap her in a sheet, and if anyone stops us to ask about it, we can say that she succumbed to her injuries and we're taking her to be buried away from camp."

"Why do we need the jeep then?" Ira asked, trying to look like she was being helpful even though her broken arm prevented her. "Can't we just say we're going to bury her and take her past the lines that way?"

"They would expect us to take her back behind our own lines," Doctor Engel said.

"She's an enemy, why would they want her buried behind your lines?" Ira persisted, and Doctor Engel's mouth thinned, and something in his eyes went flat.

"That has never stopped them before," he said, voice hard. "If you go on foot, you will not get very far. Someone will notice and shoot us. No one will be expecting an attack, but they will figure it out eventually. We have snipers, and it takes too long to get out of their range on foot."

Dounia nodded. Snipers were a major worry of hers now that she was on the ground, and she really didn't want to find out how far away they could still hit her from and be accurate enough to kill her.

"Come on," Meow said, batting at Dounia's arm with his paw. "We have to leave now, when there's still no light for them to see us by."

They carried Tanya together in the blanket, and Dounia hoped that Tanya wouldn't move around too much or it might alert people to the deception. As it was, no one looked twice as they carried Tanya through the camp. A few people called out to Doctor Engel, but no one tried to stop them. Doctor Engel gave those who spoke to them a tired smile and said a few, short words in German.

Dounia supposed that a lot of people must die on the front lines, and the sight of Doctor Engel carrying away patients to be buried was a common one.

Dounia wanted to ask what they were saying, but she dared not let anyone overhear her speaking Russian.

Tanya gave a twitch in the blanket, and Dounia glanced over at Doctor Engel. He was staring straight ahead, as if he hadn't noticed, and Dounia followed suit. Her own actions might give them away if she weren't careful. Tanya twitched again, and Dounia held her breath and hoped that no one would see.

Doctor Engel steered them into the dark spaces between tents and semi-permanent structures where they flitted from shadow to shadow. Meow finally made a reappearance, coming to sit across Dounia's shoulders.

"How far do we have to go?" Dounia risked asking, glancing around and seeing nothing but darkness to one side and the intermittent lighting of the camp from the other.

"Not far," Doctor Engel whispered back.

The doctor was as good as his word, and soon they were standing outside the back of a makeshift vehicle bay where two guards stood watch.

"What do we do about them?" asked Ira, looking at Doctor Engel.

The guards weren't particularly attentive, both of them leaning against a stack of boxes and chatting, laughing every once in a while. And why should they think they had to worry about anything being taken? If a fellow soldier came up to them, they wouldn't think anything of it.

"Can you lure them back over here?" Doctor Engel asked. "If we can knock them unconscious, they won't be able to call for help until it's too late."

Dounia wondered if Doctor Engel had ever deliberately killed anyone. Would he still be helping them if he knew how Dounia had set that patrol of Germans on fire? Or how many bombs she and Ira had dropped on top of their heads in the night? Tanya had been the one to call down the bombing run on her own position. Tanya probably hadn't told him that, either.

Dounia looked at Ira, and Ira nodded. They would try not to kill the guards if at all possible, for the doctor's sake.

"I'm sorry, I can't be the one to lure them over. If they recognize me later, they'll turn me in, and I'll be executed."

Dounia knew he was leaving out the part where he would be lucky if they just executed him. In Russia, they were not kind to traitors either.

"I can speak German. I should be the one to do it," Ira said. "You two be ready to hit them on the back of the head with something."

Dounia had her pistol, and as she and the doctor lowered Tanya gently to the ground, she looked over at him questioningly. He pulled a heavy flashlight out of his jacket pocket.

"Where do I aim to do the least amount of damage?" Dounia asked.

Doctor Engel shook his head and looked at the ground. "There isn't one. I am a doctor, and I know the human body. A blow that will knock someone unconscious is also likely to kill them. The brain is easily damaged, and even if I had the right training, putting them in a choke hold could still cause damage, simply from lack of oxygen."

"I'm too short to put someone in a chokehold," Dounia pointed out.

"There would be a chance they could escape or warn others before we could put them out. We have to knock them out in one hit. The temple, aim for the temple, and hit hard," Doctor Engel said, and he tightened his hold on the flashlight.

Ira stepped out and said something quickly in German. The two guards stopped talking, standing straighter as they listened. Ira pointed out of the camp emphatically, and the two guards looked at each other once, before standing up straight, throwing their shoulders back and pushing past Ira.

One got out a flashlight and started shining it out into the darkness. Both guards were busy peering out at the landscape beyond, and Dounia raised her pistol above her head. Aim for the temple, hit hard, don't give them a chance to cry out, she repeated to herself.

Her hand was sweaty on the barrel, but she didn't dare take the time to wipe it off.

Doctor Engel started to swing, and Dounia hurriedly brought the butt end of her pistol down on the guard's temple. The man crumpled straight to the ground, knees folding underneath him and the rest of him following. Dounia didn't even have time to catch him, it happened so fast.

When she turned, Doctor Engel was checking the head wound on his guard, lips thin as his fingers gently probed at it.

"I'll see to them in a moment. You have to be off, right away," Doctor Engel said, leaning down to pick up Tanya.

Dounia and Ira searched both the guards and found keys. Doctor Engel opened the back door of the jeep and started arranging Tanya inside.

"This isn't a jeep, it's a bucket," Dounia said.

"Yes, it is a *Kübelwagen*," said Doctor Engel with a small smile. "Or, a direct translation—bucket car."

"Will it drive over this kind of terrain?" Ira asked, her brow pinching up.

"Yes, it is a very good terrain vehicle," Doctor Engel assured them. "Your main concern should be getting past the lines without being shot."

"Good," Dounia said, testing the various keys they'd found until she found the right one to start the jeep up. "Good luck, doctor. And thank you."

"It's been an honour," Doctor Engel said, and waved them off.

The way forth was clear, with no tents or other obstructions in their way. The Germans had set up their camp so that their vehicle bay had a clear exit. It was a very efficient set-up, and one that worked in their advantage.

Dounia drove forward without the headlights turned on and made for the front lines, hands gripping the steering wheel in a death grip. This was it. They either got out, or they wouldn't.

"*Halten Sie!*"

There were more guards, and they were stepping out onto the road in front of the jeep, hands held in front of them to signal the jeep to stop.

"What do I do?" Dounia hissed.

"Just run them over," Meow suggested.

"I can't just run them over!" Dounia protested, wavering between pressing her foot on the gas pedal and slowing down.

The guards already looked suspicious, marching forward imperiously. However, they didn't draw their guns, so they still weren't alarmed by Ira and Dounia's actions. Dounia was trying to figure out how to get them to move, so she didn't have to run them over. They started coming around to the driver's side of the jeep, no doubt to check her identification.

"They're out of the way now," Meow pointed out.

Dounia slammed her foot down on the gas pedal just as the guard drew level with her window. Ira yelped from where she was holding onto Tanya in the back seat, and Meow levelled an unimpressed look at her from his seat.

The guards yelled behind them, and Dounia pressed down harder, the rough terrain jolting their vehicle up and down. Dounia wished the ride was less wild, but there was no way to avoid bumps and dips in the terrain with her headlights off.

They hadn't gone that far when behind them, the camp stirred into an abrupt uproar.

"I take it they've noticed the knocked out guards," Ira yelled from the back seat.

"Undoubtedly," Dounia said. "I hope Doctor Engel will be okay."

All at once, they were drenched with light from behind as one of the big spotlights used to highlight planes in the sky was instead turned on their bucket jeep.

"I hope *we'll* be okay!" Meow yowled.

Dounia knew how to avoid spotlights.

"Hold on tight!" she warned.

And she threw the vehicle into a wild zigzag pattern just as a shell landed close by and exploded, making Dounia's ears ring. They'd brought out a Panzer.

~~*

Dounia kept up the wildly wavering driving pattern as shells went off one after another behind them, striking far too close for Ira's comfort. She held on tight around Tanya's shoulders and tried to keep them both from being tossed around. Even strapped in, Ira worried Tanya's injuries would be jostled too much.

"The tank's going way slower than we are, at least," Meow said smugly. "Not made for our rough, Russian terrain."

"Neither was this jeep," Dounia pointed out tersely. "Also the range on that gun is—"

Another round of shells started exploding near them, but they'd driven out of range of the spotlight, so the tank could only guess their position.

The jeep jarred again, snapping Ira's teeth together. Her arm renewed its vicious throbbing, and Ira could only hope the morphine lasted a little while longer, or Tanya would be in terrible pain.

"Twelve hundred meters," Dounia continued. "We can be far ahead of them and they can still hit us."

"They can't see us," Meow argued.

"I can hardly see a thing either," Dounia said. "At least, not far enough ahead that it would do any good."

"Be thankful you have my eyes," Meow said primly, and then yowled as an abrupt turn threatened to throw him right out of the vehicle.

The tank was not giving up in spite of the fact they couldn't see the jeep very well. It was nowhere near as fast as their jeep on rough terrain, but Dounia was forced to zigzag an awful lot, and the range of the tank's guns made it a dangerous game of pursuit.

A moment later, the spattering sound of a machine gun firing tore through the night.

Meow jumped into the back seat alongside Ira and peered out over the back of the jeep. The machine gun fired another burst, but there were no telltale pings of bullets on metal, so Ira could only assume they hadn't been hit.

"They're not even aiming," Meow reported. "Just firing all over the place in the hopes that they might hit us by accident."

The next burst went off, sending high-pitched tinging noises into the air as the tank finally found their mark, if barely. The tough tires of the jeep weren't affected, and none of the rounds had penetrated far enough into the vehicle to do any real damage.

The machine gun fire was immediately followed by another round of shells, and Dounia cursed as she dragged the vehicle back into a zigzag.

The tank operator changed tactics, and stopped trying to hit them directly. He fired past them, opening up craters in front of them. Dounia wove between them as best she could, but the new attack mode slowed them considerably.

The only good thing about that was that Tanya was no longer being thrown around the back seat like a doll.

"How far is it to our front lines?" Dounia asked.

"It can't be that far," Ira said, trying to remember the maps she'd seen in the days before their disastrous mission. "The lines are pretty close together, no more than ten kilometers."

The panzer fired another burst of machine gun rounds at them, and Ira ducked down in her seat and hoped the jeep would be able to withstand the barrage.

"We should have stolen a tank," Dounia muttered.

"Can you drive a tank, dear one?" Ira asked wryly.

"I'm sure I could have figured it out, ye of little faith."

Yet another round of shelling broke off their argument, and just as Ira thought that she was getting used to getting shot at and gaining confidence in Dounia's ability to avoid them, a crater opened up right in front of them. Dounia yelped and jerked the wheel, but it was no good. Without any advance warning to dodge, there was no way to avoid this one. The brakes slammed on too late, and with a sudden dip and a vicious jerk, they were nose-first in the crater.

"Can you get us out?" Ira asked urgently.

Dounia didn't waste any time in her assessment; she tried to drive out again, but the back wheels spun uselessly. The vehicle was hung up on the edge of the crater.

"No, we're stuck," Dounia said rapidly. "No time to dig it out, we have to get out."

"But we need it!" Ira exclaimed. "We'll never make it back on foot while being pursued by a tank."

"If we stay here, the tank will shell us where we are, stuck in this hole," Dounia said. "Come on."

She ran around to the back and lifted Tanya out of the jeep, carrying her limp form across her shoulders in a way that couldn't be comfortable. Ira followed, leaping out of the jeep as easily as she did their little plane. Meow jumped out, and although he shook his paws at the wetness, he took off into the night, calling back instructions.

"More left, the ground is less rough here," Meow said.

They ran as quickly as they could, Meow circling back around to run alongside her. He warned her about anything that might trip her in the dark, and Ira ran blindly, trusting that Meow wouldn't lead her astray.

Behind them, the tank came upon their vehicle and stopped. While it paused to deliberate on its next course of action, Dounia and Ira continued to escape further into the night.

"Will they follow us?" Ira panted, not daring to complain about the stitch in her side when Dounia was carrying Tanya over her shoulders.

"I don't know," Dounia gasped back. "I don't think I can run much further."

The tank opened fire on the jeep for several seconds and then stopped. Then, someone opened the turret and examined the jeep with an ordinary flashlight. Obviously, they weren't there, and the soldier yelled back down into the tank that there was nothing.

And then the tank swivelled and began firing in a sweeping motion, trying to hit them anyway.

"Into that crater!" Meow screeched, scampering into a nearby dip in the ground.

Ira followed him, sliding in feet-first as quickly as she could. Dounia jumped in after her, pulling Tanya's head down. The Panzer strafed the area with machine gun fire for several minutes in bursts. Ira held her breath, as if keeping absolutely still would keep them safe.

"Do you think they'll give up?" Meow whispered.

Without warning, another explosion rocked the earth beneath them, but this one had sounded slightly different, at least to Ira's ears.

"That was one of ours!" Dounia exclaimed, and looked out over the top of the crater.

Ira looked as well, more carefully. "Do you want to get your head shot off?"

The Panzer had a large hole in the front that was smoking, and another anti-tank round whistled through the air, plunging deep into the armour of the enemy tank. The turret at the top opened, and two men spilled out, coughing violently.

"Oh no!" Ira hissed. "Why won't they all just stop coming after us?"

"I can't set them on fire from this far away," Dounia said unhappily.

Ira hoped that at this point, the Germans would just give up and turn around, especially since they were close enough to their lines that an anti-tank gun was in use. But to her horror, they actually started coming in their direction.

"Dounia, your pistol," she said urgently. "Quick!"

"I'm out of ammo."

Ira fumbled in her jacket, tearing the German uniform off one shoulder to try and get at the gun nestled against her side. It was on the wrong side, and her broken arm was in the way. They were too close. Any moment they would notice three girls and one cat right underneath their noses.

Ira was so panicked, she forgot that the Soviet lines were right behind them.

Two shots rang out, two shots that neither Ira nor Dounia had fired. Boths dropped, and the closest one tumbled forward into the crater next to them. Dounia flinched back from the body, dragging Tanya with her.

"You're not Germans," a voice said at the lip of the crater, and Ira had to look up and back.

Standing behind and above her was a woman carrying a pistol and a medic bag. Ira frowned and blinked at her.

"No, we're aviators," Dounia said. "And this is my sister. She's a radio officer."

"What are you doing *here*?" the nurse asked, crouching by the side of the hole. "You're a long way from the 4th Air Army, dear."

"Long story," Ira said with a sigh. "Can you help us? Tanya is badly burned, and I have a broken arm. Not to mention we're all just very tired."

"Aren't we all," the nurse said, but slid down into the crater to help Dounia carry Tanya out.

It turned out, the nurse was checking for wounded stragglers, and the front lines were actually further back than they'd thought.

"It's just your luck that one of the wounded soldiers I was tending is a gunner," the nurse said with a smile. "The gun itself is too broken to move anywhere, but it still fires. He'd resigned himself to leaving it there, but then a tank came along. I've never seen anyone so happy to be of use."

There was a small group of them with various injuries, and the nurse helped Dounia heft Tanya up and led the way back to their lines.

Ira couldn't believe they'd made it.

They weren't back yet, but they were in friendly territory once more. Relief swept over her in an overwhelming wave, and the tight feeling she'd had roiling in her gut and across her shoulder blades had lifted.

She picked up Meow with one arm, and he gave a plaintive mew as he tried to shake the mud off of his wet fur. She hadn't been able to see earlier, but their mad dash through the broken up terrain had soaked him right down to the skin. He wasn't the only one. She and Dounia were covered in mud from diving into the crater and even the nurse was mud encrusted up to the knee.

They slogged their way back to the front lines, but everyone was mostly in good spirit. Some of the infantrymen started singing a marching song as they went, and just as the sun started to rise over the mountains in the east, the front lines came in sight.

Everything was chaos as soon as everyone found out who they were, and how they'd managed to get back to Soviet territory all on their own.

Tanya was immediately carted off by several nurses, and Ira was forced to stay in the medical tent while her arm was looked at again. Dounia was torn between staying with Ira and going to find out if Tanya would be okay.

"Go, dear heart," she said, smiling. "Tanya needs you, and Meow will stay with me."

Ira distracted herself by cleaning the majority of the dirt off Meow's fur with a rag while she waited for a doctor to come look at her.

"This was set by a doctor," the doctor commented, and looked at Ira questioningly.

Ira smiled and didn't say anything.

Her arm would be fine, and when it healed in the next several weeks, there shouldn't be any complications. Whoever had set her arm—and the doctor gave her a significant look as he said this—had done an excellent job.

Ira had been thinking in between hiding, running and getting shot at, and the idea had finally coalesced into something concrete.

"I think I'll become a doctor," Ira said to Dounia, once she found her and Tanya again.

"A doctor?" Dounia asked, ears perking up. "Why? You said many times throughout the war that you didn't want to be a doctor. After all those times Doctor Glazova bothered you about it, and now you want to do it?"

"I keep thinking," Ira said. "If I knew how to treat wounds like mine and Tanya's, so many things would have gone so much more smoothly."

"Hey, we still made it," Dounia said, with a smile. "And Tanya is going to be fine, too. They're sending her to a hospital further back behind the lines."

"But what if I could help people like us?" Ira asked, waving one arm. "And you know, the war isn't always going to be on. One day, the war will be over, and what will I do with myself then?"

"No one said that you had to stop flying," Dounia pointed out. "There are lots of things you can do. Becoming a doctor would be hard."

"Becoming a doctor would be no means the hardest thing I've ever done," Ira pointed out.

"You're right. Basic training was definitely harder," Dounia said solemnly, but couldn't hold a straight face for long.

"Don't tease, I really am going to," Ira said, laughing. "Never mind anything that Doctor Glazova said."

With Tanya looked after, they finally got their long overdue debriefing, in which several officers asked them the same five questions over and over again, except with different wording. They couldn't seem to believe that she and Dounia had not only managed to survive the crash, but rescue Tanya from the Germans and then outrun a tank in a stolen jeep.

However, the evidence was indisputable, because no one could deny that all four of them, had, in fact, all made it back in one piece.

"Can we just go back to our own base already?" Dounia scowled.

"You know you'll be paired up with someone else until my arm heals anyway, right?" Ira pointed out. "I find it doubtful that they would make me fly with a broken arm."

"I wouldn't count on it," Dounia said, shaking her head. "You don't need both arms to use your navigation equipment, right?"

"I can't believe they're sending news of our story right to the top," Ira said. "I've never thought of myself as anything other than a soldier, doing my part for our country."

"Do you think they'll give us a medal?" asked Dounia.

"What, for not dying?" Meow asked. "Surely that's the point of war, right?"

"Medals are for bravery," Ira said, and laughed. "I don't feel all that brave. Do you?"

"I got mud on me," Meow said haughtily and stuck his nose in the air. "I feel like I deserve a medal on that count alone."

"Maybe they'll award us Heroes of the Soviet Union," Dounia said, bumping her shoulder to Ira's uninjured arm.

Ira rested her head against Dounia's for a moment while no one was looking and twined their fingers together under the cover of her uniform sleeve.

"I'm not a hero, darling."

"You're my hero," Dounia said, and she said it with such conviction that Ira was stunned.

It was the closest to "I love you" that the two of them had ever gotten. There was only one response for a declaration like that.

"You're my hero, too, dearest."

THE ADVENTURES OF MONKEY GIRL AND TIGER KITE

KAI SCHALK

Someone was raising the dead.

At least, that was my friend Delia's theory for the recent spree of grave robbings in our area. The police were stumped, and when I tried contacting the Hero Corps I was given an automated message of given a coldly worded automated message that implied that the superheroes would look into it without actually promising anything.

"Ingrates," Delia had declared, when I showed her the email during our lunch period. "We saved this city last June. They should be begging us to join the Corps, not sending us on our way with a pat on the head and telling us to leave this sort of thing to the grown-ups."

"Yeah, but do you really want to join the Corps at fifteen?" I pointed out. It was hard enough juggling school and softball practice. I don't know how the Hero Corps are able to have day jobs and normal lives along with their Hero lives.

Delia sighed. "Not really," she admitted. "I just wish they'd take us seriously. I guess it's up to us to save the city by ourselves. Again."

"It might be nothing," I said hopefully, though fifteen missing bodies over the course of two weeks did not seem like nothing. It sounded, as Delia had put it, like the start of a zombie army. "Or maybe it won't be zombies." I hated zombies.

Delia rolled her eyes. "Yes, because there are so many uses for a dozen human corpses. Come *on*, Sunny."

"Maybe someone is feeding them to a monster that only eats human flesh," I said. "In which case it's rather considerate of them to use bodies that are already dead."

"Flesh-eating monster, zombie army, what's the difference?" Delia replied. "It's in our town, and it's up to no good, so we need to stop it."

She had a point.

"All right," I said. "How are we going to track this guy down? Stakeout? I'm pretty close to the Roseville cemetery. We can take it in shifts."

Delia squirmed. "Well, about that..."

"Yes...?"

"Do you think you might be able to take this one on your own? There's a robotics competition coming up this weekend, and I still have a lot of work to do."

I stared at my traitor friend. "You're ditching me? For a robot?"

"Well, it's not like I'm any good to you without them," Delia said.

I winced. It was true that during the June Apocalypse, as the event had come to be called, I had fought with my powers while Delia had fought with her machines. And it was true that afterwards, I was the only one who attracted the attention of the Hero Corps to be registered in their system as a super-human. But Delia had been my best friend since middle school, and she was my partner in everything.

Or so I had thought.

"But I don't want to face zombies alone," I whined. "I hate zombies. I couldn't even get through that one episode of *The Walking Dead* with you, remember?"

Delia rolled her eyes. "I remember. All right. I'll see how much I can get done tonight, and if I'm ahead of schedule, I'll join you. Okay?"

"Okay," I said, resigned.

Delia grinned at me. "Besides, I'm working on a surprise for you."

"Oh? What is it?"

Delia laughed. "If I told you, then it wouldn't be a surprise."

I made the appropriate grumbling noises, but really, I was glad I had made her smile. Delia's life's work had been a personal flying machine, and that had been destroyed in June. She had been desolate ever since. It broke my heart to see her that way—and not just because I was completely in love with her.

So I didn't mind too much sitting in a cemetery at three in the morning all by myself, doing math homework while waiting for a zombie army to show up.

Okay, I minded a little.

While hunting through the back of my textbook to figure out why I had gotten a different wrong answer three times in a row, a strange sound drifted toward me. I paused, listening. It was an odd, irregular thumping sound, like someone stamping out a rhythmless dance. Glad for the excuse to put away my book, I got up to investigate.

When I saw what it was, I almost preferred the math homework.

The... thing was roughly man-shaped, but I could tell at a glance that it was not human. Not anymore, at least. Its limbs were stiff with rigor mortis, forcing it to move with a strange, hopping motion. It wore ragged, dirt-stained tatters, and carried a shovel. I couldn't see its face. I didn't want to. Faces were what freaked me out the most in zombie movies.

As I watched, the zombie stopped by a grave, awkwardly set its shovel to the ground, and began to dig.

"Oh no you don't," I muttered. With some effort, I swallowed my urge to vomit, took a deep breath, and shouted "Hey! You there!"

It paid me no attention, simply continuing to dig faster than I would have thought possible, what with its labored movements. "What are you doing here? Stop that!"

It continued to ignore me.

"Fine, then. You leave me no choice." I reached behind my ear and took out my secret weapon, the reason I was now a registered super-human—a golden hairpin.

Or so it looked at the moment. "Change!" I shouted.

The pin began to glow. The light spread over my body, solidifying into weightless, golden chain mail—or maybe it was just my sudden burst of super-strength that offset the heft. The pin itself expanded into a fighting staff, and I swung it a few times to get the feel of it again. It had been a while since I had fully transformed.

All this time, the zombie continued to dig.

That irked me. I raised my staff and swung it like a softball bat at the zombie's head, taking it clean off the shoulders. There were a few spatters of gore accompanied by a rancid, rotting scent. Ick.

As if that wasn't bad enough, the body kept digging. For a few seconds, anyway. Then it paused, presumably in confusion at being unable to see anything. It stood still for a moment, as if trying to decide what to do, which must have been quite difficult to do without a brain. Finally, it began to hop and stumble around, feeling for its head.

Oh no.

I shifted my grip on the staff and used it like a hockey stick to whack the head as far away as I could. No way did I want those two to join up again.

Now what? I wondered. The thing wasn't talking. And with the amount of awareness it had displayed, I doubted it was the mastermind behind the grave robbings.

Belatedly, I realized what I should have done was wait for it to dig up the body and see where it took it. Oops. Still, there was a chance that eventually it would give up on its head and go meet its master.

Which meant I had to wait and watch it until it did.

While it bumbled about, I texted Delia: *There's a zombie thing and I took its head off. Meet up w/ me to see what it does?* She never replied. Probably asleep, like I wished I was.

I sighed deeply. The zombie offered no sympathy, simply continuing to search for its head. They really weren't so scary when they were headless and you had magic armor.

"Guess it's just you and me, pal." I perched on a tombstone, and waited.

Nothing happened.

By dawn I had, by some miracle, finished my math homework, my worksheet for history, and read the novel for English. When the sun finally cleared the trees, I was reviewing Spanish verbs. This all-night stakeout thing was going to do wonders for my GPA.

As soon as the light touched the zombie, it went still and fell to the ground. I even prodded it a few times to make sure it was, in fact, back to being an inert corpse.

"So much for you," I sighed. "Useless."

I gathered my books, dispersed my armor, shrank my staff to a hairpin again, and flew home on my magic cloud. If I was lucky, I might be able to get in an hour of sleep before school.

~~*

I was not lucky.

I managed to creep back into my room through the window, replace the window screen, and then collapse into bed. A muddled dream about trying to explain to the German teacher why I only knew Spanish was only barely coming together when I heard my mom calling. "Sunny? Are you awake?"

"Mmmmawake," I mumbled. My relief at remembering that I did not in fact take German was cut short when I realized that I had ten minutes to catch the bus. "Aaaugh!"

"Are you feeling all right?" My mom asked. My mom is white, middle-aged, and a bit plump. She wears too much makeup and even though she used to be blond, has recently started dyeing her hair a clownish shade of red. People ask if I'm adopted all the time. They're usually the same people who do a double take when they find out she's "Mrs. Wong." I wish she'd go back to using her old name, now that she and dad are officially divorced.

"Fine," I said, hiding under the covers. Changing into pajamas hadn't happened as I climbed in bed, and I was hoping she wouldn't notice.

Mom put a hand on my forehead. "You feel a bit warm. Maybe you should stay home today. Your health is more important than school."

Her offer was tempting, but I needed to consult with Delia about the zombie. "I feel fine," I said. "You can go now."

"Well maybe next time I won't wake you up," my mother huffed. She was insulted. Again. Sorry I'm not your perfect little daughter who worships the ground you walk on anymore. Sorry I'm an individual now. But she left, and I got out of bed, changed clothes, and dashed to the bathroom.

As I was grabbing my backpack and a granola bar, I saw the bus zoom past outside. I sighed. "Mom?" I called. "Could you give me a ride to school?"

Three months ago...

"Mom? Could you give me a ride to school?"

"Again?" she called back from the bathroom. She had just gotten out of the shower. "You need to start getting up earlier. When you're late, I'm late, and my boss is starting to get cranky about it."

"It's the last week of school," I complained. "I promise I'll get up early tomorrow, okay?"

My mom sighed. "Just give me a minute to dry my hair."

One minute turned into ten, and then ten more spent puttering about getting herself put together. I waited, seething. Pushing her wouldn't do any good. Eventually, I had to pee, and when I came out of the bathroom the inevitable, "Aren't you ready to go yet?"

I almost snapped at her. Almost. But I'd gotten used to biting my tongue since the divorce. Mom was constantly talking about all of dad's faults, how he was inconsiderate, overbearing, apathetic, and behaved as if he wasn't in love with her anymore. It never occurred to her that maybe I had a different opinion of him. Not for the first time, I wished I had elected to live with dad instead of mom, but I knew she would never have forgiven me if I had. Besides, that would have meant switching schools, and I didn't want to leave my friends, or my crush, Delia. I had not quite worked up the courage to tell her I liked her, but I had vowed I would do so before summer break.

That gave me less than a week.

Mom drummed her fingers on the steering wheel as we crawled through rush hour traffic. The radio blared the usual morning talk shows, gossiping about celebrities and giving advice on how to date heterosexuals. I felt a little sick, and rolled down the window. There was another reason I had been snappish with my mom lately, but what with the divorce and everything, I felt it was not the best time to bring it up.

If Delia likes me back, I decided. I'll come out then. That's how it goes in YA novels, right? You come out when you get a girlfriend.

"Close the window," my mom said. "You're letting all the air out."

Staring sulkily out the window, I obeyed. As I steadfastly avoided looking in her direction, I saw something streak across the sky. A flash of intense, bright light. I squinted, shielding my eyes.

"What's that?" I said.

"I don't know," my mom replied. "Some kind of meteor? Didn't they have one of those in Russia a few years ago?"

Traffic inched along.

Suddenly, the radio began blaring the emergency signal tone, and a woman's voice spoke. I cranked up the volume.

"*This is Polly Thompson of the Hero Corps. Our sensors have alerted us that strange objects have landed in the following cities: New York, San Francisco, Paris, London, Singapore, and Tokyo. If you live in any of these cities, DO NOT APPROACH! Hostile entities have already injured several researchers attempting to gather information. It has not been determined whether these objects are human-made or extraterrestrial in origin. Rest assured, the Hero Corps is doing everything in its power to keep the people of Earth safe.*"

It continued on a loop. Mom turned the volume back down. "Don't listen to that hero nonsense," she said. "They're just a bunch of self-serving glory-seekers who drain the government's budget."

I didn't have the energy to argue with her about that. "But that thing we saw—what if it's one of the space objects?"

"They didn't mention Minneapolis or St. Paul," my mom replied, but she turned the radio up a notch anyway.

Sure enough, the radio had gone back to the regular program, but this time the DJ's weren't talking about dating. They were talking about the strange thing in the sky. Apparently it had landed somewhere in downtown St. Paul. The internet was already flooded with pictures. It was a giant, roughly egg-shaped thing about the size of a skyscraper. In the other cities, they had broken open into giant skeletal monsters destroying everything in sight. So far, the St. Paul egg was inert, but the newscasters were advising everyone to stay home, just in case.

I glanced at my mom. She stared straight ahead, but her hands were gripping the steering wheel far more tightly than necessary.

"We're almost at your school," she said. "We're not that close to the landing site. I'm sure we'll be fine."

But she walked me to the school entrance, and gave me a hug before she left. That was unusual; we were not a family that touched often.

Inside, I found everyone strangely quiet. The TV was on, and we all watched it tensely. It reminded me of the way grown-ups who talked about 9/11. Everyone thought it was the end of the world. We were used to hearing of monsters and mayhem in places like New York, but all around the world? During first period alone, the news confirmed similar eggs in St.Paul, Chicago, Vancouver, Berlin, and Cairo.

During second period, the egg began to hatch.

It was a theater elective I had somehow convinced Delia to take with me, even though she hated being in the spotlight and preferred to help out the backstage tech crew. We watched helplessly as the monster rampaged through downtown St. Paul, a bipedal skeleton-like things with demonic teeth and horns. People cringed every time they saw a landmark they recognized. One girl began crying as she saw a family member's apartment building destroyed as the monster's hand shattered a hole in the wall.

"Enough," I heard Delia mutter. "The Heroes are not enough." She looked at me, and there was a steely glint in her eyes that I had never seen before. "Are you with me?" she asked.

I had no idea what she was talking about, but I nodded anyway. I was with her to the end of the world, however long or short that might be.

"Good," Delia said. "Come on."

And just like that, she walked out of the classroom. She didn't even bother asking for a bathroom pass or anything. The teacher made as if to protest, but Delia stared her down with those scary eyes. And she left, me trailing apologetically after her.

It was strange being outside after watching the news. I felt like there should be monsters everywhere. But of course, they weren't quite that close. I did, however, see several military planes fly overhead. They came in faster and louder than the jets that sometimes passed by on their way to the Minneapolis-Saint Paul airport.

"What are we doing?" I asked Delia. We were walking to her house, but I did not know what she had in mind.

Delia was also staring up at the planes. "They're never enough. Have you noticed that? People who make things with the intent to destroy the world always make them stronger than the military. That's why we need the Heroes. It's harder to calculate what they can do."

"So you think the Heroes will save us?" I asked hopefully. I had always daydreamed about witnessing a Heroic battle in person, though my imagination had always glossed over the reality of my city being destroyed.

"No," Delia said harshly. "Weren't you watching the news? The first round was to scare them out, stretch them thin. By the second round, they've taken on all they can. And we're the second round."

Her words chilled me. "So what are we going to do?"

Delia stopped in front of her house. She pushed the code to open the garage. Inside an old truck was crowded to the side to make space for a startling array of mechanical devices.

Delia turned to me. "We're going to be our own heroes," she said.

Miraculously, I was not late, though I had missed the first bell and most people were already moseying to their classes. Delia, however, perched on a low brick wall outside the front entrance, waiting for me.

And she had coffee.

"I love you," I said, taking the cup.

Immediately I regretted my choice of words. The last time I had said that... Well fortunately, today Delia just smiled and shrugged.

"Sorry it's cold. Were you out late?"

"Until dawn." I described what had happened in as much detail as I could remember. Delia listened patiently. We missed the second bell, but all I had was gym, and I could sneak in late for that, and Delia had math, where the teacher loved her and would let her get away with murder.

"So I was right about the zombie army," Delia said, brushing dyed-red bangs away from her forehead. The color looked better on her than on my mom, maybe because Delia only used it in streaks, and let the rest of her natural black show through. Delia was not what most people would call pretty, especially not the boys at our school. She was short and stocky, with an acne-speckled face and a mouthful of braces, but there was a solidness to her body that was more than just muscle (though she had plenty of that) that made me want to just sink into her. And when she felt passionate about something I always got caught up in it as well and swept away in a wave. Even if what she was passionate about was something as gross as zombies.

"Yeah," I said. "Zombie army. Or at least one zombie."

"And you said it was hopping? Not limping and lurching like zombies in movies, but hopping?"

"Yeah." I shuddered at the memory. "Honestly, I prefer the movie zombies. *The Walking Dead* has nothing on that guy."

"*Jiangshi.*"

"What?"

"I've been reading up on zombies," Delia replied. "There's a Chinese variety called a *jiangshi*. Supposedly, if someone died far from home, and the family couldn't afford to have the corpse transported, a Taoist priest would cast a spell so that it would hop itself home."

I thought about the thing I had seen last night. "I don't think that guy was trying to find his way home."

"Well, presumably they can be raised for other purposes. Good news, though." Delia grinned at me. "It doesn't spread by biting. So you don't have to worry about becoming one."

"Ugghhh." Delia's words conjured up an image of me as a hopping monstrosity. The bitter coffee burned at the back of my throat, and I swallowed hard. "So how do we kill them? I mean, I smashed it up good, and it stopped twitching once the sun came up, but is there anything easier? Like for taking on an army of them?"

Delia squinched up her nose thoughtfully. The expression was super cute, but I would never dare tell her. She didn't like being 'cute'. "I'll have to look," she said at last. "I don't remember off the top of my head. We can consult at lunch."

"All right," I said.

By some fluke of scheduling, Delia and I had the same lunch block, despite having completely different schedules. She was taking all the advanced math and science classes, while I plodded along in ordinary everything. Sometimes we shared a table with my softball friends or her nerdy friends. But today the weather was mild enough that we could find a quiet spot to ourselves outside on the grass and talk hero business.

Delia brought her own lunch from home and waited for me to join her with a Styrofoam tray of greasy pizza and lactose-free milk. "So," I said, mopping the grease of my pizza with a spare paper napkin. "How do we kill zombies?"

"Wikipedia has a great section on that. I sent you the link," Delia replied. "It's a lot more exciting than just fire and decapitation. You can repel them with garlic, mirrors, the blood of a black dog—"

"Okay, one: ew. And two: Garlic? Are these zombies or vampires?"

Delia stared thoughtfully at her lunch. "Sticky rice is supposed to work too," she said, ignoring me. "But it has to be uncooked."

"Delia!"

"I didn't find anything about bloodsucking," Delia said. She had been paying attention after all. "I mean, they're not vampires, but they're not really zombies in the Western sense. They're *jiangshi*. Literally a 'stiff corpse'. Just one that walks. Or hops, I suppose."

I shuddered. "Ugh. *You* weren't there. You don't know how freaky those things are. I don't even want to think about an army of them."

"Can't kill what's already dead," Delia agreed. "Get a big enough army, in a city that's still trying to rebuild from the June Apocalypse, and..."

"Don't," I said sharply. Delia shut her mouth. "We need to alert the Hero Corps. But if they ignore us again, or don't get here in time..."

"What then?"

"Then I'm going after the villain myself."

Three months ago...

"You've got to be kidding me," I said, watching Delia poke around the garage. "You're going to take on an alien invasion with a flying lawnmower?"

Delia snorted. Picking up a wrench, she began to adjust something on her machine—the Kite, she called it. "It's not aliens. Clearly it's one of Dr. Mortality's bio-weapons. I bet he was growing them in space to avoid detection. He even escaped from jail just in time to see his master plan unfold."

I knew better than to argue with Delia's conspiracy theories. She was almost always right. "But what are you going to do?" I asked. "You don't have any powers."

The wrench slipped, clanging loudly against the side of the machine. Delia swore. "That doesn't stop Cat Claw or Boomeranger," she snapped, pointing the wrench at a tattered and stained poster on the wall. Cat Claw, the legendary thief turned spy turned Hero, who was so elusive there were no actual images of her, only stylized drawings of a shadowy figure with bright golden eyes staring out from behind a mask. She had been the first Hero in the Corps who did not have superpowers. I had never realized until now just how much Delia looked up to her.

I was very afraid that Delia was planning something reckless. "You haven't even tested it yet!" I was practically shouting and didn't care. "And even if it does get off the ground, what then? Are you going to kill monsters by flying circles around them? What can you do that the military jets can't?"

"God, Sunny, you're so stupid sometimes," Delia snarled. That shut me up immediately. I always felt out of my depth when she was trying to explain her latest project to me, and my grades were never anything close to hers, but she had never looked down on me for it. Delia ducked behind a wing, hiding her face. "Look. The monsters have some kind of bone-armor plating that makes them impervious to explosives. But there are flaws in anything. And if someone small enough can get close enough, they can find those flaws. Did you see how Thunderstar took down the one in Berlin?"

I had watched it on the TV in school, but I hadn't particularly noticed how. I felt stupid again.

"The heart's exposed," Delia explained. "It's most covered by armor plating, but you can see it sometimes when it moves. Wiz Kid created a diversion, and while it was reaching for him, it revealed its heart, and Thunderstar went in for the kill. It never saw him coming."

"But who's going to create a diversion for you?" I asked quietly.

Delia took her time replying. She finished the mechanical adjustments, and then searched her worktable for a can of spray paint. "Maybe the military will help me out, once they see what I'm doing," she said, but she sounded doubtful.

"Delia," I said. There was a pleading note in my voice that disgusted me, but she already thought I was stupid, so what did it matter if she thought I was pathetic and needy too? "Don't go."

Delia unzipped her black hoodie and tossed it onto the workbench. Her gray tank top stretched over her breasts and her arms were covered with not-quite-faded scars. She shook the spray can then blasted long, jagged stripes of blaze orange along the dark wings of her flying rig. "Why not?" she said furiously. "People are dying, and I'm going to do something to help. Even if it costs me my life. I can't just sit here. Give me one good reason."

"Because I don't want you to," I said helplessly. Delia continued to spray. I raised my voice. "I don't want you to get hurt."

"Believe me, I'm not eager to get hurt," Delia said grimly, starting on the second wing.

"That's not what I meant. I... I care about you. I like you."

The spray can slipped in her hand, making a large, ugly splotch on the right wing. Delia ignored it, turning to stare at me. I could not read her expression.

"What?" she said.

"I like you," I said wretchedly. Not in my wildest dreams had I imagined the conversation going like this.

"Like... like-like me?"

I almost laughed. Almost. "I think I'm kind of in love with you," I said.

Delia said nothing for a moment. She stared down at the spray can in her hands. Then she said quietly. "Oh."

I waited, but she remained silent.

"Is that it?" Now I was starting to get angry. It was the only emotion that made sense. "I tell you I'm in love with you, and you don't even give me a real word?"

"What am I supposed to say?" Delia yelled. "You want me to say that I love you too, that I want to marry you and have your adopted babies? Maybe make out dramatically as I realize that love is more important than being a hero? Than saving lives?"

"No!" I shouted. "I just want you to tell me if you like me back or not!"

"I don't know!"

"It's not that hard! Yes or no?"

"I! DON'T! KNOW!"

Delia threw the spray can on the floor. I flinched as it clattered against the cement and rolled out of sight. Delia took a deep breath.

"I just... you're my best friend. And I want us to be friends for the rest of our lives. But not, like, in a married way. And right now... Right now there's a lot going on. I don't know what I'm going to want in three or five years. I just know that right now..." Her voice choked as if with tears. I had never seen Delia cry. Then again, I had not met her until a year after her mother died. "Right now, someone is hurting my city, and I want to hurt them back. You can either help me, or get out of my way."

"You want help from a stupid, pathetic weakling?" I said bitterly. I immediately regretted the words, but there was no way to take them back. I think Delia felt sorry, but she was never any good at apologizing. Instead, she went to the table, picked up a new can of paint, and went back to striping her rig. It was a darker red-orange that did not quite match. Some of the lines were forming Chinese characters, I saw now, but I did *not know enough to say what they were. They might have been numbers. Or names.*

She did not look up as I walked away. I know because I looked back.

She spoke, though. "Tell the reporters that my hero name is Tiger Kite," she said.

I turned away and kept walking.

Staying up a second night in a row was grueling. The nap I had taken immediately after softball practice just left me muddled and jet-lagged instead of more awake. I hoped my super-strength would help me to work through that if it came to a fight tonight. I was alone again—Delia was still finishing her robot and the "surprise"—so it would have to be enough.

Still, I was yawning by the time the *jiangshi* showed up again. This time, there were two of them. Both carrying shovels.

I crept close to them, hiding behind tombstones as I went. Not that stealth seemed necessary, considering how unaware the other one had been of its surroundings. But it didn't hurt to be cautious.

The two selected a grave—by what criteria I could only guess—and began to dig, again with implausible speed. It seemed like only a couple minutes before they dragged out the coffin, forced it open, and pulled out the half-rotted corpse inside. I held my breath against the stench.

The *jiangshi* dragged their prize to a stone mausoleum and disappeared inside. They left the door ajar, and I darted in close, listening and peering into the darkness.

There was someone inside. A living someone, not just another walking corpse.

"Excellent," the person said. I guessed he was a man, judging by his low, gravelly voice. "We didn't lose anyone tonight. And I actually bothered coming out here myself this time." He sighed. "I suppose I'll have to send you out in pairs from now on. It will slow the operation down considerably, but if someone is closing in, it's only a matter of time before they call in the Hero Corps. And we wouldn't want that, would we?"

I heard a hoarse, wheezy moan. At first I struggled to catch words, but then I realized that it was just one of the *jiangshi* voicing assent with rotted lungs. They were just full of gross surprises.

I hoped the man would go on a long monologue about his plans so I could take action to stop it, but his words faded into a low mutter that reminded me uneasily of Delia when she was absorbed in a project and speaking techno-babble to herself. While I was focused on trying to figure out what he was mumbling, I failed to notice the pair of *jiangshi* come hopping out of the building.

"Hrrnghplflalf," one of them said, placing a surprisingly strong hand on my shoulder. I screamed, and tried to shake myself free, but the knuckles locked around my upper arm. Another *jiangshi* grabbed my other arm before I could snatch my staff, and they dragged me into the mausoleum.

"Glcksshplgth," the *jiangshi* announced.

Inside the mausoleum was a pile of corpses, the smell of which hit me like a slap to the face. One of them was laid out on a stone slab in the middle of the single room. A lit candle was placed at its head for some ritualistic purpose as there was also a large flashlight on the ground.

The man I had heard was standing by the stone, bent over the corpse and muttering—no, chanting—in a language I did not understand. It sounded a little bit like Chinese ground up into sharp-edged pieces like broken glass.

He looked up as the *jiangshi* dragged me inside. He had a pale face, narrow eyes, and a pointed black beard. "Ah," he said. "So you're the little mouse who had been poking around and ruining my toys."

I struggled to get free, or at least reach the needle behind my ear, but to no avail. If it was still there. I worried I had dropped it outside in the struggle. But the *jiangshi*'s grip was like iron. "Toys?" I said, hoping to stall for time. "You're desecrating the deceased. These are people's loved ones. And somehow I doubt you got permission from anyone to do this. What were you hoping to accomplish?"

He stroked his beard. Clearly he had a taste for the dramatic. I made a mental note in case I could use that against him later. He added a condescending smile to the beard-stroking, and said "What was I hoping to accomplish? Well, what does it look like?"

"It looks like you're creating a zombie army," I said.

The man sighed. "Shame. I was hoping I could put you off with some spiel about medical technology conquering death and curing grief. But I can see you're too clever to fall for something like that."

"You bet I won't," I snarled, making one last desperate grab for my needle. But as I moved, I heard the man say more broken-glass syllables, and everything went black.

~~*

"Awake."

I had been trying to explain the quadratic formula to a *jiangshi*, but once I heard the voice, I realized I was dreaming. I felt a momentary relief, until I realized that I was lying on my back on top of the stone slab. My wrists and ankles were tied, and I still couldn't tell if my needle was still behind my ear, or if my captor had recognized its importance and taken it, or if I had dropped it long since.

Not that it made much difference, under the circumstances. I cursed my inattention.

My captor chuckled. He was standing not two feet away, watching me. "Such a foul mouth for one so young and pretty," he said. Gross. He was a creep. I mean, creating a zombie army was one thing, but sexual harassment? I tried not to wonder why I was still alive.

"Who are you?" I said, trying to sound like an interrogator rather than a prisoner. Fake it 'til you make it, as Delia was fond of saying.

"An excellent question," the man said. "While I have not yet made my official debut, soon the world will know me as the Necromancer."

"Not very original," I said. "I bet I could come up with something better. Like a pun based on your powers. What is it you do, exactly?"

"Nice try," the Necromancer said. "But I won't be tricked into spilling all my secrets so easily. I think it's my turn to ask some questions." He was stroking his beard again. I wanted to rip it from his face. "For instance, who are you? And more importantly, who sent you?"

"No one sent me," I said. It was even true.

"Then how did you know where I was?"

"I just happened to be in the area." That was also mostly true.

The Necromancer said nothing but moved around to where I could more easily see him. From a sheath at his belt, he drew a long knife. A very long knife. With his other hand he took a stone from a pocket of his long black robe and began scraping it up and down the blade. My elementary school still had an old chalkboard, and every day at least one person would decide to run their nails down it. But the pain of that grating sound was nothing compared the rasp of a knife being sharpened by someone who means you no good.

"Do you often take midnight strolls in the cemetery?" the Necromancer asked casually.

"Lately, yeah." I couldn't take my eyes off that shiny, shiny knife. Wasn't it sharp enough yet? "I haven't been able to sleep."

"Hm. And I suppose you have no connection to the Hero Corps?"

"No," I said, relieved that I could answer that one honestly. I was a terrible liar. Then again, if I had been inducted into the Hero Corps, I probably would have had backup and wouldn't be in this situation in the first place. I decided to stop overthinking.

The Necromancer looked at me hard and said. "You know, I think I believe you. That makes this easier, then."

"Makes what easier?" I asked nervously.

The Necromancer smiled. "Behold, my army of the dead," he said, making a sweeping gesture with the hand holding the knife to encompass the entire shed. "Have you ever heard of a *jiangshi*?"

"Yeah, and fought them too," I said drily.

He looked at me in surprise, tinged with respect. "Ah, you're Chinese, aren't you?" he said. "I thought you might be. Still, the kids these days don't know their heritage as well as they ought. Your mother must have raised you well."

"My mother's white," I muttered, before I could stop myself.

But the Necromancer just laughed. "As was my father, may his soul burn in hell for a thousand years. He had no respect for the mystic arts. It was my mother who allowed me to be apprenticed to the local shaman in our tiny Chinese village. He saw the potential in me, and taught me most of what I know. But he never saw the potential in his knowledge. Take the *jiangshi*, for example. It is a soldier that cannot be killed, for how do you kill the dead? A soldier that needs no food, nor comfort, who has no qualms about ethics or mercy and carries no thought of rebellion. A soldier made of a constantly renewed resource. In short, the perfect soldier. There is, however, a single drawback."

"And what might that be?" I asked eagerly.

The Necromancer sighed, letting his arm drop back to his side. "They're so stupid. It's not surprising, with their brains rotted away, but it does make them damned difficult to organize in large numbers. I need a lieutenant. A chain of command. Someone to delegate to."

I had no idea where he was going, so I said nothing.

"A fresh corpse," the Necromancer said, and I suddenly figured out where he was going. "One only seconds old, the blood still warm and fresh pumping through its brain. That's what I need. By the time they make it into the ground, they're days old. And since I can't leave you alive to go to the police or the Heroes, this makes the perfect solution. Two birds, one stone."

"Oh no, that won't work at all," I said, trying to think through the cloudy panic filling my brain. My fresh, warm brain full of living, flowing blood. I bit back a whimper.

The Necromancer tested the edge of the blade on his finger, smiling in satisfaction as a small droplet of blood welled up. "We shall see, won't we? At best, I'll have a thinking slave who can control my army while I'm busy elsewhere. At worst, I'll have another zombie soldier and no witnesses."

"What if it works too well?" I asked quickly. "If I think too much and decide to plot against you?"

"Then I can simply remove the spell. It can be undone quite easily, after all."

"And how's that?" I didn't have a clue what I was doing now. I was stalling, but I didn't know what for. I just knew that I didn't want to die.

"You think me a fool," the Necromancer said. "Bound hand and foot, unarmed as you are, and you still seek to outsmart me? You'll make an excellent servant." He raised the knife. I closed my eyes, and strained against the ropes.

Then I heard a low, mechanical whine. It grew louder as I listened. I slowly cracked open one eye, and noticed that the Necromancer was listening too. More importantly, he was not killing me.

Then I heard the gurgling cries of the *jiangshi*. He must have made them stand guard outside after bringing me in. They sounded pained. I mean, they always sounded pained, but this time they sounded like they were actually *in* pain.

The Necromancer frowned, and lowered his knife. "What the hell is that?"

I laughed softly, hysterically, thinking of Delia hinting at a surprise. "That's Tiger Kite. Remember her? St. Paul's own hero, who fought the monsters on the June Apocalypse? Looks like she's still in town." I grinned at the Necromancer. "You're in for it now."

The Necromancer glared at me, and spoke sharply in that strange language. The pile of corpses in the room shuddered and began to heave themselves upright. I closed my eyes, not wanting to see their unnatural movements. "I'll deal with *you* shortly," the man said.

Then he left with the *jiangshi*, and I was alone.

With the rotting bodies no longer in the room, the deep breath I took was slightly less foul. Delia had given me a chance.

Now I just had to make use of it.

I squirmed. Then tried wiggling my ears, hoping it didn't matter if I held it in my hand or not. "Change," I whispered.

But nothing happened.

"Change!" I said, louder, more desperately.

Still nothing.

I pulled against the ropes, feeling them burn against my wrists. They did not give. I thrashed wildly then fell limp in exhaustion and frustration. Tears trickled down my face, but I was unable to wipe them away.

"I'm sorry, Delia," I whispered.

Three months ago

I sat at home, alone, watching the news. Monsters. Heroes. Monsters. Death and destruction. Monsters.

The same thing over and over. I could have changed the channel. I didn't.

Eventually, I got hungry and made myself a bowl of ramen noodles, sitting down in front of the TV to eat. I was no cook, and my mom never had the time. Delia was a culinary expert, though. Ever since her mother had died, she had been teaching herself traditional Chinese dishes and often brought them to school for lunch.

Thinking of Delia, I realized what was what I was watching for. I was waiting to see her. I was waiting to see if she would actually go through with her boast and if she would triumph, become another Hero, or if she would fall and become another Icarus.

Then I saw her.

There was the Minneapolis skyline, broken by the monstrous, skeletal figure that prowled the streets. Its bony feet crushing cars and benches and the Snoopy sculptures scattered around the city and just about anything that was unlucky enough to be caught underfoot.

But the camera was not looking at its feet now. It was focused on the thing's head—a long-snouted skull with horns and fangs. Its jaws opened and closed as it snapped at something, like a lizard trying to catch a fly.

Delia.

She looked so tiny, so fragile, but she was flying. I felt a burst of elation for her. Years of dreaming and planning and hard work had finally paid off. Her machine, which looked like an awkward cross between a hang-glider and a riding lawnmower in the garage, now dipped and bobbed with elegant movements, like a kite freed from its string. It even looked like a kite, roughly triangular in shape with brilliant streak of color on the wings. She was flying circles around the monster now, and for a moment, it looked like the tiny craft was fast enough, agile enough to keep the monster occupied without being caught.

Then I saw the thing's hand reach up and snatch at her.

"Look out!" I shouted, forgetting or not caring that she couldn't hear me through the TV. Delia saw the monster's hand just in time, pulling her wings in close and ducking aside. The clawed hand barely clipped her, but I saw pieces of metal debris crumble to the ground, heard the newscaster's shocked babbling as she tried to make sense of what was happening.

The little kite wobbled, but gamely clung to the air. Even I could tell its flight was shaky now, though. I held my breath.

The monster raised its hand a second time, ready to swat at the fly, but Delia made her move first. She dived straight at the things chest, sliding in behind the armor plate. The hand caught only empty air.

Then... nothing.

I waited for Delia to reappear. I waited for the monster to fall down dead. I waited for an explosion – something, anything other than the monster simply going on its way. But that's what happened.

"No," I whispered, sinking to my knees. "No..."

It was my fault, I thought numbly. If I hadn't told her I loved her... if I had said something else... done something else...

I shook my head angrily. Those kind of thoughts never did any good. As I shook my head, my eye caught on the small shrine my mom kept in the corner of the living room. My dad was firmly atheist, but my mom was *a hipster Buddhist and always kept a few statues and incense lying around.*

I went to the shrine and lit a stick of incense. With eyes closed, I knelt and clasped my hands—no wait that was a Christian thing right? I wished I had paid better attention to my mother. Reconsidering, I instead put them flat on the floor, and whispered. "Please. Someone. Help us. That's what you're supposed to do, right? You're the ones with all the powers. I'd go and help her myself if I could... If I could just help..."

Something banged against the window, and I screamed, certain that the monsters had arrived to kill me. Then my rational mind caught up and reminded me that I would have heard them coming from miles away. So what was it?

I looked at the window, and nearly screamed again. A face was staring at me, and not a human one. A golden-furred monkey grinned at me with sharp yellow teeth, and tapped on the window with a grimy paw.

I stared, frozen.

"Open up!" he snapped. When I still didn't move, he sighed irritably and tapped the window sharply one more time, causing it to spring open. The monkey nimbly jumped up on the sill and into my house.

I should mention that he was a chain-mail wearing, talking monkey. The absurdity shocked me into inaction and is probably the main reason I did not freak out as much as I might have at being confronted by a wild monkey.

"All right," the Monkey said. "I'm not technically supposed to be here, so let's make this quick. You want to help fight, but you need some help helping. I want to help fight, but I'm not allowed to anymore. Word of

advice, my friend, never become a Buddha. They don't get to have any fun."

"Aren't you not supposed to want fun once you become a Buddha?" I asked. Mentally, I was trying to sort through my hazy recollections of Buddhism and Chinese mythology. There was something about a monkey...

The Monkey grinned and winked at me. "Technically. But I never was much good at following the rules."

A memory of an old TV show with tacky special effects and no subtitles that I had watched with Delia came back to me. "Wait... you're Sun Wukong! The Monkey King!"

Sun Wukong, also known as the Monkey King, also known as the Great Sage Equal to Heaven, but most often affectionately referred to simply as "Monkey," was a legendary Chinese trickster hero. He had wreaked havoc in the Kingdom of Heaven, where he stole the Peaches of Longevity and the Pills of Immortality. For his crimes, he was imprisoned under a mountain for five hundred years, until he was released to accompany the monk Xuanzaang on a quest to retrieve the sacred Buddhist texts. For his service, he was pardoned and granted Buddhahood. He was the stuff of myth and legend, the hero of countless action movies, operas, and cartoon shows.

And he was standing in my living room.

Monkey bowed. "The one and only," he said. "And I'm here to offer you a bargain."

I tried to remember if there was some kind of proverb against making deals with monkeys. It seemed like there would be, but I couldn't think of any. Besides, this was Sun Wukong, the Monkey King, who had guided the holy westward to retrieve sacred Buddhist texts. That was, of course, after a number of more disreputable adventures, but he was probably trustworthy now.

Still, I decided it to play it safe. "What sort of bargain?" I asked.

"It's like this: I give you three gifts. In return, you use them to protect people. Not just now, against these monsters, but forever."

"Forever?"

Monkey twitched his tail dismissively. "Oh, well I suppose forever is a long time for you mortals. How about until your body and mind start to decay? Then you find a successor to pass my gifts down to. That way, the bargain protects people for longer than a single mortal life. Isn't that how that Irish fellow with the sword did his?"

I swallowed. "You mean Broadsword? I think he's Welsh, actually..."

"Ah well, something like that," Monkey said. "I never did get to that part of the world much. Anyway, he's just got one thing, and I'm offering three. First, my staff." He reached behind his ear and plucked out what looked like a golden needle, which he presented to me with a flourish. I took it gingerly, and promptly dropped it. It felt like it weighed a ton. I was surprised it did not leave a dent in the floor.

Monkey frowned. "I'll have a word with that in a moment. Make sure it knows you're allowed to carry it. Second, my armor." He waved a paw at himself to demonstrate. "And third, my cloud-walking boots. What do you say, girl? You want to be a hero?"

I did. Suddenly, I wanted it more than anything else in the world. I wondered if this was how Delia felt about *her machines. But I still had doubts. "Why me?" I said. "I'm sure there are thousands of people praying for the power to do something right now. Why me? And why here, in America? I'm not even fully Chinese." I also wondered why he was speaking English, but I supposed the godlike powers transcended language barriers.*

Monkey snorted. "You think I stop looking after my children just because they go somewhere else? Pssht. Besides, most folks are praying for rescue. You, though... Well, maybe I was just in a hurry and picked someone at random. Maybe it's the similarity in our names. Or maybe I got a good vibe from you, and when you're a Buddha, your vibes count for a lot more. Does it really matter? Right now, you're here and I'm here, and I'm offering you a bargain. Or are you worried there's no one else? Because there's always someone else. You don't have to carry the whole mountain on your shoulders." Monkey chuckled. "Believe me, I tried that once, and it's no fun. So, what do you say, Sunny Wong? Do you want to become the Monkey Girl?"

I looked at the TV. Monsters everywhere and not enough heroes to fight them. Delia, still trapped, still missing. Delia, who had tried to carry an entire mountain even though there were soldiers better equipped for it.

"Yes," I said. "I will be Monkey Girl."

Something was crawling up my arm.

Straining my muscles, I tried to shake the *thing* off. I could not see what it was, but my mind conjured up images of gigantic, many-legged insects that probably didn't live in Minnesota. Though with monsters falling out of the sky and necromancers raising the dead, one couldn't be sure. "Get off," I muttered. Of course it didn't listen. Instead, it stopped just where my wrists met the ropes.

The tickling and immobility were too much for me. My limbs twitch involuntarily, jerking against the ropes. I tried to lie still and regain control of my body, tried not to think of Delia out there fighting the Necromancer alone. The motor of her Kite, the Tiger Kite, was still humming faintly, and underneath it, I thought I could hear the Necromancer chanting.

I tried to focus on meditation, prayer, anything to stop the spasms in my muscles and the fear clouding my mind. I mean, it had worked last time. But I could not remember any of my mother's meditation exercises, and who did I have to pray to really? The Christian God who owned the land we were on, whose church I went to exactly once a year on Christmas with my dad? Maybe not. The Monkey King who had given me his power, who had come to my aid last time? But he had given me this power for me to help myself, and to help others. It looked like I had failed.

Sorry, Monkey, I thought, sinking deeper into my misery and despair. I pulled one last time at the ropes, and, to my complete surprise, felt them give. It was the work of moments to wiggle my hands free. I sat up quickly, too quickly. The blood rushing from my head and making me dizzy. My hands throbbed and tingled, and I flexed them to get the sensation back. My wrists were chafed and bloodied. I hadn't noticed that happen.

I looked at the ropes which had so recently bound me, and saw that they were torn and frayed. Had I done that? But of course I had not because sitting on the stone slab, next to the remnants of rope, was a tiny mouse.

We stared at each other, the mouse and I, for a long moment, and then finally I said the only thing I could think to say, which was "Thank you."

The mouse twitched its whiskers. What sort of emotion did that gesture convey?

I ran a hand through my hair, hoping against hope I would find a golden needle, but there was none. I sighed.

"I must have dropped it outside," I muttered. "Hopefully Mr. Necromancer didn't notice and decide to pick it up."

I set to work undoing the knots at my feet. I had pulled them tight in my struggling, which I now regretted, but there was nothing to be done now except pick at them with agonizing slowness that made my hand cramp.

A squeak from the stone next to me broke my concentration, causing my hand to slip off a particularly tricky knot. I swore, and looked down.

There was the mouse again. Holding a golden needle.

"I hope you don't turn out to be something bad," I told the mouse. "Because right now you're almost too good to be true." When I took the needle the mouse ran to the other side of the stone, and changed. I blinked, certain my eyes were playing tricks on me, but there was no mistaking it.

The mouse had transformed into a beautiful girl.

"Uh," I said. Eloquent as always with a pretty girl.

The girl—she looked about my age, maybe a bit older, less gawky—sat on the edge of the stone, her legs crossed neatly over the side. She had long black hair that fell past her waist and brushed the stone. Her skin was pale as the moon, but she wasn't white, not with single-lidded eyes like those. Eyes like mine. She had beautiful eyes, I realized. I had never thought that eyes like mine could look beautiful. Until now.

She was wearing a filmy white dress, and I blushed, trying not to stare, but that meant I ended up looking into her large dark eyes, and that was even worse.

"You're welcome," she said, in a voice like the opening notes of a symphony.

My brain scrambled for words that made sense. "Who are you?" Not elegant, but at least grammatically correct.

The girl smiled secretively. "Call me Kumiho," she said.

"Okay," I said. The name rang a bell, but I couldn't place it. Maybe she was in the Hero Corps? But there weren't any Asians in that organization. Not known to the public, anyway. And the only Asian supervillains I could think of were male. "I'm Sunny," I told her.

"I know. I have been watching you."

I should have been more creeped out than flustered. I really should. I swallowed. "So, Kumiho, how did you—"

A scream from outside cut through my fogged thoughts. Delia.

"I'm sorry; we'll have to talk later!" I told Kumiho, then to the staff: "Change!"

The familiar weight of the armor settled on my shoulders. The staff expanded to fighting size, and I felt magical strength coursing through my body. I ripped the ropes off my feet as though they were cobwebs and leaped, staggering only slightly, to the door of the mausoleum.

Kumiho was at my side. She put a hand on my shoulder, steadying me. "I will fight with you," she said.

I glanced at her. "How?"

She put a finger on my lips, the only part of my face visible from under my helmet. It was a shockingly intimate gesture, and while I was still trying to figure out how to react to it, she morphed into a white tiger. I stared. Were tigers always that big? I made a mental note to go to the zoo at the next opportunity to check my memory. Then I shook myself. Whoever she was, *what*ever she was, she seemed to be on my side, and I had a battle to fight.

"Let's go," I said, and pushed my way out of the mausoleum, the tiger stalking at my heels.

I gasped in horror at the scene that awaited me.

Delia stood, clutching an injured arm, among the shattered wreckage of the Kite. So much for the surprise. Yet although grounded and with a pack of *jiangshi* closing in, Delia still held her ground. With her good arm, she flung a handful of pellets at the *jiangshi*, causing them to flinch back. I vaguely recalled her saying something about sticky rice at lunch today. If that was what it was, she was running out, and the Necromancer's chanting urged the *jiangshi* on.

"Stay the fuck away from me!" Delia yelled, holding up a shiny piece of metal, broken from her Kite. A makeshift mirror.

"Give it up, girl," the Necromancer hissed. "Your little toys are no match for my powers. A piece of metal can't save you now."

"No, but someone holding one might," I said. I swung my golden cudgel at the head of the nearest *jiangshi*, severing it from the neck and sending it flying. Home run.

The Necromancer spun around. His eyes widened as he saw me. "You! But...!"

Then the tiger roared, and pounced at him. He did not say much after that, though I heard him chanting frantically. I turned my attention to the *jiangshi*.

The first one was still stumbling around looking for its head, and I quickly stabbed at a second one, impaling it on the end of my staff. That did not seem to faze it, however, as it hopped and lurched toward me, smearing blood and guts on the end of the cudgel.

"Gross," I muttered, and swung it around, knocking two others off their feet. The motion managed to shake my weapon free, and I followed up by smashing it down on the skull of the one I had staked. It crumpled to the ground, twitching like a cockroach.

I heard Delia shout a warning as three more *jiangshi* jumped on me. I struck one a glancing blow that cracked its shoulder, then I stumbled and fell as the corpses dragged me down and piled on top of me.

I gagged at the stench of them. I tried to shake them off, but their rotted, bony hands gripped at me with the strength of rigor mortis. They bit and clawed at my armor. I screamed with rage and frustration, and maybe a little fear. Just a little.

"Get away from her!" Delia yelled. She stumbled from the ruins of the Kite and charged at the *jiangshi*, beating at them with the broken end of a plastic broom. It seemed every bit as effective as my magical staff. The *jiangshi* fled before her.

I carefully levered myself to my feet. Delia came to stand beside me. "Are you all right?" she asked.

"Yeah. But what about you?" I was pretty sure her left arm was broken, from the way it dangled.

"Fine," Delia growled through gritted teeth. "Let's just kill these things and get out of here."

I smiled, shifting my hands on the staff to a more effective position. Now *that* was a plan I could get behind.

The *jiangshi* were regrouping after their flight from the broom, and started to circle around us.

"Guard my back," I told Delia, and then charged at where the crowd of them was thickest.

They never had a chance.

My staff took out two of them in mid-hop. Another gripped my arm, fouling my aim as I tried to get a good angle to strike it. A dusty, bloodied broom smacked it in the face, and it let go. I yelled, swinging my staff at the rest, but my cry was drowned out by the roar of a tiger. A white blur, she leapt into the fray, and with a few blows of her mighty paws, she decapitated the last of the *jiangshi* before I could blink twice.

I looked around. None of the *jiangshi* were still standing. "Where's the Necromancer?" I said.

The tiger resumed girl-shape. Delia gasped in surprise. "He got away," Kumiho spat. "I almost had him, and he knew it, so he spoke some more hell-words and vanished. But he can't escape me."

The anger in her voice sent a chill down my spine. I was glad she seemed to be on my side. But there were still so many questions I had for her. "Kumiho," I said. "What were you doing here? Why did you fight the Necromancer? And why were you watching me?"

She stared at me for a long moment, and I got distracted staring at her eyes, until Delia said, "Well?"

"I have a history with that man who now calls himself the Necromancer," Kumiho said tersely. "You and I seemed to have similar goals. Perhaps one day our paths with cross again."

That was not enough. I opened my mouth to press her further, but she stepped back and changed shape again, this time to a large, dark owl. I ducked down as she flew toward my face, her wingtips brushing the top of my head. Then she was gone into the night sky.

"Wow," Delia said, staring upward. "Do you think she really is a fox spirit, or is she just calling herself that because she can change shape?"

"Fox spirit?"

"You called her Kumiho, right? That's a shape-shifting fox spirit, like a *kitsune* or a *huli jing*. But I think the *kumiho* are a bit more malicious than their counterparts."

"Well, she helped us," I said. Delia nodded, and winced. "We need to get you to a hospital," I said. I summoned my golden cloud, the third of the Monkey King's gifts, and stepped onto it, helping Delia balance. It was a tricky feat, and I hadn't tried it since that past June, when I had clung to the back of that cloud as it carried me to where Delia was battling the monster. Now, I was using it to carry her with me to safety.

"I don't like this," Delia muttered. "I don't mind flying when I'm supported by something nice and solid, but this?"

I laughed as we rose up into the air and glided through the night sky. "Remember last time? When I blasted into the rib cage of the giant monster to find you hacking away at its heart with an ax? The look you gave me! And all it took was me whacking it with my stick for the whole thing to collapse. Then I had to grab you and drag you out of there before the monster fell on you."

Delia smiled weakly. "I keep trying to save your life. But you're always the one who ends up saving mine."

"That's not true," I told her. "The Necromancer would have killed me if you hadn't arrived when you did."

"Really?"

"Really."

I flew us on in silence for a while. I worried Delia had passed out, but then she said. "You'll go back and pick up the Kite for me, won't you?"

"What, so you can repair it and then smash it up *again*?"

"Please?"

"Oh, all right," I said, and was rewarded with a small smile. At the sight of it, something inside me eased. I realized it didn't matter whether she was in love with me or not. We were still a team.

We were Monkey Girl and Tiger Kite.

THE
MERCENARY

ANNABELLE KITCH

*"It was my lady's hazel eyes
It was her tresses long
It was her laugh that made me feel
That I was oxen strong
She bade me go into the west
She bade me seek the sea
She bade me seek out treasures gold
My lady Linna Lee..."*

The name "Linna Lee" snapped Pidge back to her reality, and she sneered into her mulled wine. The one night in a thousand that the Golden Schooner bothered to hire a bard, and he was the sort of silly fop who put names in the love songs. What did Linna Lee care if a tavern full of sailors and mercenaries knew how pretty she was? All it did was make it damned hard for Pidge to imagine her own love in Linna Lee's place.

Maybe it was just as well. Trina would never have asked her to leave the safety of Tamren's walls for something as frivolous as treasure. No, that was Pidge's own bad idea, and she'd caught seven hells over it.

~~*

"Three years you've been gone. And now you mean to leave again?" Trina had demanded frantically. Pidge had ignored her as she shoved clothes into her travel sack.

"You know why I have to go."

"I'm sick with worry when you do. Twice your letters came to me stained with blood."

"It is the price of making my own fortune."

"But you don't have to. You could stay. Be a part of my household."

"To be sneered at for being your pet dog?"

"To be safe, Pidge!"

~~*

Pidge winced inwardly at the memory. Trina was perhaps the most patient person under the wide blue sky, though she was a true viper when pushed beyond her limits. Half the court had seen it, too. For poor Trina, the eyes of the nobility staring so openly, so judging, had to feel like the sun burning down on her alone. Her anger had swiftly faded into mortification.

For her part, Pidge couldn't spare a bent copper for the opinions of the nobility. It wasn't the first time they'd stared at her. She was tall, her shoulders broad and muscular, and her complexion red from a foreign parentage. She was the Lady Warrior, the Dame Mercenary. Fighter Fair. Or, at least, those were the names they called her to her face. Her true nicknames were far less suitable for polite company.

Still, she was more at home here, in a second rate tavern a stone's throw from the stinking fisherman's dock, than she'd ever been in court. In Tamren, only Trina had cared for her and for Trina's sake she had to be polite. Here, nobody cared at all. That was easier.

The buzz of conversation filled the smoky room, almost drowning out the bard's song. A band of sailors who looked as though they'd had one too many trips out to sea leapt up from their seats and started singing along drunkenly, sloshing beer out of their mugs. Scarred faces and cloaked figures packed around cramped, dirty tables. Pidge could almost taste the sour taint of drink in the air. It was a good crowd for an outsider to hide in.

She drew her cloak around her tightly and reached out, catching the skirt of harried serving girl. The girl whirled around, her eyes wide, her face flushed. Wispy strands of yellow hair clung to her bright, sweaty cheeks.

"What you need, love?" she asked urgently.

Pidge pitched her voice low enough to pass for a boy's, if not a man's.

"I hear rumor that a Kimbrar's taken up residence in the caves under the Cliffside."

No, not Cliffside. But close. Just a few outcroppings over, if the church's writings on the matter were to be believed. Close enough that the locals would hopefully want to correct her. For once, she was grateful for all those dreadful hours she and Trina had been forced to read them in their youth.

The girl started back so hard she nearly slipped on a puddle of spilled beer. Pidge reached out and caught her wrist before she could fall, but the maid wrenched her hand free, her face twisted with irritation.

"Thirty-nine men in this tavern to keep fed and drunk going on four hours now and you want to waste my time with fairy stories and buried treasure!"

Pidge sank back, hiding her grin as the girl stormed off in a huff. Nearby, the drunken sailors turned their heads, murmuring to each other and vainly trying to look as though they hadn't been listening. With the group of them serving as guides, the story would spread across the tavern like the current under the waves.

And then? Pidge closed her eyes. One way or another, Trina was going to be upset. If Pidge succeeded, she'd only be angry. But if she failed? Well, she'd never have to see the stricken look on Trina's beautiful face. And her last memory of Trina would, at least, be a good one.

~~*

"I thought you were angry with me."

Trina lips had twitched up in a coy smile as she stood in Pidge's doorway. The soft, thin silk of her robe flowed over her sweeping curves like water over river stones, pooling on the floor at her feet. Too long for her. It was easy to forget how tiny Trina really was. Her towering personality made her seem as big as a mountain.

"Your betrothed would be displeased to know where you are right now."

"What, will you get me with child?" Trina teased, shrugging off the robe. It fell to the ground and settled in a heap of silk at her feet. Trina's skin, the very shade of well steeped tea, had positively glowed in the dim candlelight. Her eyes had glittered with mischief. Pidge's mouth had gone dry, her heart fluttering like a bird in a cage as gooseflesh rose on Trina's bare, bronzed skin.

"God's balls, Trina!" Pidge hissed, pulling back the covers. "Get under here before you freeze!"

Trina only laughed and jumped onto the bed, wriggling under the blankets. Her slender form had pressed against Pidge's and, all at once, Pidge felt horribly overdressed. She'd shifted, resting her callused hand on Trina's bare hip. Her skin smelled like autumn air and sweet wine.

Trina licked her lips and looked up at Pidge with the admiration every person longed to see. Heat bloomed deep in Pidge's belly, flowing like a wave through her limbs to the very tips of her fingers and toes. Of all the people in the world, Trina only ever looked at her like that.

"I'd rather you didn't call Count Cordo my betrothed," Trina had said, wrinkling her nose. "It doesn't suit him."

"Well, you're going to marry him. I'm sure that's what 'betrothed' means."

"Pidge." Trina let out an exasperated sigh and buried her face in Pidge's shoulder. The scent of autumn air washed over her like a summer storm, sending pleasure crackling through her veins. Pidge wrapped her arms around Trina's shoulders and pressed a kiss on the top of her dark head.

"You can't marry him."

"I can't not," Trina muttered. "He has the blessing of both my uncle the king and the church."

"He bought those blessings with gold."

"And we need the gold."

Pidge tightened her hold on Trina.

"Just because Isel's gone doesn't mean the whole kingdom is your responsibility."

"So you'll be our sacrificial lamb?" Trina fixed Pidge with a stern look. "You can't do it."

"Whoever slays the Kimbrar and returns the relics it stole has the right to take the hand of any member of the royal house," Pidge quoted.

Trina arched one dark, delicate brow.

"And you think they'd let us marry?"

Pidge smiled and ran her fingers through Trina's long, dark locks. She was soft. Gentle. Like a willow branch in a breeze. Sharp, but beautiful. She always made Pidge feel big and awkward by comparison.

"Well," Pidge said. "You won't have to marry Cordo."

"What are you afraid of, that you'll suddenly stop seeing me?" Trina smirked impishly and reached forward, pressing the tips of her soft fingers to Pidge's weather-beaten cheek. "I will be queen. And he will be king consort. He'll have no power over me."

"Save in your bedroom."

Trina leaned forward, her full lips tickling Pidge's nose.

"There's time enough to sort that out. Please. Leave the Kimbrar to fools and glory seekers and stay with me. This is where you belong."

Pidge smiled and tangled her fingers in Trina's hair, pulling her down for a long, slow kiss. The sweet wine from dinner lingered on her lips, and Pidge hummed in approval, slipping her tongue between the princess's perfectly straight teeth.

~~*

The memory of wine made the cider taste wrong in her mouth. She wanted sweet wine but, even if she ordered it now, it wouldn't taste right. Nothing could live up to the brilliance of memory. That could very well be her last memory of Trina. And Trina's of her. It wasn't the worst she could have.

Pidge was so caught up in her thoughts of Trina that she almost missed the shift in the chatter of the room.

"The Kimbrar has three heads," an old man insisted. "One of a snake, one of a lion, one of a fish."

"No, it has the head of a snake, the legs of a lion, and the tail of a fish."

"That's absurd," snorted a woman with so much rouge, her cheeks looked like shining red apples. She chewed on a long cheroot, her brows furrowed. "If it's part fish how can it live out of the water?"

"Well, it doesn't, does it?" One of the sailors rose, wavering back and forth. "That's why it lives out in the cave. Catches the tides. Guards the sacred treasure from all the holy ships it sank. "

"It didn't sink those ships for the treasure, it sank them to feed on the sailors. The treasure was an accident. "

"No animal steals treasure on accident," the woman snapped but the sailor guffawed in disdain.

"Well, I say it was after us poor souls of the sea. And it don't live in no caves. People would have seen it."

"No," came a soft reply. The youngest sailor stared down into his mug, his face ashen. His eyes were glazed and unfocused, seeing something that wasn't there. Pidge leaned forward in her seat, gripping the edge of the table. The sailor swallowed and took a drink. "I was a boy. Me and my da were out fishing—"

"Oh, Will," one of his companions said, but Will made a sharp gesture with his hand.

"I did," he insisted. "And it's there. We were almost in, I could see ma on the docks waving to us. Then something moved against the current. It's a big beast, see. But it's the color of the water itself. Fast as lightning. She came after our catch. We barely made it out alive."

"So why doesn't it go after every fisherman that takes a jaunt?" the rouged woman snorted. Will shook his head and, with no answer to give, took a long pull from his mug. Pidge pursed her lips. It lived in the caves. But it collected holy treasures and relics. So, it couldn't live down at the water's edge. The tide would wash out the treasures. No magpie would be so willing to sacrifice its horde. It might attack a boat, but it took only the fish, unless Will and his father had anything valuable to attract it. Most importantly, it kept to itself, such that even an eyewitness couldn't convince a town of hotheaded, money-starved dockworkers to go after it.

To her disappointment, the Kimbrar soon faded from the conversation. The musician, now sufficiently lubricated by one or five drinks from his enthusiastic patrons, began to play another unendurable folk song. Pidge dropped a coin onto the wooden tabletop and knocked back what remained of her cider as the bard started playing "A Tinker Came to Town." The crowd, more intoxicated by the minute, let out a cheer and started singing along, drowning out the minstrel's voice.

She crept through the crowd, keeping her head down until she could push through the door and onto the cobbled street. The air stank of brine and mildew, old fish and oil. After the sour stench of the tavern, however, it was positively refreshing. She breathed in deeply, willing her head to clear. She had everything she needed. She just needed to put it all together.

"Don't move," came a growl from behind her. Pidge froze, her eyes flicking down. A knife glinted in the light of the street lamps, clutched in a filthy fist, belonging to a filthier man. His lips stretched in an obscene sneer, and the reek of cheap beer hit her nose. Just her luck.

"I'm sure we can resolve this peacefully," she said, her sliding to her purse. "If you want coin—"

"Oh I'll have a lot more than that, no mistake," he huffed, jabbing the knife forward until it pricked her side. With a sigh, Pidge held her hands up, showing him her empty palms. The man's brows, like a pair of thick, unruly caterpillars, crept toward each other. "I seen you in there. Heard you. Talkin' about that man-eatin' beast.

Getting' everyone all riled up. But I know what it is you're really after."

"Eternal glory?"

"Shut it!" he snarled. "You're gonna lead me there. Take all the glory you like, but the treasure's mine."

"Yes. Unfortunately, that might be a bit of a problem." Pidge shrugged. "You see, I need the treasure myself. Holy relics are pretty important to some people, and I know some people who need it."

"Don't think you're in a position to say no."

Pidge resisted the urge to roll her eyes. How many two bit wannabe thugs in the world were going to try that on her? She wondered if he was trying to take advantage of her because she was a woman, he was drunk, or he was just a moron. Usually, his sort were some combination of the three.

"Aren't you afraid of the Kimbrar?" she asked, pitching her voice up like a frightened damsel in a morality play. The man scoffed.

"Ain't no Kimbrar," he snarled. "Just a horrible story meant to keep you away from the caves. Keep people from looking for the treasure."

"Of course. Perfectly sound theory. Which is why a woman with no skill for fighting at all is going to go after it."

"Huh?"

Pidge whirled around, knocking the knife out of his hand with her fist. His wrist joint let out a sickening *pop!* The man let out a loud cry as his bloodshot eyes widened, the knife clattering harmlessly to the filthy cobblestones. Pidge gave him a shove back and held up her hands.

"Why don't you go back on inside? Get yourself another drink before you hurt yourself, okay?"

His face, covered with dirt and stubble, twisted in drunken fury.

"You bleeding whore!" He snarled, lunging forward with his fist raised. His footing was wrong, and his thumb was tucked under his fingers. Pidge sidestepped him. The man pitched forward. With a helpful nudge from Pidge, he fell to the ground in a heap. His grimy hands scrabbled against the cobblestones for the fallen knife, but Pidge pressed her boot to his wrist, forcing his hand to open before he could even get a good grip.

A torrent of obscenities spewed from the man's lips, thick enough to make the drunken sailors inside the Golden Schooner blush like simpering maids.

"You could have at least made a real effort," Pidge snorted, kicking the knife out of his reach and stepping away. "You should thank me. I'm as good as saving your life. You wouldn't last a minute with a Kimbrar."

"Go choke on it you ugly bint," he ground out. Pidge's face burned. It wasn't the first time in her life someone had called her ugly. A woman mercenary, usually on her own, was hardly going to be known anywhere as a great beauty. That had always been Trina's place. Even so, sometimes the pettiest insults could be the sharpest when hurled at the right time.

Pidge clenched her jaw and, with an angry cry, brought the heel of her boot right down on the man's forearm. His bone cracked with a satisfying *snap* and he let out a bloodcurdling scream that faded into a useless whimper. He wouldn't try to threaten women in the street anymore.

In Pidge's opinion, she'd done a good thing. But, in the back of her mind, she could almost hear Trina's disapproval.

"He was just an old drunk, Pidge! Really, he wasn't a threat to you. Now he won't even be able to work, not with a busted arm like that. And I bet he's got nobody to look after him while it heals. He could starve."

It was just the sort of naïve, oversensitive attitude that drove Trina to adopt strays, including a pale street urchin with no family, who tended to run off and kill people for money whenever she pleased. With a weighty sigh, Pidge fished a coin out of her purse and dropped it on the cobblestones. It clanged brightly, settling just in front of the man's snot filled nose.

"Take that to a physician," she instructed firmly. "It better not go to buy more beer. Do you understand?"

The man groaned lowly, burying his face in the cobblestones.

"You're a bleeding demon," he whined. Pidge rolled her eyes and nudged his arm ever so gently with the toe of her boot. The man screamed as though she'd stabbed him with a red hot poker.

"Do you understand?" she asked again.

"Yes, yes!" He cried, his words thick with tears.

"Where are you going?"

"A physician!"

"Good." Pidge closed her purse and stepped back. "Might want to sober up, too."

He sputtered, and looked ready to spit a fresh insult at her, but Pidge flicked her cloak aside, revealing the wide, heavy sword that hung from her hip. She didn't use it often. In fact, she preferred not to. Most fights could easily be avoided or won with her hands alone, at least in a place like this. But it was useful against bandits, beasts, and the snarls of back alley thugs. What color remained in the man's face drained, and his mouth shut so suddenly, she heard the click of his teeth. Perhaps he wasn't completely hopeless after all.

She let her cloak flutter over her hanging sword and turned, heels thudding against the cobblestones. Trina would be disappointed if she found out about this. But what she didn't know wouldn't hurt her.

Pidge followed a winding dirt road up to the cliffs. The buildings grew sparser and squatter, buffeted by the high coastal winds. With each step, Pidge felt herself shrugging away the Golden Schooner and the man in the street like old scraps before she changed into a good, new gown. The stink of the docks fell behind, replaced by sweet grass and salt. It was easier to think up here. Strange, though, to think that a Kimbrar could be hiding beneath her very feet, stowed away in some cave atop a hoard of relics that belonged to Tamren and the church. Yet nobody knew for sure it was even there.

Atop the cliffs sat a windswept cluster of buildings too small to be considered a village. It was home to stubborn folk whose ancestors had been too eager to own their own land or too mulish to abide by the church's laws. Or, rather, to accept that the church treated their ancient gods as minor deities. People who denied the church tended to end up in desolate places like this.

Pidge was glad she'd cut her hair. The wind whipped her short, pale locks about, stinging her cheeks like needles and threatened to tear her cloak from her shoulders. Perhaps this was why nobody had seen the Kimbrar. The damned monster was terrified of coming out to endure the unforgiving wind.

Pidge pulled her hood up, and almost instantly the pervasive flapping of the cloth in her ears drowned out all other noise. Gritting her teeth, she staggered up to a small building with warm light spilling from the windows. An hour of walking through these winds had left her feeling worn and ragged. Besides, it was the middle of the night. There would be no more daring adventures before dawn, that much she could count on. Pidge rapped loudly against the wooden door, praying whoever was inside could hear her.

The door swung open to reveal a red cheeked woman, her face pinched with concern. She looked Pidge over then sniffed loudly.

"You smell like you just came off the docks." Her voice sounded a thousand miles away under the roar of the wind.

"I did." Pidge had to resist the urge to yell her answer. "I've come for lodging."

"Well, you'd have been better off staying down there. We've got a bad wind blowing tonight. The windows'll rattle."

"That's fine."

The woman's brows almost touched as she narrowed her eyes in blatant suspicion.

"You ain't here to try and convert us, are ya? To Coros or Malou or whatever the hell fold are calling their frippery church god these days."

"No," Pidge assured her. "Truth be told, I get a little queasy when I see a priest myself." More than once she'd had to endure the lecture about behavior unbecoming of a lady. That she should have stayed to serve as Trina's maid or sought out a good marriage, using the royal house as her connection. It wasn't fitting for a woman with her good fortune to set out on her own like a vagabond.

The woman scowled for another second, but something in Pidge's face must have convinced her because, like the sun breaking through the clouds after a storm, her expression brightened and she stepped aside.

"Well, in you come, then," she said. "My name's Madge and this is my place. Tisn't much, just a way station for locals and tinkers, mostly, but it'll get you in out of the wind."

Pidge stepped inside, instantly relieved as the wind stopped pounding against her. Her ears rang for a moment in the comparative quiet of Madge's unnamed inn. A small, poorly stocked bar took up most of the far wall, and only a couple of patrons sat at one of the rough, mismatched tables in the corner. Migrant workers, most likely, returned home to their families after a long harvesting season. Pidge couldn't imagine any sort of work on this windy patch of land that could bring in real money.

"Would you like a drink, then?" Madge asked eagerly. Pidge felt a slight squirm of guilt as she shook her head.

"Just a room."

"Of course." Madge waved her to a rickety staircase just behind the bar, tilting left and right as they made their way up to the second floor. Pidge climbed slowly, her heart skipping as each plank creaked loudly underneath her boots. Madge followed behind her, as sure as a bird on a branch.

"You look like you travel," the innkeeper remarked. "Any news of the outside?"

"Depends on which 'outside' you're referring to."

"Not those reeking docks, that's for sure."

They reached the top of the stairs, and Pidge sent up a private prayer of thanks to whatever god, lesser or greater, might be listening for her safe delivery up the stairs as Madge fished a set of keys from her pocket.

"I hear Lila Lark's got herself married," Madge went on. "Pity that. You know she came here and sang once. Loveliest thing I ever did hear."

"You don't say," Pidge said dryly. "I couldn't tell you much. I don't follow singers."

"Well, just a thing I heard." Madge sniffed and stuffed a key into the lock on one of the doors. "Heard Prince Isel went and died, too. Heard he caught a pox."

Pidge's heart stuttered in her chest. She remembered Trina's face after the funeral, her eyes red rimmed, but she didn't dare to let herself cry. She was the heir. She needed to be strong for her people.

"It was a pneumonia," Pidge explained. "He was out hunting. Got caught in a storm. His health always was poor."

"What's to become of that princess, then?"

Pidge smiled tightly. "She's got people on her side."

"Well, good on that, then." Madge waved her into the room and returned the keys to her pocket. The room itself was little more than a closet. There was a bed, a nightstand with a washbasin, a window that did, indeed, rattle, and just enough room to walk in a tight circle but not enough room for her to properly stretch her legs.

"No bag?" Madge asked. Pidge shook her head.

"Better to travel without, if you can." A bag was just a dead weight of belongings that would attract bandits and disaster. What possessions she had sat in a trunk at the bottom of Trina's wardrobe. Madge sniffed and rubbed her hands together.

"All right, then. It's ten penny for the night, extra two for breakfast in the morning."

"Got any other help around here?"

"My brother's boy, Tim. He's already sleeping, though."

Pidge nodded and patted the bed with one hand.

"I'll give you a silver talent for the room, the breakfast, and as much fish as Tim can get from the docks at the crack of dawn tomorrow."

Madge's brows flew up.

"You must be a fan of fish, then. He'll be on it first thing."

That night, as Pidge tucked herself into the cramped bed, the windows rattling in their panes, she thought back to Trina in her own finer bed. Alone. She thought of that last night they'd had, and the morning after. Trina's dark hair spread like a fan over her pillows, her supple body curled under the blankets. It was a sight she might not get to see again.

"I must be out of my mind," she hissed, her eyes sliding shut. But then she thought of Trina curled up just like that in Cordo's bed. His pretty wife. The thought of him forcing himself on her when Pidge knew Trina would be dreaming every night of a different partner...

This was the only way to avoid that.

~~*

Pidge had first entered the castle Tamren at eight years old, with dirt under her fingernails and a belly so empty it was almost concave. It had been a cold winter's night, the sort that crawled under a person's skin and settled deep into their bones, deep enough to freeze an unfortunate street rat from the inside out. For weeks, Pidge had hid in an empty basement, damp and moldy but safe from the snow. At least, until the first real storm of the season hit. If she'd stayed there, she'd be frozen through by morning.

The lights of the castle twinkled in the frigid air, warm and welcoming as a candle in the window. Perhaps it was dizziness from the hunger, or desperation from the cold, but in that moment Pidge could think of no better place to seek refuge for the night than with those warm lights. Barefoot and dressed only in rags, she made the slow, painful walk from Tamren low, with its filthy beggars and shady moneylenders, to Tamren high.

By a pure stroke of kind fortune, some bumbling stable hand had left the latch to the barn unlocked, allowing Pidge to sneak in. The stables were dry and sweet with the smell of hay, but most importantly they were warm. With a cry of relief, she'd staggered forward, easily finding the stall of the fattest, sweetest pony she'd ever seen in her life. There, she'd found oats, hard on her teeth but thick and filling, and water, which she drank until she felt her stomach might pop.

When all that was said and done the pony, apparently not minding her interloper, had even allowed Pidge to curl up next to her for warmth. It had been the best night she'd had in months, until a dark haired girl with a gap between her front teeth and messy braids stumbled upon her.

"What are you doing with my Mimby?"

Pidge had jumped to her feet, her bare toes scrabbling against the dirty stable floor as she prepared to jump out the window, but it seemed Mimby's stall didn't have one, and the girl blocked the way out. Pidge swallowed, her heart in her throat.

"Please don't rat me out," she'd begged. "It's only I got nowhere else to go."

The dark haired girl furrowed her brows, then stepped forward, her arms crossed.

"Only if you don't rat me out for being in the stables after bed," she'd said. "Strictly speaking I'm not allowed to be down here by myself. But I'm not by myself, I'm with you."

Pidge narrowed her eyes.

"You're... gonna let me stay the night, then?"

"I suppose. You don't have parents to go to?"

Pidge shook her head. The dark haired girl nodded and crossed her arms.

"Me, neither. I live here with my aunt and uncle. You look foreign. You ever been up north?"

"I dunno. I don't think so."

"Me neither." The dark haired girl's lip quirked mischievously and she held out her hand. "Come on. I know how to get in the kitchens even when they're locked up. We'll get some food then you can sleep in my room. It's a lot cozier."

"No," Pidge bit back. The dark haired girl frowned and folded her hands over her middle.

"Oh. Okay, then. Well, can I bring some food here?"

Pidge bit the inside of her lip. Offers like that always came with catches, always came with a price too high for a penniless orphan to pay. But her mouth watered at the sort of food they must stock in a castle kitchen.

"What do you want for it?" she asked, low and hesitant. The dark haired girl brightened.

"I'll be right back."

She darted off, all dark hair and energy. Pidge stood frozen for a long moment, still pressed against Mimby's side. She ought to run. The girl could come back with guards at any moment. But the thought of returning to the snow froze her limbs. Before she could bring herself to move, the girl was back, grinning from ear to ear, her arms stuffed with food and—Pidge's knees began to go weak—a fine, thick blanket.

"We can have a picnic right here!" the girl declared. "I've even brought an apple for Mimby."

The pony perked up at that. As the girl set out the blanket, Pidge felt herself beginning to relax.

"I'm Trina, by the way," the girl said, feeding the apple to her pony. "What's your name?"

"Pidgin," Pidge said, eyeing the food uncertainly. It wouldn't be the first time she'd seen a feast right in front of her and not been allowed to take a bite. Trina smiled.

"Go on," she urged. "I can't eat it all myself."

Hesitantly, she took a bit of cheese from the hoard of food. Then a bit more. Trina joined her, smiling and urging Pidge to try everything until, at last, Pidge curled up on the edge of the blanket and slept.

The moment the morning light streamed into the stables, Trina shook her awake.

"Come on," she hissed. "We ought to get out of the stables. I can't get caught here."

"But I—"

"We'll make something up," she insisted, already bunching up her blanket and the paltry remnants of the previous night's meal. Overwhelmed and, if she was honest, a little bit enchanted by this magical girl who had been so kind to her, all Pidge could do was follow her out of the stall.

At the dark hall leading back into the castle, though, Pidge halted, her gut squirming. There would be guards. There would be nobles. Any one of them could see her, grab her, hurt her for daring to set foot in their fine castle. Trina frowned, glancing back over her shoulder.

"Come on," she repeated, then shifted her load into one arm so she could hold out the other to Pidge. "I won't let anything happen to you. I promise."

~~*

Following Trina down that hall had taken more courage than anything in Pidge's entire life. Until now. She stood in front of the Kimbrar's cave with a sack of fish, the gusts of sea wind pressing her hard into the rock face. The narrow switchback leading down to the rocky beach below ended abruptly, presumably because the builders had thought better of it. Jagged chunks of stone had been wrenched free of the cliff face. The Kimbrar's path into the cave.

The things I do for that girl.

She gripped the hilt of her sword with one hand the bag of fish in the other. This was a horrible gamble. A horrible, *stupid* gamble, but Pidge hadn't made her career off a reputation for caution.

Sucking in a deep breath, Pidge hurled the bag of fish into the cave, waiting for the tell-tale squelch of the fish flying across the cave floor. Then, she waited. One breath, two, then three, her heart hammering loud enough to drown out the constant rumble of the wind. Surely it had risen to the bait by now.

Slowly, she pulled her sword free of its scabbard, and had to grab on with both hands before the wind could yank it free. The steel clanged loudly against the rock face, and Pidge froze. One breath. Two... but no serpent-headed beast appeared at the mouth of the cave.

She gripped the hilt of her sword until her fingers ached and charged into the mouth of the cave. For one horrible moment, the dark fell over her eyes like a veil. It took only a second for her vision to adjust to reveal...

Absolutely nothing. There was no hideous beast picking its way through the mountain of gold, no massive claws tearing at the stone floor, preparing to tear at her. Just a dark, shallow cave filled with heavy boulders instead of treasure. Pidge was so startled she staggered forward, stepping on one of the slimy fish before she could stop herself.

As she crashed to the ground, her sword skidding out of her reach, she reflected dimly that this was not her finest moment; sprawled out on some filthy cave floor to hunt an imaginary monster that clearly didn't live here, surrounded by dead fish. Oh, the courtiers in Tamren would have a field day if they ever found out.

Grumbling, Pidge pushed herself to her feet, her cheeks burning as she dusted off her trousers. Nothing for it, then, if there was no beast to slay. Without those recovered relics, she couldn't claim Trina's hand. Couldn't spare her the marriage to Cordo. All she could do was slink back to Tamren to face a red-faced princess ready to give her hell for taking off in the night on a fool's errand. Of course, Trina would probably forgive her. But she would still have to marry Count Cordo.

"Seven hells," she hissed, crouching down to retrieve her sword. And that was when she saw it: a glimmer behind one of the boulders. Frowning, Pidge sheathed her sword and leaned over the boulder, and what she saw took her breath away.

The way the church talked about these missing relics, one would have thought the gods themselves shit them out. Most beautiful, they always said, most precious, most awe-inspiring. Pidge had always thought the priests were blowing hot air. But, for the first time in her life, she began to suspect they were onto something.

Treasures were heaped atop each other, glittering in the gloom of the cave, untarnished by the damp or the bite of the salt in the air. Effigies to Neia, the goddess of fertility and Tor, god of the sun. Golden circlets said to have been worn by Coros during the nine days he'd lived among humanity and founded the church. A necklace all of diamonds and pearls, shining boxes and even the fine silver candelabra used on the high holy days. Each one shone as though it had been freshly polished. Whether or not these relics belonged to the gods, clearly there was more to them than the worth of their metal.

Pidge sucked in a deep breath, pulling one of Coros's diadems out of the hoard. It shone like a mirror in the dim light, casting gleaming reflections over the cave walls. For one flickering moment, Pidge wanted to put it on, just to feel what it must be like to be a god for a day. Then she thought of how peculiar it would look on a short haired mercenary in road worn clothes, with callused hands and muscled arms. She had no business wearing something so delicate.

No. This would better suit the likes of Trina. Not that the church would let even her keep it. Well, after this victory, Pidge could buy her a new one, twice as big, studded with diamonds and rubies. After today, she could give Trina the world. Pidge nearly tipped over as the full implication of her find slammed into her. What had been a flight of either fancy or foolishness, was suddenly a beautiful reality. She was going to save Trina from a marriage she didn't want. She could even marry Trina, the judgments of the court be damned. She'd found the relics stolen generations ago. Generations ago, the church had promised the house of Tamren, the family deemed the protectors of the church, to whoever could find them.

She could be the queen consort. What a bizarre notion. But, all the same. The title was hers if she reached out to take it.

Half delirious with giddiness, Pidge rushed to her bag of fish, dumping the rest of them out and returning to stuff the relics in one by one. Certainly they would stink of fish, but a good washing and they'd be right as rain. A mad smile stretched across her face, laughter bubbling deep in her throat as the relics clanged against one another.

A soft mewl echoed through the cave. Pidge froze halfway to stuffing in one of the shining effigies. God's balls, was that a child? Was someone living in this cave now? Who in all hells would live near such treasure and not touch it?

"Hello?" Pidge called, setting down the bag and gripping her sword. She expected another whine.

She did not expect the deep, rumbling growl that reverberated off the cave walls. Her blood turned to ice.

Oh. The Kimbrar.

Pidge turned slowly, her knuckles white where they gripped the hilt, to face the beast whose cave she now found herself trapped in. As it turned out, it did not have lion paws. The storytellers got that bit wrong. Nor did it have a fish's tail or three heads. Because, of course, Kimbrars really were just fairy stories.

What stood at the mouth of the cave was nothing less than a slick, black skinned, yellow eyed, massive sea dragon. Not a Kimbrar.

"Easy there," Pidge said, sliding away from the bag of relics. "These don't belong to you, and I'd say I have more use for them than you. So what say you eat your fish and I'll be on my merry way?"

The dragon rumbled again, exposing two rows of jagged teeth like spearheads. Pidge swallowed and, slowly, pulled her sword from its sheath with a sharp *shing!*

"All right, then."

The dragon surged forward, its low rumble building into a roar as it opened its mouth wide, wide enough to clamp around her head. But Pidge was already moving, ducking aside, her sword swinging through the air to connect with the dragon's slick skin. The blade slid harmlessly off as though she'd stuck it with a butter knife.

Quick as the shifting wind, the dragon whipped around, snarling as it swiped at her with one of its powerful paws. Pidge dropped to the ground in time to see the dragon belch out a torrent of boiling water, which hissed as it flew through the air, splashing harmlessly against the far wall.

Right. All the lore said sea dragons didn't breathe fire. But they'd never said anything about *that.*

Pidge scrambled away as the dragon reared, its tail whipping into the cave wall, sending bits of rock raining down from the ceiling. That was when she saw the thin red scratches just above the beast's dark breast, still pink and fresh from some other battle out in the raging ocean. Just like any other animal, its underside was vulnerable.

Pidge had lingered too long. The dragon reared back, its throat working as though trying to swallow a horse whole. It took Pidge one second too many to realize what was happening before she dove out of the way. With a deep bellow, the dragon spewed another geyser of boiling water, this time washing over the left side of Pidge's body.

For one long moment, she didn't feel anything. Just the warm rush of water, more like a bath than anything.

Then it burned.

Pidge was on the ground before she fully knew what was happening, her throat raw from screams she scarcely realized she was letting loose. The dragon snarled, stalking forward until it loomed over her. She could count every spearhead tooth in its long mouth.

The dragon's throat rumbled again and, not for the first time in her life, Pidge stared into the face of death and regretted leaving Tamren.

Well, if she was going to die here, she wasn't going to die alone.

Pushing the pain to the back of her mind, Pidge shoved herself up off the cave floor and lunged her sword through the air, slicing against the dragon's exposed throat. It let out a howl like a wounded steer, staggering back as the wash of deadly water meant for Pidge flooded across the stone at its feet.

Gasping, Pidge dragged herself to her feet, ignoring the unnatural pull of cloth against her skin as she rushed forward, burying the sword in the beast's belly. Blood spewed from the wound, flooding over Pidge's fine blade as the creature blinked its wide, yellow eyes. Then, with one last mournful moan, it collapsed against the cave floor. Pidge stared, waiting for it to rise at any moment and finish her off, but it didn't so much as twitch again. The sea dragon, the would be Kimbrar, was dead.

"Mercy of the gods," Pidge breathed, and she had to brace herself against the cave wall. It was dead, then, but she couldn't bring herself to smile. Now that it was no longer trying to kill her, she could appreciate that it had been a beautiful animal.

"Rest well," she murmured. Pidge took a halting step forward, intent on retrieving her sword, but stopped herself. The dragon was dead for the church's treasure and the hand of the princess. The least she could do was leave it a trophy of its own.

With a grunt, Pidge turned and staggered back to the dragon's small hoard. Her bag of treasures lay right where she'd left them, with circlets and fine necklaces spilling out of its lip. She bent down stiffly, grimacing against the sensation of her skin pulling uncomfortably as she hefted the bag up. Metal clanged on metal, and she prayed that the relics didn't scuff each other up before she reached Tamren. Then, she heard it again. A soft mewling sound, like a baby or a kitten begging for milk in the moment before a tantrum.

"Hello?" Pidge shifted the bag over her good shoulder and inched forward, peeking behind stones and under craggy outcroppings. She was so intent in her search that she almost missed it, but there it was. Crouched in a little hole in the wall, its yellow eyes wide and shining, was an infant sea dragon little bigger than a cat. Its dark tail wrapped protectively around its tender belly as it pawed anxiously at the stone floor.

Pidge felt ice drop into the pit of her belly. The damned dragon hadn't been protecting its hoard. It had been protecting its pup.

The bag of treasure dropped to the floor with an almighty clang and she swore, loudly and colorfully. It wasn't supposed to be like this. It wasn't even supposed to be a dragon, and she wasn't supposed to orphan some wretched beast.

The dragon mewled again, its eyes wide and pitiful as it clawed at the cave floor, its tiny claws scraping like nails against the solid stone. The dragon had probably been out hunting.

"Three damns!" Pidge shouted.

She couldn't go back now. Trina would know. Somehow, she always knew. And her gentle heard would never rest if she knew some creature had suffered like this for her sake. But what was Pidge supposed to do with it?

"You aren't my responsibility," she snapped. "I didn't… I don't owe you a damned thing!"

~~*

"You don't owe me a thing."

Trina turned, her lips quirking in that smile of hers as she threw her hair up in the most complicated plait Pidge had ever seen and without the aid of a maid.

"I know you think that," Trina said, sticking a bronze comb amidst her dark locks. "But I feel like I do. I found you. You're my responsibility."

"You already fed me."

"And I could feed you for years if you stay. Do you not want to stay in the castle?"

Pidge flushed and dropped her head, feeling altogether too clumsy and unrefined in the chambers of a princess.

"You don't have to."

"But I want to." Trina rose, shaking out her skirts and beaming. "And I do get horribly lonely. Maybe I was the will of the gods that we find each other.

~~*

Trina would never abandon a defenseless beast like this. And Pidge was acting in Trina's name.

"She's softening me from the inside out," Pidge grumbled, snatching the bag up and shoving the church relics back in. "It won't be a comfortable trip for you, but you'll not die because of me. Not when you've only started to live."

She crouched down, feeling momentarily dizzy. A trip to a physician was in order, and maybe a salve for her burns. The dragonling backed tightly against the wall, whining loudly. Of course.

Swearing, Pidge staggered over to the mess of dead fish and gathered up an armful.

"It's fine. I'm feeding you. See?" She held out one fish, dropping the rest in the bag. The priests would faint when they saw how she'd treated their precious trinkets.

The dragon perked up at the sight of the dead fish hanging limply from Pidge's hand. Hesitantly, it padded forward, sniffing eagerly. Then, delighted, it snapped the food right out of her fingers and bounced happily as it gulped it down. In spite of herself, Pidge let out a chuckle.

"Oh, Trina is going to adore you."

~~*

The shirt was a total loss. The cloth stuck to boiled bits of skin, and Pidge had to bite into the leather as the physician peeled it away. He didn't say a word, though. He simply rubbed a poultice on her burns, wrapped them up, and instructed her to keep them clean. If he noticed the occasional wriggle and whimper from her bag, he said nothing, which was just as well. Pidge had chosen him for his reputation for discretion.

She returned that night to Madge's inn and, this time, ordered enough food for three people. Madge was stunned at first, but jumped to accommodate her, positively alight with joy. Still elated by her victory, Pidge rifled through the bag, sifting through her treasures until she found a necklace that looked like it probably wasn't a holy relic and stashed it in the small chest of drawers. This inn probably didn't see much money, and Pidge felt grotesquely generous.

The dragonling perched atop the bed, mewling until Pidge tossed it a plate of mutton. To her credit, Madge had earned the money she was bound to discover in the morning. She'd need it to replace the pillow the creature had already destroyed.

It was a two day journey back to Tamren high. That meant two days of keeping off the roads, her treasure kept close, and her new companion kept closer. It also meant two days of trying to feed and tend to an increasingly irritable baby dragon. As soon as they entered Tamren and it went back in the bag, it started fussing. And it didn't stop, not even when Pidge knocked at the servants' entrance.

"Stop that," Pidge hissed as the dragon wriggled in its bag, scrabbling loudly at the treasures in. "Stop. They'll never let me in if they see—"

The door cracked open with a loud creak as one of the kitchen maids poked her head out with a tight frown.

"Oh no," she huffed. "Not you. Not on a day like this."

"What? Why?" Pidge's stomach churned. No. Not the wedding, not yet. She should have had time.

"Count Cordo's over, he and the king are in talks. And I bet you want to distract the princess, do you?"

"And what makes you say that?"

The bag rattled at her side, the dragon mewling softly as it scrabbled, no doubt confused as to why it could smell fish when there were none to be seen. The maid's eyes flicked down to the bag and she pulled a face.

"Don't tell me you brought her a cat," she moaned. "The last thing we need is another creature to bring chaos at a time like this. Do you have any idea what it's been like—"

"I'm sure the princess will want to see me."

"So you can whisk her away to who knows where exactly when she needs to be here? Fat chance."

"I won't take her anywhere, I promise," Pidge insisted. "I have a… a gift for her. Because of her upcoming wedding. Please." She tightened her grip on the bag and chewed the inside of her cheek. "You know how close we are."

The maid sighed heavily.

"You haven't met Count Cordo yet. You don't know the hell we'll catch if he finds out I let you in today."

"He doesn't need to know how I got in. Besides. Do you really want to let Trina know you kept me out?"

The maid grimaced but stepped aside, gesturing irritably down the hall. "Just hurry along. Trina's in the hall with the king. Wait in her chambers."

"Of course."

Pidge pushed through into the kitchen, where more than a few of the kitchen staff froze to look at her with varying levels of relief, concern, and alarm. More so the latter as a whining protest rose up from her bag. Pidge ignored all of them, though, as she walked straight into the corridor beyond, her heavy boots echoing off the dark stone. Her heart thudded in her chest like a hammer. Trina was in the hall with her father, being bartered like a piece of livestock. She swallowed thickly and squeezed her eyes shut.

"Trina, what in the name of... what is this in your bed?"

"Her name is Pidge, Uncle. I found her. She has no home."

"That doesn't mean she belongs in yours."

She took a shuddering breath and almost skidded to a halt. In all this time, she'd been so concerned with Trina it hadn't even occurred to her what the king would say. Would Pidge drive a wedge between them by doing this?

She froze as she came to a fork in the corridor. If she continued on, she could stop the marriage arrangements. Make a big show of presenting the relics, sweep Trina away, become the consort of the future queen... but she would also earn the wrath of the king and Count Cordo. Whereas on her left was Trina's room. It was safety above all else. Where they'd always found refuge together. She bit her lip, remembering the first time Trina had kissed her. In that room, on that bed, bright and eager, her eyes shining, her lips tasting of sweet wine and honey cakes.

"You know what, Pidge? I don't think I love anything in the world as much as you." Her hand fell to Pidge's knee. Pidge, stunned, stared back at her, her cheeks burning.

"Trina, you know we can't..." Pidge threw a glance over her shoulder, just in case someone approached.

"Oh, bugger them all, Pidge. It's time I heard an answer from you." She arched one dark brow. *"Well?"*

Pidge's mouth went dry but, before she could stop herself, the words slipped out.

"I... I feel the same."

Trina's face broke into a wide smile as she leaned forward, nuzzling her nose against Pidge's.

"Good. Then we'll always be together."

Pidge sucked in a deep breath and forced herself to move, one step at a time, into the great hall. A large, lacquered table had been set up before the king's throne, and it was littered with documents. The king read over one, his face pinched as he stroked his dark beard. Trina sat beside him, her eyes downcast, hands folded listlessly in her lap. Pidge's stomach squirmed. Where was that beautiful spark?

Cordo sat beside her, and Pidge could see immediately where Trina's spark must have gone. The count did not have a kind face. Cordo's eyes were like flecks of ice, his mouth a sharp, thin line in his face, as though a sculptor had clumsily slashed into clay with a knife and called it done. He didn't glance at Trina once as he jabbed a finger at the legal documents like a knife.

"No, consort is *not* going to be enough," he insisted. "If I'm going to marry her I'm going to need to know that my wife will not have power over me. I will be king and nothing less. It is tradition."

"Tradition cannot always be set in stone. Marriage is a complex union, particularly for royals," one of the three priests present began, worrying the frayed sleeves of his habit. Cordo turned to snap at him but froze as his eyes fell on Pidge. Pidge struggled to stop herself from squirming under his scrutiny. All the glances, all the half hidden sneers directed at her over the years were there in his eyes, with more malice than any one person should have been able to muster. It made her sick to know that the king intended to hand his niece off to such a man.

"What's this?" Cordo demanded. "Get out, woman. Can't you see we're busy?"

Pidge opened her mouth to speak, but couldn't quite push the words out. For one agonizing moment, she was a child, awkward and tall, an unfortunate tagalong to the princess. The king, Trina, and the three priests glanced up as one. Trina's eyes widened, one hand flying to her mouth. The priests gaped, and one made a small gesture of supplication, begging some god or other for the patience to deal with such a nuisance. The king let out a weary huff.

"Pidge, this isn't the time," he said evenly. "Go wait in your room, Trina will be in to see you later."

"I'm afraid I can't, Your Grace."

The king glanced up sharply. He'd always tolerated her in the past. Once he accepted that Trina's little vagrant would not be going away, he grudgingly accepted her as something of a family oddity. At times, if he was in a fine mood and had had too much wine, he even found it in him to be affectionate toward her. On this day, he'd clearly had no wine. Before the king could say another word, however, Cordo's face burned red and he slammed his fist on the table, sending a couple of papers flying.

"You dare to defy your king?" Cordo snapped.

"I dare to offer him something he needs," Pidge insisted, turning pleading eyes on Trina's uncle. "Something that might help him to reconsider."

"And what is that?" the king sighed, rubbing one hand over his face. In the bag, the dragonling squirmed and mewled, clattering against the treasure. All three priests jumped to their feet.

"What manner of... what have you got in there?" one demanded, the color draining from his face. Pidge strode forward, dropping the bag on the table, her lip twitching up as it flew open and the dragonling leapt out, papers flying from underneath its paws. Trina's other hand flew to her mouth, but Pidge caught sight of the smile that lit up her face, reigniting that old spark.

The king and Cordo both leapt from their seats, eyes wide.

"What is this?" the king demanded.

"Think of it as a wedding present," Pidge said.

Cordo's face twisted, as though she had just told him they'd be serving up the creature for supper.

"Well we do not accept," he snarled.

"It's not for you. Just for Trina."

"Pidge," Trina laughed, covering her face. Her shoulders shook with poorly contained mirth. "You utter lunatic."

"This is absurd," Cordo roared, turning on the king. "I came here to negotiate my ability to fill your coffers. Now if you aren't serious about this—"

"Pidge, you need to go," the king said evenly. "We will speak later.

"No," Pidge insisted, reaching for the bag. "There's more—"

"Not from you," Cordo snarled.

"Oh, she means well by it," Trina said. "Let her—"

"We have discussed your speaking out of turn." Cordo turned on her, his hand twitching just a hair, enough that Pidge could see the blow he was holding back. The blow he might not hold back after a wedding.

She was moving before she even knew what she was doing, her hand going to the hilt of her sword... but no. It was gone. Buried in the breast of the sea dragon. That didn't stop her, though. As she leapt up onto the table, she ripped at her scabbard hard enough to snap the straps one by one. The dragon let out a startled cry and scrambled out of the way, spilling the rest of the papers off the table.

Cordo's jaw let out a satisfying crunch under the slam of her scabbard, and Cordo dropped like a tree.

Pidge had only a moment to enjoy the sight of him on the floor, his smug face twisted in shock and pain. Then she heard the yells. The king screamed for his guards, the priests condemning such violence in a woman. The youngest one, a mousy boy who looked fresh from the seminary, rushed to Cordo's side, but looked too frightened to actually help him up.

Then strong hands closed around her shoulders, yanking her down from the table. The sparkle disappeared from Trina's eyes.

"No, wait—" she called as the guards began to drag Pidge away, but the king grabbed her shoulders.

"Throw her in the dungeon, we'll deal with her later," he snapped. The dragonling paced nervously, whining as it looked from person to person to person. Then, in a fit of rage, it began howling and scratching at the heavily lacquered table.

Nobody even looked at the bag.

~~*

Pidge stared dully at the dingy stone wall. Night had fallen, and only the flickering light of the distant torches lit her cell. It was odd, finally finding herself down here. Sure, the threat of imprisonment was common. Don't touch that cake, don't make faces at the duchess, don't kidnap the princess to go riding an hour before the state dinner, or you'll end up in the dungeon where you belong. The threat was so common she'd almost forgotten that it could be true.

What a mess she'd made. Why couldn't she rein in her temper? Maybe she'd wanted to show off, letting the dragon out first. She knew Trina would like it, and that was all that mattered at the time. If she'd pulled out a relic first, she could have staked her claim, rescued Trina from that marriage.

Smashing her scabbard into Cordo's face was probably the worst way to do that.

She ground her teeth together and squeezed her eyes shut. Stupid. Stupid! Everything was going to well. She had the damned church treasure, she had everything she needed to free Trina. Now she'd be lucky if the king didn't exile her. Oh, he'd threatened to do it plenty of times. But now of all times she couldn't bear the thought. How long would she be sent away? Six months? A year? Certainly he wouldn't permit her to return until after the wedding and then it would all be too late. Pidge knocked her head against the grimy wall and lifted her chin, staring at the stark, stone ceiling.

"If anyone's listening," she muttered. "Any gods or... or whatever you like, please. Don't let Trina suffer for my mistakes."

"I never took you for the praying sort."

Pidge's head whipped around and she leapt to her feet as she saw Trina just in front of the cell, the dragonling in her arms, curled up like a cat. Trina's coy smile was back in place, albeit smaller than it had been when Pidge released her new pet.

"Trina," Pidge gasped, grabbing for the bars of her cell. "I'm so sorry. I got stupid."

Trina shrugged. "You were fighting for my honor. Though we do now see that it wasn't even necessary." She shifted her grip on the dragon and, in the poor light of the dungeons, Pidge saw the gleam of a new, silver necklace. One of the non-holy trinkets from the sea dragon's hoard. Trina's eyes crinkled with amusement. "I hope you know that your treasure stank of fish."

"I'll explain that some time." Pidge licked her lips, her mouth going dry as it began to sink in. Of course. She'd left the bag on the table. Someone was bound to go through it. "The relics?"

"The priests were more than happy to take them. And what was leftover... well, it was almost what Cordo was offering for my hand."

"Thank every god in the stars," Pidge breathed, her eyes sliding shut as she leaned forward, pressing her head to the cool, rough bars of her cell. Trina laughed and reached forward, running her slim fingers through Pidge's hair.

"Yes, well, it's certainly complicated things," she said. "How am I supposed to tell you you're wrong when you were right about this? Next thing you know I'll have to approve of you running off in search of adventure. There'll be nothing left for me to fuss over!"

"You'll think of something," Pidge laughed, and for just that moment, she felt as light as air. Whatever happened next, Trina was not going to marry that brute. He couldn't buy her hand if the king didn't need the gold anymore. "At least if your uncle doesn't exile me for this. I am well and truly dreading whatever punishment he's planning to cook up for me."

Trina laughed, setting the dragonling down on the ground before she reached through the bars and wrapped her arms around Pidge's shoulders.

"I don't think he can do that," she said. "Not when you have my hand."

Pidge's eyes bugged wide open.

"I... I what?" she gaped. "But I just attacked a member of the court. In front of the king. After setting a baby dragon loose in the hall with three priests."

Said dragon let out an affectionate mewl and curled up around Trina's ankles, clearly smitten. Trina beamed.

"Yes, but the church oversees him in this. Their relics, their rules. Even they don't like to break their own rules. Fear of the gods and all that."

Pidge shook her head. "But I'm a woman. It's all well and good to dream it but that fact remains."

Trina threw back her head and laughed. "Yes, well, I'm sure they now regret not being more specific."

Pidge licked her lips, her heart hammering. She could have Trina every night, as long as she wanted her. No more sneaking into each other's rooms at night. Finally, finally, she would belong there. And there wasn't a soul in the court who could tell her to leave. Which was why it took everything Pidge had to pull Trina's hands down and shake her head.

"No. Your hand is yours. I want you more than the sun, but I don't want a captive queen. Not when I did this to rescue you from that."

"Then lucky you I'm no captive." Trina smiled. "Pidge, are you going to make me ask you?"

Pidge laughed and nodded.

"It would help."

"Well then." Trina smirked and scooped the dragon up off the ground. "You'll have to come by my room in the morning and hear what I have to ask you."

"Oh, so you're going to leave me here while you and your precious new pet sleep in your nice, soft bed?"

"King's orders. You're to stay the night. You did attack a very, very rich nobleman." Trina winked at her. "It's all right. Once you're out, I'm going to work hard to tame you."

"I'd like to see you try." And that was the gods' honest truth.

TREASON

ALTHEA CLAIRE DUFFY

Elunet had never quit an assignment, and she wasn't about to quit now. Not over raw hands that cracked and bled when she curled them too quickly, not over the steward giving her the switch in front of all the other servants when she broke a vase, and certainly not over Lord Kenar and Dowager Lady Isendre's utter lack of consideration for their social inferiors. She had played her role of innocent housemaid perfectly—she'd been meek and apologetic and frightened rather than coolly defiant, cried a little but not too much over the punishment, and no one had ever caught her snooping or noticed the four knives she kept secreted about her person in case of real trouble. She would continue to play the role until she found something incriminating House Mellas that she could turn over to Chal.

She'd be even happier to see House Mellas go down than Chal's masters at House Corellis and their allies at House Valen would be—and Corellis and Mellas had been rivals since the coffee trade with Nurana in the south began over a hundred years ago, a rivalry that had expanded to numerous other trade goods and resulted in public humiliations, bitter love triangles, business deals arranged largely to spite the other party, piracy, and at least two assassinations. The satisfaction would be almost as good as the payment she'd be adding to the lockbox under the floorboards of her hideaway. She'd been a spy for fifteen years, and Corellis and Chal paid her well for her expertise.

Elunet was dusting Lady Isendre's marriage chest and examining it yet again for anything that might suggest the family had a closer connection with Isendre's home city-state of Telar than fond memories and an heir attending the Collegium Arcanum there. Among the city-states of the Lirrisaran peninsula, a married woman owned in her own name only her marriage chest and everything she could fit into it; appropriately, Isendre had brought from Telar to her new home in Auragos a gilded and bejeweled behemoth, painted inside and out with scenes of wifely virtue and familial bliss by the renowned Delon Avelos, which had increased considerably in value upon the artist's death in a notorious duel. It was to be cleaned very carefully every day, along with the model ship, the curious angular statue from somewhere in the far south, and everything else in the room, but there was nothing suspicious or informative about it. Elunet was no closer to evidence of treason than she had been the day she'd arrived, and nothing in any of the rooms she cleaned was any more helpful.

"Nel." She jumped a little at hearing her assumed name from the doorway, but it was not spoken as a reprimand. Almara, head of the female servants, had a worried line between her eyebrows, not an angry one.

"Yes, ma'am?" Elunet turned around and bobbed politely--not the curtsy proper for the lords and ladies of the House, but a sign of deference to her superior.

"Lady Tavia's due home later, and you'll be helping her get settled. We had a letter from her yesterday saying that her maid quit—ran off with some young man who worked in the Collegium stables."

If Tavia was anything like her father and grandmother, Elunet didn't blame the maid in the least. "Yes, ma'am."

Almara smiled. "Since you've been a maid to a young lady before, I was thinking you'd fill her spot, at least for now."

She'd forgotten that little detail of her invented history. On the positive side of the balance, she'd have less cleaning to do, and perhaps her hands would have a chance to recover. On the negative side, she'd spend day and night catering personally to the whims of the spoiled heir to House Mellas. Elunet had never met Tavia, but the examples of her father and grandmother did not bode well—and Tavia was a student mage, too. The arrogance of nobility plus the arrogance of arcane knowledge couldn't add up to anything good. "Me? Um. Of course, ma'am."

"Don't be giving yourself any airs, now. We'll see how you do, and if her ladyship doesn't care for your service, you'll be back to dusting and scrubbing the floor."

"Certainly, ma'am. Thank you, ma'am, and I'll do my very best for Lady Tavia, I promise."

Almara frowned again. "Tuck that hair under your kerchief and clean your shoes before she arrives." She tsked. "I wish we could do something about how short your hair is. It's bad enough having the heir coming home to a strange maid without her looking like a ragamuffin."

"Yes, ma'am." Elunet pushed a thick dark lock under the cloth where it belonged and fluffed the ends of her hair around her chin, then moved on with her dust cloth from the marriage chest to the table with the pierce-work oil lamp. A ragamuffin was just what she'd been, years ago, until Chal had plucked her from the street and taught her to spy, to act roles, to fight, to read and write, and to observe and remember. Unfortunately, none of her training seemed to be leading her to anything useful just yet.

~~*

"She's here! She's here!" Evet the page raced down the hallway, his steps echoing on the marble floor, until Almara caught him and cuffed his ear.

"Well, don't just stand there. Go out and get her things." Almara made a shooing motion at Elunet with her free hand. Evet gave one perfunctory squirm and resigned himself to obedience.

Elunet hurried just enough to be quick and not enough to be undignified, past tempera portraits of Mellases past hung between grooved pilasters and out to the formal gardens bright with late spring blooms. At the end of the paved path, between two pines pruned to narrow spearheads and two armored bodyguards just as stiff on matched gray geldings, rode a young woman.

She was a little younger than Elunet, with only a circle of lace pinned to her hair and pale gold curls soft around her face. She was short, shorter than Elunet, but round and lush whereas Elunet was almost boyish. She rode sidesaddle, like a proper lady, but looked a bit unbalanced in the position. With one foot, she slipped out of the stirrup, and began to shift her weight sideways and down the side of the horse, before realizing the horse was still walking. "Oh," she said, and tugged gently at the reins. Dennel, one of the guards who had been sent to escort her home from the Collegium, helped her dismount, and she brushed dust from the spring-green linen of her skirt. By now, Elunet was close enough to notice that both the gown and her peridot drop earrings underlined the vivid green of her eyes.

Elunet was there to serve, not to stare, and dropped into a deep curtsy, hoping she had not paused too long for propriety. "I'll get your saddlebags and see to your things, my lady. I'll be your new lady's maid for now. My name is Nel."

"Oh. I... haven't seen you before. You must be new."

"I was hired while you were at the Collegium, my lady."

"Of course." Tavia's horse attempted to sniff her, and Dennel distracted him by stroking his neck. "Where did you work before?"

"For Lady Periet Kintaliar, my lady." Kintaliar was a minor House, not on the Council, whose members spent most of their time at their rural estate in the hills growing grapes and seldom visited Auragos more than once a year. She and Chal had chosen Kintaliar as her supposed former employer because no one was likely to know them well—particularly not young Lady Periet, their second daughter, who according to Chal's sources was a shy plain girl who had only been to Auragos twice in her life and spent most of her time on horseback.

"I... think I may have met her once. I can't remember; I'm not good with faces." Tavia started unfastening the straps of one saddlebag, and Elunet remembered what she was there for.

"No need for you to do that, my lady. Please, rest and enjoy the gardens or go inside, as you wish. You must be exhausted from your journey."

"Sorry. I've... gotten used to not having a maid." Tavia dropped her hands to her sides and smiled, looking a bit embarrassed.

"No matter, my lady." The saddlebags were brick-heavy—Elunet could feel the corners of several books and wooden boxes poking through the fabric—but she balanced them across the back of her shoulders like a yoke. Having more muscle than most maids could be useful.

As soon as they crossed the garden and loggia and reached the antechamber, Dowager Lady Isendre rounded a corner into the marble hallway beyond. In her late sixties, she was still tall, slim, and painfully fashionable in a red silk gown, gray hair gathered in a smooth chignon behind a matching red silk band. Daring jewelry, with Nuranan cowrie shells between the emerald cabochons, completed the picture—and picture it was: Isendre always looked as if she were having her portrait painted. "Oh, my darling, it's so *delightful* to see you home! They must be feeding you *ever* so well at the Collegium, my dear; you look like a prize sow."

"Thank you, Grandmama. I'm pleased to see you well." Tavia's smile was so obviously forced it looked painful to maintain.

"The Telarians don't give you a hard time about being from Auragos, do they? There have been such unpleasant feelings since the war."

"Not often, Grandmama."

"Oh, good. It's simply outrageous that your maid ran off with that stable boy. I'd have had her flogged if I'd known what she was about. Sometimes I *do* wish we lived in Halanor, where they aren't *allowed* to quit." She tsked. "No loyalty at all these days."

"No, I suppose not." Tavia fidgeted.

Isendre sighed. "Your father is out trying to wring at least a little profit out of selling coffee to the overland merchants. The captain of our last vessel in from Tanafel said the Tanafelan factors claim the coffee roasters are raising their prices—some sort of drought in Nurana damaging the supply of coffee and firewood—but I suspect all the extra gold is going straight into the Tanafelans' coffers. Or our captain's. If there were *really* a drought in Nurana, House Corellis would be raising their prices too, and they've been undercutting us for months. I suspect they might be colluding; Corellis has always wanted a monopoly." She shook her head. "And the price of silk is simply criminal this season, with that mulberry blight in Kazkir—which *is* real. At least wool prices are down."

Isendre kept up a long stream of news and speculation along these lines, and the saddlebags slung across Elunet's shoulders seemed to grow heavier and more full of sharp corners pressing against her back by the moment. Nevertheless, she memorized all the important points about House Mellas's ships, trade network, rivalries with other Houses, dealings with foreign merchants and lords, and future plans. For a woman so obviously astute in business matters, Isendre was remarkably indiscreet about discussing them in front of servants. There were advantages to people considering Elunet part of the furniture—as well as disadvantages, she thought, as her back cramped and the ache in her arms grew worse.

"Grandmama," Tavia finally said, "I've had a long ride home, and I wish to sit down." She looked at Elunet, and Elunet returned the most grateful expression she could manage.

"Of course you do. My apologies, dear. We must get you some wine and savories, or perhaps some fruit? Or perhaps both. We do need you at your best tomorrow; your father and I are hosting a soiree. Galatan is coming, and I'm sure we'll have plenty of guests even if only to hear him play." She motioned to Keres the footman, who nodded and set off for the kitchen.

"Nel, you may set that down if you wish." Tavia indicated her saddlebags. Elunet straightened and barely managed to avoid dropping them to the floor. Tavia raised a hand as if to offer assistance, then visibly remembered herself. "Go with Keres to the kitchen and have a rest if you like. I won't need anything for a while."

Relieved as she was to have a chance to sit down and work the ache out of her back, Elunet was a little disappointed not to be around to glean more information from Isendre's chatter. After a few minutes kneading at her shoulders by the cramped table where the servants ate between the spit and the ovens, Elunet went to put away Tavia's things in her chamber upstairs.

Tavia's large chamber overlooked the courtyard on one side and the gardens on the other, with balconies on both vistas, a polished wood floor, and walls of pale yellow stucco. Elunet had helped the other maids prepare the room for Tavia's arrival, washing and airing the bedclothes, beating the rug, and dusting or scrubbing every surface. She'd been disappointed to discover little in the way of magical accoutrements. Tavia had taken most of those with her, of course, in those damned saddlebags.

Elunet unpacked gingerly; she'd never touched a mage's belongings before. She hung two gowns in the armoire, one cream-colored lambswool and the other the deep blue student's gown of the Collegium with an eight-pointed star embroidered in white on the left breast. Stockings, three linen shifts, and smallclothes were next; an image of Tavia in shift and stocking feet teased at her mind, and she shooed it away. The boxes held some things Elunet expected (vials of metallic powders and dried herbs, chalk, ink, candles) and some she did not (a compass and drafting square, a bag of marbles).

Tavia's books were more likely to be useful to Elunet. *A History of Lirrisaran Magic. Symbols: a Primer. Glyphs and Geometric Tracings. Mineral and Herbal Properties. A Treatise upon Magical Research and Experimental Thaumatology.* She looked over her shoulder to be sure she was unobserved and flipped through each one, pausing occasionally to pick up a sense of the contents. Woodcuts of geometric diagrams, colored by hand and marked with symbols where the lines met, crisscrossed the pages like lace. Symbols, minerals, and herbs were paired with what they represented and invoked: a drawn knot for binding, iron for protection, rosemary for remembrance.

Three volumes bound in brown leather proved to be notebooks in Tavia's own hand. One was full of lecture notes, punctuated with doodled flowers and faces in the margins. The second held notes on Tavia's books, as well as other books Elunet did not recognize. The third, fattest one was a journal with dated entries detailing what Elunet guessed were magical experiments. *Tried attuning first circle to second circle with broken halves of maple seed. Placing marble in first circle caused sympathetic glow in second. Promising sign in right direction.* Tavia had drawn meticulous diagrams, undoubtedly with the compass and drafting square, and noted the results of spell after spell. Elunet understood little of it; she turned back to the first page and tried to piece together a sense of what it meant.

She had not gone far—four pages of cryptic wardings—when footsteps on the stairs interrupted her snooping. By the time Anata the housemaid reached the second floor, before she entered the room, Elunet was putting Tavia's ransacked possessions on shelves with casual ease, the rapid beat of her heart the only sign of furtiveness. In her line of work, she needed sharp ears.

~~*

Elunet held the lamp with one hand and opened the chamber door with the other. Tavia entered, crossed to the curtained bed, and sat down heavily. She unfastened her shoes, rolled off her stockings, and had just started to take down the pinned section of her hair when she paused, eyes on Elunet, and said, "I forgot. I'm supposed to let you do this." She stood up and padded barefoot to the dressing table, where she sat with her back to Elunet and fiddled with a blue glass scent bottle and a tin of powdery rouge.

Elunet felt awkwardly superfluous. She felt a different kind of awkward standing behind Tavia. She hesitated for a moment, hands hovering over Tavia's golden hair swept up in the middle with loose curls down the sides, heart pounding at the realization that she was about to touch her. A stern reminder to herself broke the hesitation, and she reached into Tavia's hair to feel for pins. Tavia's hair was silky and thick, warm with the heat of her skin, and the warmth spread in a wave through Elunet's whole body. *Duty*, she reminded herself again, and gently pulled the pins free. Soft curls tumbled down Tavia's back. Elunet reached for the hairbrush on the table and worked the tangles out gently, starting from the bottom as she had been taught.

"Did your first day back home go well, my lady?" she said, to distract herself as much as to keep up the demeanor of a maidservant.

"Well enough, I suppose." Tavia put down the scent bottle and picked up a tin of salve. "Here. You can use this, if you like."

Elunet paused. "I'm sorry, my lady; did my rough hands bother you?"

"Not at all; they just look like they hurt." She held it out to Elunet, who took it and removed the lid. The white cream inside smelled faintly of almond and rose—a scent that clung to Tavia herself. Elunet dabbed some on the backs of her hands and rubbed.

"Thank you, my lady; that's quite kind."

Tavia stood and started to unbutton the back of her gown, then stopped. "Oh. Right. You're here." She shook her head. "I'm sorry. I don't want to make you feel useless."

"Of course, my lady. I'm not offended." Elunet's fingers went to the small round buttons and unfastened them, only trembling a little. She peeled the top of the dress down, baring Tavia's white shift and corset. In the mirror, she glimpsed the high generous tops of Tavia's breasts, lifted to the low hemline of her shift like an offering to an altar, and reminded herself that this was only work. "The Collegium picked a fine time to send you home; the gardens are lovely this time of year," she said, to give herself something else to focus on.

Tavia sighed. "Sometimes I wish Father and Grandmama let me stay at the Collegium all year round. Even though I do love the gardens." She met Elunet's eyes in the mirror and added hastily, "And Father and Grandmama."

"What do you do at the Collegium, my lady? I really don't know anything about magic, but it seems so fascinating." It was a good spy question: probing for potentially relevant information, in the natural context of the conversation and without any specificity, while staying perfectly in the character of wide-eyed maid.

Tavia's eyes lit. "All sorts of things having to do with magic. I attend lectures and read about magic in the library and work on it in the laboratories. There are little stone rooms designed for practice, where you can draw glyphs on the floors in chalk and light candles and incense and even little bonfires and such without worrying about burning anything."

"And what sorts of things does your magic do, my lady? Not turn me into a toad, I hope."

Tavia smiled. "Magic only turns people into toads in stories. Nobody's ever figured out how to do that, if it's even possible. There are a lot of things no one's figured out, or no one remembers how to do. They say that in ancient Sujal, mages could make a door you could walk through and come out the other side on the other end of the empire, but no one's known how to do that in two thousand years as far as I know. The only documents describing how they did it were destroyed when the Great Library of Sujal was burned." She stood, and stepped out of her dress, as Elunet held it, revealing the smooth round curve of her hips and bottom beneath the clinging fabric of her shift and the shape of her bare calves. "I mostly do wardings and spells having to do with movement and travel."

"What are wardings, my lady?" Elunet knew what they were, in a general sense, but "Nel" likely wouldn't.

"Protection and blessing spells. A lot of times they keep things out. There's one for warding a room against flies, and a similar one for mice, and one to sound a loud alarm, and then there are movement spells to make wind blow in a certain direction or float an object across a room or... all kinds of things, really."

"It sounds like fun."

"Oh, it is. Though it's also a lot of work, especially if you're trying to figure out how to do something new." Tavia stood and yawned, and Elunet realized that Tavia's corset was still on over her shift.

"Are you... planning on doing any magic here?" *Be casual, be casual*, Elunet thought, as her fingers went to the laces of Tavia's corset. She pulled the bow undone, then loosened the laces, feeling the warmth of Tavia's back beneath her thin shift as she unlaced.

"Of course, when I can sneak away from Father and Grandmama long enough. I'd be embarrassingly rusty by fall term if I didn't. And I'm working on some research I really hope to make more progress on. You'll even get to see me do it." Tavia paused. "Unless it would frighten or bother you."

"Oh, not at all, my lady! I've always wanted to see real magic." Elunet pulled the last of the laces out, and opened the shell of Tavia's corset. Tavia sighed as she relaxed into her natural shape, and rubbed at the places where the stays had pressed, then crossed to her bed. Free of their restraints, her abundant breasts moved slightly as she walked; Elunet looked away before Tavia could see her looking at *that*, and turned down the covers. "Is there anything I can get for you, my lady? A hot toddy? A warming brick?"

"No, I don't need anything. Thank you for asking, Nel." Tavia slid into bed and gave Elunet a smile that made her breath catch. "Good night. And welcome to House Mellas. I hope you're comfortable here."

"Oh, I am, my lady. Thank you, and a good night to you as well." *Comfortable* was entirely the wrong word, but Tavia's presence seemed as if it would make House Mellas more enjoyable—if even more frustrating. Elunet closed the bed curtains and went to her own pallet in the vestibule of Tavia's chamber within easy hearing of the bed. She undressed to her own shift and curled up, breathing in the rose and almond scent of Tavia's salve on her hands.

~~*

In the morning, after rising early for a breakfast of brown bread and soft fresh cheese and taking Tavia's travel clothes to the laundress, Elunet laced Tavia into her corset and dressed her in a green silk gown with voluminous sleeves that she had not taken to the Collegium with her. Considering how many tiny buttons it had, it would have been difficult to wear without help. Elunet braided Tavia's hair and looped the braid into a high bun, then pinned on a fluttery lace veil.

"There, my lady. You look lovely as spring itself in that green. All the young men at the soiree will be fighting each other to dance with you." Elunet felt plain as a peahen beside her, in a russet wool maid's dress and apron.

Tavia met Elunet's eyes with a little smile, blushed prettily, and sighed. "To tell the truth, the only thing I look forward to is Galatan's playing. Well, and the roasted swan and almond pastries or whatever it is we're eating. Sometimes I feel like I *am* the swan— another centerpiece stuck with feathers and put in the center of the room to be doled out in pieces to all the guests."

Elunet tried to think of something to say to that. "Of course you're shown off to all the guests. You're young and pretty and clever and..."

"Marriageable," Tavia finished. "Father may have sent me to the Collegium, but a future Lady of the Council needs heirs as much as she needs education." She sighed. "I wish my brothers had lived, and that I'd been the youngest. Then Father and Grandmama wouldn't worry half so much about it, and I could spend the summers on my research instead of being taken to a hundred dull gatherings and reminded every day that I'm nearly twenty-two and can't go on being picky forever. Or being tutored in politics and endless details of foreign trade and shipping costs and all the alliances and rivalries among the Houses here and what not to say to whom. I'm bad at politics, and worse at business, and even worse at socializing."

"I wish your brothers had lived as well, my lady. It must have been dreadful to lose them and your mother both."

"Oh, one I never knew; he was stillborn. Another died as a baby. Thenian and Mother died four days apart, of the same fever. He was twelve." Tavia shivered and rubbed her arms at the memory. "Sometimes I still wake up in the morning expecting him to come in and jump on my bed... and then I remember."

"My mother and father both died of a fever when I was six," Elunet said. It was true, and she scolded herself a little for revealing something real about her own life. "Um. My lady."

"So... you understand." Tavia looked into her eyes for a long moment, then shook her head. "I'm sorry. It's terribly insensitive of me to whine about having to go to feasts and soirees in front of you, when I doubt you've ever had the chance to go to any such thing unless you were working."

That was also true... although the "work" involved had not been the sort Tavia had in mind. Elunet had attended several banquets as an obscure Lady So-and-so or one of her poor country relations, on Chal's behalf. Conversations became delightfully informative after several goblets of wine. "Not a bother at all, my lady. I don't mind watching; I still get to hear the music and see all the pretty clothes, without worrying about some overeager young man stepping on my toes all night."

In truth, she certainly did not envy the servants whose entire lives would be spent in drudgery for wealthy people who showed them little gratitude. Having Tavia's leisure and opportunity to pursue her interests would have been wonderful, and certainly would have seemed even more wonderful if Elunet's assumed role had been real and she had spent her whole life in service with no prospect of anything else, but Elunet was glad that she would never be shown off on the market like a cow in silks. Elunet herself moved easily through the intrigues of the Auragan elite, but she could tell that Tavia—easily flustered and clearly interested mostly in academic and magical subjects— was like a mouse in a snake pit. She'd seen, heard about, and read about similarly ill-suited lords and ladies who had ended up manipulated, swindled, supplanted, or assassinated once they'd inherited their titles, and did not like to imagine Tavia's future. Tavia did, however, have the self-awareness and empathy to recognize her own privileged position in relation to Elunet, and this impressed Elunet considerably.

Elunet had arranged to meet Chal at midday at an unassuming rented room close to the nearby market square. She covered her absence by offering to fetch Tavia whatever she wished from the stalls; Tavia requested cherries, and Elunet hurried just short of a run through four streets to the safehouse, where she knocked four times fast and twice slow as was their signal. Chal let her in. He was a compact man close to fifty, with a neat, short beard and the well-made, if slightly dusty, linen attire of a successful artisan; his entire appearance, Elunet knew, was calculated to be respectable but undistinguished, a man no one would notice. As soon as the door was closed, Chal cuffed her gently on the back in a half-hug and said, "Any new discoveries, Mockingbird?"

The old nickname, bestowed long ago in honor of her gift for mimicry and blending into whatever role she was playing, always made her smile. "Mellas is having trouble with the coffee trade—the ship captain reported drought in Nurana, but the Dowager thinks either he or the Tanafelan middlemen are lying about that. Silk is expensive and likely to stay so for some time, wool is cheap, and the winter's orange crop at the country estate was worth a good bundle in the north. They're hosting a gathering tonight, and they've hired Galatan to play the lute, so there should be a good turnout even if only for him. Lady Tavia came home from the Collegium yesterday, but she hasn't said much about Telar other than about the Collegium itself, though I have overheard rumors about someone catching a Telarian spy in House Amarin. However, Lady Tavia's previous lady's maid quit while she was still at the Collegium and the housekeeper's having me fill in for her." Elunet smiled.

Chal's smile was even wider than Elunet's own. "A remarkable stroke of luck, Mockingbird. Are you sure you didn't arrange things this way?"

"What, are you accusing me of driving poor Dulsa out? She ran away with a young man from the Collegium stables."

"Quite romantic. Isendre hasn't been to visit anyone in Telar?" Chal leaned against the wall, one foot on a plain wooden chest.

"Not since last year."

"Do you know who she and Kenar correspond with there?"

"Isendre's younger brothers and their children and grandchildren, and a few merchants. The letters I got a peek at were all pretty innocuous. All 'the first tin shipment arrived from Berethar two days ago' and 'Lilia has embroidered a nice cushion with hummingbirds and honeysuckle' and no 'we sabotaged that Corellis ship just as you asked' or 'when Auragos is Telar's vassal, you'll have the whole Port District.' That would be much too easy." Elunet glanced at the floor. "I'm sorry I haven't been more useful."

"Oh, no, you've been useful. Corellis will be glad to know they can anticipate an opportunity to cut into Mellas's share of the coffee trade, at least. This young heir—Tavia—what's she like these days? I remember her being quiet at social occasions and going off to the Collegium Arcanum."

"Oh, she's still not one for socializing. She told me she'd rather be working on her magical research. Being shown off and expected to impress suitors is uncomfortable for her, and she thinks she isn't any good at politics or business. In fact, she wishes she weren't the heir at all." She had an uneasy feeling in her stomach, betraying these confidences, and reminded herself that hearing private details of other people's lives and relating them to Chal was her job. She'd told him much worse about other people before.

"Now *that* is really useful. Did you find out anything about what she's doing in Telar?"

"She specializes in wardings and spells having to do with travel and movement. She seems especially interested in glyphs and geometric patterns. And she's working on some sort of magical research; I got a brief look at her notes, but didn't really understand them. I think she's making progress on whatever it is, though. She seems to be careful about writing everything down in a lot of detail."

"No word of dealings outside the Collegium?"

"None." Elunet shrugged. "I could lead our conversation in that direction in the future and see what turns up, but I got the sense she was mostly interested in her studies."

"Sounds wise." Chal smiled. "I trust your judgment. If you have nothing else to report, we'll meet here again in a month. I have a little business out of town in the meantime, so I apologize for the delay."

"Of course. Thanks, Chal." Elunet waved a quick farewell, and headed back to the market. The fruit-seller's cart was thronged with servants and housewives and at least one ragged child trying to pilfer something sweet. She'd been that child once, and been lucky enough to have Chal catch her trying to lift his purse. Elunet waited her turn for much too long, shouldered her way past two matrons who cut her in line, and picked out a bunch of cherries just at the perfect halfway point between red and black, then hurried back to the Mellas estate. Dennel the guard let her in with an indulgent smile and a "What, nothing for me?" She ran up the back stairs and to the sitting room on the second floor, where Tavia sat in an ornate leather chair with a book in her lap and loose curls of hair in her face.

Almara's hand clamped on Elunet's upper arm just as she was about to enter. "Where in the Sea-Father's name have you been?"

This was one of the lines of questioning she found truly worrying. "Out at the market, ma'am. Lady Tavia wanted some cherries." She held out the little sack as evidence.

"Well, you certainly took your sweet time about it. She's going to the Savara estate with his lordship for lunch, and her hair needs to be presentable. And Anata tells me you left Lady Tavia's room in a frightful state this morning—bed made very sloppily, and an actual garter on the floor!"

"The garter was my fault, Almara." Tavia had stood up, one finger marking her place in the book, and was approaching. "I hadn't gotten used to having a maid again, so I took off my own stockings last night. Nel hasn't been a lady's maid in a while, either, so she didn't notice. It was her first night working for me."

Elunet dropped into a curtsy. "You're very kind, my lady."

Almara looked as if she were about to sigh, but thought better of it. "My apologies, my lady. I'm sure Nel will be more conscientious in the future." A clatter, as of dropped dishes, sounded from the direction of the kitchen downstairs, and Almara hurried after it.

"Cherries, my lady, as you requested." Elunet handed Tavia the sack; Tavia plucked one out and bit into it slowly. One drop of juice ran down the side of her hand, and she licked it off before it could stain anything.

A second bite, and she was left awkwardly holding a pit and stem. Elunet held out her hand to take them, but Tavia found a little tray and deposited them there. With her other hand she pulled out a second cherry and offered it to Elunet, who took it with murmured thanks; it was round and ripe and sweet.

"Almara seems hard on you," Tavia said.

"She isn't so bad, my lady. Mostly it's that she worries a lot about getting everything just right, and sometimes takes the worry out on us." The steward was the truly unpleasant one, but he had more dealings with the male servants and the household accounts than with the female servants, for which Elunet was grateful.

"I understand. Sometimes I used to scold Dulsa when I was upset, and then I'd feel bad about it." Tavia shook her head.

"It's human nature, my lady."

"I know, but it was unkind of me." Tavia offered Elunet another cherry. "Come upstairs. Almara's right that I need my hair done, though I do wish she'd put it a bit more tactfully than 'presentable.' I don't look like a wild beast as I am—do I?"

Elunet looked at Tavia: pale gold curls escaping her lace veil, lush curves draped in green silk, lips stained deep red with juice. "No, my lady, you certainly don't," she said, then hoped her tone had not made her admiration too clear. She thought again of how everything Tavia said and did was potential information for her to relay to Chal, and felt that uneasy twisting in her stomach again. Tavia's openness and kindness made it easier for Elunet to weasel her way into her confidence; it also made it surprisingly less pleasant.

~~*

Elunet lingered at the edge of the courtyard late that night, between a trellis of red roses and a curtain of ivy that streamed down from a balcony above. Like the other serving women, she was keeping an eye out for any guests who needed assistance or any tasks that needed doing as the soiree drew to a close, but mostly using this as an excuse to listen to the music. Galatan's hands drew silken threads of melody from his lute and laced them together in an intricate counterpoint. He had entranced the guests all evening to the point that some forgot to dance and boast tastefully about their mercantile dealings or their children's accomplishments and spent much of the time watching him, heads canted slightly to the side, giving their full attention to his stately pavanes and brisk galliards. Tavia was one such. She sat at the long stone table, leaning slightly toward him, intent on the music. Elunet was studying the whole crowd as she always did at such affairs, noting who was speaking, dancing, and flirting with whom and keeping her ears open for snatches of conversation, but her eyes kept straying back to Tavia. Now that most of the guests had departed, Tavia was drawing more and more of her attention.

The threads of Galatan's fugue converged in a triumphant final series of chords, and the remaining listeners, including Elunet, applauded. He stretched his fingers and bowed his head in acknowledgment. "My final piece of the evening," he said, "will be an air of my own composition, which I call *To a Moonflower*."

It was exquisite. The few remaining conversations faded to a hush, and Elunet heard only a faint breeze in the ivy and laurel and the slow haunting melody. It spoke of beauty and mystery, of longing across a gulf one could never cross. She watched Galatan, his hands moving on strings and fretboard with fluid grace, and she watched Tavia, green eyes wide and cheeks flushed with wine and lips slightly parted. Tavia withdrew her gaze from Galatan long enough to glance around the courtyard—and meet Elunet's eyes fixed on her.

Elunet should have looked away, but the power of the music held her still. Tavia seemed held as well, and Elunet felt Tavia's eyes on her own like physical contact. *Stop*, she told herself, but she kept looking for a moment longer, a moment longer, and Tavia seemed just as caught as she was.

The last chord faded, and the courtyard held its breath for a space. Then Tavia began to applaud, and one by one the servants and the last of the guests joined her. Galatan bowed low, then set his broad feathered hat upon his head and packed up his lute.

Tavia bade the guests good night, still looking dazed, and went up to her chamber. Elunet followed.

Alone behind the closed door, they did not look at each other. Tavia went to her dressing table and sat down. Elunet picked up the hairbrush, the mahogany handle cool in her palm, but did not begin taking down Tavia's hair.

"The music was lovely," Tavia said, at last.

"It was, my lady."

Another long silence.

"Do you—have you ever had a sweetheart, Nel?"

"I suppose, my lady, but not anything that lasted." She'd feigned flirtations for a few of her assignments, and dallied with several women without ulterior motive. There had been plainspoken Teriga the fisherwoman, handsome with her hair cropped short and broad-shouldered as a man; Aundrel the northern merchant, with hair paler than Tavia's and a vast supply of traveler's tales; voluptuous black-haired Riva the tavern singer, whose voice alone had made Elunet shiver. A few others she'd kissed in corners but never saw again. "I don't have much chance to, in my position."

"I'm sorry. I shouldn't have asked."

"Don't be sorry, my lady. Grand ladies don't usually ask me questions like that, and it's... well, it's good to have nice conversation with the lady I work for."

"Grand ladies?" Tavia giggled nervously. "Grandmama is a grand lady, not me. I was so bored tonight, and probably so boring *to* everyone else, and so frustrated, until Galatan started playing, and then— then I felt like his music was expressing some part of me that no one knows about. Like I was wearing a mask, but that he could see under it, and... and you looked like you felt the same way."

Tavia's eyes met Elunet's in the mirror.

"I did, my lady," Elunet said softly. "Sometimes... sometimes I feel like I'm always wearing a mask. Sometimes I wonder if there's a real face behind it, or just empty space." She cursed the words as soon as they were out of her mouth.

Tavia rose, slowly, and turned to face Elunet. One hand went to Elunet's cheek, but only the tip of the thumb touched skin. Elunet felt that touch throughout her whole body. "Your eyes look like they did when you were listening to the music. Big dark pools. Mysterious. The sort of thing I'd draw a glyph around and dust with silver." She shook her head, and caught herself on her chair with her other hand. "I've had too much to drink."

"I... liked to hear you say that, my lady." Elunet could hear her heartbeat in her ears. "I wouldn't mind if you—if you said more things like that."

Tavia looked at her again, green eyes wide, a pink glow in her cheeks. "So—you understand. Again." She raised her hand again, to the fringe of Elunet's hair at the line of her chin, and touched it. A single blonde curl of Tavia's own hair spiraled across her face, free of its lacy coiffure; Elunet leaned forward and felt it between her thumb and forefinger. Her hand brushed against Tavia's smooth skin, and she could hear Tavia's breath come soft and rapid. They froze there, caught between caution and desire—and then Tavia kissed her.

Heat tingled through Elunet. Tavia's lips were soft and full and slightly wet. She tasted of red wine and coriander-spiced almonds, the after-dinner treats of the soiree. Tavia's lips moved as they kissed, sliding deliciously against her own, and Elunet, free to kiss back, made it as clear as she could that she invited this, wanted it. Tavia's hands found her shoulders and slid across her back, pulling her closer, and Elunet dropped the hairbrush and wrapped her own arms around Tavia's back, feeling silk and warmth and the quick rise and fall of Tavia's breathing. The hot tip of Tavia's tongue flicked against Elunet's lips, making her shiver, and Elunet's own tongue followed. Tavia's hand trailed over her shoulder, brushed against her collarbone beneath the wool of her dress, and continued lower toward the small firm swell of her breast—then stopped. For a moment they did not move at all, then Tavia pulled away and backed up, her bottom hitting the dressing table and jarring the mirror against the wall.

"I'm so sorry," Tavia panted. "I'm taking advantage. You aren't really in a position to refuse me, so it—it—

this would be wrong." She ran a hand over her flushed face, her loose curl of hair, and knocked her lace veil askew. It made her kiss-swollen lips and sweat-sheened cheeks look even more alluring.

"Believe me, my lady, I want it—I wanted that—as much as you." Elunet's own voice sounded as breathless as Tavia's.

Tavia picked up the forgotten hairbrush, pulled off her veil, and began picking pins out of her hair. Gold curls tumbled down, and she dragged the brush through them, too quickly. It tangled. She worked it free and began again at the ends. Elunet stood still and watched, unable to look away. Tavia finished brushing her hair and began undoing her buttons just as briskly, until she was struggling with the lower ones.

"Let me help," Elunet said, and Tavia went rigid as Elunet unfastened the rest of her gown and peeled green silk away from her like a husk away from grain. Tavia was holding her breath, but Elunet imagined she could feel the racing of her pulse. She certainly felt her own. The sight of Tavia out of the dress, thin shift clinging to her, low neck revealing the rounded expanse of her breasts cupped high and tempting by her exposed corset and quivering slightly with every breath, nearly made her moan. Elunet's shaking fingers went to the corset laces, pulled out the bow, and worked the binding slowly loose. Tavia exhaled deeply, eyes closed, as Elunet removed the opened corset and put it away in the armoire. When Elunet turned back to her, she had stepped out of her gown and draped it across the back of the chair. Elunet took it up, the silk still warm in her hands, and hung it up to air as well.

"Thank you, Nel," Tavia said, and slipped into bed.

"I truly don't mind at all, my lady. And I won't speak a word of anything to..." A pang of guilt wormed through her stomach at the lie. "To Lord Kenar and Lady Isendre." That much, at least, was true.

"Neither will I," Tavia murmured and drew the bed curtains closed.

Elunet gazed at the bed curtains for a moment, eyes tracing the curling patterns of the moonflower vines and white blossoms embroidered on dark blue linen. Then she turned and extinguished the lamp. She carried a candle down to the kitchen, where she found a little vial of the cook's trusted herbal tincture for hangovers, which Tavia might need in the morning. Back upstairs, she tidied a little by candlelight and turned again to the books on Tavia's shelf which she had brought home from the Collegium. When she had not heard a sound from Tavia's bed for some time, she pulled the volume of research notes and opened it slowly, being sure to turn the pages in silence. Tavia's soft fair hands had inked every one of these letters, and the handwriting reminded her of Tavia herself, rounded and making up in charm what it lacked in grace. She shook her head and focused on what the words said.

Thumbing through, she found the last page with writing in it, and started several pages back. *Elmarathan's experiments in causing an illusion he made in the first circle to reproduce itself in the second circle have been helpful. I modified his methods, and I think I'm close to discovering a means of recreating his experiments with physical objects. Using rosemary and silver and Hallendan's thorny pattern, I managed to produce an illusory marble in the second circle with a real marble in the first. The illusory marble mirrored the real one perfectly except that my hand passed through air when I tried to pick it up. I think I'm on the right path.*

The further entries detailed how Tavia had modified this spell. The rosemary and silver remained, but she had changed the other elements. She had added and discarded iron, myrrh, pine, and then finally added an oak branch—causing the marble to roll gently from one circle to the next. Then she had changed the glyph, after several false starts (one shattering a marble to sand), to an intricate spray of angles radiating outward in the first circle and inward in the second. The final lines of this entry, dated eight days ago, were *Marble disappeared from first circle and reappeared in second a heartbeat later. Next time I will place an identity marker on the marble to be sure, but it appeared to be the same blue glass marble in both locations, intact and real. I have found it!!* The last line was underlined twice, so hard it made a hole in the paper.

Elunet closed the book slowly. She was not certain, but her guess was that Tavia had rediscovered the ancient secret of the doors of Sujal: the means to transport an object from one location to another instantly without travel through the intervening space. This meant something big. She set the book back on the shelf, extinguished the candle, and went to her pallet with her mind furiously running through the possibilities.

~~*

For three days they scarcely spoke. The morning after the soiree, Tavia rose late, drank the tincture Elunet had procured, and let Elunet dress her in brown linen edged in white without words beyond "thank you." Elunet said little more. She dressed and coiffed Tavia for other social engagements—a banquet at House Amarin and the blessing of a new ship belonging to House Peria—and attended her at home, where Lord Kenar and Dowager Lady Isendre received an endless round of visitors in business dealings or entertainments. Tavia was usually expected to participate, or at least observe, and the perpetual activity kept Tavia and Elunet from having much opportunity to be alone together, which Elunet found to be a relief.

The wealth of information spilled casually before her was another benefit. She discovered that: House Peria and House Mellas were making their new and tenuous alliance less tenuous through a jointly funded caravan expedition to Bezalshan; that Lianta Amarin had plighted her troth to Benas Chiandre in the city-state of Delesant to the south after House Chiandre had made House Amarin their supplier of hazelnuts and plums; and that the unexpected death of Tenian, Lord Daliar, was rumored to be from poison administered by agents of another House, possibly even one of the seven Council houses (though of course not one with members currently present). All juicy tidbits for Chal, particularly the poison one, but nothing hinted in the slightest at treasonous dealings with Telar.

On the evening of the third day, after dinner, Lord Kenar was entertaining a ship's captain from Janagir, northeast of the cities of the Lirrisaran peninsula, and Tavia was present as an apprentice or perhaps an ornament. They sat in red calfskin chairs, drinking wine and nibbling little pastries filled with roasted lark and strawberries frosted in marzipan from a Tanafelan dish painted blue and white in patterns that reminded Elunet of Tavia's glyphs. On the opposite side of the room, the entrance hall stretched out to the front door where Dennel stood guard, haunted by its portraits of Mellases long gone. Elunet sat in a vestibule window seat off to the side, mending a tear at the seam of one of Tavia's stockings and wishing she sewed like an experienced lady's maid instead of a spy with a few sewing lessons and some hasty practice. She often looked up from her work, checking to see if her mistress required anything and watching the proceedings from beneath her lashes.

Kenar was in his mid-forties, with his mother's fondness for fashionable attire and less restraint in his taste. His coloring was dark, but his nose with the little upturned quirk at the end and his high rounded cheeks were Tavia's; like her, he was somewhat heavy, but the extra weight that looked lush and inviting on her had mostly settled into a paunch on him. He tapped a square ruby ring against the stem of his goblet. "I hope the wine is to your taste, Captain."

The captain, Lajaras, had two missing fingers on his right hand and an immense mustache shaped into two pointed wedges. "It is, my lord, even if is not like the wine I know."

"I'd be willing to trade a few casks for some of those mink pelts you import from Tevarat or some Kazkiri silk."

Lajaras laughed. "It is not so good to my taste as that! And few of my countrymen like it as sour, as... not quite bitter but something like." Elunet mentally supplied the word *tannic* or *astringent*. "It is good, but they may not appreciate."

"Well, if the Janagiri would rather drink syrup, that's their loss. I could offer figs, if they prefer something sweet. We have a country estate in the Faralai Hills, home to the world's finest figs. If you've heard the story of Clever Belen stealing the Harvest Goddess's heavenly figs—well, some versions of the story say they were the Figs of Faralai." When Elunet had spied on House Amarin five years ago, Lord Amarin had claimed the same of the figs on his estate in the Rimantar Valley, though she had to admit "Figs of Faralai" sounded better.

"Ah, but I doubt they could possibly be as sweet as your daughter." Lajaras gestured at Tavia. "She is exquisite: plump and golden as an apricot." He grinned widely, and his whole left hand traced a curve in the air, inches from the real curves of Tavia sitting on his left side. She flinched away a little, and Kenar gave her a look which no doubt meant something; she straightened, brushed at imaginary dust on her skirt, and swallowed some wine.

"My Tavia is as accomplished as she is lovely," Kenar said, "and as *polite and gracious*." The last three words had an edge, and he frowned at Tavia as he spoke them.

"Thank you, Father. Thank you, Captain Lajaras." Tavia spoke quietly, as if she were not using as much breath as was normal.

"And so demure and soft-spoken! A flower of womanhood. She must have many suitors, yes? Many men of quality who seek her bed?" Lajaras's thick dark brows went up.

"'A lady's chastity is her finest jewel and ornament,'" Tavia quoted stiffly. Elunet recognized the source: *The Book of Courtly Virtues*, which Chal had lent her to read long ago as research for her roles.

"Pardons, my dear; I meant your marriage bed." Lajaras smiled again. "And to my lord, pardons also. I am too friendly a man, you see?" His tone was anything but apologetic.

"Tavia and I understand. You have been at sea a long time, and I doubt there were any women aboard your ship." Kenar smiled, and took another pastry from the dish. "I am willing to offer you a bushel of figs for each three Tevarati mink pelts you carry. Or three bushels for a bolt of Kazkiri silk. Possibly more if the silk is well-dyed, but my factor would have to examine it. Of course, the final details of any deal would depend on inspection of the goods involved, but we can work it all out with my factor later."

"Three pelts for a bushel is too much, my lord. These are fine Tevarati mink, not rabbits any Lirrisaran peasant could poach."

"Surely mink are plentiful enough where they come from."

"And I think you have heard of the mulberry blight." Lajaras clucked his tongue.

"No doubt exaggerated to raise the prices." Kenar looked over at Tavia, and arched one brow. "What do you think, my dear?"

"Perhaps we could offer a little more for the pelts? They seem likelier than the silk. And maybe import more than one sort of goods, in case the pelts don't make us a good profit." Tavia spoke to her father, not looking at Lajaras. She crossed her legs and sipped at her wine. "Is there Arangari lambswool available?"

"Good; one must invest broadly and avoid depending on only one venture." Kenar smiled.

"I would ask for your daughter's hand as that 'little more', but I am too lowly for the daughter of such a great lord." Lajaras smiled at Kenar, then winked at Tavia, who pretended not to notice. "Arangari lambswool is good. I can buy there, no doubt, if you offer something I like."

"Perhaps Tavia knows of such a thing," Kenar said.

"Commissioned work from some of the artists we're patrons to? Lindes or Marsal? If there are collectors in Janagir who'd be interested." Tavia set down her goblet on a small round table, and pressed one hand to her stomach. "Forgive me, I—I need to lie down. I feel quite ill, and I... don't wish to disgrace myself." She stood and hurried toward the door leading to her chamber.

Elunet followed, folding her sewing into a neat little package as she went. She put one hand to Tavia's back, ready to help her if she needed it. When they reached Tavia's chamber, Tavia shut the door, latched it, and began to pace the rug in circles.

"My lady, are you unwell? Do you need anything?" Elunet was ready to get out some cold water, or the chamber pot, or run down to the kitchen to ask for one of the cook's simples, or whatever Tavia needed.

Tavia stopped, clenched her fists, unclenched them, and blew out her breath in a long stream. "I'm fine. I just couldn't bear to be dangled in front of that man like... like a piece of meat for a dog. He's older than my father, and he *smells* bad, and he's a crude lecher."

Elunet was relieved that Tavia was well, and pleased that she'd found a way to extricate herself. "Lord Kenar wouldn't truly offer you in marriage to him, would he?"

"Of course not! Even if he actually wanted to *marry* me, which I rather doubt. Father isn't going to... to sell me to a mere sea captain, especially not one so vulgar. He expects even me to find a better match than that. But he is going to expect me to nod and smile and be charming and remember every detail of the deals he's made and how best to negotiate with him in the future, no matter what he says."

"Forgive me for saying so, my lady, but that's unkind to you."

"Father has always said we have two faces: the one we show to the world and the one inside. He said never to let anything of the inner face show on the outer unless it's to the family's advantage. And offending people with whom we do business is almost never to the family's advantage." Tavia flopped down on her bed and kicked off her shoes. Elunet took them and set them on the floor. "And I try and try but I can never separate the outer face from the inner one. Sometimes I can pretend well enough to fool people, but I can never stop feeling the things that I feel. Father says feelings aren't really real, only the *things* that we can see and touch, but... that's one of the reasons why I've always wanted to do magic, because it can make the things inside me become real on the outside."

Elunet wished she could tell Tavia the truth. She wished she could speak of the iron control she had established over her own display of emotions and the elaborate lies she was always having to concoct and remember. Of how rarely she could relax and how seldom she could allow anyone to see what she truly felt and thought. "I understand exactly what you mean, my lady. What you—what we said, after the soiree, about wearing a mask."

Tavia sat up and looked at her, eyes round, and one hand went to her mouth. "I'm sorry. You *would* know. A maid isn't allowed to—to go off to her room in a snit by faking illness. Or she'd be in dire trouble if she were caught. A maid has to smile and pretend to be cheerful and obliging and work when she's angry or worried or heartbroken or has a headache and... and she has to take confessions from a silly spoiled girl like me and be sympathetic and kind and not gossip."

"You aren't spoiled, my lady. A truly spoiled lady wouldn't give my feelings a thought."

"I really am sorry. You can... well, you can go off and do whatever you like until this evening. Tell Almara and Father that I'm sick but not dangerously so and desperately want privacy. Invent whatever unpleasant symptoms you wish." Tavia rubbed both hands over her face, then grinned wickedly. It wasn't an expression Elunet had seen on her before, and she liked it. "I am going to practice my magic."

"Magic?" Elunet raised her eyebrows. "I've never seen magic before, my lady, not real magic. I'd very much like to stay and watch or help if I can... if it's all right with you."

Tavia blinked. "Oh. Yes. It is, as long as you don't disturb anything." She started taking supplies from the shelves: chalk, marbles, compass and drafting square, vials, ink, and the thick brown leather notebook containing her research notes. "I'm not working with anything particularly dangerous, but you really shouldn't touch the circles I'm going to draw."

"Oh, of course I won't, my lady. I'd just be interested to watch is all." Elunet settled herself in a blue padded armchair embroidered with white lilies. She didn't need to feign innocent curiosity. While it was untrue that she'd never seen magic, she hadn't seen much of it, and the only two mages she'd known more than very casually had been aloof as stray cats. Watching magic done by someone who might actually answer her questions was a new experience.

"First I meditate to prepare myself and call my power. Sorry, it's boring to watch. I promise it gets better." Tavia set out three votive candles in blue glass on the bare wood portion of the floor and lit the wicks with flint and steel, then sat cross-legged, her back to Elunet, her head slightly bowed and her hands palm-up on her knees. Elunet looked around the room in silence, mentally noting every detail: a portrait of a pretty blonde woman who was probably Tavia's mother, the pewter ewer and basin with the shapes of running deer in bas-relief, a Harvest Goddess carving with crops and flowers springing up from beneath the wide hem of her gown.

Fine hairs on Elunet's skin began to lift. The room was no warmer, but felt like a summer night before a thunderstorm. She looked back at Tavia. Tavia raised her hands slowly, then unfolded to a standing position. With a stick of chalk, Tavia drew one circle on the floor before her, then a second several paces behind, and then drew the glyphs. She worked quickly but precisely, as if she'd traced these same shapes many times before. Elunet had seen them in Tavia's notebook, but they were far more beautiful when Tavia drew them in front of her. With powdered silver, Tavia drew small circles at the center of each glyph; she placed an oak twig halfway to full leaf just barely outside each silver circle, the two twigs pointing toward each other, and sprigs of rosemary beside them. Finally, she took a porcelain cup painted with daffodils from her nightstand and placed it in the center of one silver circle, stepped back, and stood still, hands raised in the air as if conferring a blessing, murmuring in a language Elunet did not recognize.

Tavia brought her hands together, and a chill jolted through Elunet as the cup vanished from the first circle and appeared in the second a moment later.

Tavia raised her hands back into their former position, turned around once, and let her hands fall to her sides. Some kind of visible tension went out of her, and the charged feeling in the room dissipated. She bent down and picked up the cup, and an exultant smile lit her face.

Elunet's guess had been correct. "You moved it by magic, didn't you, my lady?"

"I did!" Tavia bounced a little. "Nobody's known how to do that since the fall of Sujal and I did it!"

Elunet wanted to run over and hug her. She settled for running over and clasping her hands, careful to avoid the glyphs. Tavia's warm skin made Elunet as tingly as the magic had.

"Or... if anyone's known they haven't recorded it." Tavia laughed. "The Elder Masters won't believe this. I'm going to have the best examination research spell in my class. I'm actually looking forward to writing the treatise on it when I get back and have access to all my notes."

"If you don't mind my asking, my lady, could you move larger things with it? Or move things further?"

"I'll have to keep testing, but I'm pretty sure yes. If the circles get much bigger I'll need more silver, and I'll need to draw the glyphs bigger, but the rest of the modifications are minor changes to wording and energy patterns." She began to clean up, sweeping the silver powder back into its vial, putting away the oak and rosemary, and erasing the glyphs with a woolen rag. "I'd have to change more things if there were a long time between when I made the first circle and the second, but maybe I'd be able to establish long-term glyphs if I got the materials right, and then..." She looked at Elunet and grinned. "Then we wouldn't need to haul around any saddlebags."

Several interesting threads of speculation began to spin themselves out in Elunet's head. "It sounds as if it could be useful for shipping, my lady."

"It would. I'd have to travel to wherever the goods originated, then back here, but after the first trip..." She dabbed a little oil on the rag and rubbed harder. "We'd never need to hire a ship again. Just a mage on each glyph."

"Begging your pardon, but the sailors won't be happy about that."

Tavia's face fell. "You're right."

"Could you send people through?"

"Maybe. In Sujal they could. I suppose I'd have to test it on spiders or mice or something."

Elunet fidgeted. "Well, it seems to me, my lady, that there would be good and bad. You and his lordship wouldn't need to hire many ships, but... sometimes ships are lost, and sometimes people die at sea. I don't know anything about magic, but this might be less dangerous than sailing."

"The Sujali literature is sparse, but there's no evidence of any problems with whatever they did." Tavia bit her lower lip. "So I'd be saving lives, but destroying livelihoods. Well, someday, if I refine this. And if Father likes the idea." She looked doubtful.

"He might. His lordship seems a... practical sort, my lady."

"He's never thought my magic would be much use to the family. Oh, it's fashionable now to have an educated heir, but he's always wished I were more like him." Tavia finished rubbing away the first glyph and started on the second. "He's barely spoken to me about anything other than business in all the years since Mother and my brothers died. Or to anyone else. Sometimes I feel sad for him about that, but... I'm not sure if he remembers how to feel sad himself."

"I'm not sure if that's a pity or a blessing, my lady. Or if it's only his outer face you ever see."

Tavia stopped cleaning away chalk for a moment, and her eyes met Elunet's. "I don't know, either."

They were silent for a time. Then Elunet said, "If you'd like to keep practicing, my lady, I'd be happy to watch. Or to mend and press your things over here, if that won't disturb you."

Tavia smiled. "I'd like that."

Tavia opened the doors to the balcony on the outer wall and called wind with dried rushes and a glyph full of curlicues. Brisk breezes flapped the curtains and ruffled both women's hair. She marked the boundaries of a warding spell with smooth river stones and drew a glyph of chains; she and Elunet could not pass through the unseen barrier it made until Tavia dismissed it by slashing a break in the glyph. After each spell, Tavia wrote in the fat leather notebook, lit the votive candles, and took several slow meditative breaths. Unseen power surged and ebbed as Tavia worked spell after spell, building a slow fire of wonder and desire in Elunet. It was strange, beautiful, and eerily sensual.

Elunet watched, fascinated, until the scent of roasting lamb in spiced wine drifting in through the window told her dinner was being served and Tavia dropped into an armchair with a heavy sigh. "Ugh. I'm exhausted. And hungry. And starting to regret telling Father I was ill."

"I'll find a way to sneak you up a tray, my lady," Elunet said, and allowed herself a mischievous grin. "I'm good at sneaking."

Tavia seemed startled by Elunet's expression, and Elunet guessed she knew why: she had broken character. She had let the mask slip, and Tavia had been surprised, again, by Elunet showing her something genuine. It was a risky move, and Elunet scolded herself for it. But the look Tavia gave her was not one of suspicion, nor was it merely an employer's gratitude to her maid. Elunet felt heat rise to her cheeks. She held Tavia's gaze until Tavia looked away, then curtsied properly and went down the back stairs to smuggle up some dinner.

~~*

Sharing Tavia's magic eased the awkward silence that had fallen between them, but not the feeling that the two of them were iron and a lodestone held an inch apart and struggling to come together. Elunet went about her tasks always aware of Tavia across the room, Tavia's clothes or hair or skin against her fingers, and she knew by Tavia's eyes and the color in her cheeks that she felt the same attraction but would not give in to it. Elunet reminded herself to focus on her duty to Chal, and she observed and memorized things that might be of use to him, but Tavia had told her many things she felt guilty about revealing. She would tell Chal only what was absolutely necessary about her, she decided, and keep most of it to herself.

The rest of the month passed, during which they spoke in private whenever they had the chance. By the fifth day, Elunet started hauling her pallet out of the vestibule and into Tavia's room, where the two of them lay long awake in their separate beds, sharing secrets like small girls. Elunet revealed real things about herself strategically, things that were safe to reveal: her early childhood, her three brief love affairs, real incidents from her life in service, her love of music. Tavia told of her family and her perpetually disappointing attempts to socialize with the Auragan elite, about realizing years ago that she was giddy about women the way other girls were giddy about men. Mostly she told stories of the Collegium, explaining magical theory, academic rivalries, the drunken escapades and ever-shifting romantic and sexual entanglements of some of the more notorious students, and what a student riot looks like when the students in question are mages. Tavia began retiring earlier and earlier when she could, to spend more time whispering with Elunet in the dark, and their nightly confidences became Elunet's favorite time. Each night, Elunet gazed at the shadow of Tavia's bed, willing away the distance between them, but they never touched.

Elunet assisted Tavia with whatever she was doing—attending social functions, practicing spells, copying multiple versions of her meticulous research notes—until her appointment with Chal arrived. She claimed to be out of thread for mending, and asked Tavia if she wanted anything at the market; Tavia requested cherries again, and gave Elunet an extra silver penny to get something for herself. Elunet kept going past the market, as before, and knocked four times fast and twice slow at the door of the safehouse.

Chal beckoned her in. "So, anything to report?"

"The soiree with Galatan was well attended. Irivina Daliar and Jerras Savara spent much of the evening together; it wouldn't surprise me if they end up married, which would link Daliar and Savara closer. That Telarian spy rumor about House Amarin wasn't quite true; there was a spy in Rivilan, which is a minor House that's good family friends of Amarin. Last I heard he was in the Guardhouse. Lord Kenar is trying to set up a trade deal for Tevarati mink and Arangari lambswool with a Janagiri sea captain. He's offering figs and possibly to connect artists to Janagiri patrons, not to mention a remarkable tolerance for the captain's lewd behavior toward his daughter."

"Kenar Mellas is, from everything I've heard, a highly mercenary man," Chal said. "How'd she take that?"

"Not well."

Chal smiled. "Are you getting along well with your new mistress?"

"Quite well. She treats me generously. And I've even gotten to see the magical research she's working on. She's learned to transport objects between one point and another without crossing the intervening space, which as far as she knows—or I know—no one's known how to do for two thousand years."

Chal's eyebrows twitched upward. "Impressive."

"Very. She's working on moving larger and larger objects, and interested in working the spell over larger distances. Possibly even attempting to transport living creatures, even people. She talked about how it could replace a lot of shipping, and is excited about the possibility of making travel safer, even if she is worried about possibly putting sailors out of work. She's also well aware that this could make House Mellas a lot of money." Even if talking about the nature of Tavia's research was fairly impersonal, she felt sick about revealing it. Tavia is going to share this knowledge with the world sooner or later, she reminded herself; Chal is just getting to know it before everyone else.

Chal chewed his lower lip for a few moments, which he did when he was thinking. "Any other foreign dealings on Mellas's part?"

"Not with Telar. A letter to the Duke of Varnos offering condolences on the death of his son. An agreement with the Ilaran family in Emerac for reciprocal use of harbor berths for ships."

"Emerac? They anticipate more trade with the northwest?"

"Presumably."

"Anything else to report, Mockingbird?"

"The Dowager spent lunch yesterday complaining about how she thinks House Corellis has convinced the customs house to charge our ships extra, and dinner complaining about how House Valen has lured away her favorite goldsmith. In two days, Tavia is attending a banquet at House Amarin, and I'll probably get to escort her and play chaperone. Things are mostly quiet at House Mellas, but I'll try to unearth whatever I can."

"Oh, things sound interesting enough. Thank you, as always. I'm proud of you." His smile was warm.

Elunet headed back to the market, her pleasure in Chal's recognition vying with uneasiness.

~~*

"That was the first banquet I've been to where one of the host's dogs has tried to pull off the tablecloth, my lady," Dennel the guard was saying as he escorted Tavia and Elunet home. Only the crescent moon and a few lamps in windows lit the city; this late, the broad boulevard they were taking down from the Amarin estate on Redstone Hill was empty. Tavia nodded a little as she rode, visibly sleepy; Elunet trudged along on foot beside her, and Dennel rode a short distance ahead.

"Oh, that's Hammer. He does that sort of thing, but Lord Amarin is absurdly attached to him and insists on having him in the room with guests because otherwise 'he'll feel left out'." Tavia smiled.

Dennel whistled. "Remind me never to feed him, my lady."

"Probably wise. He once tore Elsana Valen's skirt halfway off her bodice. Brocade, too, and very expensive." Tavia looked down at Elunet, and quirked an eyebrow. "I've made sure never to wear anything too nice to House Amarin ever since."

A wet thunk sounded just ahead of them, followed by a strangled sound. Elunet turned toward it. Dennel teetered, and fell out of the saddle. A knife handle protruded from his eye. Time froze in an instant of horrific unreality.

"Get down!" Elunet yanked at Tavia's stirrup. Tavia's eyes went wide with shock and confusion, but she jumped free, landing nearly in Elunet's arms. Elunet pulled her to the ground, and crouched low beside her, right hand at the top of her boot where one of her knives was concealed.

Elunet listened and looked for possible sources of danger. Ahead, in the direction where the knife must have come from, two figures emerged from an alley. Behind, she heard footsteps.

"Come with us quietly, Lady Tavia, and no one gets hurt," said a voice ahead of them.

Elunet reflected grimly that it was a little late for that.

"Elunet. Chal sent me," said a voice behind. Time froze again, and the world seemed to fall even further apart. She knew that voice. It was Hennic, another street kid Chal had discovered, five years her senior. Chal preferred that each of his agents knew few others, and she was not sure how many he had, but Hennic was one of the four she'd met, and they had sparred a few times over the years.

"What? Why?" Her voice was too high, too scared.

"You know why. With what she knows, House Mellas will take over the city."

She pitched her voice lower. "So Chal sent you to murder an innocent man who doesn't even know what the hell she's doing." The thought sickened her. Chal wouldn't. Chal was a spymaster, not a master of assassins. He'd trained her to fight, expecting she would face danger sooner or later, but he'd never sent her to kill anyone.

Hennic scoffed. "You expect us to face down an armored guard with a sword?"

"Chal's going to have your heads for this." Elunet turned so that she could see Hennic to her right and the two others to her left.

"Chal said to kill her guard if she had one. He said to get the lady any way we had to."

It hit her then: she had gotten Dennel killed. She had told Chal that Tavia was researching how to move objects instantly from one place to another. She had told Chal where Tavia was going to be tonight. And now Hennic—and presumably Chal—was expecting her to hand over Tavia.

"You aren't getting her."

Hennic stiffened and paused a moment. "So you're betraying Chal."

"I didn't think I was working for a kidnapper. Or a murderer."

"So you'd rather let Lord Mellas take control of all the shipping and make himself prince of Auragos. Because he's no fool. He's going to use what his daughter has discovered."

"She moves cups across the room, not shiploads between continents." She made her tone sarcastic and dismissive.

"You yourself told Chal she was working on increasing the size and distance of what she transported. Sooner or later, it's going to be useful if she keeps it up."

"And sooner or later she's going to go back to the Collegium and share her knowledge with the other mages. Then we'll all be on an even footing again."

"That's even worse. Because then, the mages—in *Telar* no less—are going to be transporting goods instead of using ships. *Instantly*. Can you imagine what that would mean to a port city? And what power it would give the mages, not to mention the city that nearly conquered us?"

"That's all speculation. Dennel's corpse in front of me is fact." Elunet drew a knife from each boot and held them low, in case she needed them. "And I'm not letting you kidnap a harmless research mage because you're worried about what she *might* do in the future."

"So your loyalty to Corellis means nothing."

"I barely know them. I was loyal to Chal, but maybe I didn't know him well enough." Turning her back on the man who had taught her so much was the hardest decision she'd ever made, but one of the quickest. She glanced at Dennel, at the spreading pool of blood beneath him and his horse snorting and prancing skittishly, and at Tavia. Tavia was still prone, but her right hand was moving in front of her, doing something on the ground that Elunet couldn't see.

"And you know this girl better?"

"I know she didn't just kill an innocent man and kidnap someone out of fear for her employer's purse. That's got to be worth something."

Elunet heard the knife coming from her left before she saw it, and dodged. Moonlight flashed on the blade, and it hummed past her ear and landed in the dirt. She retaliated with her own knives, aiming at the tall man who'd attacked her. The first missed. She switched the second to her right hand while the first was still in midair and threw, concentrating all her attention on lining up point and target. It split the tall man's throat, with a horrible gargling noise. Elunet's stomach roiled and she heard Tavia retch.

The shorter figure who had been at the tall man's side—a woman with her hair in a long braid—charged at her from one side and Hennic from the other. Elunet drew her two remaining knives from lined pockets concealed in her skirt, and parried an attack with each hand, then leaped back out of the way of Hennic's left-hand counterattack.

Tavia was on her feet, backing up, a faint red glyph full of jagged lines where she had been lying. It was made from her rouge, Elunet realized.

Elunet's kick caught Hennic in the kneecap. He staggered, and she thrust, piercing his right shoulder. The tip of her blade jarred against bone. He managed to parry her left-hand follow-up, but his right arm was now all but useless.

Pain sliced across Elunet's ribs, under her right breast, as the woman's dagger tore through her dress and skin. The cut was shallow, but pain was distracting. She leaped back again, and the woman followed, pressing her hard. One more step, and Elunet's back hit the wall of a house. She heard Tavia speaking words she didn't understand as she parried thrust after thrust; the woman with the braid was a ferocious fighter, and Hennic was coming up behind her, left hand at the ready.

A terrible shrieking wail, louder than any human voice, split the night. It was coming from Tavia's direction. Tavia's horse bolted past, running at full speed for home, and Dennel's horse followed. Hennic, the woman with the braid, and Elunet all jumped, but Elunet recovered first and took advantage of the distraction to attack. She rammed her knife into Hennic's chest, and caught him just below his left clavicle, missing vitals but hampering his uninjured arm. As blood welled from the deep wound, he backed up several steps, then turned and fled.

When a set of shutters banged open beside Elunet's head and a bellowing voice, almost drowned out, demanded to know what in the Sea-Father's name was that ungodly racket, the woman with the braid backed up as well. Other shutters and a door opened along the street, and the woman ran.

Elunet and Tavia ran in the other direction, as startled citizens began to investigate. They were two streets away when Tavia shouted, "It was the only thing I could think of to do that I had materials for. Are there more of them waiting for us?"

"I don't know!"

"Then we'll take a back route!" She led Elunet through an alley and out to a back street overshadowed by jutting second stories and hung with clotheslines. A chicken, pecking in the dirt, flapped away from them with a startled squawk. They proceeded down Redstone Hill in a jagged sideways motion, zigzagging from street to narrow street, then through the vicinity of the market close to the Mellas estate, avoiding the market square itself.

When they got to the Mellas gate, Dennel's fellow guard, Parric, looked at them with alarm. He unbarred the gate, opened it just enough for them to squeeze through, and then promptly shut it again. "Lady Tavia! It scared the life out of me when I saw your horse galloping back without you!"

"Parric. I don't know how to tell you this, but... we were attacked by—by thugs. They killed Dennel, and they nearly killed us. I'm so sorry." Tavia's voice was shaky.

Parric's face went slack with shock. He looked out to the city beyond the gate, and back at Tavia and Elunet. His eyes went to the dirt staining Tavia's dress, and the bloody rent in Elunet's. His mouth moved a little, as if he were trying to speak but words would not come.

"Go upstairs and get cleaned up, my lady. I'll make sure no one gets in."

"I'll find the guard post and get you a partner. You shouldn't be standing watch alone tonight."

The other six guards the family employed were sleeping in their bunks in a spare barracks lined with chests and racks of swords, hammers, spears, and armor. The one Tavia woke was equally horrified by the news of Dennel's death, and went to the gate without complaint.

They crept upstairs as quietly as they could, so as not to wake the rest of the household. Tavia closed the door of her chamber quietly, and stood leaning against it. She stared at Elunet for a long time before she finally spoke. "You lied to me," she said.

Elunet dropped to her knees. "I did. And I'm sorry, my lady. There aren't words to express how sorry I am."

"It's a little late for sorry. And you can drop the 'my lady,' 'Nel.' You were a very convincing lady's maid, whatever you really are." Tavia's voice dripped acid.

"Yes, my—yes." Elunet bowed her head. "I'll accept whatever punishment you give me. You have every right to turn me in to the Guardhouse and have me banished or executed, and I won't resist. I got an innocent man killed, and I nearly got you kidnapped."

Tavia looked startled by Elunet's surrender. "Who the hell is Chal? Who were you working for?"

Elunet sighed. "Chal is a spymaster. He has agents all over the city. He originally worked for House Corellis, but since they allied with House Valen he's been feeding secrets to both. I told him some things about your father's business dealings, about the gossip I heard, and about—about you."

"What in the *darkest caverns of hell* did you tell him about me?" Tavia's voice rose with anger.

"What your research was about. That you didn't like parties and would rather be working on your research. That you don't think you're good at business or politics. That you didn't appreciate your father letting Captain Lajaras slobber over you. That you..." She swallowed hard. "That you don't want to be heir. Absolutely nothing else."

"Nothing else?" Tavia picked up a pale green porcelain vase and threw it at the wall, where it shattered. "*Nothing else?*"

"I... I felt like it would be wrong to tell him anything else, like—like about your life, or that you liked women or kissed me. More wrong, I mean. Like he didn't have any reason to know it." Elunet realized she was backing away from Tavia.

Tavia's face had gone from pale with fear to crimson with fury. "Reason? What *reason* did he have to know anything about me?"

"He was afraid House Mellas was committing treason by conspiring with the Duke of Telar. The—the other Houses on the Council asked him to investigate. He thought your grandmother was selling Council secrets to the Duke—which I found absolutely no evidence of—and he thought you might be involved too since you spend so much time at the Collegium there." Elunet was talking fast, too fast, her heart hammering.

Tavia's red fury cooled slightly—but only slightly. "Who were those—those *brigands*?"

"That man who recognized me was Hennic, another one of his spies. I first met Hennic when I was nine. I didn't know the others."

Tavia's eyes widened. "*Nine*?"

"That's how old I was when Chal caught me trying to cut his purse. He took me in and taught me to spy—to play roles, to recognize potentially useful information, to read, to fight."

"So you used to be one of his thugs. His hired killers." She spat the words.

"What I said to Hennic was completely true. Chal never had me kill or kidnap anyone, and as far as I knew he never had anyone else do those things either."

"But you've fought before. Not just for practice, but in earnest."

"I have killed two men before tonight. One was part of a gang of robbers beating me with clubs down by the docks when I was spying on someone else. The other was trying to rape a girl behind a tavern who didn't look more than thirteen."

Tavia was silent for a while. "What you said to me when I told you about my mother and brother—that your parents both died when you were six—and when you told me later that you ended up on the streets—was that true?"

"Yes. I was on the streets for three years before Chal found me. It really was like I said. I begged, stole, delivered messages, whatever I could do to get food and keep out of trouble. I started dressing as a boy to avoid... the worst trouble. Then Chal took me in."

"I can't even imagine. So he raised you." Tavia's voice was a little softer.

"Sort of. Sometimes he taught me lessons, and sometimes he sent me off on assignments. I've been in service off and on since then. I started as a kitchen helper in a minor House, then moved up to the seven Houses on the Council."

"And you just betrayed him. For me." Tavia shook her head.

"I didn't want to work for someone who had Dennel killed in cold blood. And I didn't want to work for someone who was going to hurt you for... for discovering something wonderful that's been lost for two thousand years."

Tavia caught Elunet's gaze and held it for a moment, then looked away. "You saved me from being kidnapped. And possibly saved my life."

"I was afraid they were going to torture you for information. And the way they were talking, I was afraid they'd kill you to keep you from telling anyone about your research. Or telling anyone what they'd done to you." Elunet looked back at Tavia. "I couldn't let that happen."

"I suppose I should thank you." Tavia met Elunet's eyes reluctantly, then grimaced. "And I suppose they'll be after you now."

"Yes. And I don't even know all of Chal's agents, or even how many he has. They could be anywhere in the city, and they'll know where to find me." A chill swept across Elunet's skin. "You aren't safe either. Maybe you're safe in House Mellas, but when you go beyond its walls..."

Tavia hugged her arms to her chest. "Yes. I see." She looked at the walls, the bookshelf, the window. "They wouldn't dare to attack me at the Collegium. I don't know any hexes and I don't have any talent for destructive magic, but there are other mages who do." She began to pace. "Father and Grandmama are going to be so angry. They might even pull me out of the Collegium if they find out my research has caused all this trouble. And if I'm not there... either they'll keep me locked up like a prisoner here under constant guard, or they'll ship me off to—to I don't even know where. Marry me off to some old man in Varnos or Emerac— whoever will take me sight unseen. And I don't even know what they'd do with my research—encourage it because they thought it would make them rich, or forbid it because they don't want the mages to control shipping."

"I can pay your fees at the Collegium. I have a sapphire necklace I keep hidden in my bodice, and a lockbox with some other jewels hidden under the floorboards of a little room I rent by the docks. They're from all the money I've been saving since I started spying."

Tavia stopped pacing and stared at her, eyes wide. "You'd really do that?"

Elunet nodded. "It would be the least I could do to try to make up for deceiving you. And putting you in danger by telling Chal about you." She shivered, feeling a sick hollow in her stomach. "Protecting you would be the least I could do for Dennel. If he has any family, I'd like to... to give them whatever's left over."

"For what little it's worth." Tavia started to pace again, tight little circles on the wooden part of the floor, then stopped. "How would I explain the money to Father and Grandmama?"

Elunet smiled, just a little. "You've received a scholarship for your extraordinary research. I'll forge documents for it."

"You can do that?" Tavia shook her head. "Of course you can do that. I'm not sure I want to know everything else you know how to do."

"Climb walls, if they're rough enough. Among other things."

"Father and Grandmama won't be pleased to hear I've taken up full-year residence at the Collegium, but it's best if I'm not in Auragos for a while, and I think they'll come to understand that once I've sent them an explanation. Someone tried to assassinate Father in his youth, and he spent four months visiting cousins in Delesant while Grandmama made sure it wouldn't happen again."

"Full-year residence?"

"I can rent a room for the summer term. Some students do." She smiled. "Almost more of a cell. The rooms are tiny compared to this one. I don't blame Dulsa for leaving."

"I don't mind." Elunet stopped. "I'm sorry. That was horrible effrontery on my part, to assume I'd still be serving you after... after spying on you and nearly getting you killed."

"And betraying your mentor to save me." Tavia shook her head and stretched. "I expect you'll be leaving Auragos as well—considering that there's probably a whole group of people after you and you don't even know who most of them are."

"Definitely."

"I'm planning on leaving for Telar at dawn, and I'd rather not tell the guards until I'm out of Father and Grandmama's reach. I suppose that would make you the closest thing to a guard I have."

Elunet's heart seemed to flip over. She couldn't believe it. "I'd be honored to serve you, my lady. And I know the path where the goatherds drive their goats down from the hills; we can take that and avoid the road."

"I'm... a little worried by what else you probably know. But if you were going to kill me or have me kidnapped, you'd have turned me over to those... those people, not risked your life for me." She ran a hand through her hair, and pulled her veil off. "And I can't let anything happen to someone who risked her life for me."

Hearing Tavia say that felt like warm sun on her skin.

"Speaking of which... you're hurt."

"A little. I've had worse." The cut was a long stinging line across her ribs, but it was no longer bleeding.

"I'll wash it with brandy."

"Brandy!" Elunet winced.

"It's something I've learned at the Collegium. It hurts, but they say it helps it heal clean."

Tavia found a flask of it in the drawer of her dressing table; Elunet was amused by the thought of Tavia keeping a hidden flask of brandy. Elunet sat in the blue armchair, and Tavia spread open the tear in her dress. Her fingers were a little cold against the bare skin of Elunet's chest, but the touch sent warmth through Elunet. Tavia wet a lacy handkerchief with brandy and touched it to the wound. It burned; Elunet drew in a hissing breath through her teeth and held it as Tavia cleaned.

With the blood washed away, the cut on Elunet's chest was very thin and shallow at the ends, with only a small place in the middle that gaped red and open. Tavia's fingers rested against Elunet's skin for a moment, and Tavia looked up at her, face softening. Elunet thought about how close to her own lips Tavia's were and how much she wanted to kiss them, and how inappropriate it would be. Instead, Elunet stood, went to the washstand, poured water into the basin, and began trying to soak the blood out of her dress as well.

Tavia started to pack for the journey. Elunet mended her own dress, cleaned Tavia's dress and stitched a few small tears, and helped Tavia finish packing. Tavia lay down very late in her bed, but kept turning restlessly; Elunet sprawled in the blue armchair and awaited the dawn, uneasy.

She remembered her days on the streets of Auragos: the filth, the terror of violence, the gnawing hunger and cold nights when she crawled into middens to keep warm. If Chal had taken her in and asked her to kidnap or kill for him, would she have done it? She didn't think so, but she wasn't sure. She remembered the tall man with her knife in his throat, and Hennic's wounds, and shuddered. Maybe she could have been in their place.

~~*

As black sky began to fade to gray, they readied themselves to leave. The whole room seemed tight with tension as they spoke, still uncomfortable with looking at each other. Tavia asked Elunet to tell her everything she knew about Chal: the places he frequented, his other associates who might be dangerous, and how he might be found.

"Please don't have all his agents killed or arrested," Elunet said. "Most of them are like me, as far as I know. They spied for him, maybe they stole for him, but they didn't kidnap or kill for him. They don't deserve to die, and I don't want to be responsible for having them killed."

"I won't. I'm not sure I could order anyone's death. It's one of the reasons I don't think I'm well suited to the Council." Tavia rearranged books and boxes in her saddlebags. "Father took me to a nobleman's execution when I was twelve, and I threw up all over some unfortunate person's shoes when the head came off and the body started..." She grimaced. "He never took me to another."

"I didn't sleep at all for two nights after I killed that robber," Elunet said quietly. "I just kept pacing and straightening my things over and over and washing my hands and clothes and... it felt like something was chasing me and I'd never be able to get away." She scrubbed her hands over her face. "Maybe I was right."

Elunet explained Chal's methods to Tavia: his safehouses scattered around the city, the few other agents she knew of, the types of assignments she'd had in the past. Tavia listened, nodding grimly.

When they left, Tavia left a note on the silver tray by the front door explaining her departure. Elunet didn't read it. Tavia could easily have put in all the details needed to apprehend and hang a certain spy in maid's clothing, if she wished. If Tavia changed her mind and chose to denounce Elunet to her father, she had every right to do so, and Elunet wasn't going to invade her privacy any more than she already had.

They crept out as the sun was rising. Parric was still on guard duty at the front gate; he looked at them with surprise.

"I couldn't sleep after what happened last night," Tavia explained. "Nel and I are going to stay at the Rillans' country estate until tomorrow. Perhaps we'll be able to rest outside the city." Her voice was subdued, but her lie was no more awkward than her usual interactions with family. "I'm terribly sorry. I know you and Dennel were friends."

"Thank you, my lady." Parric was stiff, emotionless, and Elunet ached for him, knowing he was not in a position to get away from his duties and the reality of Dennel's death. "Roscan and I are going out soon, to... find him."

Tavia looked as if she wanted to say more, but did not. Elunet looked back once at the estate as Tavia mounted her horse, at the marble loggia framed between the columnar pines lining the path through the gardens and the balconies overflowing with ivy, and turned away, following Tavia.

Once they were out of sight of the walls, Elunet led Tavia toward the docks and her hideaway. As they moved further from the high ground at the center of the city where the seven Houses on the Council had their estates, the buildings grew shabbier and the dwellings grew smaller and more closely packed. People had started building upper stories so far out into the streets that little sunlight got through, especially this early. Elunet kept her hands close to her two remaining knives in her concealed pockets. She'd have to replace the ones from her boots later. In the distance, the shouts of dockworkers and the creaking of pulleys echoed over the water. The air smelled of the sea, of fish and tar and, unfortunately, the sewage dumped into the water and streets and the effluent from tanners' and dyers' shops. Tavia pressed a handkerchief to her nose with a look of distaste, but did not complain.

They rounded the corner of one tanner's shop, tied Tavia's horse to a wood railing bristling with splinters, and climbed two flights of rickety stairs to the roof of the building, which was high enough that Elunet could see the dromonds and galleys and newfangled caravels at anchor in the harbor. Atop the building with the tanner's shop, someone had built a ramshackle set of tiny rooms, a jumble of shacks nailed together.

"This is where you live?" Tavia said.

"Sometimes. If I'm not on an assignment that requires me to live somewhere else."

"I... like the view." It was definitely faint praise. Tavia had likely seen little of the world outside her own wealthy circles.

"I like that it's not a place anyone would consider worth robbing too carefully. I keep my valuables in a lockbox under the floorboards disguised as a prop to keep the floor from creaking." Elunet smiled, and fished her door key from a little pocket sewn into her bodice.

Inside were a straw-filled pallet, a tiny stone brazier, a small chest, a pot, pan, and spoon hanging on the wall, a chamber pot, and a candlestick on a three-legged end table. And Chal, behind the door.

"Hello, Elunet," he said, his voice cold. "I guessed you might show up here sooner or later. And Lady Tavia—it's an honor to finally meet you." He sounded surprised, but not dismayed, to see her.

Elunet and Tavia both went deathly still. Time slowed down, dilated like a vast hole opening to swallow them.

The point of a knife pricked Elunet's back. Someone else had crept up behind her.

"I raised you. I taught you everything. Without me, you'd likely be dead in a gutter somewhere, or a street whore, or a thug. And for this you betray me and kill one of my men?" Despite everything, the hurt in his voice felt like a punch to her gut. She'd looked up to Chal for so long, and she owed him so much, and this was how she repaid him.

Elunet spoke as calmly as she could. "I'm sorry, Chal—but if I hadn't betrayed you, I *would* be a thug. A kidnapper. And possibly responsible for getting Lady Tavia killed, as well as her guard, because I was afraid you might not let her live."

Chal advanced until Elunet could see the sleepless red that flecked his eyes, drew his knife, and held it to her throat. "Jenira says you told Hennic—who's in pretty bad shape, by the way, and might not live if those wounds take septic—that you didn't care about Mellas taking over the city with their advantage. Or the mages turning into merchants and making us irrelevant."

Elunet swallowed, feeling the edge of the blade cold against her skin. It felt as if it were already pressing in.

"That's not quite true. I do worry about those things. I just don't think speculations like that are a reason to kill innocent people."

"But your personal feelings are a reason to murder your own comrades."

"That man was throwing knives at Lady Tavia and me, and had just killed her bodyguard. And Hennic was trying to kill me."

"For siding with someone who threatens us, our whole city, our entire way of life." The knife bit into her, and she felt a warm trickle of blood running down her neck into her collar. Chal's voice rasped in her ear; she closed her eyes and prayed silently to the Harvest Goddess, who shelters the dead, for forgiveness. "I've only had to do this to an agent once before. You were so bright, so skillful... and you threw it all away. I'm sorry, Elunet, but I can't allow you to live."

"You can't allow her to die either." Tavia's voice shook a little, but it was strong and clear. "If you kill her and let me live, I will have you hunted down myself. She risked her life to save mine. And if you kill her and kill me as well, my father will find you. You're not the only one who has spies."

"Really. And how would he know where to find me? Or you?" Chal's voice was contemptuous—but held a faint hint of worry.

"I left Father a letter explaining everything. I gave him this address, and your name, and the names, locations, and... and cover identities of all your other agents that Elunet knows about. I gave him the locations of—of all your safehouses. I told him everything Elunet told me about you, including all her previous assignments and every other bit of spying you've done that she could think of. Either he'll find all your agents and track you down through them one way or another, or I will."

So Tavia had turned her in after all, and turned in her former associates. She'd lied about not planning to do so. But then, Elunet was hardly one to complain about people she'd deceived lying right back at her. The details were odd, though: Elunet had certainly not given Tavia the locations of any safehouses or the cover identities of any agents, and had only told her about working as a servant in places that fit "Nel's" invented history.

"But Father's not an early riser. If you let Elunet and me go, I'll go back to House Mellas, burn the letter, and forget I ever met you... as long as you never threaten anyone else again."

Now this Elunet had not expected.

The edge of the knife dropped a little away from Elunet's throat. Chal still held it pointed at her, but she no longer felt cold metal against her skin. Feeling a little dizzy, she gulped down a breath and resisted the urge to put a hand to the place where the knife had been. Drops of blood were still oozing out of the cut.

Tavia's face was white and damp with sweat. She took a deep breath to compose herself, and continued. "Killing us also wouldn't accomplish anything except making you a hunted man... because I've already shared my research with the mages at the Collegium. I've taken notes. Immensely detailed notes, and there are multiple copies, in both House Mellas and the Collegium. I always thought all the lost knowledge from the burning of the Great Library of Sujal was one of the saddest things I'd ever heard of, and I've always been careful to make sure nothing I discover would ever be lost, no matter what happens to me. Any other mage who knows a lot about motion spells would be able to duplicate what I did." She smiled, and the smile was not entirely forced. Chal's arm lowered slowly, as if it were deflating. "This secret's already out. You can't stop it from spreading."

Chal had gone pale and sweaty, too. He stared into Elunet's eyes a moment longer, but his stare no longer had any menace in it. "She's right, Jenira. Put the blade down. We're getting out of here."

The knife at Elunet's back eased away, and she breathed out fully. Chal and Jenira—the woman with the long braid who had fought with her during the night—went quietly out the door. She could feel the vibrations of their footsteps as they headed toward the stairs.

She waited until she could no longer hear them before moving or speaking. Tavia sat or fell down on the lid of the chest with a thud. She was shaking visibly. Elunet realized she was shaking too.

"You just saved my life," Elunet said. "As well as your own." She did not mention that Tavia had previously promised not to turn in Elunet's fellow agents.

"I can't believe I just did that. I can't..." Tavia let her face sink into her hands, was still for a few moments, then looked back at Elunet. "It was all true. Well, except for the bit about what's in the letter. And meaning to go back for it." Tavia spoke very quietly, as if she were worried that Chal and Jenira might still overhear.

"So there really are research notes in multiple places?" Elunet managed a smile. "Clever. Maybe you should have been a spy too."

"Yes—with me right now, back at the estate in my chamber, and deposited in the library at the Collegium. And the letter for Father and Grandmama only says I don't feel safe in the city because of what happened last night, and that I'm going back to the Collegium and taking you." She smiled weakly back. "All also technically true."

Elunet remembered their conversations after the soiree, after Captain Lajaras's visit. "Sometimes masks can be useful. But as an occasional disguise... not an everyday face."

Tavia was silent.

"I only wish we could get some kind of justice for Dennel. But trying to prosecute Chal and Hennic and Jenira would mean that a lot of other people would probably hang or be beheaded as well. Some of them are people I know. Some of them—maybe most of them—aren't any worse than I am." Elunet sat down on the floor next to Tavia.

"Dennel used to play stones with me. We hired him when I was ten, and we used to play games where he'd chase me around the gardens until the steward made him stop." Tavia's voice was soft and sad.

"I don't want anyone else to die because of this," Elunet said. "Because of me." Her throat was tight, and she felt tears prick her eyelids. She swallowed hard and forced them back; she was *not* someone who cried.

"I don't ever want anyone to die because of me." Tavia paused. "I'm an unfit heir. I'm too soft. Too academic. Too impractical."

"Too *good*," Elunet said. "But I'm not sure that's a bad thing. Provided we can keep you from getting assassinated."

"I hope Father lives a very long and healthy life. I don't want to be Lady Mellas until I'm as old as Grandmama."

"At which point you'll be so wealthy and powerful because of your research that no one would dare to harm you."

"Ha." Tavia turned her head to Elunet, still lolling against the wall. "I'm rather flattered, actually, by how much Chal overestimates me. It'll be years yet before my spell is useful for shipping anything. If it ever is."

"Chal always did take the long view. A good spymaster is as patient and prepared as a spider in its web." Elunet smiled. "He views all his people as long-term investments."

"Long-term investments don't always pay off. Father would say it's a good thing he has a lot of them." Tavia returned the smile, and her hand found Elunet's and gave it a squeeze. "At least this one paid off for somebody."

Nothing could have felt more welcome just then than Tavia's hand in hers. They sat in silence for a moment, allowing the moment to be what it was.

"I'd better get you those jewels," Elunet said, "and we'd better get going." She lifted one corner of the pallet, pulled a slim prybar from beneath it, and worked a floorboard free. Beneath was an unassuming, completely unadorned block of wood, slightly gnawed by rats, with a keyhole and catch hidden behind a sliding panel. With another key pulled from a hidden pocket in her bodice, she opened it. Tavia's eyes went wide at the jumble of jewelry coiled inside: a fat sapphire ring to match the necklace Elunet concealed on her person, a pendant with tiny rubies arranged into a wild rose, pearl earrings, a bracelet in three braided ropes of gold, aquamarine and amethyst necklaces with silver beads worked in the shape of lilies.

"My life savings," Elunet said, and handed it all to her.

"You'd better hold on to some of it for now, or I'll rattle when I walk." Tavia handed back the necklaces and bracelet, and slipped the rest into her purse.

"Spying paid well, but I'm done with it," Elunet said, sliding the remaining jewelry into her hidden pockets next to the daggers. "I'm tired of lies. I'm tired of wearing a mask all the time."

"So am I." Tavia stood, brushed off her skirt, and turned toward the door. "Let's find a place that smells better."

~~*

Elunet led Tavia and her horse along the goat path over the hills toward Telar. Spring was easing into the dry heat of the summer; the grass in the highlands was turning parched and gold. They passed terraced fields ringed with stone walls, olive groves and vineyards, high pastures and cottages. By midday the path was narrow, winding, and steep enough that Tavia had to dismount and lead her horse. The heady rush of danger and flight gradually left them as the sun climbed high, and the afternoon was a hot misery of exhausted trudging up and down rocky slopes; they had carried bread and hard cheese and almonds and water flavored with a little brandy, but only the water in quantity. By sunset, Elunet was in a daze of sleep deprivation, and Tavia was stumbling as well, but they were over the highest crest of the hills and on the long slope down toward Telar. They found a wide rock outcropping sheltered by trees and a grove nearby, where they tied Tavia's horse close enough to grass for him to graze, rubbed him down, and climbed up into the stony perch with their saddlebags and tack. Elunet let Tavia sleep first, and kept herself awake by pacing about despite her aching legs and envisioning bandits approaching in the darkness. By the time it was Elunet's turn to sleep, she was so exhausted that she fell asleep on hard stone covered with a blanket as easily as if it had been a bed.

It was already midmorning when Elunet awoke, stiff and aching but much more clearheaded. She and Tavia shared the last of their food and continued down the goat path to Telar.

Elunet had been to Telar before, in the course of her work, but not for four years. It was a slightly larger city than Auragos, with limestone walls describing an S-curve along the harbor. She realized that she was on the opposite side of the Lirrisaran peninsula, and an image came to mind of the path that she and Tavia had followed marked in red dashes on a map of the Inner Sea. Telar was not so different from Auragos within; people spoke with a different accent and some of the words were strange, the architectural styles were not quite the same, and there was a duke's palace at the center of the city rather than seven rival merchant lords' estates, but it was still a port city on the coast of Lirrisar. There were wealthy and influential merchants, though they were not (officially) the rulers; there were the rich on horseback and the poor on foot; there was a rough district by the docks; the whole place smelled far less pleasant than the countryside, but it smelled like home.

There was also the Collegium Arcanum. Tavia managed to wangle them a room in an old estate within the Collegium walls that had fallen on hard times and been chopped up into tiny student residences; it was the size of Elunet's hideaway, but the walls were stone.

Tavia took to setting warding spells on it when they slept; she said that they could never be too careful. Within days, once Elunet had pawned one of the bracelets, they were able to pay two masters who lectured in the summer, and to pay Tavia's library and laboratory fees. Tavia set to work, spending hours bent over books or practicing in the laboratory; Elunet was rather at loose ends. She cleaned their room and did their laundry and mending and cooked their meals, but there was only so much cleaning one could do in a room so small and sparsely furnished. They sometimes spoke, but not the way they had during the magical month after the soiree at the estate. At night, Tavia slept on a pallet and Elunet on a blanket by the door; she gazed at Tavia in the darkness and remembered the silky warmth of Tavia's lips, the softness of Tavia's body against her own.

One evening after dinner, Elunet was scrubbing the floor with a brush on hands and knees, for lack of anything more useful to do, when Tavia laughed.

"You do realize that you're not my maid any more, now that you're paying my school fees, don't you?"

Elunet stopped scrubbing and dropped the brush into the bucket. "I'm not?"

Tavia shook her head. "I suppose you're my benefactor now."

"I prefer to think of myself as doing penance."

"Benefactor sounds better if we have to explain our arrangement to other people."

"Arrangement? Is that what this is?" Elunet raised an eyebrow. "There's something charmingly scandalous about that word. If... if you want there to be. Because that night—the soiree—when we kissed—I..." She was babbling, foolish, pathetically nervous. This was stupid.

It was utterly stupid and ridiculous to hope. "Nothing about it was just me being obedient, and all I really wanted was... to keep going." Her cheeks burned.

Tavia stared for a long space, another one of those terrible moments when time froze. Finally she said, "You... aren't my maid any more, Elunet." And a slow, wicked smile spread across her face.

Elunet got to her feet, and kissed her.

Tavia kissed back hungrily, her lips soft and full and her tongue flicking against Elunet's own lips with maddening sensuality. One hand pressed hard into Elunet's back and slid down to grasp her bottom. Elunet gasped and slid her own hands around to Tavia's buttons. Her hands were shaking, her breath was shaking, as she fumbled with buttons again and again and couldn't get them undone fast enough, and at the same time Tavia was undoing her buttons too, and then she was pulling down bodice and sleeves and Tavia was pulling off hers and they were tangled in wool and linen and had to separate for a frustrating moment to free each other of their dresses. Tavia was as delicious as ever in her corset, generous breasts high and round with a deep valley between and broad hips curving out from her cinched waist. Elunet yanked out the bow, tore at the laces until they were gone, as Tavia undid Elunet's own bodice. Free of constraining garments, they tumbled toward the pallet, Elunet already feeling at the full ripe richness of Tavia's breasts free beneath her shift, burning. Elunet was on top and Tavia pulled her shift up over her head, and then they rolled and Tavia was on top and Elunet pulled *her* shift off, and then they rolled again.

Sweet Harvest Goddess, Tavia was beautiful naked, with her golden curls spilling over her bare shoulders and her face and chest flushed clear down to her rosy nipples, gasping and panting. They writhed, Elunet's olive skin against Tavia's fair skin, Elunet's slim body firm with muscle against Tavia's voluptuous glory. Elunet's hand found Tavia's thigh, and Tavia gasped; slid up, and Tavia moaned. Elunet kissed in a long damp trail all the way down until lips and tongue and hand all met and moved together and Elunet felt an echo of Tavia's shuddering ecstasy.

Tavia lay back trembling, recovering, and then her hands slid down, the perfect size to fit Elunet's small breasts, and one slid down over her taut belly to her thighs and where they met, and Elunet whimpered with need. Tavia's lips were hot on her earlobe and then her neck and then her breast and then she felt Tavia say something between her legs and she didn't know or care what because her warm breath there felt so good. And then Elunet's world was building tightness and unbearable pleasure and intense, astonishing release.

Lamplight cast flickering shadows on the wall as they lay spent and cooling on the pallet. Elunet lay with her head on Tavia's shoulder, playing with a curly tendril of her hair. It looped around her fingers like a golden ring.

"What do you think the future will be like?" Tavia murmured.

"Better than the past, I hope. I was saving for the future, but I never really decided exactly what I was saving for." Elunet smiled. "I suppose this is as good as anything."

"I never really liked to think about the future," Tavia said. "After I started at the Collegium, at least. Before that, I spent my whole life hoping Father would let me go. Now, I've spent the last few years with a terrible dread in the back of my mind—graduation."

Elunet chuckled, and closed her eyes, breathing in the scent of Tavia—rose and almond and woman—and feeling her bare warm skin and the gentle rise and fall of her chest as she breathed. But eventually the past intruded on Elunet's mind, and she contemplated it for a time, and then spoke.

"For years I seldom thought about the future, or about—about the larger implications of what I was doing. Oh, I knew about city politics, but I didn't really connect what I did to how the information I gathered might be used." Elunet shivered, and Tavia's arms encircled her. "I hope it hasn't gotten anyone else hurt."

Tavia was quiet for a time. "I don't know what my magic will mean. It'll take me a long time to work up to long-distance transport—probably years, if I get it to work that way at all. And if it does... I remember one of our ships carrying a cargo of spices sank when I was a little girl. Father was very upset about how much money we lost, but all my brother and I could think of were the sailors that drowned in the ocean." She turned her head toward the small open window in the middle of the wall. "Everything we do, every change, can have repercussions that we don't expect. We need to think about them before we act—but we can't stop *acting* out of fear of what our actions will lead to. Because the only way to do that is to stop living."

"I think this change will lead to good things," Elunet said. "I'll find work, and you'll study magic, and we'll live in Telar and think about what's going to happen when you're Lady Mellas some other time." She paused. "If you want me to keep living here."

"I think it's best if we keep an eye on each other. And not many people would dare to harm us in a whole Collegium full of mages." Tavia laid her left hand gently on Elunet's breast—not stroking, just cradling it. No urgency, just tenderness. "And I... I'd like you to be with me. And we can do that here."

Elunet's eyes went wide. "Openly?"

"More or less. I know a lot of mages who... who are women who like women. Or men who like men. Or people who like both men and women." Tavia sighed. "It's a different world, here."

"I've always liked exploring new places," Elunet said.

"Oh, *have* you?" Tavia's tone turned Elunet's remark into innuendo she hadn't intended.

"Yes. I have." Elunet smiled and kissed Tavia again, without lies, without masks, without betrayal.

Fin

About the Authors

S.S. Skye is an engineer moonlighting as an author, filling the margins of her notebooks with fluff and stuff. She's been writing m/m and f/f romance (with a few dalliances with m/f) since discovering it in eighth grade, due in no small part to the founders of Lt3. She's delighted to be able to share the fruits of many nights interrupted by inspiration and many hours she should've been studying, and is speechlessly ecstatic to be doing so among authors of such a high caliber.

Every week, she tries to further hone her fluff 'n stuff skills by writing short ficlets for the Sunday Snuggles community. Further works by her can be found at the following:

http://skeptics-secret.livejournal.com/   and http://sundaysnuggles.livejournal.com/tag/author%3A%20skeptics_secret

Caitlin Ricci was fortunate growing up to be surrounded by family and teachers that encouraged her love of reading. She has always been a voracious reader and that love of the written word easily morphed into a passion for writing. If she isn't writing, she can usually be found studying as she works toward her counseling degree. She comes from a military family and the men and women of the armed forces are close to her heart. She also enjoys gardening, hiking, and horseback riding in the Colorado Rockies where she calls home with her wonderful fiance and their two dogs. Her belief that there is no one true path to happily ever after runs deeply through all of her stories.

Website: www.CaitlinRicci.com

Cari Z. is a Colorado girl who loves snow and sunshine. She has a wonderful relationship with her husband, a complex relationship with the characters in her head and a sadomasochistic relationship with her exercise routine. She feels like Halloween should be every day, and hopes that you enjoy reading her stories as much as she enjoyed writing them in the first place. Find out more about Cari and her books here: www.carizerotica.blogspot.com, https://www.goodreads.com/author/show/2989189.Cari_Z_, or on twitter as @author_cariz.

Camilla Quinn is an English major from South Texas. When she isn't saving the world one insurance policy at a time or scribbling scenes between phone calls, she's tending to a hyperactive corgi or referencing obscure movie quotes.

Anastasia Vitsky is cookie queen, wooden spoon lady, and champion of carbs, She specializes in F/F erotic fiction. She hates shoes and is allergic to leather. When not writing about women who live spankily ever after, she coordinates reader and author events such as Spank or Treat, Love Spanks, and Sci Spanks. Her favorite event is Ana's Advent Calendar, a month-long celebration of books, community, and making a difference.

She is too afraid to watch *Dr. Who*, but she adores *The Good Wife* and anything with Audrey Hepburn. In her next life, she will learn how to make the perfect pie crust.

Living in Sin is her seventeenth publication. Other notable works include *Taliasman, Mira's Desire, Simple Gifts, The Way Home, Lighting the Way, Becoming Clissine,* and *Mistress on Her Knees.* Forthcoming books include *Ana Adored, Freiya's Stand, Seoul Spankings,* and a sequel to *Taliasman*.

Valerie Mores (aka Val) has been creating stories for a little over a decade and frightening her few readers just as long. While the dark and sometimes depressing nature of her words has greatly dimmed down, it still lies in wait, just biding its time until the appropriate moment to reappear comes about. Until then, she continues to push the boundaries and ensure that a little pain and angst still makes its way on paper along with that enticing happy ending.

But writing takes up only a small chunk of her time, the rest being filled by putting her fashion degree to good use costuming in the film industry.

Alex Powell is an avid writer and reader of sci-fi and fantasy, but on occasion branches into other genres to keep things interesting. Alex is a genderqueer writer from the wilds of northern Canada who loves exploring other peoples and cultures. Alex is a recent graduate of UNBC with a BA in English, and as a result has an unhealthy obsession with Victorian Gothic literature. Alex has been writing from an early age, but is happy to keep learning to improve on their writing skills. Feedback and comments as well as any questions are appreciated! You can reach Alex at aa.powell.author@gmail.com

Kai Schalk lives and writes in Minnesota. They are a recent graduate of the University of Wisconsin – Eau Claire with a B.A. in German, and are currently trying to learn Cantonese in order to communicate properly with both sides of their family. In their spare time they enjoy crocheting dragons and becoming proficient in multiple types of weaponry.

Annabelle Kitch used to think she was a normal girl. Then she found out 'normal' was a lie, threw her pretenses to the wind, and went streaking through life wearing the proud banner of 'odd'. One of the only constants in this life was an unrelenting passion for storytelling, and she's traveled the world (or worlds, if you count the ones in her head) in pursuit of this. As an avid fan of, well, everything, she naturally stumbled upon fanfiction. Therein she came upon slash and, after initially resisting, ultimately said 'why not'. Depending on your point of view, it was all downhill or uphill from there.

These days, Annabelle works a desk job, which is a pretty good cover for the nonsense that goes on in her head. Pretty soon, she's going to strike it big, but for now the writing of passionate fiction will be relegated to evenings and weekends. And lunch breaks. And times when the work is slow and there's nobody looking at her monitor.

Althea Claire Duffy is the pen name of a 30-something librarian from a one-stoplight town in western Massachusetts. She spent her childhood dreaming of being a writer, acquired an impractical degree in a fit of youthful naivete, worked too many different jobs, and moved to Boston for grad school in her mid-twenties. After some floundering and a lot of getting lost, she fell in love with her adopted city and never left. For years, she wrote little and finished less, but an early midlife crisis of sorts pushed her back into writing—and, for the first time since age fourteen, pursuing publication.

She's an introvert, an eclectic reader, a computer and tabletop roleplaying gamer and occasional game master, an amateur mezzo-soprano, a fan of classical and international/world music, and a metalhead. A soft, fuzzy center is hidden beneath her cynical, prickly exterior, sort of like an artichoke. She likes art museums, eccentric vegetables, and snarking Z-grade movies.

Website: http://www.altheaclaireduffy.com
Tumblr: altheaclaireduffy.tumblr.com
Twitter: @AltheaCDuffy